John Gideon lives in Oregon in the United States and is the author of GREELY'S COVE and GOLDEN EYES, both available from Headline. Of the kind of fiction he writes, he says, 'Stephen King and others have suggested that horror fiction is cathartic, because it lets the reader vent anxieties and fears within the safe confines of an armchair. Reading horror lets you face evil of a species that does not exist in the real world of freeways, desert war and deadline journalism. When you close my books, you can take comfort that nothing in this world could be as bad as what you've confronted between its covers.'

Also by John Gideon

Greely's Cove
Golden Eyes

Red Ball

John Gideon

KNIGHT

First published in 1994
by HEADLINE BOOK PUBLISHING PLC

First published in paperback in 1995
by HEADLINE BOOK PUBLISHING PLC

A HEADLINE FEATURE paperback

This edition published 2003 by Knight,
an imprint of The Caxton Publishing Group

10 9 8 7 6 5 4 3 2 1

ISBN 1 86019 6187

Typeset by Letterpart Limited, Reigate, Surrey
Printed and bound in Great Britain by
Cox & Wyman Ltd, Reading, Berkshire

The Caxton Publishing Group
20 Bloomsbury Street
London
WC1B 3JH

For Pooski,
Who rode her bicycle down to the sea
And lingered in the sand to talk with me.

INTRODUCTION
May 1992

During the last seventeen minutes of his young life, Ron Payne got laid. A hundred heartbeats after the final jolt of orgasm, he ran his fingers along the backbone of the undulant creature stretched on her belly next to him, savoring the down in the small of her back and the sweet smell of sex. He relished the satin-feel of her skin, the whisper of her breathing, as well as each lazy moment, never dreaming that he had so few of them left.

'Want a toot, babe?' he asked. He felt compelled to play the host now that they'd gotten to know each other.

'I don't do drugs,' she answered, gazing through the floor-to-ceiling window at the lights of the city below. 'I'll take a smoke, though, as long as you're up.'

With exactly fifteen minutes left to live, Ron Payne shook a Camel filter from the pack on the bed table, lit it and gave one to her. 'Don't set the bed on fire, okay? I don't have renter's insurance yet.'

The woman sighed and stroked his bare thigh, her cigarette flaring orange in the dark as she inhaled. 'Ronnie, I can't tell you how good I feel right now,' she said, her words flowing languidly like Southern honey. 'This is what we were both made for, don't you think?'

Ron grinned in the dark and squeezed her breast. 'It's what we were made for,' he agreed.

Within a mere month his life had come together like the knitting of a broken bone, bringing him money, respect, a shiny future. This woman, too, had become his, willowy and dusky, her eyes exotically mismatched. She'd fallen into his hand like a sun-ripened berry, suddenly and unexpectedly. He'd seen her around the clubs during the past few months, always alone, always mysterious, and he'd fantasized over her more than once, imagining with great precision the exact moves he'd made only moments ago in this very bed. That she'd shown up an hour earlier in his apartment without benefit of a key, unannounced and unplanned for, seemed like the kind of miracle that only happened to guys who wrote letters to *Penthouse*.

Amazing what a little fame and money can do for a man – right, pard?

Down on the streets of Portland he'd been just another grungy metal-man with tattoos and wild rock-and-roll hair, someone to avoid, someone to protect your teenage daughters from. Only weeks ago he'd lived as a squatter in the basement of the warehouse where his band had practiced, in a musty room with concrete-block walls and paint cans for furniture. But that sojourn into purgatory was behind him now, all part of a past and increasingly irrelevant life. Up here the air was sweet, and the stars burned clean and sharp like tiny lasers.

God, is it good to have money, or what?

Ron Payne, twenty-four, was the lead singer of Demon Beef, a 'particularly corrosive' heavy-metal band, in the words of a local underground-newspaper writer. For the past six years he and his cohorts had made the rounds of every sleazy venue in Portland, Oregon, rocking and rolling their hearts out for a slim percentage of the gate and all the drinks and bar food they could cram into their faces.

Ron had lost count of the apartments from which he'd been evicted for nonpayment of rent, not to mention the meals he'd missed. He'd lost count of the drummers, keyboard players and rhythm guitarists who'd come and gone, not to mention the rapacious scumbags who called themselves managers. He'd lost count of the girlfriends who'd given up on him and walked away, leaving him to endure his restless nights alone.

Over the years Demon Beef had gathered a following among Portland's metallic rock hounds, and Ron had become a minor local celebrity – reputation-rich but cash-poor. A year ago the band had started playing regularly at Satyricon, a rock and roll club in northwest Portland, where an executive of Kaleidoscope Records eventually heard them. The rest was fairy-tale stuff, right out of a small-time rocker's wet dream. The executive had offered them a chance to cut a demo at Kaleidoscope's studio in L.A. The tape had turned out good (*damn* good, in fact), and had brought an offer of a recording contract. Kaleidoscope had then bought two dozen of Ron's songs for sheet music and had booked Demon Beef on a national concert tour as the opening act for Megadeth, one of the heaviest heavy-metal groups in the land.

Demon Beef was now big news in town. A week ago, the Portland *Oregonian* had run a long feature on the band in its Arts and Entertainment section, replete with color photos, a tribute to local boys made good. *They're doing the Devil's bidding*! read the tongue-in-cheek headline, a play on the group's Satanist themes and visuals. The piece included a color close-up of Ron in full snake-skin make-up, snarling into the camera like a thing possessed. 'That ought to generate some letters from the religious right,' he'd quipped to the photographer.

Since receiving his first hit of money only a month ago, Ron had leased a used Porsche, rented this showy apartment in fashionable Washington Park and acquired a closetful of new clothes. He'd scored more cocaine than he could use in a year and bought two new guitars, a Fender Stratocaster for the stage and a Martin acoustic to write songs on. He felt as if he had everything he would ever need.

'Tell you what, babe. I'm going to do my nose, and then I'm coming back to bed to let you do my hose.'

The woman laughed softly. 'I suppose that sort of thing comes naturally to you songwriters.'

'Hey, I'm just getting warmed up. Stay put, okay? And don't set the bed on fire.'

'You've already told me that.' She pulled his hand to her lips and kissed his palm. Ron grinned: he had no inkling that his life would end in a mere six minutes.

Wearing only a pair of leather wristbands studded with pure silver rivets, he padded into the bathroom, where he switched on a light and pulled a Glad freezer bag from a drawer. He poured a mound of white powder onto the marble countertop. With practiced ease he used a shiny straight razor to pulverize any lumps, then channeled the powder into four straight lines.

'Want to know something, babe?' he asked, his voice bouncing harshly off the bathroom tiles. 'This success trip scares me a little. I keep wondering if I'll still be able to write good music, now that I'm a man of means. My tunes are pretty angry, right? When you get beyond all the shit about demons and devils, I'm talking about the world like it really is, and there's a lot to be pissed off about out there. But I'm not *out there* anymore – I'm in here where it's clean and warm and comfortable. I'm a little worried about staying pissed off.'

He fetched a small chrome tube from the drawer and bent low, holding the tube in one nostril. He sucked up a line of cocaine, took a few deep breaths, and moved onto the next. After sucking up this one, he stood upright a moment. A stirring reached his ears from the bedroom, leading him to believe that the dark woman was moving around on the bed, making herself comfortable, getting ready for him.

'You needn't worry about losing your anger,' he heard her say in a voice husky and low. 'I would be willing to bet that your anger outlasts you.' The coke ignited a chilly fire in Ron's nasal passages, which he enhanced by breathing hugely. He had less than four minutes now.

'I don't know about that, babe. It was easy when I spent every fuckin' minute wondering where my next meal was coming from.' He sucked up the remaining two lines, the last cocaine he would ever do. The cold fire exploded again, producing sparks behind his eyelids.

Jesus, this is good shit.

After massaging his gums with the last stray grains of the drug, he tucked the Glad bag and his utensils into the drawer, killed the light and padded into the bedroom. His eyes took a moment to readjust to the gloom, and he was momentarily blind. A breeze licked his naked skin, telling him that the woman had opened the sliding glass doors that led to the deck.

'What's the matter, babe, did you get a sudden case of

the hots?' He chuckled to himself as her sprawling image gradually took shape in the dark. His dick started to get hard again.

He lay down beside her, but she made no move to welcome him. She lay as silent as a Nordstrom mannequin, except for her breathing, which seemed weirdly guttural.

Ron endured a sudden, irrational thrill that clawed its way to the front of his mind and hung there like a big ugly spider. He'd not felt anything like it since he was a little kid, when some tiny, nonspecific sound had sometimes stirred him awake in the dead of night, leaving him trembling under the sheets, dreading the slavering thing that surely lurked behind the half-open door of his closet.

She's changed.

His hard-on withered, and his throat constricted. He reached for her tentatively, and found her skin slick with slime, found her eyes staring at him with an eldritch light behind them – unmatched, one eye warm with bloody fire and the other a glacial blue. She sat up suddenly, a lunatic shape that might have escaped from one of Ron Payne's songs.

'There's magic in your anger, Ron,' she rasped, 'but it's not enough for me. I'm sorry.'

Unlike the images of his screaming music, this thing had breath. It breathed rage. Ron stared stupidly at her, his mouth dry as cotton, his jaw working and yawning. The final few seconds of his life ticked away as moonlight glinted off her teeth, as something sliced through the dark with a faint hiss. He felt it pass over his throat, and suddenly his windpipe was clogged with blood.

PART I

'Whoever fights monsters should see to it that in the process he does not become a monster.'

Friedrich Wilhelm Nietzsche
Beyond Good and Evil
Chapter IV

CHAPTER ONE
The Man with the Deep Blue Shadow

i

Though the blast occurred at least a thousand meters away, it rattled Lieutenant Lewis Kindred to his core. A dark speck caught his eye, rocketing upward through a geyser of gray smoke. 'What the fuck . . . ?' he breathed, his stomach flopping. 'Is it incoming or what?'

'Engine block,' muttered Specialist Jesse Burton, the most seasoned fifty-caliber gunner in the platoon, his marble-hard eyes following the speck as it fell to earth. 'Some poor motherfucker ran over a mine or something.'

Lewis keyed his radio headset and ordered the platoon to halt. His four squad leaders relayed the order, and the ten armored personnel carriers, or 'tracks' as the men of the scout platoon called them, growled to a stop. He switched frequencies and called the battalion tactical operations center, which lay in a laager some ten kilometers from this noxious, tangled corner of Vietnam: 'Main Rancho Six, this is Tango. I'm approximately five hundred meters north of Charlie Papa Five. I've just observed an explosion about one klick to my west, lots of debris in the air. Looks like someone hit a mine or a booby-trapped artillery round . . .'

'That was no mine,' muttered Lewis's driver, PFC Danny Legler, a squat lad who spoke with the ponderous, commonsensical monotone of the rural Nebraskan that he was, 'and it sure as hell was no artillery round. That was at least a goddamned five-hundred-pound bomb.' He clucked and wagged his large blond head.

'Leg, what the fuck do you know about five-hundred-pound bombs?' demanded Specialist T. J. Skane, the M-60 machine gunner, a lanky black kid from L.A. 'You wouldn't know one if it crawled up and licked your dick.'

'Cut the man some slack,' said Jesse, standing now in the cupola of the track to get a better view. Tall and bull-shouldered, he wore a fragment of an olive-drab T-shirt tight around his head, a 'do-rag,' which was de rigueur among young black GIs in Vietnam. Beneath his flak jacket he was bare-chested but for his dog tags and a plastic peace symbol on a chain. 'The gooks can handle any fuckin' thing we throw at 'em, man. Charlie finds a dud five-hundred-pounder out in the bush somewhere, and presto, it ends up buried in some fuckin' road, converted into a fuckin' mine.'

He turned to the fifth man on the track, a boyish little soldier with high cheekbones and severe almond eyes. Tran Van Hai was a 'Kit Carson,' a former Viet Cong who had joined the American side. 'Ain't that right, No Bick?' asked Jesse. 'Fuckin' NVA don't sweat no little old five-hundred-pounder, do they?'

Hai apparently knew little English, and he usually responded to questions with a phrase that to American ears sounded like 'No bick.' In the hybrid lingo that Americans and Vietnamese used on one another it meant simply, 'I don't understand,' but Lewis's men suspected he understood much more than he let on. They'd pinned

No Bick on him as a nickname.

'So how about it, Hai? Did your old home-boys bury a five-hundred-pounder in the road and booby-trap it?'

'No bick.' The little man stared back at Jesse with a defiant gleam in his eyes.

'Why bother askin'' him?' ventured T. J. Skane, grinning savagely around his granny glasses. 'He'll just sit there like a frozen jar of piss and say "No bick" until his hair falls out and his ass drops off.' Danny Legler guffawed when he heard this. He thought T. J. Skane was the funniest man on God's green earth.

Lewis adjusted his headset so that one earphone rested atop his steel helmet, leaving one ear uncovered. After listening to a short radio message, he nodded unenthusiastically toward the gray mushroom in the western sky. 'The Old Man wants us to go over there and check it out.'

'Why doesn't that surprise me?' grumbled Jesse.

Lewis unbuckled his seat belt, stood, and made circles with his hand above his head, signaling his squad leaders that he wanted a meeting. They dismounted and gathered at the rear of his track for a confab that lasted a mere two minutes, long enough for Lewis to tell his NCOs to approach the blast site in a disciplined tactical formation. Sergeant Marino's squad would take the left flank, Sergeant Hillman's the right. The platoon sergeant, a profane old lifer named Markowski, would lead the two remaining squads in the center.

'Maintain strict fire discipline and stay alert,' said Lewis, wrapping up. 'That device, whatever it was, could've been command-detonated, which means the bad guys might still be in the area. And make sure your people are wearing shirts, flak jackets and steel pots, for Christ's sake. The Old Man's gonna be in a chopper overhead, and I don't want to get my ass chewed because somebody's out of uniform.'

The 'Old Man,' which is what the troopers of the 2nd Battalion of the 22nd Mechanized Infantry Brigade called their forty-year-old commanding officer, was notorious for his temper, and nothing could set him off faster than the sight of a GI without a shirt or helmet.

ii

Lieutenant Kindred's scout platoon rumbled westward out of the Ho Bo Woods, leaving behind a wasteland. Since 1965, the Americans had saturated the area with the defoliant Agent Orange, pounded it with B-52s and artillery, and bulldozed it repeatedly in a futile effort to deprive the enemy of their bunkers and tunnels. By 1970, the once-lush jungle had become dusty and desolate, a riot of dead and broken tree trunks, useless to any but the enemy, ironically, who found the revised terrain easier to negotiate and more suitable as a staging area for guerrilla attacks on Saigon and its environs.

Belching black diesel fumes, Lewis Kindred's tracks emerged into an open area sectioned into orchards of nut trees and gardens of manioc, sweet potato and peanuts. Though the monsoons had ceased in early September, a month ago, the twenty-ton fighting vehicles left wet ruts in the red laterite soil. The soldiers rode atop the vehicles, sitting on ammo crates and flak jackets, or, as in Lewis's case, actual passenger seats cannibalized from wrecked trucks or downed helicopters. To ride inside a track meant certain death if it hit a mine or took a rocket-propelled grenade, so even the drivers sat topside with everyone else, using extensions made of metal tubing to work the throttles.

Lewis pointed his platoon northwest toward the column of gray smoke rising from a dirt road. Behind the cloud, Nui Ba Den reared purple against the warm morning, an extinct volcano that Westerners knew as Black Virgin Mountain. Many old folks among the Vietnamese believed that Nui Ba Den was a sleeping goddess who would someday awaken to unleash destruction upon the land. Lewis sometimes wished that the legend were true, that the Black Virgin would send out rivers of lava and blizzards of ash to sweep away the madness that had seized her realm, and in so doing free his own life from its grip. Gazing now at her war-scarred face, he felt a premonition squirm like a snake in his gut.

A light observation helicopter, or 'loach,' orbited overhead as the platoon approached the mysterious blast site. In it was Lieutenant Colonel Gilbert Golightly, the commanding officer of 'Triple Deuce,' as the 2nd of the 22nd was known. Over the radio he tried to describe what he saw on the ground below, what Lewis and his platoon would find when they arrived.

But the scene around the crater defied words.

iii

At a distance of two hundred meters from the blast site Lewis and his men found twisted shards of metal, engine parts, and ragged chunks of human bodies. As they drew closer, the grisly wreckage became denser and more ghastly. The explosion had showered the land with bits of clothing, luggage, watches, eyeglasses, jewelry, arms, legs, heads.

The crater, which was easily thirty feet across and six feet deep, lay a quarter-mile outside an unnamed hamlet, where a dirt road passed between a stand of bamboo and a rice paddy. The demolished frame of a civilian bus hunkered near the rim of the crater, a twisted skeleton with its sides blown outward, its roof shredded. The scene was eerily silent, except for the furious buzzing of flies that had attacked in legions to feast on the atrocity.

Lewis deployed his platoon in a tight defensive circle and ordered the men to dismount, leaving behind one man on each track for security. The scouts approached the bus on foot, taking great care where they stepped, their weapons ready. Jesse Burton stayed close on Lewis's heels, for Jesse was his RTO whenever they dismounted – 'radio telephone operator' in the acronymic language of the army. Using the radio strapped to Jesse's back, Lewis stayed in touch with his men in the tracks and with the Old Man in the chopper overhead.

'Main Rancho Six, this is Tango,' he said into the radio handset while stepping carefully over a fragment of an old woman. 'The vehicle looks like a civilian bus, one of those old Isuzus you see everywhere. Apparently it hit some kind of high-explosive device, equivalent to three hundred, maybe four hundred pounds of C-4, judging from the crater and the damage. There don't appear—'

He gagged as his eyes alighted on the remains of a young woman. Her body was gone below her rib cage, though her yellow *ao dai*, the traditional full-length tunic worn by young Vietnamese women, was mostly intact. Her pretty face appeared unharmed except for the gray neutrality that signified the fleeing of life. Death, Lewis had learned during his six months in Vietnam, leaves the human face void of emotion, as blank as a round of cheese.

14

'—to be any survivors.'

'Tango, this is Rancho Six. Can you estimate the number of casualties?'

Lewis's stomach roiled. The bus, he figured, could have carried thirty passengers by Western standards, by Vietnamese standards at least three times that many. They would have clung to the top of the vehicle and perched on the edges of windows, huddled in the step well of the door, jammed themselves into the aisles, wedged themselves two or three deep in the seats. They would have smoked and joked and listened to their tinny, discordant music on their portable radios, never suspecting . . .

'I estimate ninety dead,' Lewis heard himself answer.

Colonel Golightly informed him that a company of 'Little People' was en route from the town of Trung Lap, just a few miles to the south. 'Little People' was American code for ARVN (pronounced 'Arvin'), which stood for Army of the Republic of Vietnam. Their job would be to clean up the mess, and – while they were at it, maybe – to mourn their butchered friends and neighbors. Some of the ARVNs from Trung Lap likely had relatives among the dead.

'I want you and your men to un-ass the area as soon as the Little People get there,' continued Golightly. 'They're liable to be tetchy when they see what's waiting for them, and the last thing we need is some kind of incident with our allies. Then I want you to conduct a sweep of the hamlet to your north. I'll bet you a case of George Dickle that the guys who did this are hiding up there, and we better find 'em before they do it again. Got a good copy?'

'This is Tango. Good copy.'

iv

Lewis Kindred had arrived in Vietnam barely six months earlier, a newly graduated philosophy major from the University of Oregon. Beyond his next-to-worthless sheepskin he owned little but the distinction of being a next-to-perfect poker player, a status that he'd pursued ardently since his early boyhood. He'd landed in the war zone just in time to participate in the U.S. Army's 'incursion' into Cambodia, where he'd received his baptism of fire. While the Ohio National Guard was busy killing and maiming antiwar demonstrators on the campus of Kent State, Second Lieutenant Lewis Kindred learned how to kill and maim NVA in the wilds of Southeast Asia.

After the Cambodian Incursion, Triple Deuce received assignments in the notorious Michelin rubber plantation, which lay in the shadow of Black Virgin Mountain; in the Boi Loi Woods and the Ho Bo Woods; in the infamous Iron Triangle; on 'VC Island' south of Saigon; and finally, back in the Ho Bos again. Lewis had seen his share of corpses during the first half of his tour, and he'd seen enough suffering, destruction and accidental casualties to last three lifetimes.

But *this* was by far the worst he'd ever seen. Anywhere, anytime.

'Careful where you step, L.T.,' warned Jesse Burton, grabbing his arm. The nickname was simply the abbreviation for lieutenant. Lewis glanced down and saw a severed arm so filthy with red mud that he'd almost failed to recognize it for what it was. The dead fist gripped the handle of a wicker cage, into which the owner had crammed four or five live ducks, a common way to transport fowl in Vietnam. Incredibly, several birds were still breathing and quacking loudly, having somehow survived a blast that had killed every human being on the crowded bus.

Suddenly Tran Van Hai darted in front of Lewis and snatched up the cage. He wrenched the dead arm off the handle and tossed it away as if it was so much garbage. *'Numbah one chop-chop,'* he said, holding up the cage and grinning into Lewis's face. *'Numbah one,* okay?'

Good food, yes, in the Pidgin English of Vietnam. *Numbah one* meant good, just as *numbah ten* meant bad. *Chop-chop* meant food. The Vietnamese wasted nothing, left no potential victual to spoil, not even a clutch of ducks gripped in the fist of a dead man.

Lewis glared back at No Bick, loathing him ferociously. He loathed him for stealing ducks from a dead countryman and laughing about it, for being practical and opportunistic in the midst of unspeakable carnage. He loathed him for the madness that raged throughout this painfully beautiful land, as if No Bick was somehow responsible for it all.

'Let him be, L.T.,' soothed Jesse Burton, his grip tightening on Lewis's arm. 'He's just doin' what he's doin', same as you, same as me.' Lewis's anger drained out of him, and for a panicky moment he feared that his eyes would gush tears, that he would sob and quake like a two-year-old. But he fought back the torrent. No way would he let himself go to pieces in front of his men.

The afternoon was well under way before four trucks arrived, bearing the company of ARVN from Trung Lap, all wearing grim, anxious faces and carrying their M-16 rifles tensely with their fingers on the triggers. The air around the crater was now gaggy with death. As the ARVNs piled out and started poking through the carnage, the American scout platoon saddled up and headed north for the hamlet, grateful to leave the tension and the stench behind.

'It won't piss me off if I never see anything like *that* again,' said Danny Legler in his slow, Midwestern way. 'Anyhoo, nobody back home would believe me if I told them about it.'

'Fuck it,' replied T. J. Skane, lighting a Kool. 'Don't mean nothin', man.' Which was GI slang for: *Don't think about it, man, because it means plenty.*

Lewis reported to the Triple Deuce tactical operations center that his men had found no coaxial wire leading away from the crater, so the explosive device had not been command-detonated. Still, the Old Man suspected the presence of enemy in the hamlet, and ordered a thorough 'cordon and search.' Triple Deuce's Alpha and Bravo Companies had established blocking positions north, east and west of the hamlet, ensuring that the bad guys couldn't escape when Lewis and his men went in after them.

v

A cruel tropical sun beat down upon the citizens of the hamlet, about three dozen strong, all of them women, children and old people, since draft-age males either served in the South Vietnamese military, fought on the side of the Viet Cong, or hid out to evade conscription whenever allied units were in the neighborhood. The people squatted in a tight bunch around a stone well, cowering under the guns of the Triple Deuce scout platoon. Lewis ordered his medics to give them water every half hour.

'Main Rancho Six, this is Tango,' he said into the

handset of Jesse Burton's radio. 'We've searched all the hooches and found nothing incriminating. We've questioned the villagers, and nobody admits to knowing anything about the mine in the road. All their IDs check out, and they all have nice tans. Over.' Someone with a tan obviously hadn't been holing up in a tunnel during the daylight hours, which meant that he probably was not an NVA soldier or a member of an active Viet Cong unit. Lewis felt that his platoon was wasting time here, and his tone of voice said as much.

Colonel Gilbert Golightly answered from the shade of the headquarters tent in the tactical operations center, between sips of ice-cold Mountain Dew. 'Tango, this is Six. Somebody's not being square with you, son. No way in hell the bad guys could bury that much explosive in the road without being seen by somebody in the hamlet. My guess is there's a squad of NVA hiding in a bunker somewhere nearby, and the folks in that hamlet know where they are. You stand your ground, y'hear? I'm sending you an India Papa Whiskey.'

India Papa Whiskey stood for *interrogator of prisoners of war*, a man trained by the U.S. Army to extract information from uncooperative captives. The 25th Infantry Division, the parent element of Triple Deuce, teamed its IPWs with specially selected ARVN interpreters. On a moment's notice, the IPW teams went by helicopter from the sprawling division base camp in Cu Chi to wherever they were needed.

Lewis felt his gut twist, because he'd seen them at work before – several times in Cambodia and again near the city of Dau Tieng, which lay on the edge of the Michelin rubber plantation. In his mind, IPWs were out-and-out sadists. They had informal license to commit acts that the Geneva Convention didn't allow, presumably under the pretext of *exigent need* or *tactical emergency*. In Cambodia he'd watched an IPW dislocate the elbow of an NVA soldier who refused to reveal where his unit had cached its food and ammo, then break both the man's eardrums by firing a .45 caliber pistol mere inches from his head – this without ceremony, first the right ear, then the left. The same beast had permanently crippled another prisoner, a boy no older than sixteen, by pulverizing his kneecaps with a crowbar.

Torturing enemy soldiers was ugly business in and of itself, but uglier in Lewis's mind was mistreatment of civilians. U.S. Army units frequently 'detained' civilian Vietnamese encountered during reconnaissance-in-force operations. Such detainees sometimes knew about enemy activity in the area but were understandably reluctant to share information with the foreign devils who had just plowed through their houses and gardens with tanks and armored personnel carriers. Lewis strongly believed that turning loose an IPW on civilians, as often happened – on helpless old mamasans and papa-sans, and at times even children – was unconscionable. But what could he do, if the Old Man was bent on sending an IPW? A lowly lieutenant couldn't tell a light colonel to take his IPW team and stuff it sideways up his ass, not if he wanted to stay out of Leavenworth.

'Sit tight,' he told his men through grinding teeth. 'There's an IPW inbound.' A smattering of *yeows* went up from the platoon, the kind that Lewis figured you might hear at a cock fight.

vi

A helicopter settled to earth at the edge of the hamlet, whipping up dust on the road and scattering ripples across the nearby rice paddy. An American soldier and an ARVN jumped out and jogged toward Lewis, their fatigues flapping in the rotor wash. The helicopter ascended again, dipped its nose and thundered away.

'Sergeant Gamaliel Cartee reports,' said the American, saluting smartly. 'Sir, I understand you need someone who knows how to ask questions. That's my speciality.' A striking man of indeterminate age, Cartee was as young as twenty or as old as thirty-five, as tall as Lewis but hard-looking in a rangy, sinewy way. His accent was thick Southern syrup. He was apparently racially mixed, for he had the features of an African and the complexion of a Greek or an Arab. His tailored fatigues were crisply laundered and his boots spit-shined, as if he'd moments ago stepped out of a recruiting poster, except for his jaunty bush hat, which had one edge of the brim bent-up flat against the crown in the fashion of the Australian Army.

Though he wore reflective aviator-type sunglasses, something potent poured from his eyes that Lewis couldn't define. *You're still freaked-out from this morning*, Lewis told himself, fighting down crazy notions. He pulled himself together and briefed Cartee concerning the suspicions of his battalion commander, that someone among the huddled civilians knew where to find the bastards who'd planted the monster-mine in the road.

'But you don't agree with the Old Man, do you, lieutenant?' offered Cartee, grinning. 'You're thinking they're all innocent civilians, right? I'm surprised that anyone who's spent more than a week in this stinking hell could believe there's such a thing as innocence anymore.'

'It doesn't matter what I think, sergeant,' answered Lewis. 'What do you say we get to work and do our jobs, okay?'

'The question of guilt is important to you, isn't it, sir?'

Lewis stared at the man openmouthed, as one might stare at a levitating dog. How could Cartee know, he wondered, that he had come to feel personally guilty for America's involvement in this hopeless, unwinnable war? His recurring fantasy about an eruption by the Black Virgin was really a yearning for pyroclastic *cleansing*, a fiery baptism that would wash away the guilt. Or that's what he'd told himself time and again, drawing from what he remembered of an undergraduate psychology course.

'Well, I'd better get to work,' said Cartee, removing his sunglasses, which he handed to his ARVN interpreter. 'There's no worse crime than waste of time, the old ones say.'

With the glasses no longer hiding Cartee's eyes, Lewis saw that the right one was a stony blue and the left one a deep, somber brown. He'd known more than one person with different-colored eyes, but he'd never before found the effect so unnerving. As Cartee walked toward the knot of civilians, Lewis saw something that his brain rejected, a spectacle so wildly illogical that it failed to register more than superficially in his consciousness: Cartee's shadow, cast by a blazing afternoon sun on the clay-paved apron around the village well, was a deep, almost iridescent *blue*. It had a grainy texture that seemed somehow alive, like an inky swarm of microscopic insects. Lewis looked away from it and stared instead at Nui Ba Den, the forlorn Black Virgin Mountain, telling himself that he'd not seen anything out of the ordinary. The premonition he'd endured earlier squirmed again.

Jesse Burton's low voice tugged him back to reality. 'That's one strange mother-fuckin' dude, L.T. If you want to know the truth, that's maybe the strangest mother-fuckin' dude I ever saw in my life.'

vii

Gamaliel Cartee began by addressing the civilians as a group – in Vietnamese, which came as a shock to Lewis. Americans who could speak more than a few words of real Vietnamese were rare as hen's teeth in Vietnam and, until today, he'd never met one. He wondered why Cartee even bothered to bring along the ARVN interpreter.

'What's he saying?' he asked the interpreter, a spidery sergeant in tiger-striped camouflaged fatigues. The man pursed his lips and shook his head as if brushing off a boy who dared to meddle in grown men's business. But Lewis wasn't about to be brushed off. 'I asked you a question, sergeant, and I'll get an answer, damn it! What's he saying?'

Suddenly Tran Van Hai, his own Kit Carson, was at his side, whispering urgently, his stare riveted on Cartee. 'He tells the people they must keep silent, because he wants the pleasure of beating the truth out of them. He tells them he will give them such pain that their dead ancestors will cry out from their graves.'

'Jesus, I hope this isn't his idea of winning their hearts and minds.' Lewis glared at Cartee, then turned back to Hai again, his own mouth dropping open in shock. He'd never heard his Kit Carson string together so many words of English – good English at that, only mildly accented.

All this time, it seemed, No Bick had only pretended to *no bick*.

'Sergeant Cartee means merely to frighten them, sir,' offered the interpreter glaring a dagger at Hai, the former Viet Cong. 'They are much more willing to cooperate if they are afraid. They understand nothing so well as they understand fear.'

Cartee waded into the squatting mass of civilians, his voice rising to a shriek, the liquid syllables of the language rolling over his white teeth like lava over stones. The people cowered before him, bowed their heads and pressed their palms together in front of their eyes, an Oriental gesture of respect and supplication.

Cartee selected one of them, a spindly old woman with a walnut face and silver hair knotted at the back of her head. Like nearly all the others she wore loose trousers of black silk, a white shirt with long fitted sleeves, and a conical hat that hung down her back on a string. Her lips were stained red and her teeth black from chewing betel nut, a mild stimulant favored by many elderly Vietnamese. Cartee's fist closed around her shirt and lifted her upward as if she weighed nothing. Another flood of words flowed from him, harsher now, more threatening. The old woman groped ineffectually at his forearm and issued a low moan, while Cartee's other fist closed around the knot of gray hair and pulled her head back, causing obvious pain.

'*Yeoww!*' screamed someone among the spectators of the scout platoon. 'Don't take no shit from that old mama-san, sarge! Break her fuckin' neck if you need to!'

'She is the elder of this village,' whispered No Bick, his face dark with hatred. 'She will tell him nothing. She will die before giving in to him.'

Lewis's fingernails bore deep into the skin of his fisted palms. He watched Cartee slap the old woman across the face twice, three times; heard her gurgling screams, heard the cries of the huddled civilians. One among them, a young woman whom No Bick identified as the old woman's granddaughter, leapt up and flew at Cartee with her hands spread into claws. Cartee whirled smoothly and slammed a fist into her face, and she went hard to the ground, where she lay sobbing, bleeding. More approving yells went up from the crowd of GIs.

'He demands the names of those who placed the explosive in the road,' No Bick translated. 'He commands her to show him where their tunnels are.' But the old woman only wailed pitifully and raised her pressed-together palms to her forehead, begging mercy.

Cartee appeared cool and unruffled. *This is just another day at the office to him*, thought Lewis, his rage mounting. *He's enjoying this, the cocksucker!*

Cartee beckoned to the interpreter, who jumped to his aid with a length of cord, and they tied the old mama-san's hands behind her back. Cartee snatched up the young woman from the ground by her hair. They dragged both women to a nearby ditch, which carried brown river water to the surrounding rice paddies. Cartee then announced his intentions to the mama-san loudly enough for all to hear, and No Bick translated for Lewis: Unless she gave him the information he wanted, he would kill her granddaughter – slowly and painfully. He promised that the old woman would hear the girl's dying screams in her sleep until the end of time.

'He ain't really gonna do that, is he, L.T.?' asked Jesse Burton, having overheard No Bick's translation.

'I think he's just trying to scare them,' Lewis answered lamely.

Cartee asked for a sandbag, and Lewis's own platoon sergeant, Frank Markowski, fetched one from his track. 'I've seen this trick before,' Markowski announced to the crowd. 'This is gonna be good!' Bumptious laughter went up from some GIs, while silent stares issued from others.

Cartee launched a spit-shined boot into the young woman's chest, where it landed with a thud, and the girl drew herself into a ball, gagged and gasped for air, writhing like an impaled worm on the muddy bank of the ditch. He hoisted her by the hair again, and Markowski, grinning with his bad teeth around the butt of a Pall Mall, forced the sandbag over her head. Cartee cinched the bag tight at her throat and thrust her down toward the muddy water.

The old mama-san filled the hot afternoon with her wails, and Lewis needed no translation of the words she hurled at the American. The granddaughter fought back as her head neared the water, flailed and kicked and grabbed fistfuls of Cartee's fatigues, but the man was like granite, unyielding, almost preternaturally powerful. Her head slipped below the surface of the water, held firmly by Cartee's hand at the back of her neck, and her screams died amid a flurry of bubbles.

A full minute dragged by, during which Lewis groped for images of sanity from his past life, where no mines destroyed busloads of people and no handsome monsters like Gamaliel Cartee tortured young girls. It was a life of American Bandstand with Dick Clark, poker in the friendly card rooms of downtown Portland and matinee movies with his fiancée, Twyla. It was a life of laughter and pizza and deciding whether to attend graduate school. At this moment, the quiet world of Portland, Oregon, the City of Roses, seemed so inaccessible as to have been impossible.

Somewhere on a distant rice paddy a water buffalo bellowed. A dog barked. A GI's cassette player poured out the Beatles' 'Come Together.' Gamaliel Cartee jerked the girl's head out of the water, and the fans cheered. The girl gulped for air, but the wet sandbag clung to her mouth and nostrils, letting in only enough to tease her burning lungs.

T. J. Skane, looking fragile under his bulbous Afro, turned away from the spectacle and retreated toward Lewis's track. 'Fuck me,' he breathed, shaking his head in utter dismay. 'This shit's no good, man.'

Danny Legler followed close on his heels, like a little blond mongrel with its tail between its legs. 'Don't mean nothin',' he murmured helplessly.

Cartee shouted more threats, more evil promises, and his fans clapped him on while the old woman moaned and wailed, her voice hoarse, her red-stained mouth contorted into a tragic yawn. As Cartee repositioned himself to renew the torment of the girl, his shadow fell across her body, a shadow that seemed implausibly deep and blue, full of wriggling strands of ink. The girl shivered, as if a blanket of ice crystals had fallen over her shoulders.

Am I the only one who sees this? Lewis asked himself. *Doesn't anyone else understand what's happening . . . ?*

He happened to catch Jesse Burton's eyes, and their stares locked together like radar beams in the night. *Jesse knows*, said a voice in Lewis's head. *He sees it, too . . .*

Cartee pushed the girl's head beneath the water again, shrieking like a demon, the whites of his eyes showing wholly around the mismatched irises. Then he jerked her upward again and dug his knee into the small of her back, as if to garrotte her with the tie-string of the sandbag. He glanced at the old mama-san, whom his interpreter held tightly, and hurled another stream of words at her.

'He tells her that he will break the girl's back,' translated No Bick, and Lewis thought he could hear vertebrae popping. 'She must immediately tell him where the NVA are, he says, because the girl cannot endure much more . . .'

'Man, this shit's got to cease,' hissed Jesse Burton.

'You're right,' said Lewis, his voice thick. He chucked aside his steel helmet and strode toward the bank of the ditch, teeth grinding, fists balled tight. He no longer cared whether he incurred the wrath of the Old Man or even whether he was about to jeopardize the success of a combat mission. He could not stand by quietly and watch the commission of an atrocity.

As a student of philosophy he knew the hopelessness of trying to define concepts like *truth, good* and *evil*, and he'd set himself against the absolutists who claimed monopolies on such definitions. But now he felt as if he'd found a genuine absolute – right here in a dusty little hamlet just north of the town of Trung Lap, the Republic of Vietnam, maybe the last place on earth where a philosopher would expect to find absolute *evil*. There it stood, wearing the uniform of the U.S. Army, a man who had one blue eye and one brown. A man who cast a deep blue shadow.

'That'll be enough, Cartee!' Lewis thundered, surprising himself with the timbre of his own voice. 'Let the girl go, and stand at ease!'

The platoon sergeant, Markowski, strode forward and caught hold of Lewis's arm. 'You better wait a minute, sir,' he said, his nostrils flaring and issuing smoke from the Pall Mall that clung to his lower lip. 'This man is executin' an order given to him by the commander of this battalion. Now if you don't have the intestinal fortitude . . .'

'Take your hand off me, Sergeant Markowski, or I'll have you standing in front of a summary court-martial.'

'You're making a big mistake, sir. The man's just doin' his duty!'

'I said take your hand off me!' Frank Markowski's hand fell away, and the war-ragged old veteran stepped back, scowling furiously. A chorus of boos went up from the spectators.

Gamaliel Cartee had not released the young woman, who still struggled and choked in his death-grip, while the grandmother hung limp in the arms of the interpreter, spent. Cartee himself gazed at Lewis expectantly, smiling just enough to show the tips of his ivory teeth, his mismatched eyes twinkling.

'You heard my order, sergeant. Release that girl.'

'You're wrong to direct your anger at *me*, Lieutenant Kindred,' Cartee replied softly, grinning now. '*I'm* not the problem.'

Lewis unholstered his service .45, pulled back the slide to chamber a round, and leveled it at Cartee's forehead. 'Let her go, or I'll blow your fucking head off, I swear.'

'Do you want to know who to be angry with?' asked Cartee. 'Be angry with yourself, because that's where the problem is. You've gone to war, Lieutenant Kindred, and you've killed people. You'll kill again before you're finished. You'll tell yourself it's your duty, and you may even believe that . . .'

'You have two seconds, Cartee. If you don't shut your

fucking mouth and let go of that girl, you're dead.'

Sergeant Frank Markowski piped up again, his face purpling. 'Lieutenant, you're committing an assault against a noncommissioned officer who's acting in the line of duty! According to the Uniform Code of Military Justice, I can relieve you of your command to keep you from—'

'Don't quote the UCMJ to me, you shit-brained old lifer! Sergeant Cartee has committed blatant violations of the Geneva Convention, which I've sworn to uphold as a commissioned officer, and you're a fucking accomplice, as far as I'm concerned. I could blow you both away and probably get a medal.'

Smirking as if he'd just achieved some private satisfaction, Cartee let go of the girl, and she sank to her knees in the mud, engulfed by her tormentor's swarming shadow. The ARVN interpreter loosed the hands of the old woman, who twisted away from him and went to her granddaughter. She tore off the sopping sandbag and cradled the girl's head in her arms. Lewis shouted for his favorite medic, a brawny Wyoming cowboy named Scott Sanders, who instantly showed up at his side with a first-aid rucksack.

'Make sure they're both okay, Doc,' he instructed, 'and give them something for the pain. If either of them is hurt bad, we'll dust them off to the Twelfth Evac.' *Dust-off* meant evacuation by helicopter to the Twelfth Evacuation Hospital in Cu Chi.

'You got it, L.T.' The young medic started toward the huddled women, but turned back briefly to Lewis. 'Nice goin', sir. You did right.' Lewis wanted to thank him, wanted to shake his hand and hug him, but he didn't. He glanced briefly around at his men, seeking out the friendly faces – Jesse Burton's, T. J. Skane's, Danny Legler's – while avoiding the others, chief among them the beetle-browed face of Sergeant First Class Frank Markowski.

CHAPTER TWO
The Orb

i

Nothing much came of the incident north of Trung Lap, at least not at first. Sergeant Cartee returned to his headquarters unit in Cu Chi, seemingly unruffled and bearing no grudges, which Lewis found hard to comprehend, given that he'd come close to blowing the bastard's head off. The Triple Deuce scouts went back to conducting routine reconnaissance-in-force operations in and around the Ho Bo Woods. During this period they located no NVA and engaged in no firefights, found no mines or booby traps, suffered no casualties.

Lewis struggled to put the incident with Cartee behind him, and would have succeeded if, a few days later, Sergeant First Class Frank Markowski hadn't complained to Triple Deuce's command sergeant major about his 'no-guts' platoon leader and hinted that he might bring a formal charge against Lewis for assaulting an NCO with a deadly weapon. The command sergeant major relayed the complaint to the Old Man, who called Lewis to his track one evening for an informal chat.

Colonel Golightly smoked a pipeful of rancid-smelling tobacco and delivered a 'GI-issue' lecture on the moral dilemma that confronts every officer – how to avoid becoming a killer and a thug while carrying out warfare. Warfare is basically an honorable pursuit, he insisted, one worthy of officers, gentlemen and lesser humans, notwithstanding that it occasionally demands bending the rules of decency. A good officer does this, said the colonel, only in accordance with something called the 'law of war.' He will never let civilian notions of morality get the better of him, or worse, interfere with his mission. He will suffer no pangs of guilt or sleepless nights, quite simply because he understands that any outrage he's forced to commit is honorable within the formal context of warfare. Golightly advised Lewis to forget about 'rightness' and 'wrongness,' and concern himself instead with 'honor.'

The lecture, short and neat as it was, merely hardened a conclusion that Lewis had reached months earlier: only killers and thugs go to war.

ii

A week later the scout platoon rolled into Cu Chi Base Camp for a three-day stand-down, which gave the scouts a chance to pull maintenance on the tracks, drink some beer and get their laundry done. Located on Highway 1 about twenty miles northwest of downtown Saigon, the camp was a veritable city. It had movie theaters, USO nightclubs, restaurants, swimming pools, bars, barber shops, tennis courts, baseball diamonds, gyms, massage parlors, a PX and even a bowling alley. Unfortunately it was severely lacking in the one comfort that GIs longed for above all else – round-eyed girls.

Because it housed the headquarters of the 25th Infantry Division, Cu Chi Base Camp enjoyed heavy security.

The Americans could move around unarmed inside the perimeter with little worry about snipers, booby traps or mines, thanks to a two-story fortified berm that surrounded the complex. Still, the enemy occasionally lobbed in a mortar round or a 122-millimeter rocket just to keep them honest, and occasionally a REMF, or rear-echelon motherfucker, went home in a body bag.

Lewis welcomed the chance to sleep indoors on a mattress with actual sheets, but even so, he never slept soundly in Cu Chi: too many helicopters coming and going at all hours – surveillance ships, gunships, troop ships, dust-offs, cargo carriers and couriers. The air was always astir with the *whup-whup* of rotor blades, and he'd come to think of the base camp as a massive hive, the helicopters as bees.

After getting his men safely settled in the Triple Deuce battalion area, he staked out a bunk in the company-grade officers' hooch, which boasted a day room with a pool table, dart boards and a television set. He took a leisurely shower, dressed in freshly laundered fatigues and ambled by the Headquarters Company orderly room to pick up his mail. En route back to his bunk he paused in the day room to catch the evening news on AFVN, the Armed Forces Vietnam Network, which operated the only English-language television station in the region. The station ran all the latest American network sitcoms and action shows, and, like its counterpart on the radio, served as a little slice of home reality for war-weary soldiers, sailors and airmen.

An Air Force sergeant with a sober broadcast voice read an item that made Lewis feel slightly ill:

'*A spokesman for the Criminal Investigation Division reports no leads yet concerning the grisly serial murders that have occurred during the past four months in and around the Saigon area. Army Major Vernon Karsten says that U.S. Military Police have formed a joint task force with the Saigon District Security Police to investigate the murders of twelve young women . . .'*

God help us, said Lewis to himself: We've brought more than Coca-Cola and Marlboros to Vietnam. The very idea that serial murder could occur here seemed absurd. Serial murder seemed so gut-wrenchingly Western, so unworthy of the inscrutably subtle Southeast Asians. I'll bet it's a GI, he thought.

'. . . and CID investigators are at a loss to explain the brutality of the crimes. One investigator described a murder scene as looking as if some kind of animal had attacked the victim . . .'

Lewis left the day room, shaking his head, and went to his bunk to read his mail. A letter had arrived from his fiancée, Twyla, and it improved his mood even before he cracked the envelope. She hadn't written in over two weeks, which would have unnerved him if he'd not known that she'd just started graduate school at Portland State University. Her schedule, no doubt, was a heavy one, and he didn't begrudge her some time to settle into a new routine. *She's not the most organized person in the world*, he said to himself, smiling.

As was his custom, he saved Twyla's letter for last, opening first a letter from his maiden aunt Juliet, who owned an apartment building in Portland. He didn't get far into it, for Aunt Juliet was a flaming born-again Christian who never missed an opportunity to 'witness.' Her letters were mostly sermons peppered with scriptural quotes – boring beyond belief.

More exciting was the one from his mother, which

promised a 'care package' full of home-baked butterscotch cookies within the coming week. She also shared some important family news with him: his younger brother Ken had taken a job on a drilling rig in the Gulf of Mexico, leaving his mother alone in the big family house near Laurelhurst Park in southeast Portland. Reading between the lines, Lewis surmised that she was desperately lonely. His father had died of cancer only two years earlier, and though his mother had many friends, and was active in her church and garden club, she missed having family around, missed having someone to look after. *She can live with Twyla and me after we're married*, Lewis resolved right then and there. *She can help with the kids we're going to have . . .*

Which brought him to the last letter, Twyla's. With a thrill of anticipation he held the envelope to his nose and inhaled, expecting the usual rush of Chanel No. 5. He'd given her a bottle of the costly stuff for her birthday more than a year ago, and she'd taken to scenting her letters with it after he'd gone into the army. Lewis now craved that warm fragrance nearly as much as the words of the letters themselves. The envelope that had arrived today, however, lacked any trace of Chanel No. 5.

He suffered a tiny, nonspecific dread as he stared at it. Twyla's neat cursive handwriting seemed neater than usual. Too, the return address was new, closer to Portland State, but Lewis himself had written to her and urged her to find a new apartment closer in, so this was nothing to worry about, surely. *Get control of yourself, man. She forgot to spray the letter with perfume, that's all. Stop being so damn paranoid.*

He tore the envelope open. Carefully. Slowly. Took out the single page, unfolded it.

> *Dear Lewis,*
>   *I've been dreading telling you this, and I've been searching for the right words, because I didn't want to hurt you . . .*

Ah, yes. A Dear-John, the bane of every GI who has ever slogged through a combat zone. Lewis barely skimmed the body of even handwriting, his eyes snatching up only the operative words, devouring them, then racing on in a rush to get this nightmare over with.

> *. . . someone I met at a party in August . . .*
> *. . . can't help it, but I love him . . .*

An ache developed somewhere near his solar plexus and spread throughout his chest. He felt numb, as if his blood had turned to sludge.

> *. . . no one you know . . .*
> *. . . moved in together . . .*

He set the letter aside and stared through the screened window of the officers' hooch, from which he could see the trailing edge of a tangerine sun slipping behind the berm of Cu Chi Base Camp. The sky looked angry, as he supposed he himself should be. He braved a final glance at the evil thing on his bunk.

> *. . . sent the engagement ring to your mother's house . . .*

A helicopter thundered across the bunker line of the base camp, spraying for mosquitoes, and Lewis glanced up at it. Within the few seconds that he followed it with his eyes the sun slipped completely away, leaving only the angry redness behind.

The numbness gradually left him, and the sky darkened to a velvety purple. Night devoured Vietnam. Lewis didn't cry, though he was alone in the hooch and could have done so without shaming himself. Hell, he *wanted* to cry, even felt as though he should, but he felt drained of whatever it took to muster tears.

He dug through his duffel bag and found the spare shaving kit he'd bought at the PX when he first arrived in Vietnam, in which he'd kept all the letters Twyla had written to him since then. Among them was a photo portrait taken during her senior year of college at the University of Oregon, the most recent one he owned. He took a moment to study the heart-shaped face inside the brass frame, the intelligent blue eyes and the straight golden hair. That she'd thrown aside the vow she'd made – the promise to be true, to keep him uppermost in her mind and heart – pained him unspeakably.

'Taxi girls' were a dime a dozen in Vietnam, lithe and willowy beauties, many of them, and for the equivalent of five dollars Lewis could easily have relieved himself of his sexual itch. He could have done so a hundred times, in fact, but he'd never been seriously tempted. He hadn't procured so much as a hand-job, because whenever he felt the longing, Twyla's beautiful face leapt into his head. The mere *thought* of her was enough to see him through the tough spots, along with the assurance that she would be there for him when he came home from this hellhole. He'd kept *his* promises . . .

What a chump I've been. What a stupid, fucking chump . . .

He zippered the portrait and the letters into the shaving kit, then left the hooch, carrying the kit under his arm. He followed a cement walk to an asphalt road and turned toward the Triple Deuce motor pool, which was a cluster of Quonset-type garages near the base camp perimeter. Here the air stank sharply of Vietnam, a mixture of petroleum fumes, mildew and burning shit. The army handled the product of its temporary latrines in a most direct, if not environmentally sound, manner – burned it with kerosene. The worst duty a GI could pull was the 'shit detail,' which involved dragging the brimming barrels out of the latrines, pouring in the kerosene, and setting them afire.

Lewis strode past a row of latrines and circled around behind them, taking care to stay on the walkway made of perforated steel planking lest he blunder into putrid, ankle-deep mud. He approached a flaming barrel, which was a fifty-five-gallon drum cut off to fit under the toilet seat of a latrine. Ghastly orange and green flames licked its inner edges. The stench was overpowering.

Without stopping to think further about it, he lobbed the shaving kit into the barrel, where it thudded softly into the molten excrement. A swarm of sparks rose into the night as the leather kit caught fire. In mere seconds Twyla's portrait and perfumed letters burned away to nothingness. All the words she'd written to him, the lavish dreams and her starry-eyed forecasts of their future together, the promises of children and familial bliss – all became part of the stink of Vietnam.

iii

The game was well under way when Lewis arrived in the motor pool. The players squatted on ammo boxes or sat in folding chairs around a low metal table in the center of the aluminum building – black guys, white guys, a Hispanic or two, even Tran Van Hai, the Kit Carson. Half a dozen spectators loitered on the periphery, smoking and joking, trading small talk about the 'World,' which was anywhere outside Southeast Asia.

As Lewis approached, one of the players glanced up, saw him, and shouted a '*Ten-hutt!*' but Lewis quickly replied, 'Carry on, carry on,' which obviated the enlisted men's leaping to attention. A light bulb hung on a cord from the ceiling, shrouded in a metal shade that directed a conical blast of light on to the table. Nearby stood a garbage can full of beer and ice. The garage smelled tartly of diesel oil, beer, sweat and cigarette smoke. From somebody's tape player issued the voluptuous voice of Aretha Franklin, as black as the Vietnam night but full of life.

'What's happenin', L.T.?' asked T. J. Skane, keeping his eyes fixed on his cards. 'You slummin' tonight, or did you clean out all the officers already, and you're lookin' for a new game?' A wide-tooth comb with a long handle protruded from his 'Fro.

'Hell, those college boys know better than to play cards with the L.T.,' said Scott Sanders, the good-natured medic from Wyoming. 'They ain't as dumb as they look, y' know.' The men all laughed. Most had heard how good Lewis was at poker, and several had experienced his prowess firsthand.

'I'm just looking for a low-stakes game,' Lewis replied with a sad smile. 'I don't intend to clean anyone out.' This brought another round of chuckles.

Most of the seven or eight sitting players were members of his scout platoon, among them Skane and Sanders, as well as Jesse Burton and Danny Legler. Several others were REMFs who worked in the motor pool. Lewis had not yet seen the face of the man who sat with his back to him, the one who hadn't bothered to turn around and acknowledge his presence.

'I'm gettin' the fuck out of here,' said Jesse, slapping down his cards and standing. 'I'm down my last paycheck and most of my next one.' His eyes met Lewis's and conveyed something stronger than disgust over losing money.

The man whose face Lewis had not yet seen turned around and grinned, his eyes glittering blue and brown. 'Why don't you join our game, lieutenant?' he drawled in his syrupy New Orleans accent. 'I can let bygones be bygones if you can. We promise not to rat on you for fraternizing with us degenerate enlisted types – as long as your money's green, that is.'

Lewis's mouth went dry and his voice caught like a fish bone in his throat. He understood what he'd seen in Jesse's face a few seconds earlier – the same revulsion he himself now felt. For a mad moment he saw the grinning Sergeant Gamaliel Cartee as the cause of the ugliness he'd suffered over the past few weeks, starting with the atrocity on the road north of Trung Lap, continuing with the barbarity in the hamlet and culminating with the arrival of Twyla's Dear-John letter. But this was craziness, he told himself.

'L.T., I need to talk to you a minute,' said Jesse, moving toward him around the table. 'It's a personal problem, okay?'

'Save me a seat,' said Lewis to the group, then turned to follow Jesse outside. They talked under a yard light that was under siege by a horde of anopheles mosquitoes.

'You don't want to get into a card game with that motherfucker,' Jesse warned. 'He plays poker like most dudes breathe. Now I know you're good—'

'I can handle myself in a card game.'

'I know that, sir, but—'

'Don't sir me when no one's around, goddamn it. How many times do I need to tell you that?'

'Would you *please* fuckin' listen? You're good at poker, maybe the best I ever saw before tonight, and I'm from the South Side of Chicago, man. I've *seen* some good poker players in my life, hear what I'm sayin'? But this motherfucker is like nothin' I've ever seen. He knows what cards you're holdin' in the hole, like he's got X-ray eyes or something. And he's lucky like nobody has a right to be. He's lost maybe two hands so far, and we've been playin' a good hour. He's already—'

'How much are you down?'

'Never mind that, man. What I'm worried about is—'

'How much are you down, damn it?'

'Six hundred and change – so fuckin' what? Cartee is some kind of fuckin' *machine*. He won't walk out of here until he's wiped out every swingin' dick in that game.'

'Hang tough. I'm going to get your money back for you.'

Lewis turned and strode back toward the Quonset, but Jesse grabbed his arm. Under the glare of the yard light his black face shone with sweat. 'It's not the money, L.T. It's – it's—'

'It's what?'

'I don't know. It's something else. You feel it, too, I know. Cartee isn't . . . *right*. My old gran'ma-ma would've said he ain't a natural child. It's best to stay away from people like him.'

Something cold tickled the base of Lewis's spine, and he hoped it was merely sweat running down the crack of his ass. He needed to say something sane, if not for Jesse's sake, for his own. He needed to hear sane words issue from his own lips. 'You're talking like a little kid, Jess. There's no such thing as the boogy man, in case you haven't heard. This is the real world, okay?' He dragged his fingernails across his closely cropped scalp to scratch a nonexistent itch, thinking, *That wasn't enough. I haven't convinced myself yet, much less Jesse.* 'Why should we go looking for a boogy man, for Christ's sake?' he added, hissing the words. 'We've got *Vietnam*, right? We've got NVA and VC. We've got assholes like Gilbert Golightly, Frank Markowski and that son of a bitch in there.' He nodded toward the door of the garage, meaning Cartee. Then he grinned a bit too broadly, as he often did when angry. 'Do you want to know something else, Jess? These assholes drop their trou and take a shit when they need to, just like you and me. They eat, they fuck and they get malaria if they forget to pop their little white pills. They *bleed*, Jesse, and they lose at poker.'

'Say what you want, but you've seen it, too – I know you have. You saw it when Cartee was beating the bejesus out of that little girl out by the Ho Bos. You saw his *shadow* . . .'

Lewis pulled free of Jesse's grip, no longer grinning. 'I don't want to hear any more of this. Stick around, and I'll get your money back for you. You can buy me a beer later to show your gratitude.'

iv

At the age of five Lewis Kindred learned the game of five-card draw from his father, Lyle Kindred, a beer-swilling, cigar-chomping civil engineer who'd built bridges and trestles on five continents and had played poker on six. By the age of ten Lewis knew the rules of a dozen poker games, but his favorite was seven-card stud, because it required much betting and allowed for massive bluffing. In the same way some kids become passionate about baseball, tennis or chess, and go on to devote major shares of their lives to those passions, Lewis became passionate about poker. By the time he reached high school he could hold his own in games with seasoned adults, thanks to his father's loving tutelage, and by the age of eighteen he was competitive with most professionals.

'That kid is the most natural poker player I've ever seen in my life,' Lyle Kindred had often bragged to his buddies. 'He figures odds like a computer. I swear he could bluff a honey bear off a beehive.'

Having reached his early twenties and having played ten times as much poker as most people play in a lifetime, Lewis understood the game on a level that few even know exists. He knew that winning requires much more than luck, that the laws of mathematics distribute good cards and bad cards with remarkable evenness. To win, a player must not only figure the odds of getting the best possible hand, but also calculate the probability of taking the pot with that hand. Lewis appreciated that winning at poker takes *courage*, the quality that separates good players from bad ones. A winner has the guts to back his good hands with his hard-earned cash.

Like all strong players he played conservatively, avoiding dramatic showdowns over big pots, never sandbagging his opponents to stimulate betting, never raising or calling too often. He quietly kept track of his position in the betting order and memorized the cards that showed in every hand. As the game went on he monitored the betting and bluffing patterns of everyone at the table. After losing a hand he put the loss behind him, knowing that no player wins every hand, no matter how good he is. He seldom put his trust in mere luck, and he almost never left money on the table.

Gamaliel Cartee welcomed him to the game with the offer of a beer, but Lewis never drank anything stronger than Pepsi when he played poker. Neither did he smoke or eat. He shunned anything that could conceivably cloud his judgment or distract him from the cards. From the moment he sat down, his mouth elongated into an amiable little smile that he would maintain until the very end of the game, come hell or high water, win or lose. It was his game face, his poker mask.

'Dealer's choice, lieutenant,' said Cartee, lighting the biggest green cigar that Lewis had ever seen. 'Dollar ante, maximum bet of ten, jacks or better to open.'

'Don't call me lieutenant tonight,' said Lewis through his poker smile. 'Everybody's a sir in a card game, all right?'

'How egalitarian of you. We'll call you Lewis then.'

'Call me anything you want, as long as you do it with a smile – sir.' This brought laughter from all around the table.

v

They played on a table covered with an olive-drab army blanket, using the brightly colored 'Military Payment Certificates' – MPC – with which Uncle Sam paid the troops in Vietnam. The government printed the stuff and used it in place of greenbacks, in order to keep the latter from falling into the hands of indigenous civilians and ultimately those of the enemy, who needed hard currency for buying weapons. GIs, of course, referred to MPC as 'Monopoly money.'

During the next hour players dropped out like flies, casualties of Gamaliel Cartee's murderous betting strategy. Lewis detected what most others at the table did not – that Cartee often faked a weak hand to entice bettors. Nearly every hand quickly became a big one, and Cartee won far more than his share, driving most of the players out of the game.

Lewis won enough hands to stay afloat, keeping his thin little smile in place, trading 'card-talk' with the others while hiding his knowledge of what was happening. He knew that Cartee occasionally folded to let someone else win a hand, even though he held stronger cards, just to keep people in the game and enhance his chances of cleaning them out – sandbagging on a grand scale, in other words.

'This is gettin' too rich for my blood,' drawled Scott Sanders, sounding like a refugee from a John Wayne Western. He tossed in his cards and gathered his rawboned frame to rise from the table. 'I've never seen anybody so lucky in my whole life.'

Gamaliel made a show of thanking him graciously and promised that next time things could be different. 'Every dog has his day,' he said, grinning around his green cigar.

'Ain't gonna be no next time for this dog,' muttered the cowboy.

Now only Danny Legler and T. J. Skane were left, in addition to Gamaliel and Lewis himself. Most of the spectators had wandered off to bars or movies. While Gamaliel dealt the next hand of seven-card stud, Lewis scrutinized his every movement, trying not to be conspicuous about it despite his mounting awe. If Gamaliel was cheating, he was the best cheat Lewis had ever seen, bar none. If he was *not* cheating, then his luck was nothing short of unholy.

Leg was the next to go. He shook his corn-colored mop of hair and declared that Mama Legler hadn't raised any dummies. T. J. Skane managed to last another three hands before slapping down his hole cards and getting to his feet. 'Ain't no fuckin' justice,' he murmured, eyeing the mountain of MPC in front of Gamaliel. By this time Lewis, too, was substantially down.

'Justice has nothing to do with poker, brother,' replied Gamaliel. 'It doesn't matter whether you're a good man or a bad one, you win if you hold the right cards.'

'No way I'm your brother,' said Skane, shambling off with exaggerated soul. Several other blacks went with him, as did Leg, leaving but two spectators – Jesse Burton and Tran Van Hai.

Gamaliel's laughter reverberated off the metal walls of the building and finally died among the shadows. He took a long moment to relight his cigar, then stared at Lewis with his mismatched eyes. Lewis became intensely conscious of the shadow cast by Gamaliel's hand on the olive-drab tabletop, but he stopped himself from looking directly at it, fearing what he might see. 'Just you and me now, Lewis. We've separated the sheep from the goats, it seems.'

Jesse moved close to the table and placed a hand on Lewis's shoulder. 'Time to pack it in – right, L.T.? Everybody has a bad night now and then.'

'Let's not try to make his mind up for him,' protested Gamaliel, fanning the deck of cards expertly with long, snaky fingers. 'The lieutenant – I mean *Lewis* – is a big boy now, and he's perfectly capable of making his own decisions. Isn't that right, Lewis?'

Like all strong players, Lewis knew exactly how much money he had left, so he didn't need to count it – $39, which meant he was down more than a hundred. His smile faltered, but he quickly shored it up again. Jesse was right: even the best player has a bad night occasionally. A prudent man resists the impulse to throw good money after bad, but Lewis could not bring himself simply to give in to Gamaliel Cartee. Men like Cartee shouldn't be allowed to walk off with the spoils unopposed, he told himself, a conclusion that was neither logical nor prudent.

Suddenly he suffered a mental snapshot of the bloody scene on the road north of Trung Lap, the pieces of human bodies littering the countryside like the leavings of some unfathomable carnivore. He saw the hamlet where Cartee had terrorized a spindly old woman and nearly killed an innocent young girl. He heard again the words of the AFVN announcer, describing the handiwork of a serial murderer who had struck a dozen times in and around Saigon. And finally he saw himself toss a shaving kit into a burning barrel of shit only hours ago, a fountain of sparks rising into the night, the dying remnants of his future with the woman he'd loved.

All these were threads of a psychotic tapestry, he imagined, one that depicted a scene in which he and Gamaliel Cartee were the main figures, the antagonists. Either figure represented something that was antithetical to all that the other stood for, and neither could simply walk off the field, leaving the other to win by default.

'I know what you're thinking,' said Gamaliel. 'You're

thinking that no man can possibly be as lucky as I am. You suspect I'm cheating.'

'I haven't seen you cheat, and I know what to look for. I'm not exactly new at this.'

'I don't doubt that for a moment. In fact, I recognize that you're a great poker player, Lewis, much better than I am, believe it or not. You understand odds and bluffing. You've got card sense, I think it's called. I don't.'

'Are you saying you're just lucky?'

'Not at all. What I lack in skills and knowledge, I make up for with this.' His hand slipped into the side pocket of his crisply starched fatigue jacket and brought out a crystalline globe of brilliant red, which he placed on the table next to his mound of MPC. Lewis stared wide-eyed at the object, for its innards swarmed with stuff that brought to mind living protoplasm. Slightly larger than a golf ball and perfectly spherical, it thudded on to the army blanket as if it was much heavier than it looked.

'Motherfucker,' breathed Jesse, leaning over Lewis's shoulder. 'What in the hell is it?'

'Exactly what it appears to be, just as I am,' answered Cartee, exhaling cigar smoke.

'And what in the hell is *that*?' demanded Jesse.

'Call it a gemstone or an orb. Call it a good-luck charm. It doesn't really matter what you call it, I suppose. All that matters is what you *do* with it.'

The poker smile on Lewis's face shrank. Something about the gem, perhaps the impression of movement deep inside it, reminded him of Gamaliel's shadow.

'There's nothing to be afraid of, Lewis,' soothed Gamaliel, touching the thing with a long finger. 'We're only playing poker here. I hope you don't judge me wholly on the basis of what you saw a few weeks back.'

Lewis felt an eyelid flutter, felt a muscle in his cheek start to twitch. *Jesus, the son of a bitch reads minds, too.* Judgment, he feared, was beyond his capabilities now.

'What do you want from me?' he managed to ask.

'To play to poker with you, that's all. It's what we're here for, isn't it – a small diversion from the cruelties of the real world? Since we're the only two left, let's lift the betting limit and make things more interesting.'

'I don't have that kind of money with me.'

'No problem. You're an officer and a gentleman, so I trust you. If you lose, you can owe me. I have almost nineteen hundred dollars on the table, but let's start with an ante of say, ten dollars. We can cut for the deal.'

'Don't do it, L.T.,' pleaded Jesse. 'Let's get the fuck out of here, okay? You don't need this shit, man. You don't want to *owe* this cocksucker . . .'

'Shut up, Jesse,' Lewis hissed. He cut the cards and came up with a deuce. 'Deal, Cartee. I'm in for ten.'

'Then it's five-card draw,' said Gamaliel, grinning wickedly around his cigar. 'We've played enough stud poker tonight, I think. I'm in the mood for something more pure, aren't you?' Lewis didn't protest. Given his small cash reserve, he welcomed a game that didn't require at least four rounds of betting with every hand.

Gamaliel dealt five cards each to himself and Lewis, face down. Lewis drew the deuce of clubs, three of hearts, four of diamonds, five of hearts, and jack of spades – a potential 'double-ended' straight, meaning that he needed either a six or an ace to complete a strong hand. He bet ten dollars, knowing that in order to get that hand he must overcome five-to-one odds to draw either of those cards. Under normal circumstances he never would have trusted in pure luck, but these didn't seem like normal circumstances.

Gamaliel saw the bet and called instead of raising, apparently in deference to Lewis's shaky financial position. Lewis discarded the jack and, lo, drew the precious six he needed, giving him a six-high straight. Gamaliel, too, drew one card, but his handsome face gave no inkling whether it was a good card or a bad one.

'The bet's to me,' intoned Gamaliel, laying aside the rest of the deck. 'I'll bet eighteen hundred and thirty-one dollars, which is everything I have on the table. As I said earlier, your credit's good.'

Lewis checked his hand again and felt a bolt of anticipation. The odds were finally with him. He'd gotten his card to complete the straight, which was a mind-boggling achievement in a game of five-card draw, one-on-one. The chances of Gamaliel beating this hand were mathematically remote. 'If my credit's good, I'll see you and call,' he answered, feeling a droplet of sweat crawl down his neck.

Gamaliel leaned back from the table and puffed on his cigar, making the atmosphere even more poisonous. He knitted his long-fingered hands on his stomach. 'Let's engage in an experiment before we show our cards, Lewis. It's a simple one, and it requires absolutely no effort on your part. I'll guarantee that you'll find it very entertaining.'

'What kind of experiment?'

'It has to do with tasting power and the possibilities it offers. Not everyone gets a chance like this – only a privileged few. Are you game?'

'I don't like mixing poker with parlor tricks.'

'This isn't a trick, I assure you. All you need to do is put your cards down and wait. I'll do the rest.'

Lewis was wary. Something about the proposition smelled vaguely Faustian. A taste of *power*? Suddenly it all seemed overly theatrical and downright funny. Gamaliel Cartee was obviously some sort of performing prestidigitator, and the red orb was a mere prop. Lewis had heard about sleight-of-hand artists who could cheat at cards so smoothly that not even the most experienced players could catch on, and Gamaliel was clearly one of these. Casinos routinely barred Gamaliel's kind. Lewis felt like a country bumpkin who'd lost his wad to a big-city card sharp. The boy-wonder poker player, it seemed – the kid who could bluff a honey bear off a beehive – had met his match not in Las Vegas or Paradise Island or Monte Carlo, but in a dingy motor pool in South Vietnam!

He felt a smile tug his face, felt a laugh grow in his gut. A giggle squirted out between his lips, and suddenly he could contain himself no longer. He laughed long and loud, slapping the table with his hand and stomping the floor with a boot. He laughed until the tears came, until his cheeks hurt and his ribs ached. He hadn't laughed like this in months, maybe years. Gamaliel watched him for a time, a perplexed look on his face, but then he too started to laugh, and soon the pair of them were roaring like drunken lodge brothers. The hilarity halted abruptly, however, when Lewis caught sight of Jesse Burton, who stood like a pillar of ebony outside the cone of light, his face grave. Deeper in the shadows stood No Bick, equally somber, a sharp-eyed wraith. Lewis turned back to Cartee, who immediately fell silent.

A few seconds ago Lewis had verged on admiring this handsome man who was neither black nor white and yet was both. But Gamaliel was *evil*, as the citizens of a tiny hamlet north of Trung Lap could testify, and evil was no laughing matter, not even to a philosopher who was trying excruciatingly hard not to believe in absolutes.

'About the experiment,' said Gamaliel, flicking the ash of cigar into an empty beer can. 'You know that if you turn down the invitation, you'll never forgive yourself. You have the curiosity of a cat, Lewis, just as I do.'

Lewis sat silent a long moment, staring at the orb. 'I'll agree to it under one condition,' he answered. 'You don't touch the cards.'

'Agreed. I have absolutely no need to touch the cards – not in the physical sense, anyway. Now please take one last look at your hand and place it face-down on the table in front of you.' Which Lewis did. He expected to be nearly $2,000 richer very shortly, as long as Cartee kept his hands in plain view.

'The experiment begins,' said Gamaliel. He picked up the orb and placed it on Lewis's side of the table, next to the face-down cards. 'The bauble is now yours to keep, Lewis. I hope you enjoy it. I have no doubt that you'll make good use of it in the years ahead, as I have. But I believe you called, didn't you?' He turned over his hand, card by card, and Lewis developed a sudden, blinding case of nausea. Gamaliel had drawn one card to complete a full house, jacks over nines, a phenomenal display of luck, considering that a lowly pair of deuces was statistically good enough to win more than half the hands in a one-on-one game of draw. The feat dwarfed Lewis's taking one card to fill a straight.

With his tongue feeling large and cottony, Lewis croaked his concession. He put his palms on the table and tried to stand, but his legs felt leaden. His vision went fuzzy. His own stupidity appalled him: he'd stayed in a game with someone he knew to be a sleight-of-hand artist and a cheat. No one had held a gun to his head – he'd stayed of his own free will, against Jesse Burton's warnings, merely to satisfy an unhealthy curiosity. Now he had the devil to pay.

'You may wish to check your hand,' said Gamaliel. 'With so much money in the pot, it would be a shame to make a mistake.'

'I know what my hand is.'

'Yes, but I don't.'

'I'm under no obligation to show a losing hand,' Lewis retorted bitterly, which was true according to the rules of poker. A good player never displays a losing hand, because a good player never reveals anything about his betting and bluffing strategies, even in defeat. 'I'll pay you tomorrow, after the post American Express Bank opens. I assume you can be reached through division headquarters.'

'Let's not get ahead of ourselves – you agreed to the experiment, remember? You even accepted my gift.' Gamaliel gestured toward the orb that sat in its place near Lewis's hand, still emitting its toxic red light. Lewis glanced quickly at the thing and ground his teeth. He hadn't considered it a gift and didn't plan to accept it even now. He doubted whether it had any material value, not that this mattered.

Jesse moved close and whispered, 'Can we *please* get the fuck out of here now? Haven't you done enough damage for one night?'

'I didn't take you for a man who would go back on his word,' said Gamaliel Cartee. 'I assumed that someone like you, an officer and an expert poker player, would care about his honor. Apparently I underestimated you.'

Lewis didn't care about any officers' code of honor, but he *did* care about his honor as a poker player. His father had instilled in him the belief that a dishonest man has no business at a poker table, because poker is an honest game and true poker aficionados are honorable to the core. It was true that he *had* agreed to the experiment, which implied that Gamaliel was entitled to see his cards. Besides, he would never again play poker with this man, so what did it matter if he showed his hand?

Lewis turned the cards over all together and involuntarily sucked a deep breath when he saw them: four sixes and a stray five. He looked up at Gamaliel, then at Jesse, then at the bloody red orb, his mouth working soundlessly. The room seemed to tilt.

'Well, shut my mouth!' exclaimed Gamaliel, letting the Louisiana syrup flow freely. 'I do believe that you've been trying to sandbag me, Lieutenant Kindred. You've been trying to set me up for a big old double-or-nothing bet, haven't you? Oldest trick in the book, but I must say, you're good at it – *damned* good, in fact! I'm sad to say that I've reached my limit for one night, so you'll need to find yourself another pigeon.' He pushed his mound of MPC to Lewis's side of the table. 'Thank you for the game and for your participation in the experiment. It's been a stimulating evening, to say the least. Now, if you gentlemen will excuse me . . .'

'Wait!' said Lewis hoarsely. He snatched up the orb and held it toward Gamaliel. It was heavy and disturbingly warm, as if it contained newly taken blood, and he intensely disliked the feel of it. 'This belongs to you.'

'*Au contraire*, my friend. I gave it to you in return for your participation in the experiment. It's yours to keep.'

'Negative!' shouted Lewis. 'It's *not* mine! I don't want it!'

Gamaliel took a long moment to extinguish his cigar butt, exercising care not to let any ashes fall onto the army blanket. 'You surprise me, Lewis. You've seen what this little bauble can do. The possibilities are limitless. In the hands of someone like you – well, you can just imagine what you could accomplish. All you have to do is *accept*.'

'I don't accept! I don't want anything from you. I hope to God I never lay eyes on you again, Cartee, and you'd better hope the same about me.'

A long, turbulent silence followed, during which Lewis heard neither the background *whup-whup* of helicopter blades nor the thudding of his own heart. Silence muffled his senses like falling ashes. He glared defiantly at Gamaliel, as if to blink first would be to surrender. Finally Gamaliel rose from the table and placed his bush hat squarely on his head. He straightened his fatigue jacket and smoothed out the wrinkles. He took the orb in his hand and tossed it a few times in the air before slipping it into his pocket.

'Good night, Lewis. Good night, Jesse, and Sergeant Hai.' He turned and swaggered slowly toward the door, but for one fraction of a second his shadow fell across the table, and Lewis was certain that it made a sound as it slid across the army blanket, a soft rustling sound, like living skin on fabric. Gamaliel halted a moment, spoke again. 'I knew you would be here tonight, Lewis. That's why I came – to have a game with *you*, not with these other poor fools. And I'm glad I did, too, despite the outcome. We'll play again sometime – if not poker, then another game – and maybe things will be different.' Grinning, he slipped out the door, and the night swallowed him.

CHAPTER THREE
Blood in the Night

i

Because the home base of the 25th Infantry Division was in Hawaii, the main recreation area in Cu Chi Base Camp was known as Waikiki East. The restaurant there had torches for light, potted palms for atmosphere, and locally hired waitresses dressed in muumuus and leis. The food, however, was Chinese, since Hawaiian cuisine was beyond the range of locally hired cooks. Whatever its pretensions, the place was pure Vietnam, right down to the stooped mama-sans who bused the tables and the skinny boot-shine boys who accosted every customer to come through the door.

Jesse felt like celebrating, and he badgered Lewis into joining him there for dinner. Between bites of pot-sticker he said, 'I feel like I just walked through a trip-wire, but the booby trap didn't go off. It's like I got a new lease on life. That Cartee is one dangerous son of a bitch, L. T. Don't ask me how I know this – I just know.'

Lewis nodded, but kept quiet while Jesse sipped his fifth Pabst Blue Ribbon. He wanted to talk about Gamaliel's shadow, but he couldn't bring himself to broach the subject, not even with a bellyful of beer.

59

'You got my money back for me,' Jesse went on, 'and here I am, wearing a clean uniform and pushin' Chinese chow into my face, drinking beer like there's no tomorrow – I gotta say it, man, I feel good!' He laughed deeply, his bull-shoulders lurching, but then he became serious and put down his chopsticks. 'I'm grateful to you, L. T. It looks strange, a soul brother gettin' tight with a white lieutenant, but I don't give a fuck what anybody thinks. You've been straight with me. I want you to know I appreciate it.'

Lewis grinned sloppily. He hadn't drunk this much beer since his freshman year in college. 'I can't take any credit for getting your money back, Jess. It was all part of Cartee's trick to get me to take that big red marble.' He leaned on his elbows and massaged his eyeballs through closed lids. 'I've *never* seen anybody cheat that well, not in all my years of playing poker. The way that son of a bitch handles cards, he should be on the stage.'

'Why do you suppose he was so all-fired determined to give that thing to you, anyway?'

'I don't have a fucking clue.'

Jesse paid for dinner, and they retired to the bar to listen to a Vietnamese band from Saigon render a passable version of the Jefferson Airplane's 'White Rabbit.' Lewis wondered briefly if the Kewpie-doll singer understood the lyrics she was singing, then decided that it didn't matter – in Vietnam live music was live music. He stared absently across a torch-lit patio full of GIs dressed in baggy jungle fatigues, crammed cheek by jowl around tables laden with beer bottles. Cigarette smoke blanketed the area like a tropical fog. Without knowing exactly why, Lewis felt as sorry for them as he felt for himself.

'Something's eatin' at you, L.T., and I don't think it

has anything to do with Cartee,' said Jesse, lighting a Kool. 'I don't doubt he rattled you as bad as he rattled me, but I think there's something else, too.'

Lewis felt drunker than he wanted to be and wished he was in his bunk, alone in the dark. Despite the beery fog in his head, the painful reality of Twyla's betrayal came to him again and again, like the tide on a dark shore. His face must have displayed the pain.

'You okay L.T.?' asked Jesse.

'Yeah, I'm okay – I guess. I . . . uh . . . was just thinking. I've told you about Twyla, haven't I? She's my fiancée, or at least she *was*.'

'Right. I've heard you talk about her.'

'Sent me a Dear-John. Got it this afternoon.'

Jesse shook his head, studied his newly polished jungle boots and eventually hissed a *Motherfucker!* To the troops in Vietnam only two things topped a Dear-John on the scale of personal catastrophe – getting wounded and getting killed.

'She steppin' out with Jody?' asked Jesse, referring to the mythical thief of women's affections after their men had gone off to battle. The army's marching songs were full of references to the loathsome Jody, who was rich, handsome, and for some reason immune to the draft. Lewis nodded and bluntly summarized the Dear-John. He recounted matter-of-factly how he'd thrown his entire stash of Twyla's letters into a shit-burner out by the motor pool, along with her picture. Jesse listened sympathetically, nodding as if he'd heard many such stories. When it was over, he said, 'Didn't waste any fuckin' time doin' it, did you? Throwin' her letters and pictures into a barrel of burning shit seems pretty final, not to mention symbolic, if you get my drift.'

'I wanted to insult her, and I wished like hell she could've been there to see me do it. But afterwards I felt – empty. All I wanted to do was play cards, because the world gets real small and manageable when I play cards.' He drank deeply of his beer, lowered his eyes, tried not to be dizzy. 'Trouble is, a poker game doesn't last forever.'

Jesse crushed out his Kool and lit a fresh one. 'Let me ask you a question, L.T. Could you ever forgive the bitch for this? Could you take her back if she apologized and promised to be true for evermore?'

'I – could *forgive* her, maybe, but take her back? I don't think so. I'd always wonder if I could trust her. Whenever we were apart, I'd imagine her in the sack with some graduate student, or some professor, or some fucking pizza delivery boy. And I don't think I could ever forget what it was like, sitting on the bunk tonight, reading that letter.'

'I hear you, man. Now, I'm gonna suggest something, and don't say no until you've thought about it. You need some *therapy*, and I'm not talkin' about mind-altering substances. I'm talkin' about pussy, which I know from personal experience is the best damn therapy for just about anything that's hurtin' a man. You gotta do the one thing that proves you can make a new start, L.T. – you gotta put the boots to some stranger.'

'Get serious. This is Vietnam, remember?'

'I *am* serious. I'm gonna take you to a place in Cu Chi City – it's called Mama Dao's – where a dude can get himself a first-rate blow-bath and a steam-job. The girls are pretty, they got tight asses, and in the immortal words of Jimi Hendrix, they're *experienced*, hear what I'm sayin'? It'll make a new man out of you, I swear.'

'I know the place you're talking about. It's outside the wire, for Christ's sake.'

'Of *course* it's outside the wire. They couldn't run a place like that inside the base camp – what's wrong with you, college boy? Now listen up, 'cause this is important. For a few bucks the MPs on the east gate will let us out, and all we gotta do is double-time a couple hundred meters right into Main Street Cu Chi. Mama Dao's is only a block this side of the big ARVN compound. We slip inside, get our bananas peeled, have ourselves a relaxing bath and massage, and slip back into the base camp before sun-up. Nobody's the wiser.'

For a maniacal moment Lewis imagined himself going along with the scheme, slipping into the city of Cu Chi with Jesse, finding himself a lean little whore with long, satiny hair and strong, knowing hands. He saw himself submitting to her ministrations, tasting her lips, feeling her fingers on him, and suddenly he had a hard-on, right there at the bar in Waikiki East. He knew then that Jesse was right, that throwing Twyla's letters into the shit-burner hadn't been enough.

'I can't believe I'm about to say this, Jess . . .' It was the beer talking, he knew, but he couldn't help it, not when his dick was doing his thinking for him. '. . . but you better lend me one of your shirts and some rank insignia. It might cause a stir at the gate, a lieutenant sneaking out of the base camp to visit a cathouse.'

ii

They made their way over the potholed asphalt road to the outskirts of Cu Chi, past a jumble of huts built of flattened American beer cans, testaments to the fact that Vietnamese could find good uses for just about anything the U.S. Army threw away. They halted briefly at an ARVN roadblock manned by a trio of soldiers with 'QC' on their helmets, which was the abbreviation for the Vietnamese equivalent of 'Military Police.' The senior QC gave them the once-over before waving them on with a grin and a wink. He knew exactly what they were up to.

Further on stood shops and stalls, secured for the night with barred gates of wrought iron. Lewis caught glimpses of people peering out through the bars, saw their cigarettes flare in the dark, heard their sing-songy voices as they chatted among themselves. Closer to the heart of the town he saw more people on the streets, papa-sans and mama-sans, kids, ARVN soldiers. The lights were brighter here, the buildings more substantial. Commercial signs covered virtually every square inch of wall space, hawking Coca-Cola, Marlboros, Michelin tires and a thousand other products in Vietnamese, English and French. A banner strung over the street bore the likeness of President Nguyen Van Thieu. A moped zipped past, carrying two scrawny young men. Dogs barked and babies cried. Vietnamese music drifted on the evening air, mingling with the soft light of colored lanterns and the smells of oily cooking.

Jesse led him into the main market place, beyond which lay the ARVN compound. During the daylight hours this market teemed with townspeople and farmers who carried a brisk commerce in everything from American-made flashlight batteries to roasted monkeys. Seeing it deserted gave Lewis a chill.

They stopped at a two-story building fronting a narrow side street, flanked by lush tamarind trees. Shrapnel had pocked the pink stucco walls here and there, marks of the Tet offensive of 1968 when the VC rocketed the hell out of the city, but otherwise the building was in good repair. A wide balcony overlooked a courtyard, where the management had strung colored-paper lanterns between the pillars. Bougainvillea grew in a leafy riot along the walk, and someone inside was playing the Carpenters' 'We've Only Just Begun' on a stereo.

'Welcome to Mama Dao's, L. T.,' said Jesse, patting Lewis on the shoulder. 'I'm gonna get you inside and make sure the good mama-san fixes you up with somebody real nice. Then you're on your own, my man.'

iii

The girl was exactly as Lewis had fantasized, lean but not skinny, tall for a Vietnamese and raven-haired, maybe nineteen. Her huge almond eyes bore a faint hint of European blood, suggesting a French colonialist in her family's past. She wore an elaborately embroidered *ao dai* of powder blue and, beneath it, white bell-bottoms and a New York Yankees T-shirt that some grateful soldier had given her.

Her name was Thuy Thanh, but she instructed him to call her simply Thanh, and she laughed sweetly as she talked, making Lewis feel as if he was the greatest joy she'd yet found in life. 'You gee-eye boucoup horny, yeah? You want boom-boom one hour, fie dollah MPC. You want boom-boom all night, only twenny-fie dollah MPC, okay?'

Yes, he had to admit, he *was* one very horny GI and under the circumstances he probably *could* boom-boom all night. The fee was just fine. At this moment he thought Thuy Thanh was the most beautiful creature he'd ever seen, and he would have given all he owned for a night with her. He dug into his wallet and handed a wad of MPC to Mama Dao, who was a chunky mama-san well under five feet tall with huge brass hoops through her earlobes. She took his money with a grin blackened by decades of chewing betel nut, and made a production of linking Thanh's hand with his.

Thanh led him up a flight of narrow stairs to a small, candle-lit room that stank of incense and marijuana. A low bed lay against an interior wall, and French doors opened on to a shallow balcony with a filigreed railing, beyond which stars twinkled like gems. On a low mahogany table was a clutter of religious appurtenances – a small jade Buddha, colored candles, punky sticks of incense and framed photos of dead relatives. Thanh undressed him, carefully folding his clothing. She then pulled him into a standing position, wrapped him in a clean Turkish towel, and giggled at the lump that his hard-on made beneath it.

She steered him down the hall to the steam room, which was little more than a closet with a bench in it. She deposited him on the bench and ordered him to stay put. The room was excruciatingly hot. The steam reeked pungently of rotting wood and some toxic spice akin to ginger. Before long he was thoroughly soaked with sweat, and his stinging eyes ran like faucets. But he also felt as if he was sweating out the evil humors he'd poured into himself at Waikiki East, along with a multitude of worries and anxieties. This was good. He felt mentally sharp and acutely sober.

Fifteen long minutes later Thanh reappeared, having changed into a flowered two-piece bathing suit. She shepherded him to a tiled room with an ancient bathtub in it. Following her orders, Lewis lowered himself carefully into the soapy water and suddenly felt pliable as a wet noodle.

Somewhere a stereo played a Byrds album, and his mind drifted in a fog of purely physical sensation, where no worries of the past or the future could intrude. Thanh gave him tea and sugary little rice cakes, scrubbed his back raw, lathered his hair, rinsed him thoroughly, dried him. She then led him back to the bedroom.

Silhouetted against a fulgent moon that had risen behind the tamarinds, she slipped out of her swimsuit and stood a moment at the foot of the bed, letting Lewis survey her. He did so slowly, hungrily, marveling at her satiny skin, her graceful limbs, her beautiful little breasts and the mound of dark silk between her legs. He marveled too at her smile, the warmth in her flawless face, the way the candlelight burnished her skin and made her look like something off the cover of a fantasy novel.

He now appreciated fully the addictive effect of the Orient on countless Westerners over the centuries – not just because of women like Thuy Thanh, but because of the culture that produced such women; a culture that ignored deadlines, bureaucratic decrees and other Western devices inimical to true human nature. If not for this insane war, he felt he could live out his life in a place like Cu Chi City, probably with a woman like Thanh, and become intoxicated with merely being alive. He could see himself basking forever in the coppery sunlight of this land, drinking in the fragrant colors of the landscape, reveling in the velvety nights. He could see himself growing fat on the zesty food and fathering a platoon of exquisite Amerasian kids. Unburdened of the demands of modern Western life, he would read philosophy and bloat his intellect on the idealism of Kant and the pragmatism of Nietzsche; maybe synthesize the two with the Asian mysteries that he yearned to unravel, and emerge as the great philosopher of the twentieth century. The thought made him smile.

Thanh lay down on him suddenly, covered his mouth with hers and thrust her tongue deep. So much for philosophy. The touch of her breasts against his chest nearly catapulted him to orgasm, but he somehow managed to hold back the flood. He rolled her over and went to work on her nipples with his tongue, making her moan softly. His cock was between her legs now, and she was already driving her groin against it, seeking it. Her fingers found it and pressed it into service, taking only the tip at first, but urging it deeper with every thrust. Ten such thrusts, and he was wholly inside her, engulfed in her heat. With practiced pelvic muscles she held his cock and coaxed it, squeezed it, twisted it this way and that. She sighed and moaned, licked at his earlobes with her tongue, and dug her fingernails into his buttocks as she pulled him ever tighter and deeper. Their bellies made kissing sounds as they slapped together and pulled apart.

Suddenly his orgasm exploded like a grenade launcher, and Thanh yelped as she rode him out, grinding against him until finding completion herself. Afterward they lay together a long while, their sweaty skin cooling in a breeze that whispered through the open window. Only one of the candles remained alive, the others having burned themselves into shapeless piles of wax.

'You gee-eye make me come,' she whispered in the near-dark, touching his cheek. 'I not come with other gee-eye, but you make me come, okay?'

'I'll bet you say that to all the boys.'

'No, I not say it before. You good boom-boom, okay?

You make me come. You gee-eye numbah one.'

'You too, Thanh.' He kissed her face and gently smoothed her long black hair. 'I've never known anyone like you.'

He wasn't lying. He and Twyla had slept together countless times, but Lewis had never felt with Twyla or anyone else the sheer sexual exhilaration, the total immersion and release, that Thuy Thanh had given him. The fact that he'd paid for the girl's services didn't matter in the least to him. He wondered whether he would feel this good in the morning, when the afterglow had worn off. *Who the hell cares what I feel in the morning?*

Sometime later he detected a flicker through closed eyelids, as if something bright had passed near his face. He reached for Thanh, but found only a tangle of damp sheets. He assumed she'd gotten up to go to the bathroom, that she would soon return, since he'd paid for a whole night with her. A glance at his watch told him that it was only minutes past one in the morning.

He became conscious of the *silence* – a silence that deadened the chirping of crickets in the foliage beyond the balcony and the *whup-whup* of helicopters landing and taking off from the base camp nearby. He raised himself on his elbows. Something was wrong, but he couldn't fathom what it was.

A red glow caught his eye as the door opened slowly and threw a wedge of bloody light over the bed. Lewis watched in amazement as the source of the glow came into view, and suddenly his heart began to thunder like a kettledrum.

A sphere of red crystal hung in the air over the threshold, unsupported by anything visible, glowering like a crimson eye and casting its refractive rays over the bed and walls, over Lewis himself. It was slightly larger than a golf ball. It moved lightly from side to side and up and down, as if riding a languid wave over an invisible tropical ocean. If it wasn't the same gemstone that Gamaliel Cartee had tried to give him earlier in the evening, it was identical to it.

For what seemed an eternity Lewis stared at the thing, disbelieving, blinking to purge what he hoped was a hallucination. He tried to swallow, but found that he had no spit. His scalp prickled as his brain flipped through a list of rational possibilities – invisible wires? Mirrors? A projected image? He rose from the bed and approached the orb, but it moved deeper into the black corridor as if it feared his touch. He took another step toward the door, and it floated down the corridor to his right, bouncing lightly along on invisible currents.

No lights shone under the doors of the other rooms, which seemed terribly wrong, because Mama Dao's whores and their johns should have been coming and going, so to speak, no matter how late it was. Too, a light should have burned over the staircase at the end of the corridor, but the staircase was as dark as a mine shaft. The whorehouse had plunged into a coma, seemingly.

Leaning through the door into the corridor, Lewis saw the orb halt near a room two doors away, and something made him wonder if that was the room Jesse was in. Apparently the object was waiting for him to follow, and he decided to oblige. Some scientific explanation lay behind all this, he was sure, and he decided that he must find it. He stepped into the corridor, naked, feeling as vulnerable as he'd ever felt in his life.

He approached the orb slowly, cautiously, and wondered whether it would let him close enough to detect the thin wire that must hold it. The orb did not retreat from him, but only bobbed lightly on its invisible wave. Sweat beaded Lewis's forehead, and he felt the splintery old floorboards bite the soles of his feet, heard the wood creak under his weight. Gooseflesh rose.

When he'd drawn to within an arm's length of the orb, he heard sounds from the room next to which the thing had halted – breathy, greasy sounds; the sounds of sex, he thought, and maybe something more . . .

He reached for the orb, and it didn't flee. His outstretched fingers moved to within an inch of it, but he stopped himself, for his heart was trying to climb into his throat. The image of Gamaliel Cartee loomed vivid in his mind, tall in the hot sun of a nameless hamlet near the Ho Bo Woods, casting a shadow swarming with microscopic vermin, just as the interior of this bauble swarmed with life. Somehow Lewis forced his hand to close around the thing, and the orb surrendered itself, warm and heavy, feeling just as it had felt earlier in the evening when Gamaliel had tried to give it to him. He found no wires attached to it and no threads, saw no tracks along the floor or on the ceiling through which a stage magician or a trickster could have guided the device. The damned thing had indeed levitated, a reality that gave Lewis a sick feeling in the back of his skull.

He turned toward the door. The sounds of passion in the room beyond it were becoming stronger, more violent. He tasted an unreasoning fear that filled his gullet and threatened to choke him. He labored to shape words, tried to call out, but his vocal cords balked. 'J-Jesse?'

He tried again, harder this time. 'Jesse, are you in there?' Near total darkness engulfed the corridor, since Lewis held the only source of light clenched tightly in his fist. A few crazy beams of crimson escaped between his fingers, enough to show him that the door of the room was slowly swinging open. The greasy sounds became louder still, and moonlight spilled through the balcony of the room into the corridor.

'Jesse, for Christ's sake, are you . . . ?'

Now the door stood open wide. Blood was everywhere, spilled over the floor, slung in great inky dollops across the walls – flowing from the body of Thuy Thanh, who crouched on the low bed as something took her doggy-style from behind, something that didn't look human.

Whatever this was, or *whoever* he was, he hunkered over the poor little whore like some freakish canine, his monstrous cock plunging in and out of her like a piston, literally splitting her up the middle and scattering strings of blood in all directions. His hands had long, gnarly nails that had left parallel tracks of red across the girl's skin.

While fucking Thanh to death, the thing tore strips of meat from her neck with his teeth and bolted them down like a wolf. Incomprehensibly, the girl appeared to verge on orgasm, even as the thing bit into her again and again. Lewis stood stone still, his eyes unblinking, his senses overloaded, until at last Thanh shuddered and slumped forward into the swamp of blood that had pooled on the bed. The beast pulled out of her, sated, turned his face toward Lewis and grinned with a mouthful of dazzling teeth, all pointed like a crocodile's. His brow was a bony exaggeration, his nose flared, his jaw was almost dog-like. He wore camouflaged jungle fatigues that were soggy with the girl's blood, sewn with the rank insignia of a sergeant. His atrocious cock stood out from his body like a medieval instrument of torture, throbbing and glistening in the moonlight, dripping blood.

Lewis caught the glint of the beast's mismatched eyes – the right one blue, the left one brown. *No question about who this is, is there, Lewis-old-boy? – not anymore! Did you have any doubt . . . ?* Light fluttered behind those eyes, almost as though Gamaliel had a candle inside his skull. Lewis sucked a huge lungful of air and screamed his revulsion until his throat cracked and his lungs burned.

Through lips and teeth ill suited to speech, Gamaliel whispered, 'I knew you would come, Lewis. I knew you'd be here, just like I knew you would show up last night in the motor pool to play poker. You'd be surprised how much I know about you . . .'

Lewis crossed a threshold of some kind. He reared back like a pitcher on the mound and hurled the red orb with all his might at Gamaliel's head. The thing flew as straight and true as a major-league fastball, but halted abruptly a mere foot from Gamaliel's face – arrested by some invisible force. Gamaliel grinned and plucked the object out of the air, held it a moment in his clawed hand as if to savor the glittery red ghosts of light. Then he stared again at Lewis with those cold-hot eyes, probing him, reading him, maybe even *loving* him, and Lewis could endure no more. He doubled over and retched.

Gamaliel turned away and leaped nimbly through the open French door, perched a moment on the railing of the balcony like a huge dark bird, and bid Lewis goodbye with a wave of a talon. Through blurry tears Lewis imagined that he saw his face shifting, rippling, returning to its normal shape and features, but he couldn't be sure of this. A heartbeat later Gamaliel plunged into the night as though he could fly, and perhaps he *could* fly, for Lewis heard no crash in the courtyard below, only the songs of insects and the faraway whipping of helicopter rotors.

Kneeling in the corridor outside the room, shaking so badly he could hardly breathe, Lewis covered his face with his hands and cried. He cried for Thuy Thanh and whoever else had suffered Gamaliel's lethal hunger. He cried for a world that could produce such a beast. And he cried for himself. He sobbed so hard that he didn't hear the approach of Jesse Burton behind him, and he scarcely felt Jesse's hand on his shoulder.

CHAPTER FOUR
In the Shadow of the Mountain

i

Throughout the following day and most of the next, Lieutenant Lewis Kindred went about his chores as if nothing extraordinary had happened. He attended briefings by the brigade operations officer and conducted perfunctory inspections of his platoon. He drafted morning reports, disposition forms and requisitions of new equipment. He approved and denied requests for leaves. In short, he did everything that a scout platoon leader would do during stand-down and astounded himself that he could carry on in a normal fashion, having seen what he'd seen at Mama Dao's.

On the final afternoon of the stand-down he used the land line in the Headquarters Company orderly room to call division headquarters and ask whether a particular IPW, one Sergeant Gamaliel Cartee, would be available to participate in combat operations during the coming weeks. Most assuredly, answered the grouchy warrant officer who'd answered the phone – all IPW teams were available for duty anywhere within the 25th Division's area of operation, including Sergeant Cartee. Lewis hung up before the man could ask who was calling and why.

Specialist-4 Jesse Burton had assumed a low profile since the episode at Mama Dao's, which Lewis found understandable. On the final night of the stand-down Lewis found him in the enlisted men's day room, sitting zombie-eyed in front of a TV set, chain-smoking Kools. The news was on, and there was an update on the latest serial murder in the vicinity of Saigon, the thirteenth such killing. The victim was a young prostitute in Cu Chi City . . .

Lewis lowered himself into a frayed armchair and listened in silence. He tried in vain not to conjure images of Thuy Thanh's wonderful face, all bloody and slack, made *un*wonderful by Cartee. A sudden ache in his chest took his breath away. 'We need to talk,' he said finally.

'I suppose so,' replied Jesse, absently poking through a pile of magazines on the coffee table in front of him. 'So talk.'

'Not here. Too many ears.'

'Somewhere else, then. What the fuck do I care?'

They went out into the dark and walked toward the bunker line of the base camp, past the Triple Deuce motor pool into the 2nd of the 34th Armor's tank park. Helicopters thundered overhead with typical regularity, like worker bees attending the hive, even in darkness. Parachute flares popped here and there near the horizon, accompanied by the faraway *chunk* of grenades and the *crump* of mortar fire, indicating encounters between the enemy and allied ambush patrols. Red tracers arced silently into the night, barely coming into view over the edges of the berm. Men were dying out there, Lewis knew. While he and Jesse ambled casually along the bunker line, others were suffering shattered limbs, sucking chest wounds and ruined dreams.

'This should be private enough, don't you think?' asked Jesse, propping a jungle boot against the road wheel of a parked tank. He lit a fresh Kool, and the flame from his Zippo briefly reflected in his hard, glistening eyes. 'So what do you want to talk about?'

'You know as well as I do.'

'What's there to say, man? I mean, there's nothing we can actually *do*, is there? We've already talked about goin' to the MPs, but you said yourself that nobody would believe you about seein' Cartee doin' what he was doin' to that girl. There's nothin' we can accomplish, except maybe gettin' your ass court martialed and me busted. Isn't that what we decided?'

Yes, that was what they'd decided, while running in blind panic from Mama Dao's cathouse, pulling on their clothes as they stumbled toward the base camp gate, chased by the screams of a whore who'd discovered Thuy Thanh's body. Lewis and Jesse had barely slipped into the safety of the berm when the sirens of QCs' jeeps erupted back in the city, the sounds of cops on their way to the scene of the crime.

'The long and the short of it,' Jesse went on, 'is that we were damn fortunate to un-ass that place without gettin' ourselves arrested. Hell, we might even have been suspects in the murder. If you ask me, the best thing we can do is let sleeping dogs be.'

'We can't do that, and you know it.'

'Why the hell not?'

'Because Gamaliel is *evil*, that's why. We've both seen it. We've both felt it.'

'Of course he's evil. He's a fuckin' GI, right? We're *all* evil, man. I mean, think about it: We're over here in this stinking little country, shootin' the shit out of everything that moves, knocking down people's houses, breakin' heads and splatterin' little yellow dudes all over the landscape – and for what? For Nguyen Van Thieu and his fat generals? Hell, half his people are dealin' smack to the U.S. Army. The other half are runnin' whores, or stealin' from the government and salting it away in Switzerland. If you ask me, it's evil to kill for these motherfuckers.'

'I won't argue with that. But Cartee's different from the rest of us, Jesse. I wish you could've seen his face when he was . . . when he was with Thanh. He wasn't even human. He was something else . . .'

'Come *on*, L.T. He's a trickster, that's all – a performer. He should be on the stage. You said so yourself.'

'What he did to Thanh was no trick. I'm telling you he was some kind of animal, the kind you had nightmares about when you were a little kid. You saw what Thanh looked like when he was finished with her. He's a *monster*, Jess. I've never believed in things like this, but I know what I saw. I can't just walk away from it, and neither can you.'

Jesse disagreed. He pointed out with dry logic that fighting men left Vietnam daily by the planeloads, returning to their homes, families, and girlfriends after putting in their tours. Every one of them, he was willing to bet, left a piece of himself in this smelly, rat-infested purgatory. Every one of them had suffered a day or a night or a moment that he wished to God he could take back, a snapshot in time that couldn't have happened anywhere but Vietnam, during which he'd sunk to something less than human. But in the end, every swingin' dick managed to walk away without looking back, just as Jesse himself intended to walk away when his time came. 'When I get back to the World, the air's going to smell sweet, man,

78

not like burning shit,' he declared. 'I'm goin' to a *good* place, man. Vietnam won't even exist for me.'

'Don't be so sure about that. As long as Gamaliel exists, so will Vietnam. There'll never be a good place, Jess – not while he's alive. Not for you and me.'

'How can you be so fuckin' sure of that? What makes you the fuckin' authority, huh, college boy?'

Lewis rested his forehead against the cool hull of the tank and wondered whether he was about to taste his friend's knuckles. He breathed in smoke from Jesse's cigarette, his eyes clamped tight. A mosquito stung his cheek, but he didn't care. 'He tried to give the red ball to *me*, remember? I think that's important somehow.'

'And why would you think that?'

'I don't know. I just do.' He opened his eyes. 'Remember when he left the motor pool – after I made him take it back? He turned around and said he'd *known* I would show up to play cards that night. He said he'd come to have a game with *me*, not with all you other poor fools.'

'He was fuckin' with your mind, that's all.'

'But later at Mama Dao's he said the same thing. After he'd . . .' Lewis gagged and took a slow breath. '. . . after he'd killed Thanh, he looked at me with those . . . those weird fucking eyes of his, and said that he'd known I would be there, too, at Mama Dao's; just like he'd known that I would show up in the motor pool to play poker. "You'd be surprised how much I know about you," he said, and it was like he was inside my head, Jesse, like he'd singled me out from everybody else in order to . . .'

A helicopter flew over low, a Cobra gunship outbound for some firefight deep within the seamless night of

Vietnam. Lewis let its thunder fade before continuing. 'He has *plans* for me. I don't know what they are, but I know he has plans for me. I can't wait around and let him carry them out. I know you can understand that. You've seen the red ball. You've seen his shadow. You've seen what he . . .' His voice petered out, as if the words tasted too foul to utter.

Jesse sucked deeply from his Kool, blew the smoke out slowly, harshly, and kept quiet a long time. Finally: 'So what do you want to do about him?'

Lewis reached under his fatigue shirt and pulled a blunt semiautomatic pistol from his belt, a Chinese-made K-54 that he'd taken from a captured NVA captain several months earlier. It had unusual pearl handle grips that marked it as a source of pride to its original owner. Moonlight glinted off its oily surfaces as he held it up so Jesse could see it. 'There's only one thing we *can* do, I think.'

'Oh, Jesus,' the black man breathed, his eyes round and wide. 'You don't need to say any more – I know where this is goin' . . .'

ii

Lewis got the opportunity he needed six days later on the southern edge of the Michelin rubber plantation, near the town of Dau Tieng in the shadow of Black Virgin Mountain. Colonel Golightly had sent the scout platoon on a mission to recon an overgrown area that had once been a string of hamlets, where plantation workers had lived before the U. S. Army decided to move them out in order to cut off their support of local Viet Cong units. According to intelligence reports, the NVA had since dug tunnels and built bunkers where houses once stood, and now used the area to stage attacks on Dau Tieng and the surrounding communities.

A pale rain fell as the tracks crawled forward through the low brush, their engines growling and belching black smoke as they ground down wild banana trees and pepper bushes.

Black Virgin Mountain loomed close in the mist like a remembered dream, and Lewis found himself gazing at her time and again, getting lost in fantasies about eruptions of lava and ash. *Do it!* he implored the goddess under his breath. *Do it, and make all this unnecessary*.

Noon. The scouts circled the tracks in a comparatively flat area and broke for chow. 'This is supposed to be the fuckin' dry season, man,' groused T. J. Skane, tearing open a rain-soggy box of C-rations. 'And it ain't supposed to be cold in Vietnam. It's supposed to be *hot*. This place is so fucked up that even the weather don't know how to act.' Danny Legler laughed so hard at this he almost fell off the track.

Lewis noticed that No Bick wasn't eating, that he was behaving as if he was on sentry duty. He sat rigidly on an ammo box with his rifle at the ready, his slitted eyes scanning the dark wall of rubber trees in the distance. Since the episode with Gamaliel Cartee in the hamlet north of Trung Lap, Lewis hadn't heard the Kit Carson utter more than two consecutive words of English, even though all the scouts knew by now that Hai spoke English better than most Americans. The nickname that T. J. Skane had given him still stuck – 'No Bick' – and nearly everyone in the platoon called him that. If Hai took any offense to this, he didn't show it.

He senses something out there, Lewis said to himself, studying the small man's austere face. *He knows how the bad guys think, because he's been one of them. And he's scared . . .*

Lewis set aside his cold can of 'Beef with Spiced Sauces,' and moved next to No Bick, who acknowledged him with a faint nod. 'What is it, Sergeant Hai?' he asked simply. 'I've got to know.'

No Bick gazed silently at the rubber trees as if Lewis didn't exist, his eyes sweeping slowly from side to side, water dripping off his bush hat. '*No bick*,' he replied flatly, as if this would make Lewis go away.

'Give me a break, Hai. I've heard you speak the King's English like an Oxford don, remember? This *No bick* routine doesn't pack it for me.' Hai's expression hardened, became decidedly defiant. It reminded Lewis of the faces painted on targets at the firing ranges at Fort Knox, caricatures of the villainous Viet Cong – a wily and bloodthirsty enemy who needed killing. 'Okay,' said Lewis, holding back his anger, 'have it your way. But if you see or hear something I should know about, my door is always open.'

He moved back to his own spot, where Jesse Burton was engrossed in the chore of eating pound cake from a small green can with a plastic spoon while trying to keep it dry. Their eyes met, and each knew that the other was asking himself: *Is this the day?*

Lewis hoped ardently that this *was* the day, but he'd begun to wonder if it would ever come, whether the right combination of circumstances was too much to hope for. He needed the proper tactical conditions and a suitable detainee. If he was to do the deed and get away with it, he needed a situation that would make believable the story that he and Jesse would tell. *What are the odds*, he wondered with his poker player's brain, *that it will all come together? Ten to one? A hundred to one?*

Half an hour later the platoon was under way again, sweeping close to the boundary of the plantation. Soon the scouts were near enough to make out the spiraling grooves cut into the bark of the trees, from which oozed white, rubbery sap that dripped into buckets hanging from pegs driven into the trunks. The rain relented around two o'clock and the sun broke through, generating a steamy mist that lay heavy on the land.

'There!' shouted Jesse, standing up in the cupola, pointing ahead. 'We've got movement, gentlemen!' Lewis unbuckled his seat belt and craned to see what he was pointing at. A hundred meters or so to their front stood a makeshift hooch nestled in the ground fog, one built mostly of thatched elephant grass. A man stood near it, casually eating a banana, apparently without fear of the approaching Americans and their thundering war machines. He wore a faded Hawaiian sport shirt, dirty blue trousers and a ragged conical hat. His right arm, Lewis noticed with a cringe, ended just above the elbow.

'Yeah, it's movement, all right,' he said sarcastically. 'This guy's a real menace.' But he was thinking: *The odds just improved . . . !*

Over Lewis's headset came the gravelly voice of the platoon sergeant, Frank Markowski, reporting that he too had seen the man. 'This guy's no little kid,' said Markowski, 'and he's sure as hell no old papa-san, so he must be fair game. I recommend we recon by fire. Over.'

Lewis nixed that idea, which he was certain only reinforced Markowski's conviction that he was a spineless puke and unworthy of leadership. He then ordered the platoon to halt and instructed his squad leaders to form a tactical perimeter not closer than a hundred meters from the hooch. Jesse, who also wore a headset that was plugged into the track's radios, overheard the transmission, and cast a knowing look at Lewis. *This is it, isn't it?* said his eyes, but Lewis tried to ignore him and told Markowski that he wanted a meeting with the squad leaders at his tailgate as soon as the perimeter was secure.

'Okay, gentlemen, listen up,' he told the gathered sergeants. 'Jesse and I'll interrogate the guy in the hooch. He's obviously an ARVN vet who's been wounded and discharged, but he may know something about the NVA activity around here. Sergeant Hillman, I want you to take six men on foot and set up a listening post a hundred meters west of that hooch. Sergeant Marino, I want you to do the same a hundred meters east of it. Make sure you each take at least one M-60 machine gun, and bring radios so you can stay in contact with me. The rest of you stay here with Sergeant Markowski, and keep your eyes open. Be ready to move out when I give the order, and maintain fire discipline. Also, make sure every swinging dick is wearing a steel pot and a flak jacket. Got a good copy?'

They all had good copies. And the odds were getting better and better.

iii

Lewis called battalion headquarters on the radio and advised Colonel Golightly of his situation, saying that he was about to detain and question a civilian, to which the Triple Deuce commander gave his blessing. The two foot patrols left the perimeter as Lewis had ordered, and a few minutes later he and Jesse set out on foot for the hooch, where the civilian stood as if he was waiting for them, unruffled, sunning himself.

The twenty-minute 'interrogation' took place inside the hooch, while Jesse stood guard in the doorway, his PRC-77 radio strapped to his back and his M-16 locked and loaded. The one-armed detainee's identification card verified what Lewis suspected – he was an ARVN veteran who had lost his arm in combat. Through sign language and Pidgin English Lewis learned that the man was destitute, having lost his family to the war, along with his home and most of his friends. He now lived by poaching rubber sap from the plantation and selling it in nearby Dau Tieng, earning barely enough in combination with his veteran's pension to subsist alone in this dilapidated shack. Lewis felt intensely sorry for him and wished there was something he could do for him.

The sun now blazed hotly, and inside the hooch the air was dank and smelly. Flies buzzed and bit, mosquitoes stung. The ARVN veteran incessantly scratched the severed stump of his arm with his fingernails, causing Lewis's own skin to tingle and itch.

'Okay, it's been long enough,' said Lewis, glancing at his watch. 'Time to call the Old Man.'

'Sure you want to go through with this?' asked Jesse.

'We've talked about it a hundred times. We don't have a choice, remember?'

The big black man clamped his teeth together, causing the muscles in his jaw to ripple. 'I remember.' He unhooked the radio handset from his chest strap and handed it over, avoiding Lewis's eyes.

'Main Rancho Six, this is Tango . . .' Lewis prayed his voice wouldn't quiver. '. . . I think this situation calls for an India Papa Whiskey. I have a feeling that this detainee knows more than he's letting on . . .' He told the lie smoothly and even embellished it, improvising as he went, but at length he got to the crux of the matter – the fact that he wanted not just *any* IPW. He wanted Sergeant Gamaliel Cartee, whose name he spelled out in code, the accepted radio procedure in Vietnam. Golightly, who by now was orbiting high above the Michelin rubber plantation in a loach, said he would be delighted to send an IPW, but he wondered whether sending *that* particular man was a good idea, considering the man's history with the scout platoon.

Lewis was ready with an answer, having rehearsed it thoroughly in his mind and having crafted it to appeal to Golightly's soldierly sensibilities. 'This is Tango. Sir, I can appreciate your concerns, but I want a chance to make things right with the man, to show him that there're no hard feelings on my part. I think we both deserve a chance to prove we can work together like professionals. When it comes right down to it, we're both in the same army, and despite whatever differences he and I've had, he's the best damn India Papa Whiskey I've ever seen. Over.'

There. He'd spat it all out, but he feared that it had sounded too canned, not to mention out of character. Golightly was no dummy, and he undoubtedly knew that you can wash a pig but you can't teach it to make doilies. When the colonel keyed his radio to answer, however, he was chuckling merrily, much to Lewis's relief. Golightly promised he would do all he could to bring *that* particular IPW on station.

Lewis lowered the handset and took several deep breaths in an effort to bring his pulse back to normal. *Okay, what are the odds that I'll actually get Cartee? One in three? One in five?* The enormity of what he was doing had only just begun to sink in, and the ease with which he was doing it was scary.

The Vietnamese veteran squatted in a dark corner of the hooch, his mouth twitching with worry now, for he'd seen how Americans often handled detainees, having been a soldier himself, and he clearly knew the term 'India Papa Whiskey.' Lewis tried to smile at him, tried to assure him that he wouldn't be harmed, but he didn't do a very good job on either count.

Jesse's radio crackled, and he answered it. 'It's Skane,' he muttered, holding the handset toward Lewis. 'Something about No Bick starting to talk.'

Lewis took the handset. 'This is Tango. What's going on? Over.'

Skane answered from the cupola of Lewis's track, which was parked the length of a football field from the hooch. 'That *dinky-dau* Kit Carson of yours has started to talk a blue streak, man, and he's usin' good English, you dig? Says we're parked near a big bunker complex, probably the headquarters of a regimental-size NVA unit. I say again – *regimental* size November Victor Alpha. Ain't that a bitch? Over.'

Lewis recalled the tension he'd seen in No Bick's face earlier in the day. The fact that the Kit Carson had decided to break his near-legendary silence was indeed cause for worry, regardless of whether he was right about the size of the enemy unit in these parts. Equally worrisome was the possibility that No Bick was working for the other side. The little man's sudden decision to start behaving like a real Kit Carson might have been a trick to mislead the scouts about what was really here – a cache of NVA weapons, possibly, or an underground hospital, or any of a dozen other things that a spy wouldn't want the Americans to find. Lewis keyed the radio, called Frank Markowski, the platoon sergeant, and asked whether he had monitored the transmission from Skane.

'This is Delta,' answered Markowski, his voice hard with derision. 'That's affirmative, I monitored the whole damn thing. Seems to me we should get ready to un-ass this location. I don't like to think about what might happen if we get hit by a regimental-size unit of November Victor Alpha, do you? Over.'

'This is Tango. Don't go off half-cocked, Delta – it might be a trick. Stand fast for now, but stay alert. If you see any movement, call me before you fire. I say again, call me before you fire. Got a good copy?'

'This is Delta. Roger that. We're standing fast and staying *alert*. We're also wearin' our steel pots and flak jackets. Out.' The sneer in Markowski's voice was damnnear palpable.

Twenty minutes later Lewis detected the faraway throb of rotor blades, which grew steadily louder until the sound was directly overhead. Jesse went outside to 'pop smoke' for the chopper pilot, which meant tossing a colored smoke grenade into a clear area to mark a suitable landing spot. The big slick touched down only for a moment, scattering miniature tornadoes of bright red smoke in all directions, barely long enough to disgorge two men – a Vietnamese and a tall American who was neither white nor black and yet was both.

Lewis watched from the doorway of the hooch, squinting to see through the swirling veils of red. Not until the helicopter rose again was he able to confirm that the tall man was indeed Gamaliel Cartee, immaculate as always, his creases like razors and his boots like mirrors in the hot sun. The spidery ARVN interpreter trailed him like a dutiful manservant.

Jesse slipped back into the hooch. 'We've still got time to change our minds,' he whispered.

'No way,' answered Lewis, watching the IPW team approach. The sight of Cartee made him feel cold in his guts.

The radio crackled again. 'Markowski wants to know what the fuck is going on,' said Jesse. 'Wants to know why you're not setting up security on all sides of the hooch. What should I tell him?'

'Tell him to mind his own business.'

'Lewis, I can't do that. He's the fuckin' platoon sergeant. Besides, he's got a legitimate point – we're hamburger if there's a big NVA unit out here.'

'Tell him whatever you think sounds good, but make sure he stays his distance. Now go do your thing, like we planned.'

Jesse puffed his cheeks and blew out air, making obvious his misgivings. He relayed Lewis's orders to Markowski on the radio and turned to head out the door, but held up a moment. 'What we're gettin' ready to do – it's right, isn't it?' he asked Lewis. 'I mean, we're not becoming like *him*, are we?' He motioned with his head toward the approaching IPW.

'What we're doing is good,' answered Lewis, and having heard this from his mouth, he believed it wholly.

Jesse intercepted the IPW team and told them that the lieutenant wanted only Cartee in the hooch with the detainee. 'Hey, this detainee's one spooky gook, man,' he lied. 'He used to be an ARVN, but we think he's workin' the other side of the street now. The L.T.'s afraid that if he sees an ARVN uniform he's gonna clam up, hear what I'm sayin'?' Smiling his most disarming smile, he offered the ARVN interpreter a cigarette, and the two of them put their feet against a stump and lit up. *Christ almighty*, thought Lewis, watching from the door, *Jesse's a natural-born actor*.

Cartee apparently swallowed the line and walked on toward the hooch alone. Lewis backed away from the door as he came near, having glimpsed his shadow, a colony of blue-black lice that rustled faintly as it swarmed over the ground. For a moment Lewis plunged into pure panic, the kind he thought a mouse must feel when cornered by a toothy cat. He sucked in several huge lungfuls of air, forcing himself to concentrate on what he must do, step by step, one small action at a time, and the panic evaporated as suddenly as it came.

He took a glove from the side pocket of his fatigue shirt and pushed his right hand into it. Then he pulled the pearl-handled Chinese pistol from his belt, chambered a round, and held it in the small of his back.

Cartee ducked his head to pass through the door, straightened to his full height and grinned ruthlessly at Lewis, who stood against the far wall of the cramped hooch, the ARVN veteran squatting at his feet. Saluting crisply, he said, 'Sergeant Cartee reports, sir. Nice to see you again. Played any poker lately?'

Lewis felt the heat of anger building inside him, like lava inside a volcano. He remembered Thuy Thanh as he knew he would remember her all his life, not as an exquisite young woman, but as the gory victim of the smiling monster who now stood before him. The northern slope of Black Virgin Mountain was visible through the open door of the hooch, behind Cartee, and Lewis mouthed a silent prayer to the goddess: *Do it! Erupt now, or I will!*

'With all due respect, sir, you don't look at all well,' drawled Cartee in his sickly-sweet New Orleans accent. 'You haven't been forgetting to take your malaria pills, have you?'

Lewis tried to speak, but couldn't. His mouth and throat had gone completely dry, which was fine, because he didn't have any idea what to say to someone just before blowing his head off.

'Well, you're a big boy now, aren't you, Lewis?' Cartee went on, dispensing with the military courtesy. 'You can take care of yourself, I'm sure. You take *all* the proper precautions, don't you? – like brushing your teeth after every meal and using foot powder to prevent jungle rot. I'll bet you wear rubbers when you're with whores to keep from getting the clap, don't you? Is that what you do, Lewis, when you go to Mama Dao's – wear a rubber? I don't use rubbers myself, because I don't worry about things like the clap, but I can certainly sympathize with people who do.' His mismatched eyes glittered like jewels. 'I'll bet you take other precautions as well. You're probably wearing a glove on the hand you plan to kill me with, aren't you? That way, you won't leave any fingerprints. This assumes, of course, that the Criminal Investigation Division will actually check for fingerprints, which they won't. Better to be safe than sorry, though, isn't that right, Lewis?'

Lewis brought the pistol from behind his back and pointed it squarely at Cartee's forehead. '*Ong!*' he said to the Vietnamese squatting at his feet, which meant *man* or *sir*. It was what Vietnamese men called each other. 'You *di-di mau*, okay? Take off now. Go!' He gestured north, indicating the rubber plantation, and used a hand signal to advise the man to stay low, to keep his head down. 'You're number one good guy. You're no VC, no NVA, you *bick*? You *di-di mau*.'

The man was clearly confused. He probably feared that he would be gunned down while trying to 'escape,' which was not unheard of in the annals of dead detainees. For whatever reason, he cowered even lower on the clay floor of the hooch, pressing his one hand against his stump in an awkward simulation of the Southeast Asian gesture of respect and supplication. The more Lewis hissed at him to *di-di mau*, the more he cowered and scraped.

Cartee found all this amusing and laughed wickedly. 'Lewis, Lewis. Surely you can see that the miserable wretch has no intention of cooperating with you. You may as well get used to the idea that you'll need to kill us both. You sure as hell can't shoot me and leave him as a witness.'

Lewis's lower lip trembled. 'What *are* you?' he demanded hoarsely. 'What in the name of God *are* you?'

'Invoking the name of God now, are we? That surprises me – an educated man like yourself, a naturalistic philosopher and a confirmed humanist. I thought God doesn't exist for people like you.'

Lewis's eyes began to tear, and beads of sweat skittered down the sides of his face. He knew he could kill Cartee easily, but he wasn't about to harm the innocent man at his feet. The question now was whether he was ready to spend the rest of his life in federal prison, or maybe even face a firing squad for doing the world the service of exterminating Gamaliel Cartee. He wondered what the odds were that the ARVN vet would testify against him, if the U. S. Army's Criminal Investigation

Division sought him out and questioned him.

'What's this?' asked Cartee, taking a step nearer, his mismatched eyes flashing. 'Is your anger fading? Don't let it fade, Lewis, please. Anger is *magic*. It's *power*. Don't dilute it with reason. It smells so delicious when it's pure, like yours was a moment ago.'

Lewis again urged the ARVN veteran to flee, to *di-di mau*, but the man was paralyzed with fear. Lewis's own resolve weakened, and his right hand started to shake, the one holding the pistol. He steadied it with his left one, gripping the wrist tightly.

'Really, Lewis, you're beginning to disappoint me. You called me all the way out here from Cu Chi, promising me a detainee to play with, and I hadn't been here two minutes before you pulled a gun on me. You teased me with all that sweet-smelling anger, and just when I'm starting to think, Hey, this is getting interesting, you start shaking like you've got malaria or something, and your anger goes limp. What's going on, Lewis? Are you losing your conviction, or are you just losing your nerve?'

Lewis now shouted at the Vietnamese veteran to *di-di mau*, not caring whether Cartee's interpreter heard him. But the vet curled into a fetal ball, shut his eyes tight and shivered.

Gamaliel made disgusted clicking sounds with his white teeth and shook his head. 'I swear that in all my years I've never seen a more sickening display than this, Lewis. I've severely overestimated you, I'm afraid. You've got no balls. I suppose I have no choice but to help you along . . .' Gamaliel drew his own pistol, a clubby service .45, clicked off the safety and leveled it at the head of the ARVN veteran. Lewis's eyes widened as Gamaliel took precise aim. Fire exploded from the barrel, and Lewis felt a blast of heat on his face. Loud laughter issued from Gamaliel and hung in the air like the stink of rotting meat. Lewis stared down at the twitching body of the veteran, and saw the man's brain spilling on to the hard clay floor, watched dark blood spread like a plague. Lewis's own boots had bits of the man's scalp stuck to them.

Anger like Lewis had never known filled him. Through hot tears he sighted on Gamaliel's face and squeezed the trigger of the Chinese-made K-54. The pistol bucked and spat fire. The bullet hit Gamaliel just below his left eye, the brown one, and he went down gracelessly, as if he was a marionette and someone had cut his strings. He lay on the floor of the hooch, squirting a stream of blood through the hole in his face with every failing heartbeat, until the heart stopped.

Lewis watched himself move as if detached, a disembodied spirit observing a body on autopilot. He went to the rear wall of the hooch and kicked a hole in the thatched elephant grass. He took a hand grenade from his webbed pistol belt, pulled the pin and rolled the grenade through the hole. Footfalls came from beyond the door, and shouts – Jesse and the interpreter, having heard the shouting and the pistol shots, rushing to investigate. Now he heard the pop of the grenade's fuse, and he threw himself to the floor, mindless of the lake of blood there.

The grenade exploded with a bone-crunching *chunk!* Shrapnel whistled overhead through the thatched walls of the hooch. Lewis fired into the ceiling with the K-54 again and again and again until the clip was empty. Scrambling to his feet, he snatched up his own M-16 rifle and fired a burst through the far wall, punching a score of holes through which poured shafts of sunlight. He rushed out of the hooch, his fatigues gooey with blood, none of it his own, and saw Jesse toss a grenade into the brush, then another. Both men hit the dirt, and the explosions showered them with clods and twigs.

'Where's the interpreter?' yelled Lewis, wiping dirt from his eyes.

'He's un-assing the area,' answered Jesse. He pointed to the ARVN, who ran toward the circled tracks as if a demon was on his heels. 'The man thinks this is the real thing! He likes to beat up old mama-sans, but he wants nothing to do with the fuckin' NVA!'

Lewis actually laughed, and laughing felt good. The interpreter's cowardice made things tidier. The worst was behind him, he was certain, and he felt liberated, cleansed. He glanced at Nui Ba Den and imagined that the goddess too was laughing, despite the fact that a U.S. artillery battery occupied her summit. He locked a fresh magazine into his rifle and peppered a grove of bamboo, celebrating. 'Come on – let's make this look good!'

'And sound good, too!' Jesse joined him in spraying the brush harmlessly with rifle fire. They filled the sky with their ricocheting tracers.

'We were in a firefight, okay? – just like we talked about,' shouted Lewis over the noise. He wanted to make certain their stories meshed. 'We'll say we were probed by a squad of NVA, and one of them fired into the hooch. They killed Sergeant Cartee—'

'He's actually dead?' Jesse wanted to know, his face full of wonder. 'You really put smoke on him?'

Lewis beamed from ear to ear, and let fly another burst of ammo into the brush. 'I put a round through his head, Jess. I watched his heart stop beating. This blood all over me – it's mostly Gamaliel's!' His cheeks darkened a shade, but his grin did not. 'The detainee didn't make it, I'm afraid. Gamaliel blew him away, the murdering cocksucker. He blew him away just to give me some pain, but it was nothing compared to what I gave him . . .'

Jesse grimaced, but loaded another magazine and resumed firing. Together they did an excellent job of simulating an encounter with a nonexistent unit of the NVA. After another full minute of noise and fury, which approximated the average length of a firefight in Vietnam, Lewis flipped the pearl-handled pistol into the brush, hoping that it would never be found, but not really caring. No one could prove it was his. He tossed aside the glove he'd worn, which, as Gamaliel had pointed out, had probably been a needless precaution against fingerprints. 'Let's get our asses out of here,' he said to Jesse.

iv

Never in his life had Lewis run this hard, his legs pumping like pistons as he dashed through the shimmering heat. He vaulted low shrubs, dodged clumps of bamboo and crashed through an ocean of elephant grass, loving the sting of sweat in his eyes and the tang of adrenaline in his veins. He ran as if he really had something to run from, heading for the dark green shape ahead – his armored personnel carrier. He could see T. J. Skane standing tall in the cupola, a hand shading his eyes as he tried to make out something of the 'firefight' that had erupted in the hooch to his front. Leg sat atop the driver's hatch, his hands on the laterals, ready to spin the vehicle and speed away, if the order came. *Where in the hell is Hai?* Lewis wondered.

A dozen strides later the other nine tracks came into

view, circled like a wagon train under threat of Indian attack, their crews standing on the topsides and craning in the direction from which they'd heard explosions and small-arms fire. Gamaliel Cartee's interpreter had scrambled atop Sergeant Markowski's track, and was gesturing frantically toward the hooch, no doubt trying to tell the platoon sergeant that the lieutenant and his own boss, Sergeant Cartee, had blundered into an NVA ambush.

When Lewis and Jesse had only twenty strides left to go, the afternoon suddenly crackled with a sound that reminded Lewis of a hundred Flamenco dancers shaking their castanets with no attention to rhythm or time signature. He had heard the damnable sound many times before, and as always it nearly stopped his heart – incoming small arms fire. Green tracers laced the sky and kicked up chunks of earth around him. Green was the color of tracer rounds that the NVA used, in contrast to the red that spewed from Americans' guns. The Triple Deuce scout platoon was under attack by an element of the North Vietnamese Army, a *big* one, judging from the volume of fire.

A whoosh of blue fire nearly blinded him, and the concussion of the resulting explosion knocked him onto his back. A rocket-propelled grenade had slammed into Lewis's track, and even before he comprehended this, the vehicle's fuel tank exploded, sending arcing trails of fire and smoke high above him. He rolled to his chest and pulled himself onto his hands and knees, braving an onslaught of enemy rifle fire. He saw T. J. Skane on the ground, having been blown off the vehicle, whirling and writhing, a human torch. His flesh burned away as Lewis watched.

Jesse dashed toward the fiery hull, screaming for

Danny Legler, but the vehicle was an inferno now, and its load of ammo began to cook off. A case of hand grenades exploded, hurling a blizzard of shrapnel outward from the track. Jesse fell back on the ground and covered his head with his hands.

T. J. finally lay still but for an occasional twitch, and Lewis started to go to him, but Jesse grabbed a fistful of his shirt and forced him down. Lewis twisted out of his grip, no longer caring about the danger. 'We can't just leave him!' he screamed. He bolted away and immediately tripped over what was left of Legler – a mere torso and a head of dirty blond hair hidden in the tall elephant grass. Lewis's knees buckled. His eyes flooded and his throat seized up. He went down beside the body.

The guns of the scout platoon erupted on all sides, firing in many directions – heavy machine guns and light machine guns, M-79 grenade launchers, M-16s, light antitank weapons and thrown hand grenades – a mind-shattering display of firepower. But the enemy was apparently well dug in, and the deadly fire response didn't stop them from launching a barrage of mortar rounds at the scouts. The earth shook with the detonation of every incoming round. Though he couldn't see over the brush, Lewis was certain that he heard secondary explosions, meaning that at least one track had taken a direct hit, either from mortars or rocket-propelled grenades.

He came to his tactical senses and snatched the handset of the radio off Jesse's shoulder strap. He called 'Delta,' the platoon sergeant, and asked for a 'sitrep.'

'This is Delta!' shouted Frank Markowski into the radio, his voice high and tight with the near-panic of combat. 'I thought you'd gotten blown away, Tango!

Welcome to the fuckin' Vietnam War, you no-nuts little puke. Here's a sitrep for you – we're getting hit by a regimental-size element of November Victor Alpha, and we're getting the shit kicked out of us! Unless you can think of something better to do, I'm going to take our people and execute a controlled retrograde movement, so's maybe we can get our shit together before we all get fuckin' killed . . . !'

Lewis saw GIs running past him, low to the ground, hugging the brush and trying to dodge green tracers. He recognized Sergeant Hillman, and remembered the foot patrols he'd sent out earlier.

'Negative, negative!' he shouted into the handset. 'Don't leave until we've recovered the foot patrols . . . !'

Scott Sanders, the amiable cowboy-medic from Wyoming, followed close behind Hillman. Blood covered his hands and forearms, either his own or that of someone whom the squad had been forced to leave behind. Sanders happened to see Lewis and Jesse, and he halted suddenly, turned and jumped into the brush alongside them.

'Thought you were a goner, L.T.!' he shouted above the clatter of battle. 'Where you bleedin' from?'

Lewis glanced down at his own fatigues, filthy with the blood of Gamaliel and the one-armed ARVN veteran. He tried to explain the situation to Sanders, whose young face seemed so earnest – and he *would* have explained, but a bullet fired by an NVA soldier ripped through Scott Sanders's ribcage and blew his heart out through his back. The cowboy's face went instantly slack and his forehead thudded onto Lewis's shoulder.

Lewis and Jesse ran, knowing they could do nothing for Sanders, knowing that if they stayed in that spot another thirty seconds, they too would die. Lewis tasted tears that splashed into the corners of his mouth with every stride. All around him lay dead and wounded GIs, or pieces of them among the chunks of aluminum armor that only minutes earlier had been tracks. Lewis recognized many of the bloody faces, and shouted their names as he ran, feeling that he must do this, as if shouting their names would somehow honor them and ease the guilt that was squeezing the breath out of him. They were dead or maimed because of *him*, because of his insane obsession with killing Gamaliel Cartee. If he'd kept his head on straight, he would have paid attention to his tactical responsibilities, and would have called for gunships and artillery support before halting his platoon near the suspected location of so many NVA.

But he'd *not* kept his head on straight.

Something made him turn toward Nui Ba Den – a voice in his head? He would wonder about this for many years afterward, whether a voice had called his name.

Lewis . . .

He saw the volcano wearing her misty cloak, holding a rainbow as a queen might hold a scepter. 'You didn't do this, did you?' he asked, waving a hand to indicate the chaos all around him.

Lewis . . .

Movement to his left: he saw Tran Van Hai scurry through the brush, whether chasing the enemy or fleeing to the enemy's welcoming arms, Lewis could not know. Suddenly Hai came to a dead halt and stared straight at him. Lewis felt the fury in the little man's eyes, and he wondered if it was hatred, or—

The eruption cut off his stream of thought, and he assumed it was the work of the Black Virgin, that she had finally tired of the madness and had decided to put an end to it.

v

When he opened his eyes he felt terribly cold, as if his legs were submerged in ice water. A shape came slowly into focus, metamorphosing into a soft face clothed in a surgical mask. It had clear brown eyes that were unmistakably feminine. And kind. And *warm*.

How beautiful! he thought, yearning to reach up and touch that face, to steal a bit of the warmth from those eyes and wrap himself in it.

'Lieutenant Kindred, can you hear me?' the nurse asked. Her voice barely penetrated through a twanging in his ears, the result of having stood too close to an exploding volcano. Lewis managed to nod, though his body felt leaden. *Morphine. They've given me morphine.*

'Good. You're in the Twelfth Evacuation Hospital in Cu Chi. You've had surgery, and you're in the recovery room. Do you remember what happened to you?'

'I-I think so.' His tongue felt as if it belonged to someone else. Probably the effects of the general anesthetic, he figured. 'What about Jesse – Specialist Burton? And Sergeant Hillman? And . . .'

Another face came into view, which he recognized instantly, despite the surgical mask it wore. It belonged to Lieutenant Colonel Gilbert Golightly. 'Take it easy, son,' said the colonel, placing a hammy hand on his chest. 'You're going to make it. Feeling okay?'

Again Lewis managed to nod, though he felt far from okay. The ringing in his ears was driving him crazy, and he felt like a stranger in his own body. 'What about Jesse and . . .'

'Your country owes you a man-sized debt of gratitude, Lewis, and I want you to know that I'm proud to have soldiered with you.' He reached into a pocket of his starched jungle fatigues and took out a pair of medals, which he proceeded to pin to Lewis's blanket. 'This one's the Purple Heart, which is probably the greatest honor a soldier can receive – it shows he bled for America. There's nothing better a man can do for his country than bleed for it – I believe that with all my heart. And this one is the Silver Star with Oak Leaves and "V" for "Valor" . . .'

'Fuck you and your medals!' Lewis spat. His legs were so very cold, and his left arm felt like a block of stone. He sensed a boulder of pain hovering precariously over him, held by mere threads of morphine. He couldn't abide Golightly's military drivel just now, not when there were things he needed to know. 'What about Jesse? Is he okay? Can you tell me that much?'

'Specialist Burton was only lightly wounded,' answered Golightly, his eyes brimming. 'He carried you from the field on his back, Lewis, after you were . . . *wounded* by that mortar round . . .'

So it was a mortar round, was it? – and not the Black Virgin after all. Too bad.

'. . . I'm recommending him for the Congressional Medal of Honor. I've seen uncommon valor in my time, but never anything like his.'

'What about the others – Hillman, Marino? Markowski and . . . ?'

'Sergeant Markowski took an AK-47 round through his head. I'm told he didn't suffer. As for Hillman and Marino—' The colonel said no more, but only bowed his head.

Lewis clenched his eyes for a moment and suffered an insane mix of emotion – numbed relief that Jesse survived in one piece, laced with fiery grief over his fallen men. He wanted to cry, to laugh, to scream. He feared seriously that he might piss himself. The moment passed, mercifully, and he looked into Golightly's stricken face again. Something in the colonel's expression frightened the living hell out of him.

'One thing more,' said Golightly, his voice hitching. 'Two men are missing in action, and we're afraid they're prisoners of war – Sergeant Tran Van Hai, your Kit Carson, and Sergeant Gamaliel Cartee. I want you to know, Lewis, that I'm proud as hell of the way you treated Sergeant Cartee. It showed me the kind of soldier you are, the kind of man you are, and I'm . . .'

Lewis turned his head away. He knew now what he saw in Golightly's eyes that frightened him so. It was *pity*.

Mustering every ounce of will, he reached down to touch his leg, struggling to make his right hand cooperate against the deadening effects of morphine. He expected to find the skin there as cold as ice, because his feet actually ached, they were so cold.

Panic scurried through him as he pawed and groped with his unwilling hand, finding no legs, no legs at all, not even knees, for Christ's sake – only heavily bandaged stumps. But still his feet felt so cold, which was insane. *How can you have cold feet when you don't even have legs?* He didn't realize just yet that he was screaming, that the nurse was trying to hold him down, that Colonel Golightly was yelling for a doctor to bring more morphine . . . more morphine . . .

vi

How long he floated in an ocean of featureless gray, he didn't know: hours or days, perhaps – as long as it took for someone to decide that he'd absorbed enough morphine and that it was high time Lewis Kindred woke up and faced the music. He regained consciousness in stages as the drug wore off, crossing a region of dreams that many years later he would insist were more than dreams.

He talked with his father, two years dead of cancer, and tried to make him understand why he'd had no choice but to kill Gamaliel. His father listened sympathetically, rubbing his high, narrow forehead with the tip of his index finger, a mannerism that Lewis himself had inherited. *Just remember, Lew, that nobody ever figures the odds right all the time. When you figure 'em wrong, you live with the consequences. There's no way to get the shit back into the horse, once it's on the ground . . .*

When he finally burst into full consciousness, the first thing he saw was an expanse of corrugated aluminum that curved over his bed like a canopy. He lay in a bed with crisp white sheets. A chrome i.v. rack towered over him, holding a clear plastic pouch full of something yellow. The ringing in his ears had subsided to a jangling of five or six intermittent tones. Other beds lay in a row to his right, maybe eight or ten of them, all holding men heavily bandaged like himself. Now and then someone coughed or groaned.

Yes, it's a hospital . . .

His feet and ankles itched maddeningly, but he couldn't have scratched them, even if he could have moved his arms. His legs weren't there. He thought of the ARVN veteran in the hooch near the Michelin plantation, who had endlessly scratched the stump of his arm.

Doctors and nurses quietly came and went, tending the patients as in any other hospital. Underlying the clean hospital smell was the unmistakable reek of Vietnam. Upon discovering this, he knew that he was still in the Twelfth Evac in Cu Chi, where he would probably stay until he was strong enough for transport back to the World. Then he could launch a new career selling pencils from a wheelchair.

A fragment of a dream crossed his consciousness, in which he saw No Bick staring at him in the moments before the mortar round exploded, boring holes in him with those rat-shrewd eyes of his. For a short while after the explosion, Lewis floated above his own body like an angel, surveying the scene and watching the 174th Regiment of the North Vietnamese Army decimate the Triple Deuce scout platoon. He watched No Bick crawl close, a rodent on the prowl, then skitter away, spider-like, having snatched up one of Lewis's severed legs.

Numbah one chop-chop, okay . . . ? The very notion that the Kit Carson had stolen the leg to eat it was beyond sanity, and Lewis knew this, but he couldn't make it go away. Some rural Vietnamese ate dogs; others ate monkeys. Still others ate unborn chicks still in the eggs, for Christ's sake, and drank coffee made of beans vomited up by weasels. Nowhere in Vietnam, though, did people eat people, and Lewis had absolutely no reason to think that Tran Van Hai, obviously an educated man, would make off with an American lieutenant's leg to make a meal of it.

But Hai isn't like other men, said a voice inside him. Hai was the kind who let himself be called No Bick even though he spoke immaculate English. The kind who stole ducks from a dead man. The kind who let his commanding officer circle the tracks on the doorstep of an NVA regimental tunnel complex, withholding any warning until it was too late. The long and the short of it was that Hai, in addition to being disrespectful of the dead, was still a VC, an unrehabilitated enemy soldier who saw the advantage of playing dumb. He was sneaky, duplicitous, untrustworthy. And the little bastard had run off with one of Lewis's legs . . .

vii

The window of the recovery room faced the Black Virgin. He couldn't see much of her, though, thanks to the high berm that enclosed the base camp, but he could just make out the tip of her summit, purple and forlorn in the mist. Actually he didn't care to look upon her anymore. He'd lost all faith in her. She'd failed him, left him a hopeless cripple, even though he'd declared himself her ally.

Lewis watched helicopters crisscross the sky, listened to the engines of tanks and tracks, heard occasional shouts from GIs as they passed by the Twelfth Evac. The world was carrying on without him, and the realization staggered him, bringing hot tears that he couldn't hold back. He felt more insignificant than he'd ever felt in his life.

He must have napped briefly and he opened his eyes to discover a man silhouetted against the window, dark and tall, whose features he couldn't quite see. 'Jesse, is that you?' he croaked. 'How in the holy hell did you convince them to let you in here?'

The man stepped toward the bed, casting a deep blue shadow on to the white sheets that covered the hillocks of Lewis's stumps, a shadow that seemed to rustle as it moved. 'I didn't have any trouble getting in here,' he replied in a deep Southern voice that gurgled horribly. 'But then I seldom have trouble going where I want to go.'

Lewis narrowed his eyes and nearly swallowed his tongue. The man's cheek was crusty with dried blood. Beneath the left eye, the brown one, was a small round hole with ragged edges, a bullet wound. Lewis could smell the rotting gore that still clung to the visitor's camouflaged fatigues.

This wasn't Jesse.

The man, or whatever it was, ran a long finger over the medical chart that hung on the foot of Lewis's bed. 'You certainly managed to get yourself messed up, didn't you, Lewis? It says here you've lost both legs above the knees. You've suffered a shattered ulna in your left arm, a perforated spleen, fractured vertebrae in your lower lumbar region and assorted lacerations over your entire body. Sounds to me like you're about to become one of the world's experts on scar tissue.'

'How . . . how did you . . . ?' Lewis's mind balked at the hellish truth standing at the foot of his bed, and for a moment he let himself believe that he was dreaming. This couldn't be Gamaliel Cartee. He'd watched Gamaliel's heart stop beating, for the love of Christ. He'd watched the geyser of blood subside to a mere trickle through a bullet hole in the man's face.

Someone at the far end of the room coughed, and Lewis knew then that this was no dream. He remembered Colonel Golightly's revelation that two men were missing in action, Tran Van Hai and Cartee. Could this mean . . . ?

'I won't keep you awake long, Lewis. I know how very tired you must be. I just wanted to drop by and give you my regards.' Gamaliel came around the side of the bed and leaned close, affording Lewis a clear view of his ruined face. The blue and brown eyes glittered, despite the sickly yellow where white should have been. His breath made Lewis want to vomit. 'To prove to you that there aren't any hard feelings, I want to give you this.'

Lewis felt something pressing into his right hand, something hard and round and disturbingly warm. He lacked the strength at the moment to hoist it up to look at it, but he knew what it was. The orb.

'No need to protest, Lewis. I want you to have it. You need it now. You've *earned* it.'

Earned it? The idea was ghastly.

'Good-bye, Lewis and take care of yourself. I look forward to seeing you again, though I'm not sure when that will be.' Gamaliel touched Lewis's cheek with a long, blood-crusty finger. The touch was lifeless and cold, that of a dead man. Lewis felt his gorge rise, forced it down and clamped his eyes tight. He heard footsteps fading, and when he opened his eyes again, Gamaliel Cartee was gone.

PART II

'For madness as a blessing – tis denied me.'

Lord Byron
'Manfred: A Dramatic Poem'
Scene II

CHAPTER FIVE
Dream Creature

i

On September 12, 1992, the crowd was shoulder-to-shoulder at the Rockaway Lounge in downtown Portland, Oregon, an untidy mix of American subcultures that gyrated, thrashed, stomped and slammed in time to the cannonading music of the new Demon Beef. There were punks with neon-colored hairdos and safety pins through their ears, hard rockers with riveted leather straps around their necks, and deadheads who looked like anemic spiders in their white skin and black clothes. There were skinheads with bristly scalps and Nazi jewelry. There were grungies wearing ultra-baggy shorts and layers of deliberately ruined shirts. There were modern-day hippies in tie-dyed jeans, preppies in rugby shirts, and denizens of subcultures that pundits had not yet named.

Seventeen-year-old Josh Nickerson wore the uniform of 'grunge,' replete with a frayed flannel shirt and a battered Minnesota Twins baseball cap worn backwards. His choice of footwear, however, gave him away as something less than a dedicated follower – costly Nikes that qualified as anything but grunge, an unconscious statement, maybe: *Hey, I look this way because I want to. I can afford better . . .*

He was tall, lean and auburn-haired, almost a redhead – a little gawky in the baggy clothes but smooth in his movements, and sure of himself in a way that made him seem older than he was. His green eyes snapped with a restless intelligence as he scanned the crowd, poking his stare into every dark booth and corner, searching.

Not everyone at the Rockaway Lounge that night was a disciple of Demon Beef, but everyone there had at least one thing in common: curiosity. This was the band's first public appearance since the sensationally gruesome murder of its lead singer, Ron Payne, four months earlier. With his passing, Demon Beef's lift-off toward stardom had abruptly belly-flopped, but the surviving members of the band had immediately enrolled a new front man and had doggedly set out in quest of the big time once again. Portland's rock-and-roll faithful had turned out in droves to catch the band's new act.

The final song of the set ended with an eye-popping barrage of colored laser beams, shredding guitar riffs and a molten scream from the throat of the group's new singer, Darren Busby. The applause was polite but not frantic – only a smattering of *yeows* and an occasional *woof!-woof!* As the musicians plodded off the stage through a fog produced by smoke machines, Josh Nickerson and his companion drifted with the crowd toward the front exit.

'It's not the same without Ron,' he muttered. 'They're just another band now. When they lost Ron, they lost their soul.'

'I don't know how you can stand this kind of music,' said Nicole Tran with a cute sneer. 'It's nothing but screams and mind-shattering guitars. I think you're regressing, Nickster.'

'I'm here for professional reasons, you know that – not because I'm into death metal. Besides, if you hate it so much, why did you come along?'

'I like to watch you when you're stalking.'

'I didn't come here to stalk anyone.'

'Oh, right.'

'I'm here to do research, Nicki. That's all.'

They sidled past the pair of no-neck bouncers they'd conned an hour earlier with their fake IDs, and slipped outside. The cool night air felt good on Josh's face, and he drank deeply of it, grateful to breathe free of the sting of cigarette smoke in his throat. He took a moment to scan the crowd that still poured from the Rockaway Lounge into the street. Apparently many others felt as Josh did: without Payne, the band no longer had a soul. The crowd was voting with its feet.

'See, you're doing it,' said Nicole.

'Doing what?'

'Stalking.'

'I'm *not* stalking anyone. How many times do I have to tell you?'

'I'll bet she has big snoobs, doesn't she?'

Josh tried to hold back a grin, but couldn't. Nicole had been doing this kind of thing since they were little kids. He didn't doubt that she knew him better than his own sister did, and sometimes he wondered if Nicole could actually read his mind. 'It's not what you're thinking,' he allowed, chuckling. 'She's part of the story I'm working on, I swear. She's some sort of Demon Beef groupie, or at least she was before Ron Payne got killed. I was sure she would be here tonight.'

Nicole grinned slyly, keeping her lewd suspicions to herself.

They walked north on Fourth Avenue toward the lot where Josh had parked his old Escort. High above the sleek office towers of downtown Portland, stars peered feebly through a haze of urban light pollution, and the night air tingled with a hint of autumn, which was not unwelcome, because the summer had been long and scorching. The streets were chaotic with traffic, this being a Saturday night – carloads of teenagers, mostly, cruising and trolling, their stereos thudding with rap music.

'So tell me how this babe with the big snoobs figures into the story,' pressed Nicole, unable to douse her curiosity.

'I don't want to get into it right now – it's too complicated. You can read all about it when *Rolling Stone* prints it.'

Nicole laughed, but not derisively. She was one of Josh's strongest supporters in his bid for a career in investigative reporting. She'd seen the pieces he'd written for his high-school newspaper and had found them compelling and gritty, well-researched, passionate. Josh Nickerson was nothing if not passionate. Nicole had remarked, though, that his writing seemed over the heads of most high-schoolers, that his targeted audience simply didn't appreciate him. She'd suggested that he undertake a freelance project, something entirely of his own choosing, and that he submit it to magazines.

He'd taken the suggestion seriously and had hit on the idea of covering the flight to stardom of the hometown rock band, Demon Beef. The subject matter was close to his heart, inasmuch as he'd been a devotee of heavy metal as a young boy. He knew rock and roll, the inside terms,

the jargon. The story of Demon Beef was right up his
alley.

He'd talked to the group's manager, attended rehears-
als and interviewed each of the musicians, including Ron
Payne. The group had allowed him backstage during
several local gigs, and he'd become friendly with many of
the people involved with the band. He'd taken reams of
notes and had begun cobbling together the beginnings of
a feature story when catastrophe struck.

Someone killed Ron Payne mere weeks before the
band was to embark on a national tour. Not just *killed* –
ripped him to pieces, devoured parts of his body, left him
looking as if a pack of wolves had set upon him. The
Portland Police Bureau withheld the bulk of the grisly
details, but the news media gleaned enough to convey the
savagery of the crime, and the good people of Portland
lapped up the coverage like good chowder.

All this had happened last spring, when Josh and
Nicole were finishing their junior year in high school.
Feeling crushed and defeated, Josh had toyed with aban-
doning his project. But Nicole had argued that the story
of Demon Beef was still worth pursuing, even if the band
didn't manage another serious shot at stardom. The
police hadn't found Ron Payne's killer or even a clue
about the motive, according to the news coverage.
Whether or not Demon Beef ever achieved stardom, the
tragic story of Ron Payne was a juicy one, an unsolved
mystery that a good writer could turn into gold. Nothing
captures a reader's attention faster or holds it longer than
an unsolved mystery, she'd said.

All this was true, Josh agreed. A good writer would
find a story in the impact of Ron Payne's murder on the
lives of those who had known him and depended on him.

A good writer would explore the ins and outs of the mystery and relate the theories offered by those close to the victim, then lay out a theory of his own. The tale of Demon Beef was a mother lode waiting to be mined, no question about it.

He'd never told Nicole this, or anyone else, either, but he knew something about the murder that the police and the news media did not know, and he was sure that this knowledge gave him an edge, an exclusive angle that would make his version of the story an unqualified hit. But he needed to develop it, uncover more details. He needed to find a certain tall woman . . .

ii

'Damn this piece of shit!' he hissed. He twisted the key in the ignition lock one more time, pleading under his breath. 'Come on, babe, you can do it . . . make me proud now. Come *on*, babe . . .' The old Escort's starter groaned and wheezed, but refused to turn over. It gave a final *thunk!* to announce that the cause was hopeless. 'Fuck you, car.' Josh thumped the steering wheel with the heel of his hand.

'You really should watch your mouth, Nickster,' scolded Nicole. 'It's not the car's fault that you didn't buy a new battery.'

'Who has money for stuff like that? I'm a struggling writer, remember? I finance all my own investigating.'

'You know perfectly well that your father would buy you anything you asked for. If you were to say the word, you'd find a brand-new Miata in your driveway, and your car troubles would be over.'

'And you know perfectly well, Nicole,' he answered, parroting her preachy tone, 'that I cannot accept gifts from that sanctimonious, hypocritical douche bag. It's bad enough that I let him pay my tuition at Gavin Dell, which I do only because my mom insists on it. Enough said, okay?'

A central feature of Josh's life was his hatred of his father, Gregory Nickerson, a successful insurance executive. Greg had divorced Josh's mother a decade earlier, having found a pretty young secretary who was eager to play house with an important officer of a big corporation. Eventually he'd jettisoned the secretary as easily as he'd jettisoned the mother of his children.

Over the years Josh had nurtured his bitterness toward Greg Nickerson like a favorite pet, until it had grown big and unruly and downright ugly. He'd come to loathe his father and everything he stood for. He'd stopped accepting gifts from him several years earlier, which was his way of declaring that a son's affection wasn't something to be bought. He allowed one exception to the policy, however, mainly because his mother insisted on it: he let his father pay his tuition at Gavin Dell, an exclusive private school near Portland's Sylvan Heights. He would have gladly attended Lincoln High, the neighborhood public facility where Nicole Tran went to school, but his mother was adamant on the matter: her two kids would get the best education money could buy, and her philandering ex-husband would pay the freight.

'Why don't we walk?' suggested Nicole.

'You mean to tell me you're up for hiking twenty-five blocks, most of it uphill? I think I'm about to have a seizure.'

'Hey, we're young and strong, and we're not exactly pressed for time. Come on, get out. The sooner we start, the sooner we'll get there.'

They strolled three blocks west to Broadway, the main thoroughfare that ran through the heart of downtown Portland, then turned south. The street swarmed with Saturday-nighters both young and old, movie-goers and symphony patrons, bar-hoppers and plain old sightseers. The mood of the crowd was decidedly festive. The Northwest's legendary wet season was just around the corner, and everyone seemed glad for a last fling on a starry weekend night.

Josh's mood improved as they walked. He and Nicole conversed with an easy familiarity that comes only with long years of friendship. Theirs had begun more than a decade earlier, when they were both in the first grade. Immediately after her divorce, Josh's mother had moved with her brood into a venerable old Colonial Revival apartment building in Gander Ridge, a woody hillside on the southern fringe of the southwest business district. The Tran family lived in a house down the block.

Josh soon became best friends with Nicole, who was then an elfin tomboy with lively Asian eyes and a mouth that wouldn't quit. They became known throughout the neighborhood as the 'Dynamic Duo of Gander Ridge,' for one was seldom seen without the other. Though they attended different schools, they spent most of their spare hours together. Josh called her 'Nicki,' and she called him 'Nickster.' Their friendship never developed into a boy-girl thing. Josh now had a girlfriend named Laurel, a classmate at Gavin Dell whom he'd dated more or less steadily during the final months of his junior year and throughout the ensuing summer. Nicole had never dated, though her willowy Asian looks attracted glances from males of all ages.

As Josh and Nicole crossed Salmon Street two blocks

south of the Pioneer Courthouse Square, a Olds Cutlass with faded yellow paint and cheap chrome wheels turned abruptly off Broadway and nearly ran them down. Josh grabbed Nicole and hauled her back to the curb just in time, having seen the car approach from the corner of his eye. He was about to give the driver the finger when the car halted with a shriek of rubber on asphalt. The passenger door burst open, and a tall teenage boy jumped out, scowling malevolently.

'Why don't you watch where you're going, you fuckin' gook-lover?' he screamed at Josh, his voice shrill with hatred. 'What's the matter – ain't white babes good enough for you? Or are you so hard-up for a piece of ass that you've got to hit on gooks?'

The guy's thin face was a mass of pimples, and he wore a camouflaged military-surplus field jacket over a black T-shirt. His hair was shaved almost to the scalp, and he sported a chrome Nazi swastika on the pocket flap of his field jacket. Josh thought: *This guy's a skinhead with a capital S, no doubt about it, and he's probably wasted on beer or drugs, or both . . .*

Unlike their comparatively harmless imitators for whom neo-Nazi gear was little more than a fashion statement, real Nazi skinheads carried lethal toys – guns, knives, aluminum baseball bats and God knew what else. They cruised the streets in search of excuses to use those toys. What offended them most, apparently, was the sight of a racially mixed couple.

'So, what are you – deaf – you race-mixing shit bag?' The skinhead pounded the top of the Olds with a fist, and immediately his cohorts inside the car began pounding back. The effect was that of stampeding horses. 'I want to know why you're out with a gook cunt instead of an honest white girl – and I want to know *now*!'

'Don't say anything to them,' whispered Nicole, clutching Josh's arm hard enough to hurt. 'Let's turn around and go the other way, okay?'

'The son of a bitch can't get away with calling you that.' Josh's muscles tensed involuntarily and a knot formed in his gut.

'Hey, the man asked you a question, gook-lover . . .' The driver was out of the car now, a fireplug of a man who looked twenty, maybe twenty-two. His square jaw was blue with stubble, like his scalp, and he wore a brown leather jacket, faded jeans and spit-shined Doc Marten boots that reached to mid-calf. 'You *better* be deaf, because if you're givin' us attitude, you're going to be one sorry mother-fuckin' gook-lover.' He started toward them, and Nicole pulled furiously on Josh's sleeve, urging him away.

Suddenly horns started honking. Cars had queued behind the Cutlass and the skinheads were tying up traffic. Then a police siren whooped, and red and blue beacons flashed, and Josh's heart leapt with relief. A unit of Portland's finest pulled around the queue of cars and halted behind the Cutlass, upon which Pimples and Fireplug plunged back into their car. As they roared away, Fireplug shouted something obscene through the driver's window, but Josh didn't quite catch it. The police car gunned away in pursuit.

Nicole exhaled a long puff of air, her eyes huge with excitement, and for a giddy moment Josh thought she was the most beautiful thing he'd ever seen. 'You okay?' he asked her.

'I think so, yeah. I hope to God the cops put those jerks in jail before they hurt somebody.'

'Never happen. Unless they've got drugs or open beer in the car, they'll only get a lecture.'

Nicole let go of his arm, and Josh regretted this. Her grip had felt strangely good. He stared at her a long moment, wondering how in the hell anyone could object to someone as pretty as she was, or as smart, or as wise. 'Come on,' he said. 'We better cruise, or we'll never get home.'

iii

They cut over to 13th Street, which bordered I-405, a busy freeway that skirted the west-side business district. Turning south again, they headed up the hill toward Gander Ridge. It was not yet 11:00 P.M., so traffic was still heavy. A steady stream of cars flowed past them on the one-way street, bound for the on-ramp of the freeway.

'It's been a long time since anything like that has happened to me,' said Nicole of the incident with the skinheads. 'God, I can't even remember the last time someone called me a gook.'

Nicole's father and mother had come to America from Vietnam in 1976, when Nicole was an infant. They'd been 'boat people,' refugees from a cruel new order that aimed to 're-educate,' imprison or kill anyone who had supported the old one. They'd arrived in Portland, Oregon, with little more than the clothes on their backs and a determination to build decent lives for themselves. Mr Tran had worked with a city road crew by day and a janitorial service by night. Within five years he owned the janitorial service, and had built it into a thriving business. Within the next five years he'd tripled his revenues and had become a moderately wealthy man, a walking illustration of the American dream.

'Face it,' replied Josh. 'Some people are ignorant jerks. They'll never quit hating, because hating is so much more convenient than loving. In order to love someone, you need to *know* him, right? – and that takes effort, and maybe even some brains. But you can hate someone without even knowing him, or for that matter, without knowing *anything*. Ignorance and hatred go side by side.'

'Sounds like you've been talking to Lewis again.'

'Why is it whenever I say something halfway smart, you think it's something I've gotten from Lewis?' He feigned being insulted, then laughed and punched Nicole lightly on the arm. 'But you're right, that was something Lewis said. I think he was on his third bottle of Beck's, and he was starting to wax eloquent.'

Lewis Kindred, a veteran of the same war that drove Nicole's family from their homeland, was a middle-aged double amputee who lived in the apartment immediately below the Nickersons'. He was also the nephew of Miss Juliet Kindred, who owned the building. If someone had asked Josh to name his best friend, he could not have chosen between Nicole Tran, who was like a sister, and Lewis Kindred, who was like a big brother in some ways and a father in others.

'Oh God,' breathed Nicole. 'It's them, isn't it?' An old yellow Cutlass cruised past on 13th, headed up the hill, its smoked-glass windows obscuring the faces of its occupants. Approaching the next corner, its driver signaled left, slowed to a crawl, then tromped the accelerator and took the corner on two wheels.

'Yeah, it's them, all right,' said Josh. 'I'm sure they saw us.'

'I can't believe this! There's over a million people in

this city, and we meet those Neanderthals twice in the same night. Do you think they'll come after us?'

'Let's not take any chances. We don't want to be here if they come back around the block.' He steered her into the parking lot of an apartment building, and they cut through it to an alley. Josh felt certain that once he and Nicole made it to the campus of Portland State University, which was now less than a block away, they could elude the skinheads among the campus buildings and make their way safely to Gander Ridge.

Suddenly Josh heard the roar of a big V-8. He whirled and saw the yellow Cutlass approaching from behind, having rounded the block and turned into the alley. Its headlights caught them straight-on, casting his and Nicole's shadows huge against the bricks.

'This way!' he shouted. They darted to their left, hoping to cut between two buildings and emerge onto 12th Street, forcing the skinheads to get out of their car in order to follow, or round the block yet again, or better still to give up the chase. But two figures stood in the way, one of whom Josh recognized as Pimples. 'Damn it! They must've let two guys out on 12th . . . !'

Nicole caught his sleeve and pulled him around toward the opposite direction, and he gathered himself for an all-out sprint back toward 13th Street, but two other figures blocked the way, both carrying metal baseball bats. Josh felt his testicles constrict and his mouth go dry as he realized that the skinheads had deployed men on his and Nicole's flanks to cut off their escape.

The Cutlass skidded to a halt scarcely ten feet from Josh and Nicole. The engine shut down and the headlights went black, leaving purple splotches on Josh's field of vision. The driver's door opened and Fireplug stepped out, an ugly smile twisting his mouth. His jaw rippled as he chewed what must have been a fist-sized wad of tobacco.

'Well, if this ain't a happy little coincidence,' he said in a voice that seemed too small and high to belong to someone as broad and blocky as he was. 'We were just talking about you guys, y' know? – talking about how nice it would be to meet up with you again. I mean, it's not every day you catch some chicken-shit little white man walkin' the street with a mud woman. It's sort of frustrating to get all primed to beat the dude's head in, only to have the fuckin' cops show up and give you a lecture about tying up traffic. But I don't see any cops around now. Do you see any cops, chicken-shit?'

Josh's mind worked furiously while Nicole clung to him, her face pale with terror. *There are five of them, and one of me. I have a brick wall at my back, one of them in front, two on each side. God, what I wouldn't give for a baseball bat or a tire iron, or a . . .*

Or a gun. For the first time in his young life, Josh Nickerson actually wished for a gun, something big and deadly, designed specifically for combat. Something like a Tec-9 semiautomatic pistol with a large magazine, or better yet, a Hechler and Koch submachine gun. What horrified him was knowing that he would readily use one right now, if he had it; that he would gladly spray slugs into Fireplug's fish-white face, then wheel around and mow down Pimples and the others. He hated these creatures with a fury that both mortified and exhilarated him.

Lacking a gun, however, or a baseball bat or a tire iron or even a pocket knife, he needed to rely on his wits. And his mouth.

'Hey, are you dudes *good*, or what?' he said to Fireplug, forcing a smile. 'I should've known better than to think we could outrun you. You guys are pros, right?'

Fireplug spat on the ground, scowling ferociously. 'You tryin' to flatter us, chicken-shit? You tryin' to get on our good side so we won't bash your fuckin' heads in?'

Pimples spoke up now, walking slowly forward from Josh's and Nicole's right, flanked by a black-jacketed young man who wore his bleached-yellow hair like Adolf Hitler. 'Save your breath, gook-lover. You can't talk your way out of this. You just stumbled into the worst fuckin' night of your life.' For some reason his cohorts found this funny, and they all laughed uproariously.

'Nickster, what are we going to do?' hissed Nicole, pressing her cheek against his shoulder. Josh struggled to keep his smile in place. It seemed too crazy to be true – a pair of young friends out walking on a beautiful summer evening, bothering no one, and for some incomprehensible reason thugs attack them with crowbars and bats. But it *wasn't* too crazy to be true: several years earlier, skinheads had bludgeoned to death a young black student from East Africa in the parking lot of an apartment building in northwest Portland. This was reality, crazy or not, in the handsome, liberal-minded city of Portland, Oregon, and in hundreds of other cities across the country where hate-mongers had gotten a toehold.

'I'm not trying to flatter you guys,' Josh managed to say, still holding the smile that Lewis Kindred had taught him to use while playing poker. 'I'm expressing my admiration, that's all. Hey, could you dudes use a beer or something?'

Fireplug stepped forward and spat a brown stream of tobacco juice onto Nicole's bright green pullover. Josh felt her flinch, and his anger burned so hot he could barely breathe.

'You think we would drink with filth like you?' asked Fireplug, pulling a set of brass knuckles out of his leather jacket. He slipped them on his right hand and flexed his stubby fingers. 'You think we'd dirty ourselves by drinking with some chicken-shit who sticks his dick into a mud woman?'

Josh gulped loudly. He felt himself go dizzy with rage and terror. 'I was only thinking that you dudes might be thirsty . . .' His voice cracked, and he knew now that he had no choice but to fight for his life and Nicole's, using only his fists. Maybe he could wrench a bat away from one of the attackers, he thought, then do enough damage with it to drive the others off. Maybe . . .

'You're trying to bribe us, ain't you, chicken-shit?' said Pimples, now only an arm's length away. 'You're trying to bribe us with *beer*!' The others laughed and whooped and spat on the ground. 'For your information, gook-lover, we're real Americans, and we don't take bribes.'

'Know what I think?' asked Fireplug. 'I think he's a Jew. First thing a Jew tries to do when he's in trouble is bribe somebody. Jews are a lot like slopes that way. What we've got here, troops, is a double bonus – a dirty slope-headed mud woman and a slimy Jew. We better get busy, because we've got our work cut out for us.'

All five started forward en masse, converging on Josh and Nicole like wolves on a pair of frightened deer. The blond Hitler raised his aluminum baseball bat, Fireplug drew back with his brass-knuckled fist, Pimples wound up for a swing with a tire iron. Josh launched himself straight at Fireplug, screaming like a banshee, meaning to rip the animal's throat out. Suddenly the roar of an engine rolled over them, and the alley lit up under the glare of headlights. The sound and light distracted Fireplug, and his brass-knuckled fist missed Josh's head, glancing off his shoulder. But Josh's fist didn't miss – he drove it hard into Fireplug's larynx, and Fireplug went down, gagging and choking, clutching his throat with both hands. Nicole screamed and ducked under the roundhouse swing of Pimple's tire iron, then darted into the shadows.

Josh leaped over the writhing form of Fireplug and whirled on the other attackers, who seemed confused in the noontide glare of the headlights. He heard movement over the asphalt and saw a blur of white, a woman, tall and dark-skinned, dressed in a dazzling white minidress that barely covered her torso. Moving like a panther, she waded into the knot of skinheads, caught the blond Hitler by the hair and hurled him against the wall, where he impacted with a thud and slid down beside a dumpster. She caught Pimple's tire iron in mid-swing, wrenched it from him and broke his arm loudly, causing him to vomit all over himself. He hit the ground unconscious and lay motionless in a pond of his own filth.

The woman moved so quickly that Josh's eyes couldn't quite fix upon her, so smoothly that she seemed like some sort of dream creature whose shape shifted and flowed with her purpose. Her strength was nothing short of supernatural. She went after the two thugs who'd cut off Josh and Nicole's retreat toward 12th Street, caught them by the collars of their leather jackets and smashed their heads together. They collapsed in a heap of knees and elbows and stubbly scalps. Fireplug pulled a blunt pistol from a shoulder holster inside his jacket and assumed a shooter's crouch, using both hands to level the weapon at the woman. Josh kicked him in the side of the head, putting every ounce of his weight into it, and Fireplug went sprawling, but he held onto the gun and struggled upright again. Suddenly Nicole flew out of the shadows, waving a baseball bat that one of the skinheads had dropped, and brought it down hard on the top of Fireplug's bristly skull. He buckled to the asphalt face first, and lay twitching like a dog having a bad dream.

Silence now, warm and heavy. The traffic on I-405 and 12th Street seemed distant and inconsequential. Nicole pressed herself into Josh's arms, and he held her as she sobbed, liking the feel of her cheek against his chest. He became conscious of his own heartbeat, his own breathing, and gloried in the feedback of his senses, thankful beyond words to be alive and in one piece. He owed his survival, he knew, to this dazzling woman who had burst on the scene like a guardian angel.

He squinted against the brightness of the headlights and saw that her car was a sleek Jaguar convertible, blacker than night and sinfully shiny. A giggle tickled his throat: Josh Nickerson's guardian angel drove a Jag. And she wore the sexiest minidress he'd ever seen. Her legs were long and brown, not quite the color of milk chocolate but more like . . . what? It came to him suddenly: her skin was the color of cocoa with marshmallows in it.

She examined each of the senseless, bloodied skinheads, kicking away their weapons lest they wake up and decide to renew the fight. Then she stood in front of Josh, her arms folded across her ample breasts, a smile twitching her red mouth, a beauty who might have been twenty, thirty, or any age in between. She was racially mixed – neither white nor black. Her face was long and strong, her lips full, her wide nose gracefully curved and flared. Her cheekbones were high, severely contoured, and her rusty hair tumbled to her shoulders in intricate dreadlocks. Most striking, however, were her eyes, which were deeply set and huge – eyes that captured light and tossed it back into the world like finely honed gems. They were mismatched, which only heightened her exotic appeal: the right one was a frosty blue, while the left was the color of warm brown earth.

iv

Josh recognized her instantly. She was the woman he'd hoped to see tonight at the Rockaway Lounge. She'd been an admirer of Demon Beef, of Ron Payne in particular, perhaps *more* than an admirer. Josh had never before gotten close enough to taste the magic of her eyes.

She'd attended all the band's gigs, lingering alone in the shadows near the stage, staring intently at Payne with an expression full of something that Josh had assumed was lust. Josh had admired her from a distance, imagining how it would be to insinuate himself between those deliciously long legs. And he'd encountered her on the night of Ron Payne's murder.

He'd needed to talk to her, to ask her why she'd been in Payne's apartment that night, a fact that he felt certain no one else in the world knew. He'd searched for her throughout the summer, contacting people who'd been close to Payne and Demon Beef, asking who she was and where she lived. But no one had been able to give him any answers. He'd figured that she would likely show up for tonight's gig at the Rockaway, but she'd disappointed him. Josh had considered the evening a waste of time.

Until now.

Did he dare ask her *now*?

'I want to thank you,' he said lamely, his voice shaking.

'I don't know how you did it . . .' He glanced around at the broken and bruised skinheads. His breath caught as the enormity of the facts started to sink in. A lone woman in a minidress had taken on five heavily armed neo-Hitlerites and had reduced them to this mess.

Nicole had collected herself by now, and was no longer blubbering against Josh's chest. 'No kidding, thanks for helping us,' she said, wiping moisture from her eye with the back of a hand. 'If you hadn't come along when you did, God only knows what would've happened to us.'

'We would've gotten snuffed,' Josh put in simply.

'Don't thank me,' said the woman in a deep contralto. 'You would've done the same for me, I'm sure.' Her accent was Southern with a hint of Caribbean flavor.

'How did you happen to come by?' Josh asked. 'This alley isn't exactly on the beaten track.'

'That's a long story – too long to tell you tonight, I'm afraid. Perhaps another time.' She looked each of them up and down with narrowed eyes, first Josh and then Nicole. 'Are either of you hurt?'

They both shook their heads, though Josh knew he would have a nasty bruise on his shoulder where Fireplug's brass knuckles had landed.

'I'm sorry that the pig spit tobacco on you, Nicki.' The woman smiled sympathetically, and Josh gasped when he saw how white and perfect her teeth were, like luminescent pearls.

'How did you know my name?' asked Nicole.

'Everyone knows the Dynamic Duo of Gander Ridge,' answered the woman, laughing. An uneasy feeling sliced through Josh – he would wonder later whether it was a premonition or simply shock that she knew what the neighbors had called Nicole and himself when they were kids. 'If I were you, I would be more picky about who I hang with from now on,' the woman joked, and Josh and Nicole chuckled with her.

'I don't think we've ever been introduced,' said Josh, offering his hand. 'My name is . . .'

'I know who you are, Josh. I'll admit that it's no coincidence that I'm here. I've been looking for you. I was hoping that you might do something for me.'

'Do something for *you*?' He stared at her blankly. 'I – uh – you bet. I'd be happy to do anything . . .'

'We'll do anything you ask,' put in Nicole.

'Good.' The woman turned and strode to the open door of her Jaguar. Josh noticed for the first time that she was barefoot. She'd apparently kicked off her stilettos while jumping out of the car. As she slid in behind the driver's seat, Josh couldn't help but watch the parting of her long brown legs. Her minidress rode high up on her hips, and he saw that she was without underwear. He felt himself go instantly hard and forced himself to look away.

She retrieved something from the glove box and returned. She held something out to him, a sphere of bright red crystal about the size of a billiard ball. The thing caught the glare of the headlights and produced a thousand shards that flitted and darted with every movement of her hand, almost like living things. Josh glanced at Nicole, who stood transfixed, the rays from the orb dancing across her face.

'What's inside it?' she breathed, venturing to touch it with a cautious finger.

'I can't honestly say I know,' replied the woman. 'Someone gave it to me a long time ago, but it wasn't mine to keep. He made me swear that I would eventually return it to its rightful owner.'

'And who's that?' asked Josh.

'A mutual friend of yours and mine, I think. His name is Lewis Kindred.'

Josh shook his head, incredulous. '*You* know Lewis?'

'In a sense, yes.' She reached down and caught Josh's right hand, raised it and pressed the dazzling orb into his palm. The weight and the warmth of the thing struck him immediately – a disquieting warmth that made him think of sinking his hand into the guts of a freshly killed animal. He wanted to pull away, but the power of the woman's blue-brown stare held him. He remembered the glimpse of the area between her legs a moment earlier, and his hard-on raged anew. She withdrew her own hands, leaving the orb with him. 'Give it to Lewis as soon as possible,' she urged. 'Tell him that all good things come to he who waits.'

'Should I tell him who it comes from – I mean, who you are? He'll want to know.'

She leaned against the graceful fender of the Jag and slipped her shoes on her feet. Josh watched her every move intently. 'My name is Millie. You can tell him that. You can also tell him that Millie would greatly enjoy playing poker with him.'

'If you're a friend of his, why don't you give it to him yourself?'

Millie stood up straight, walked slowly back to Josh and laid her palm against his cheek. 'You're a curious young thing, aren't you? – so full of questions, so passionate. You're capable of great anger, aren't you, Josh?'

'I guess so.'

'That's good. *Very* good, in fact. Never try to hold your anger in, Josh. Always let it out. Let it grow. Let it become strong and hard. *Use* your anger, and great things will happen for you.'

He felt an icy spot burrow between his shoulder blades, though Millie's touch was as warm as the orb in his hand, and exciting. He felt as if his life had changed from the moment Millie touched his face. Something major was happening to him, he knew, but he didn't know what it was.

'You still haven't told me why you can't give him this – this *thing* – yourself? Why do you need me?'

Millie lost her smile, and her mismatched eyes became hard. 'I'm afraid that he wouldn't accept it directly from me. But from *you*—' She caressed his cheek again, and he just managed to keep himself from reaching out to touch her breasts. Something in her expression told him that she wouldn't stop him if he did. '—Lewis trusts you. It's better if it comes from you.'

She walked back to the car, her heels popping on the pavement, her buttocks rolling smoothly inside the white minidress. Before getting in, she advised Josh and Nicole not to loiter too much longer. Then she grinned a good-bye and whooshed off in a smear of gleaming black metal.

Watching her taillights disappear down the alley, Josh could not suppress the lunatic suspicion that Millie had planned everything that had happened.

CHAPTER SIX
Gander Ridge

i

The apartment building in which Josh Nickerson lived stood on a gentle, wooded hillside named Gander Ridge. Built by a prominent Portland judge, James Sloan, in 1892, the building was situated on Gander Circle, a cul-de-sac that overlooked Portland State University and the downtown business district.

Painted a dazzling white and surrounded by monumental New England elms, the house had a look of four-square sturdiness. Tall Georgian columns flanked the front entrance, and an expansive terrace swept across the front to open porches on either end of the structure. Massive chimneys rose high above the hip roof, and dormers jutted out from the third story, where the present owner, Miss Juliet Kindred, had her quarters. Free of Victorian artifice and filigree, Sloan House appeared bleak and institutional to some, but others saw elegance in its stark, imposing lines.

The Nickersons' apartment occupied half the second floor. From the window of his room on the east end of the house, Josh could look across Gander Ridge to Goose Hollow, the home of Civic Stadium, where the Triple-A

Portland Beavers played baseball, and where a massive fireworks display occurred every Fourth of July. Further east, the gleaming towers of the central city seemed almost close enough to touch, as did the Fremont Bridge, a colossus of arching girders that spanned the Willamette River. Josh could look eastward and see a forested mound named Mount Tabor, which stood like an island in southeast Portland's urban sea. On the far horizon loomed majestic Mount Hood, an extinct volcano that wore a coat of snow in winter and served as a playground for Portland-area skiers, climbers and trekkers.

Miss Juliet Kindred, the seventy-two-year-old owner and landlady of Sloan House, had two passions: evangelical Christianity and gardening. When not doing volunteer work for various causes of the religious right, she labored in the gardens. In one she grew fragrant roses and giant trillium; another was devoted to western azaleas and Pacific rhododendrons with big, bold leaves and lavish trusses of purple flowers. Every fall Juliet harvested Oregon grape and made preserves, which she distributed to her renters in Kerr jars with hand-lettered Bible verses on the labels. Not without good reason, Miss Kindred called this place 'my little Eden.'

The drought of 1992 had played havoc with her gardening. The grass around Sloan House had turned brown and Juliet's gardens had devolved into tangles of brittle leaves and ragged branches. She deemed the drought an omen of the Last Days, a sign from God to warn his faithful that the world would soon end in accordance with the New Testament book of Revelation. Her faith notwithstanding, she promised her tenants better grape preserves next year, assuming the Lord would keep the earth in its orbit

136

for at least another year and restore normal rainfall to the Willamette Valley.

The Nickersons' apartment had three small bedrooms and two baths, a kitchen, a dining area and a living room that opened onto a railed deck, where they often ate their meals and spent warm summer evenings. At night a soothing breeze usually whispered across Gander Ridge, rustling the foliage and clearing out the haze of rush-hour pollution. Josh spent hours at a stretch out here, sprawled in a reclining patio chair with the headphones of his Sony Discman on his head, a book in his lap and the breeze in his face – fighting his restlessness with visions of places far away from Portland, Oregon.

His room was small and cluttered, a 'wasteland,' his mother called it. She'd long ago given up trying to force him to keep it clean, and the cleaning lady who came once a week refused to enter it, apparently fearful of what she might encounter amid the mounds of books, fast-food wrappers and dirty clothing. A small wooden desk stood against one wall, on which sat a computer he used for his homework and his writing projects. A year ago he'd bought a metal filing cabinet in which he kept his 'background' files – items from books or periodicals that he thought he might need someday for one yet-to-be-written story or another, catalogued by subject. Shelves lined another wall, crammed with reference books, almanacs and how-to books on writing and research. There were tomes on past obsessions: the Civil War, photography, remote-control model airplanes, classical Rome, others. Within the past year he'd taken down the poster-size photos of his heroes on the Portland Trail Blazers and replaced them with travel posters that showed dreamy views of London, Hong Kong, the delta of the

Amazon, the canals of Venice – places he hoped to visit someday on assignment as a journalist.

He vaguely remembered what life was like before the family moved here ten years ago, a life in the affluent suburb of Lake Oswego, where his important father had built a big house with a view of the lake. He remembered playing T-ball with other little boys who had important dads like his. He remembered a Bernese mountain dog named Otto, who had black and tan fur and a happy grin, an *important* dog, his dad had said, because he belonged to Josh Nickerson and to nobody else. Beyond these comparatively few details, he recalled little, except for an intense contentment that he'd not felt since. The Nickersons had been a real family in those days, a good old-fashioned straight-ahead family with a mom, a dad, an important boy named Josh and a baby sister named Kendra. Things had gone swimmingly until one summer evening, out of the blue, Mommy announced that Daddy didn't want to live with them anymore. The family sold the big house with its view of the lake, and the kids moved with Mommy to Gander Ridge. And Daddy, damn his hide, had taken Otto, the important dog who'd belonged to Josh and to no one else, and had moved into a house with another woman.

Josh, it seemed, wasn't so important after all, or his father would've kept him.

ii

On Sunday, September 13, 1992, Josh got up around ten-fifteen and herded himself into the shower, drowsy and bleary-eyed after an uneasy sleep. He'd dreamed repeatedly of Millie and her mismatched eyes, how she'd handled the skinheads and, afterward, the way she'd stroked his cheek. Inevitably the dream had taken another direction, in which she'd stroked more than his cheek and had offered him more than her pearly grin. He'd awakened barely in time to grab a fistful of Kleenex from the stand next to his bed. Even after *that* he'd not slept well, for his brain had refused to shut down, humming with questions about who Millie really was, her connection to Lewis Kindred, to Ron Payne, and to Josh himself.

After showering he pulled on a pair of acid-washed Levis and a T-shirt imprinted with the face of the Portland Trail Blazers' Clyde Drexler, and ambled into the kitchen. His mother had attached a note to the refrigerator with a magnet in the shape of a duck, telling him that she and Kendra had gone to church, that they planned to grab brunch at Papa Haydn's in northwest and return around one.

Cheryl Nickerson, his mother, was a career woman, a human-resources executive with a large wholesale food distributor. Her salary, when combined with the ample child-support payments from her ex, enabled her to give Josh and Kendra a comfortable life – a moderately upscale home, cutting-edge clothes and occasional vacations in places like Mexico and Hawaii. Josh's only real material complaint was the dilapidated Escort his mother had given him for his seventeenth birthday. Cheryl had agreed that if he didn't like the Escort, he could have any car that he himself could pay for and insure. But then she'd forbidden him to get an after-school job, which would have been his only hope of saving enough to buy a decent ride. No son of hers, she'd declared, would spend valuable time flipping hamburgers or delivering pizzas when he should be studying, at least not for the sake of a *ride*.

A fair-skinned redhead of forty, Cheryl Nickerson worked out three times a week at the Multnomah Athletic Club. Yet she was losing the war against shapelessness, which Josh lamented silently, for he feared that his mother would never attract a husband if she lost her youthful figure.

Josh had often envisioned the man he wanted his mother to marry. The man would work not for a blood-sucking insurance company, but for some nonprofit foundation that helped needy people around the world. He would ply Josh and his sister not with expensive gifts but with intelligent conversation, showing that he actually cared about what they thought, even if they were mere kids. Most important, he would worship the ground Cheryl walked on.

But the vision had begun to fade. Josh was rapidly losing hope that his mother would ever meet such a man. He'd reached the point where he would have endorsed a marriage to *any* guy who really loved his mother, since he no longer cared so much about getting a new dad. He was almost grown, after all.

After poking around in a bowl of Wheaties he went back to his room. He couldn't put off any longer a task that he didn't look forward to doing. The baggy shorts he'd worn the previous day hung on a bedpost at the foot of his bed, and he plunged his hand into one of the pockets, half hoping that he wouldn't find what he knew was there.

He pulled out the orb and held it up to let the morning light filter through it. The interior of the thing swarmed with texture, but the moving bits were too small to actually see.

Was it his imagination, he wondered, or was the orb warmer than it should be? He pocketed it hurriedly.

He unlocked his file cabinet and found a file jacket within another file jacket, labeled 'Demon Beef' and 'Ron Payne,' respectively. From the inner folder he pulled four envelopes he'd received in the mail over the past summer, together with the newspaper clippings they'd contained, each from a newspaper in a different city. One had come from the South, another from the Midwest, a third from the East and a fourth from the West Coast. The envelopes bore no return addresses, so he had no idea who had sent them. The stories concerned murders that were startlingly similar to that of Ron Payne. Shuffling through the clippings, biting his lower lip and rereading each for the hundredth time, he debated with himself about whether to keep these little horrors a secret any longer.

iii

Josh knocked on Lewis Kindred's door, then pushed through it as he usually did, needing no invitation. Inside, a television set was on, providing the kind of background din that Lewis liked when he was working. As a freelance 'desktop publisher,' Lewis designed and edited newsletters, brochures and manuals for small corporations and independent businesses throughout the Portland area, using a Mac IIci computer to generate graphics and typesetting. Combined with his veteran's pension and his weekly poker winnings, his business income gave him a decent living and the one luxury he valued above all else: independence. He kept his 'studio' here in his apartment, and often worked on weekends, as he was apparently doing today.

'It's me,' Josh called out to Lewis. 'Want anything from the kitchen?'

'I'm in the studio. Get us a couple of Diet Rites, why don't you? Make mine a red raspberry.'

Lewis Kindred's apartment lay immediately below the Nickersons', but it had two bedrooms instead of three, one of which served as the studio. Because it was on the main floor, the apartment didn't boast as spectacular a view of the city as the Nickersons', but Mount St Helens and Mount Hood were visible from the window of his studio, a fact that would have added substantially to the rent if Lewis wasn't the landlady's nephew.

The furnishings were of high quality and almost austere, leather furniture, oak miniblinds and cabinets, plain earth tones in the upholstery and rugs and lamps. Lewis abided no figurines or knickknacks, but he kept a veritable jungle of potted plants, the most prominent of which was a spreading ficus tree that was much too large for the tight living room. Except for a few groups of framed pictures on the walls, the apartment contained nothing that a man couldn't reach while sitting in a wheelchair. Bookcases and shelving lay low to the floor. The closets had been customized to accommodate someone who couldn't stand, as had the bathroom. Even the kitchen sported the 'low look,' as Lewis called it, which, together with his motorized wheelchair, enabled him to cook for himself and the occasional visitor.

He looked up from the computer screen when Josh came into his study and gave the thin smile that was his trademark, one that said he knew some delicious secret or that he held a deadly poker hand that you must pay dearly to see. 'It's about time you joined the world of the living, mahatma. I thought we had a breakfast date at nine.'

'Sorry,' said Josh, handing over a Diet Rite and flopping into an easy chair next to the computer desk. 'I didn't get up until after ten. I was late getting in last night.'

'You missed a truly amazing batch of blueberry and banana pancakes. I hope she was worth it, whoever she was.' He winked and backed his wheelchair away from the computer in order to face Josh.

'It wasn't that kind of date. I was working.'

'Your Demon Beef story?'

Josh nodded, then looked away. Through the window he could barely make out the conical hulk of Mount Hood, which was about to disappear behind a thickening haze. A change in weather was under way. 'Something weird happened last night, Lewis.'

'Weird as in silly or weird as in scary?'

'Weird as in I wouldn't've believed it if I hadn't seen it myself. I'm not sure I believe it now, except Nicki was with me, and she saw it, too.'

Lewis leaned forward in his wheelchair, his gray eyes sharp with curiosity. He had a long, narrow face and a naturally drooping mouth that had a tendency to look sad. His hair had gone mostly gray, prematurely so for a man in his mid-forties, but it was still thick and lustrous, combed straight back from his high forehead. Josh's mother had often said that Lewis Kindred would be a 'striking' man if he were – well, if he had both legs and two normal arms. Shrapnel from the same mortar round that crippled him had left scattered pits of scar tissue along his jaw and above one eye, giving him a slightly disreputable look that many women thought was sexy.

'Try me,' Lewis said. 'I know weird when I hear it. In fact, I'm an expert on weird, as all my past girlfriends can testify.'

'There's something I haven't told you about the Demon Beef thing, Lewis. I probably should have told you a long time ago.' Josh pulled the bundle of envelopes out of the waistband of his jeans and flipped them into Lewis's lap. 'These came in the mail, addressed to me. They arrived a month or so apart. The postmarks are from the cities where the newspapers are . . .'

'I can see that. Give me a minute, okay?' Lewis took his horn-rim reading glasses from the computer table and started reading the articles, his brow wrinkling. He stroked his temple with the fingers of his right hand, the good one, as he often did while concentrating hard.

Josh got to his feet and wandered around the study as Lewis read, absently fingering the edges of the books on the shelves, thick volumes by scholars like James, Nietzsche, Wittgenstein, Foucault, Quine, Kuhn, Sellars, Derrida, Rorty, Scheffler. Stuffed between them were xeroxed copies of articles and monographs that claimed insights into such burning issues as the reconciliation of post-modern antifoundationalism with scientific human-ism – things that only dyed-in-the-wool philosophy buffs like Lewis Kindred could appreciate.

Josh was no dummy. He was an A-student at a tough school, someone whom several of his teachers considered 'gifted.' But when he'd tried to read some of this stuff, he couldn't plow through a single paragraph without being derailed by words like 'incommensurable' and 'ontologi-cal' and 'epistemological.' The issues of philosophy, it seemed, lay submerged in tortured syntax and five-dollar words, beyond his immature intellectual reach, and he found this frustrating. Still, he admired Lewis's intellect and respected the fact that his friend cared so ardently about *ideas*. Josh wished his father cared more for ideas and less about money.

He stared at a grouping of framed photographs above a low bookcase. One was the wedding picture of Lewis's parents, Lyle and Bonnie Kindred, a handsome couple standing at the altar of a church, surrounded by flowers. Next to it was a portrait of Lewis's younger brother, Ken, square-jawed and bright-eyed like Lewis – a high-school yearbook picture, presumably. Josh glanced over at his friend and felt a stab of sadness: the three faces in the pictures belonged to dead people. Lewis's father had died of cancer before either of the boys reached adulthood. His mother had died of a stroke five years after Lewis returned from Vietnam. An oil-rig fire off the coast of Scotland had taken Ken's life in 1987, leaving Lewis without family, except for his maiden aunt Juliet.

Lewis cleared his throat and looked up at Josh, having finished the last article. 'What do you make of all this?' he asked.

'I was going to ask you the same thing.'

Lewis took off his reading glasses and laid them aside. 'You're telling me that these clippings have something to do with whatever it is you saw last night?'

'I'm not sure, but I think so. Do you think there's a possibility that all these murders are – connected some-how?'

'That's hard to say. According to the *Atlanta Constitution*, a man died in Athens, Georgia, in much the same way Ron Payne did, if you can believe the reporter. He was a night watchman, it says. Cops thought he'd been mauled by a big dog at first, but they later came to suspect some kind of cult involvement.' Lewis's smirk became a full-fledged grin. 'Have you noticed that whenever something really bloody happens, somebody always suspects cult involvement?'

'The guy was killed about a month after Payne was killed,' said Josh, not smiling.

'So he was. And next came . . .' Lewis squinted to read the date on a clipping. '. . . the dentist in Des Moines, Iowa, according to the *Des Moines Register*. Same kind of deal, except this guy wasn't attacked in an alley. The police think he picked up some babe in a bar and went to a hotel with her.'

'But they don't think a woman could've done *that* to him.'

'No. They don't.' Lewis's face went ashen, as though a horrible memory had sparked to life deep inside his head. When he spoke again, his voice was thin. 'And then there was the guy in Burlington, Vermont.' When he held up the clipping from the *Burlington Free Press*, his fingers shook. 'Sales manager of a Toyota dealership, divorced, lived alone in his condo.'

'They found him in his hot tub, torn to pieces. *Massive tissue loss*, the coroner said, like some kind of animal had eaten parts of him.'

'And last but not least, the windsurfing instructor from Lake Tahoe, found dead in his car outside Sacramento. The physical condition of the body was more or less like the others, judging from this story in the *Sacramento Bee*.'

'That one came just last week.'

Lewis stared a long moment at the control console of his motorized wheelchair. When he looked up again, his normal color had returned. 'We've got two big questions here, it seems to me,' he said, sounding more like himself. 'The first is whether these murders are related, like you said earlier. The second is why someone would go to the trouble of clipping these stories and mailing them to you, of all people.'

Josh sprawled into the armchair again. 'I've been asking myself the same two questions ever since the first envelope came. But there's more to this thing, Lewis. I was at Ron Payne's apartment on the night he was killed.'

'You were *what*?'

'Hey, don't have an infarction, man – no way I was hangin' with him or anything. In fact, I wasn't actually inside the place.'

'Then where were you – *actually*?'

'I was parked in the lot, kind of like staking the place out. I'd heard this rumor that some major-league rockers were in town – people from a big-time black-metal band, right? The rumor was that they were planning to meet at Ron Payne's place and do some partying. If it was true, I wanted to be there to document the meeting. This might've been the kind of thing that could be significant in the future, especially if Demon Beef ever hit it big. Groups break up and merge all the time, you know, and if Ron Payne ever ended up playing with some combination of those guys, I wanted to be the one who wrote a story about an early meeting.'

'Sounds reasonable. Go on.'

'Anyway, the rumor turned out not to be true. Or at least, if any heavy-metal stars were in Portland that night, they didn't come to see Ron Payne.'

'But someone else did come to see him, unless I miss my guess.'

'Yeah. The only trouble is . . .' Josh shook his head, as if he himself didn't quite understand what he was about to say. He started again. 'Okay, this doesn't seem logical, but here it goes. At eight-thirty I followed Ron to his apartment up in Washington Park. Nothing happened for the next two hours or so. Ron shut off the lights, and the place stayed dark. At about ten-thirty I started to get a sore butt, because my ride doesn't have the most comfortable seats in the world, you know? I was getting ready to give up on the whole idea, because it was pretty clear that the rumor about big-time guys had been a crock. Then I saw somebody come out to the deck of Payne's apartment, so I dug out my binoculars to see who it was.'

'Wait a minute. This was at ten-thirty? It must've been dark as hell.'

'It was dark, yes, but not *that* dark. There were yard lights around the apartment building.'

'Okay, so who did you see?'

'A babe – a *major* babe. She walked out of Ron Payne's bedroom onto the deck and just stood there awhile, like she was having a cigarette or something.'

'Do you know who she was?'

'I recognized her, but I didn't know her name at the time. She was a groupie I'd seen around the clubs. I saw her at all the Demon Beef gigs, always right up near the stage, always giving the dreamy eyes to Ron. She's world-class gorgeous, man – half-black and half-white, I think. Wears really cool dreadlocks and minidresses that don't leave much to the imagination.'

'I doubt that she's the first groupie to end up in a rock singer's apartment,' offered Lewis.

'No kidding. After I watched her for a minute or so she moved over to the far side of the deck, where I couldn't see her. I thought that she'd probably gone back inside, but then, before I knew what was happening, she walked around the side of the building on the ground – didn't even come out of the front entrance.'

'Probably went out the back door.'

'No way. There wasn't time. I'm talking maybe six or seven seconds here. And get this: Ron Payne's apartment was on the *third floor*.'

'Are you trying to tell me she rappelled off the deck or maybe parachuted down to the ground? I hope that's not what you're trying to tell me, mahatma.'

'I don't know *how* she got down, Lewis. All I know is that she got down, and she walked within two feet of my car on her way out. She looked right at me, but I just sat there like a dweeb with my mouth hanging open. I watched her in my mirror, and she . . .' The vision came back to him momentarily, of Millie's buttocks rolling inside the tight dress as she walked. His groin suddenly became warm.

'I'm still listening.'

'She disappeared before I was able to get my head together enough to go after her. I mean, I didn't know anything had happened to Ron—'

'You still don't know that this woman had anything to do with the murder. Maybe it hadn't even happened yet. Did you see any blood on her?'

'No, I didn't. But I wanted to ask her if she'd heard the rumor about heavy-metal stars. I felt like I halfway knew her, because I'd seen her around the band so many times, and I figured it was time to introduce myself. So I went after her, but when I pulled out of the lot onto the main road, she was . . . *gone*.'

'What do you mean? She was on foot, wasn't she?'

'She was on foot,' Josh confirmed. 'She must've parked her car somewhere away from the lot, maybe along the main road, but I hadn't noticed any cars parked out there when I drove in. Anyway, she was gone, like she'd vanished into thin air.'

Lewis leaned back in his wheelchair, took another long swig of Diet Rite and offered the opinion that nothing Josh had told him qualified as Weird with a capital W. He was concerned, though, over the fact that Josh hadn't told the police what he'd seen that night. The groupie might not be responsible for Ron Payne's death, but she might have information that the police would find useful. Lewis worried that by withholding what he knew, Josh might be guilty of obstructing justice. He urged the boy to take what he knew to the cops.

'No way,' Josh answered. 'If the cops ask me what I saw, I'll tell them, but until they ask me, this information belongs to me. It's my exclusive angle, Lewis. If the babe knows anything, I want her to give it to me before anybody else. That's why I've spent all summer looking for her.'

'So who do you think sent you the newspaper clippings?'

'Probably someone who knows I was outside Ron Payne's apartment that night.'

'Like the black-white woman, maybe.'

'Maybe, but it could be someone else. She might've told someone she saw me.'

'Or she might know who the killer is, and she might be trying to tip you off to some of his other crimes by sending you those clippings . . .'

Josh's green eyes brightened. 'Hey, I like that! She wants to remain anonymous, right? She doesn't want to get involved directly, because she's worried about becoming a suspect. Or maybe she's scared that the killer might try to silence her.'

Lewis shook his head; his nose wrinkled as if something smelled bad. 'This is all blind speculation, mahatma. Face it: we don't have any idea who's sending you these clippings or why. The postmarks came from the cities where the murders happened, remember? It might be the killer himself, for Christ's sake.' He crushed his empty soda can with his good hand.– just wadded it up as if it was a paper cup – and hooked it into a wastebasket on the far side of the room. When a man has only one good hand, that hand becomes very strong.

'I still think you ought to take this thing to the cops, Josh. You ought to call them right now and tell them everything you've told me. For all we know, Payne's killer might be watching you. He might be playing with you, testing you, seeing how far he can push you. God only knows what makes a maniac like that tick, or what he might do next.'

Josh swallowed heavily and for a long moment studied the carpet between his sneakers. Outside a cloud bank moved over the sun, and the room darkened a shade. 'I haven't told you what happened last night.'

'Christ, I'd forgotten about that. Okay, tell me now.'

Josh related what had happened in the alley downtown. He described how Millie had waded into the gang of Nazi skinheads, saving Josh and Nicole from a brutal beating or worse. He described the woman herself in great detail – her long legs, her full breasts, her mismatched eyes of warm brown and frosty blue. Then he dug into the pocket of his jeans and took out the orb, and that was when Lewis Kindred became violently sick.

iv

He wouldn't touch the thing.

He flinched back as if someone had thrown a jar of ammonia in his face, and begged the boy to put the fucking thing away, to get it out of sight. Then he made for the bathroom as fast as his wheelchair could go and got there barely in time to spew the contents of his gut into the toilet bowl. He continued retching painfully for nearly ten minutes behind the locked door, as if trying to vomit out a gutful of poisonous memories.

Josh thumped frantically on the bathroom door. 'Lewis, should I call an ambulance? Are you okay? Is there anything I can do? Lewis, *answer* me, damn it!'

Finally he came out, feeling shaky as a newborn lamb and cold, his mouth tasting sour. His phantom feet itched like crazy, and he wanted nothing more than to roll up his cuffs and scratch the hell out of his stumps with his fingernails. But he didn't do this, because this was the kind of thing a man without legs only does when he's alone.

'I suppose you're wondering what the hell that was all about,' he said finally to Josh, who had made tea. The warm cup felt good in his cold palm.

'I've never seen you like this before, Lew. It . . . uh . . . *scared* me.'

'Well, it scared me, too. A little.' He put on his poker smile and tried to hide behind it. 'When you showed me that – that *thing*, I got a blast of memories, that's all. It reminded me of Vietnam, and – and some things that happened there.' His gaze wandered to a near wall, where a framed photograph showed a knot of GIs sitting on a mound of sandbags under a hot Vietnamese sky. Josh's gaze followed his and alighted on the picture.

Lewis had told him the names of the grinning men so often that Josh felt like they were friends of his.

T. J. Skane, the baddest of the bad dudes from East L. A.

Danny Legler, the chunky little Nebraskan with corn silk for hair.

Scott Sanders, the Wyoming cowboy.

And Jesse Burton, the streetwise brother from South Chicago.

Sitting in the midst of them, his fingers spread into a V that meant 'peace' in those days, was none other than Lieutenant Lewis Kindred, the dark-haired, gangly kid who played poker like most folks breathe. In the picture he was tall and tan and unscarred. He had two good legs and two good arms, and he was grinning like a mischievous little boy.

'That's not all it was, Lewis,' said Josh heavily. 'It took more than a blast of memories to do that to you.'

'You think you know me pretty well, don't you, mahatma?'

'We've been hangin' together a long time. I know it takes more than a fucking "blast of memories" to make you spazz out like that, man.'

'Watch your mouth. The English language is too precious a thing to abuse. You of all people should know that. You're a writer, for Christ's sake.'

'Look who's talking about bad language. Where do you think I learned it?' He leaned closer to Lewis, his face grave. 'But let's not change the subject. There's something you need to tell me, isn't there? You know something about the red ball, and I need to know it, too.'

'I suppose you won't leave until I spit it all out.'

'I suppose you're right.'

Lewis took a deep breath to steady himself, to order his thoughts. He drained his cup and asked for a refill. Then he leaned back in the wheelchair, holding the warm cup against his chest, and told Josh the story of Gamaliel Cartee, leaving nothing out.

V

'. . . So you see, you've been hangin' out with a murderer all these years, mahatma – either that or a crazy man. I've been willing to let myself think that I imagined all the business about killing Cartee . . .'

'That wouldn't be so hard to understand. I've read that combat does strange things to your head. Plus, you got wounded pretty bad.'

Lewis laughed. *Pretty bad*, yeah. Bad enough, he supposed, to rob him of his sanity for a time. He knew now that after coming home from Vietnam, he'd endured all the various phases that Elizabeth Kubler-Ross had described in her book, *On Death and Dying*, except he hadn't grieved for a lost loved one in the usual sense. He'd grieved for the man he himself had been before a certain mortar round exploded. Denial. Rage and anger. Bargaining. Depression. Acceptance. Lewis had tasted them all. In the end, he'd forced himself to believe that nothing he remembered about Gamaliel Cartee had been real, that it had all been the product of a psychotic dream induced by a combination of physical trauma and massive doses of morphine.

'What did you do with the orb he gave you when he came to see you in the Twelfth Evac?' Josh asked.

Lewis rubbed his high forehead lightly with his fingertips, thinking. He recalled that he still had the thing when he arrived at the Portland Veterans Affairs Medical

Center after Vietnam. Perched near the crest of scenic Marquam Hill in southwest Portland, the VAMC was a toilworn facility that séemed more like a prison than a hospital – dingy, drafty in winter, stiflingly hot in summer. Lewis had hated the place. He'd yearned desperately to go home with his mother, who visited him every day while he was there. But the doctors had insisted on keeping him at VAMC for the full six-month program of physical therapy and recovery.

'I kept the orb in a drawer next to my bed,' he went on, the recollections coming back, 'and I sometimes took it out and looked at it. I never liked the feel of it.'

'I know what you mean. It almost feels like it's alive or something.'

Lewis shook his head and paused. 'I played some cards with the other patients, penny-ante games, nothing big. I didn't want to add to any of these guys' problems by cleaning them out. Then one day they brought in a guy from New York, only lightly wounded, a loud talker who claimed he couldn't be beaten in poker. He organized a big game among the patients . . .' His voice trailed off as he tried to establish whether he was remembering a dream or an actual event. His recollections swirled and whirled inside his head like a tornado.

'What did you do?'

'I asked for a seat at the table. Then I took the orb with me to the game, and . . .' Lewis wanted intensely to believe that this hadn't really happened, and his face showed it. '. . . And I played cards. I could feel the thing in my pocket while I was playing, warm and – like you said, *alive*. Sometimes I even thought I could feel it move.'

'It was like you were repeating the experiment you did

with Gamaliel Cartee in the motor pool at Cu Chi, right?'

That was exactly right. And the outcome had been the same. Lewis could not lose a hand without consciously trying to do so, not with the orb in his pocket. He'd silenced the loudmouth, and there'd been some small justice in that, but he'd also cleaned out everyone else at the table. 'What I did made me sick, mahatma. These were wounded GIs, none of them rich. Some of them were like me, missing arms and legs. One guy had lost the hearing in both ears and the sight in one eye. I had no business taking these guys' money, but that's what I did. I took it and I didn't give it back, almost as if the orb wouldn't let me do anything else.'

'What did you do then?'

Again Lewis struggled with the boundary between fact and fantasy. Had he actually bribed an ambulance driver to take him to the Sellwood Bridge in the wee hours of the morning? Had he *really* reared back and pitched the orb into the black waters of the river, watching it arc downward like a red neon streak on black velvet, until it winked out far below? He saw the replay in his brain so clearly that it might have happened yesterday.

'Until you pulled it out of your pocket a few minutes ago, I'd hardly even thought about the thing since then,' he added, almost whispering. 'It was all part of another time. I'd assumed that I was free of it.'

Josh's green eyes moistened, and he patted his friend's arm. 'I'm sorry, Lewis . . .'

'You had no way of knowing.'

'Nothing needs to change, does it? I'll find Millie and make her take the orb back. I'll tell her you don't want it.'

'If I were you, I'd throw it in the river.'

'She said you were a friend of hers, that you and she go way back together. She wanted me to tell you something—' He looked away, remembering. '*All good things come to he who waits*. That's what she said.'

'I've never known anyone named Millie. She's no friend of mine, I can say that for sure. I was serious when I advised you to throw that thing in the river, Josh. Promise me that's what you'll do. Promise me you'll throw it in the river today.'

'What should I tell her when she asks me if I've given it to you?'

'Tell her the truth. And tell her I made you do it. Then tell her you never want to see her again.'

CHAPTER SEVEN
Uneasy Night

i

Nicole Tran phoned shortly after dinner that night, tearing Josh away from his homework. Getting right down to brass tacks, she asked whether Josh had given the red orb to Lewis, as the woman in the alley had instructed, whether Lewis and Millie were really friends, and whether he'd shed any light on who she was or where she'd come from.

'I can't really talk about it now,' Josh replied, incurring a pouting silence on the other end of the line. 'I'll fill you in next time we get together, okay?'

Could he at least say whether he'd given the orb to Lewis? A simple yes or no?

'I . . . uh . . . not exactly. I sort of still have it. Like I said, I can't talk right now. I'll give you a call tomorrow, okay? – better make that Tuesday. I have an editorial board meeting tomorrow after school. I guess I forgot to mention it, but I'm the news editor of the Gavin Dell paper this term.'

Well, whoopee-shit for him, retorted Nicole. Didn't he care that curiosity was eating her alive?

'I *do* care, but—' But his mother was sitting in the

living room, not ten feet away, her eyes glued to a book and her ears glued to his conversation. What could he do? 'I'll call you first chance I get, Nicki, I swear. Take care.'

Later his mother came to him in his room and pressed her palm against his forehead. 'Are you feeling all right, kiddo? You don't seem to be running a fever. Are your allergies acting up?'

'I feel fine, Mom. Do I look sick?'

'Not really,' she said, standing back to survey him in the way that mothers do. 'It's just that you don't seem like your normal bull-by-the-tail self, that's all. What are you studying tonight?'

'Calculus. It's an honors course. You gave me written permission to take it, remember?'

She remembered and nodded. Then she stepped behind him and started massaging his shoulders with strong, motherly fingers. Josh loved it when she did this. 'I hate to broach the subject,' she said, 'but we really do need to get cracking on your college applications, kiddo. It's not something we can put off much longer. I know you're committed to finishing your piece on Demon Beef, but some things can't wait.'

'I *know*, Mom. I'll finish the Northwestern application next weekend, I promise. By the way, I had to buy a new battery for my car today. The old one conked out in a parking lot last night. I need about seventy-five bucks to get me through the week.'

Cheryl Nickerson stopped massaging her son's neck and went to find her checkbook, muttering something and shaking her head. Josh went back to his differential equations, but concentrating was hard as hell.

ii

At 12:15 A.M. Josh awoke in his bed and stared at the webwork of shadows thrown against his walls by a yellowing New England elm outside his window. The weatherman on the eleven-o'clock news had promised the arrival of a coastal low-pressure system late tonight, with the likelihood of winds, lower temperatures and rain. The beginning of the end of the drought, the guy had dared to suggest. The wind had arrived about half an hour ago, rousing the limbs of the old elm and making their shadows dance, and Josh wondered if this was what had woken him.

Though the Sloan House had excellent interior insulation, Josh could still hear faint noises, like the gurgle of drainpipes whenever Juliet Kindred flushed her bedroom toilet, which she'd just done. And the rumble of the elevator as it alighted on the second floor, as had happened only moments ago, betraying the arrival home of the young bachelor stockbroker who lived in the apartment next to the Nickersons'. And the whir of the D' Arcys' window-mounted air conditioner, which Josh could hear even though their apartment was on the first floor next to Lewis's.

None of these sounds were keeping him awake, however. What kept him awake was the sound of breathing that wasn't his own, the breathing of someone very near.

iii

Lewis Kindred parked his Action Power 9000 next to his bed and plugged in his twenty-four-volt battery charger, ensuring that the wheelchair would be fully fueled and ready to go in the morning. Then he tucked his damaged left arm against his ribcage and expertly rolled forward onto the bed, ending up in a sitting position with the stumps of his legs protruding only inches over the edge of the mattress. If he needed to use the bathroom during the night, which was probable, he would go crablike on hands and stumps, pulling himself along the handrail affixed to the wall in the hallway, then hoisting himself onto the toilet by grabbing the stainless-steel bar bolted to the wall above it.

A man without legs becomes something of an acrobat.

Before turning out the light, he opened a drawer next to his bed and took out the Colt .45 military service pistol he kept there. He ensured that it was loaded, that it had a round in the chamber, and that the spare magazine was both full and handy. After engaging the safety he laid the weapon in his lap and switched off the bedroom light, using the remote-control device that his aunt, the land-lady, had installed for his convenience.

His eyes adjusted slowly to the dark, seeking out the shifting shadows thrown by the elms and oaks in the yard. Leaning against the wall that his bed abutted, he listened for the sounds he'd heard earlier in the evening, the ticks and scrapes of someone moving around in the dark of his porch, the squeak of old floorboards outside his front door, the soft rustle of clothing against skin. Not in years had he heard such sounds or sensed that someone was stalking him, spying on him, waiting for an opportunity to finish what had begun more than two decades ago on the edge of a rubber plantation in Vietnam. He couldn't help believing that the return of the *haunting* had something to do with the orb, with laying eyes on it again for the first time in nearly two decades.

In past years he'd come close to seeing the man half a dozen times – a smear of movement half glimpsed from the corner of his eye, never straight-on and never in the full light of day. He'd seen enough, however, *sensed* enough, to know that it was a small man with rat-shrewd eyes, wiry limbs and dark hair.

He'd seen enough to know it was No Bick.

Lewis didn't doubt the irrationality of this conclusion, but neither did he try to rid himself of it. After all, he was far from alone in clinging to a belief in the preposterous.

The notion that No Bick had stolen one of his severed legs on the battlefield, said one part of Lewis's brain, was nothing more than a figment of a morphine-induced dream, a sick fantasy brought on by trauma. To think that No Bick had stolen the leg to *eat* it was nothing short of psychotic. In another compartment of his brain, however, Lewis believed not only that No Bick had stolen the leg to eat it, but also that he'd followed him from the laterite meadows of the Iron Triangle to Portland, Oregon, U.S. of A., to *finish his meal.*

Like many combat veterans Lewis kept a loaded gun in his home. He'd often bolted awake in the dead of night, shaken by some horrific memory that had wormed its way into a dream, and wondered for a shrieking moment if he was back in the 'Nam. Falling asleep again required the comforting touch of gunmetal on his fingertips. It wasn't as if he was worried about the North Vietnamese Army anymore. He was worried about something else . . .

Numbah one chop-chop. Numbah one, okay . . . ?

He first detected No Bick's prowling back in 1976, shortly after his mother had died. He'd sold the old family house in Laurelhurst and, at his aunt Juliet's insistence, had moved into this apartment. The prowling nearly always occurred at night. He'd never called the police or told his aunt about the intrusions, simply because he knew precisely what he was up against. Vietnam had done things to him, left its disease in his heart. *You're not seeing No Bick, you idiot, you're seeing the Asian-immigrant janitor your aunt hired to clean the halls and stairways*. This was the rational explanation.

The other explanation, however, required that he keep a loaded .45 in his bed table. For it was in this particular compartment of his brain that he saw the vision of the rat-shrewd Kit Carson creeping up to his bedside in the dead of night, a bayonet in his fist and hunger glittering in his eyes. If that vision ever materialized, if it ever became real, Lewis was ready.

iv

Fear settled against Josh's chest, heavy like an anvil. His ears magnified every sound that filtered into his room from the surrounding apartments and the outside world – the faraway whoop of an ambulance, the whoosh of wind in the trees, the bong of his mother's heirloom clock on the living room mantel.

And close by, the breathing. Steady and smooth, feminine in texture.

It wasn't his mother, and it wasn't his sister, for he knew their sounds. They were his own flesh and blood, for Christ's sake. That one of them would hide in the shadows near his bed, uttering not a word, was unthinkable.

Who, then?

Something made him think of the orb. Before going to bed, he'd placed it in the right top drawer of his cluttered desk, not knowing what else to do with it. He would make that decision tomorrow, he'd told himself.

Thinking of the orb, of course, made him think of the

gorgeous Millie and her mismatched eyes. He felt again the dizzying power that flowed from those eyes, the *authority* they conveyed. He remembered the way she'd moved, as smoothly as a shadow but with the power of a lioness. Who was Josh Nickerson to disobey her?

He realized that he was shivering, for under the single sheet he wore only boxer shorts. The sound of rain came to his ears, the pitting and patting of droplets against his windowpane, the stirring of papers on his desk. The window was open, strangely, and a chilly wind was wreaking havoc with the loose clutter of the room. No wonder he was shivering, he said to himself.

With adrenaline pounding through his veins he swung out of bed and padded to the window, meaning to close it, meaning to prove to himself and whoever might be watching that he wasn't about to cower in his bed like a frightened boy. He discovered that the screen was missing. Bracing himself against the window frame, he leaned out and saw the screen on the grass below, the rain pounding cold against his neck and shoulders. The courage he'd mustered a moment ago disintegrated like a cupcake in a hailstorm.

Without knowing exactly why, he opened the top right drawer of his desk and rummaged around inside it for the orb. He heard Lewis's voice in his head urging Josh to throw the thing into the river. Maybe he shouldn't put off getting rid of it until tomorrow, Josh thought. Maybe he should get rid of it *tonight*.

The problem was that he couldn't find the fucking thing. He knew he'd put it in this drawer, which held old baseball cards, disused pens and pencils, wadded Snickers wrappers – all of which his fingers touched and ignored. The orb wasn't here now, which was crazy, because no one had come into his room since he'd snapped off the lights, except . . .

'Looking for this, Josh?' whispered someone behind him.

The back of Josh's neck tingled. His heart thundered crazily. He forced himself to turn around, to open his eyes. The night was red. Millie stood so close to him that he felt the soft heat of her breath on his bare chest, and she held the orb in her fingers only inches from his face. The thing was like a beacon, casting its crimson strings of light over the walls of the room.

'Jesus Christ . . . !' Josh croaked, his voice pinching. 'How did you get in here?'

Millie smiled wickedly. Her mismatched eyes came alive, the left one brown, the right one blue. *Earth and ice*, thought Josh, his mind fluttering like a trapped moth. She wore a simple shift of black, very short and cut low at the neck so that the tops of her breasts were visible, and Josh couldn't stop himself from staring at them. Her rusty dreadlocks tumbled around her shoulders, and she smelled of some sweet perfume mixed with musk. She wore open-toed stiletto heels, and the red of her toenails matched that of her long fingernails. The glare of her white teeth terrified him, but he was getting a hard-on nonetheless.

'Let's not waste time, Josh,' she said, and she slipped her hand into his shorts and wrapped her fingers around his cock. 'I asked you to do something for me, didn't I? Do you remember what it was?'

'Y-yes, I remember. You asked me to give that – the *orb* – to Lewis.' She stroked him with strong fingers, for he was hard as a rock now, and he could hear her breathing, her breasts rising and falling.

'But you didn't do it, did you, Josh? You let him refuse it, didn't you?'

'I-I didn't have a choice. He wouldn't take it. H-he told me I should . . .' His hips started pumping involuntarily, heat creeping from his groin upward into his abdomen, downward into his thighs. It was delicious. '. . . throw it in the river.'

'It's very important to me that you do what you agreed to do, Josh. I helped you, didn't I? Didn't I save your life? Now it's time for you to help me.' She pressed the orb into his hand, then caught his other hand and pulled it to her breast. She quickened the pace of the stroking. 'Try again, Josh,' she said huskily, urgently. 'Make him take it, Josh.'

He felt her nipple harden like an olive pit, and in his other hand the orb grew very warm. His hips thrust back and forth violently as he fucked her fist, and through his half-open eyes he saw that her body, too, was undulating, pumping, and he imagined himself pushing her onto the bed, lifting up the dress. Surely she wore no underwear, as she'd worn none last night. He imagined her legs spreading eagerly for him, long and brown, glossy with sweat, her ankles locking in the small of his back.

'Try again, Josh,' she rasped, her body shuddering, and Josh's orgasm exploded. He clutched the orb tightly as Millie slipped away, a hissing shadow. In the space of three heartbeats she was gone, apparently having left the way she'd entered, through the open window. Josh stood dazed and sticky, holding only the orb, which still glowed red but not as brightly. A chill settled over him as his sexual heat subsided and the red glow faded.

CHAPTER EIGHT
Pilgrimage

i

The journey to Tay Ninh from Cu Chi has been long and dangerous, but you've come to think of it as a pilgrimage, even though you're not a Cao Dai believer. Tay Ninh is the Holy See of the faith that once virtually ruled the province, at one time boasting two million believers and its own army. Ever since you were a small boy in Saigon, you've heard whispers of an underground sect of Cao Dai priests who know answers to questions best unasked. But you've chosen to ask such questions, having seen what you've seen, having heard what you've heard. If a pilgrimage is a quest for enlightenment and truth, you're indeed a pilgrim.

By traveling mostly at night and hiding during the day, sometimes in the same tunnels and spider holes that concealed you from the Americans when you fought for the VC, you've evaded the endless green and tan columns of NVA soldiers streaming south to Saigon for the final battle. You've walked nearly all the way, using twisty back roads, trails along rice dikes and paths through forests. Your 'Ho Chi Minh' sandals – sections of tire treads with rubber loops for your big toes – are worn nearly useless. Your feet are masses of blisters and sores. Your stomach burns with hunger.

Surrounding the Holy See is a high stone wall covered with lichens and vines, pocked here and there by bullets and shrapnel. You slip through one of the side gates and press your back against the stones, half expecting the sounds of footsteps behind you or the voices of soldiers raising the alarm. But you hear only the sounds of the night. You've made it safely – this far, at least. The city of Tay Ninh, which surrounds the Holy See, is silent. All but the bravest citizens have elected to stay inside their homes and thus minimize contact with the occupying NVA.

The triple-canopy jungle inside the enclosure effectively denies the light of moon and stars, so the gloom is profound, but gradually your eyes adjust, and you're able to pick your way along the brick-covered path that leads toward the temple. Occasionally a night bird calls or a monkey screams, raising gooseflesh on your arms and neck, but you press on. A lantern winks through the foliage ahead, and you follow its light until you reach the shapeless stone hulk of the temple, where you encounter a wrought-iron gate, which is unlocked, fortunately. A few meters beyond the gate stands a heavy wooden door, also unlocked. You shoulder it open.

Your eyes aren't ready for the assault of several hundred candles bedecking the altars and alcoves of the chamber you've just entered. The atmosphere here is spicy with smoldering joss sticks and hot candle wax. The icons of Cao Dai hang on the walls or perch on the altars, festooned with freshly cut strings of orchids – portraits and statues of its deities, their images softened by the ambient smoke: Victor Hugo, the foremost. Lao-tzu.

Jesus of Nazareth. Sun Yat Sen. William Shakespeare. Many others.

You've always thought it ingenious that the founders of Cao Dai chose such culturally varied gods to worship, thereby broadening the appeal of their creed and offering something to virtually anyone in search of a religion. Perhaps it was for this very reason that Cao Dai eventually attracted the enmity both of the Buddhists and the Catholics of South Vietnam, who joined together in brutal campaigns to stamp it out. Cao Dai has withered under the attack, but a stalwart core of believers still holds fast to this 'Third Alliance between God and Man,' and the Holy See still functions.

A man emerges from the shadows, his head shaved, his oily skin gleaming in the candlelight, wearing a loose white robe over his round body. After staring at you for a full thirty seconds, he says simply, 'Welcome.'

Suddenly you feel weak and wobbly. The travail you've suffered during the week-long trek from Cu Chi has taken its toll. You try to speak, but you can only croak. The man sees what a sorry state you're in and calls to summon his brother monks, who swarm on you from all sides, materializing like wraiths from the shadows, their bare feet whispering over the stone floor. You feel their hands on you, shoring you up, guiding you to a place where you can eat and sleep. But before you get very far, your consciousness flutters away, and you swoon into a cloud of incense and candle smoke.

ii

Having slept through the next day and into the following night, you take a meal of rice, a green bean cake and an orange that the monks set reverently before you. You sip a cup of lotus tea and wait for a visit from the 'elder brother,' as the monks know their leader. The cell where you've slept is deep within the interior of the temple, but it isn't dark. An elaborate electric chandelier hangs from the vaulted ceiling, which is decorated with terracotta filigree and mystical paintings that look almost medieval. You recognize the images of Christ, the Buddha, the angelic *apsara* of the ancient Cham civilization, and someone you can only assume is Victor Hugo.

You have a radio and a television set, but the latter is useless, because the Saigon television stations have been off the air ever since the Americans started evacuating their embassy days ago. Listening to the radio reports, however, you learn that the North Vietnamese Army is poised to enter Saigon, that General Duong Van Minh, known far and wide as 'Big Minh,' has assumed the presidency of the Republic of Vietnam. The end of the war is very near, everyone knows by now, for Big Minh has nothing to preside over.

The elder brother silently enters the room and sits on a bamboo mat across from your own. His face is round and serene, his eyes glittery with intelligence. He calls you 'little brother,' and warns that although you're welcome to the hospitality of the monks of the Holy See, it isn't safe here for a political refugee. The NVA have regularly inspected the premises ever since entering the city more than a month ago. For that matter, several of the monks have close connections to the Marxist National Liberation Front; they may even *be* Viet Cong, for all the elder brother knows. Only their reverence for the Third Alliance would prevent their turning you in.

You assure him that you have no intention of staying here, that you've come as a pilgrim. After finding the truth you seek, you plan to leave, for you have a wife and a newborn child who wait for you in Cu Chi. Naturally the elder brother wants to know more about the truth you seek. You sip slowly from your teacup, searching for exactly the right words, because you want to avoid saying anything that he could possibly consider disrespectful or blasphemous. Not being a religious man, you're uncomfortable with such things.

'I've seen a man whose right eye is blue, but whose left one is brown,' you answer slowly. 'His shadow hisses like a snake. He delights in causing pain, and he . . .'

'Say no more,' says the elder brother, holding up a palm. 'We don't speak of such things here, for we aren't shamans.'

'I've been told there are those among your brothers who can answer questions about such things. Is this true?'

'We will take you where you must go to learn your truth. You must promise, though, never to tell anyone that we have helped you. And you must promise to follow the instructions you receive to the letter . . .'

iii

With your head shaved and oiled, and wearing a flowing white robe, you easily pass for a Cao Dai monk, and the NVA soldiers in and around Tay Ninh don't glance at you twice. You're nervous though, because you know that sooner or later one of them will stop the Lambretta and ask for papers. Since you can show nothing, you will undoubtedly be shot without ceremony, simple as that. The driver, a giggling middle-aged monk with thick bifocals, seems oblivious to the direful possibilities, and handles the scooter as if he's running a motocross. On occasion he actually waves to the NVA soldiers as if they're long-lost friends of his, and they wave back, beaming. Most of them have the open, innocent faces of children, but they carry the weapons of men.

You head north out of Tay Ninh, past tumble-down military compounds that once housed ARVNs, Regional Forces, Popular Forces, National Police and GIs. The NVA haven't bothered to occupy these recently deserted relics, or even to hoist the North Vietnamese flag on the poles. Rather, they pitch their tents in school yards and on soccer fields, having no need of bunkers or barbed wire anymore. They all have deep suntans.

Your driver chooses back roads and trails through tiny hamlets that nestle in groves of bamboo and coconut palms, and you cling nervously to his waist, for you can well imagine that any of these might be booby-trapped or mined. Every time the scooter jounces through a pothole you brace for an explosion.

You enter a rubber plantation that has gone to jungle, and the April sun disappears behind the overhead canopy. The silence of this region dulls even the braying of the Lambretta's engine, and you feel as if you've entered a dream. At some point the plantation falls behind, but the narrow trail winds on, mounting low hills here and there, twisting around languid ponds and ancient, forgotten pagodas. Finally you burst into a clearing where the sunlight slants in on a deserted French villa with rusting iron gates and rotting porches. The yard is overrun by elephant grass, but a sturdy jackfruit stands proud near the front walk, its branches bending under the weight of fruit. Red jasmine abounds, and crimson butterflies flit among the blossoms.

Your driver cuts the engine and motions you on, telling you that from this point you must go alone.

iv

You step through the front door of the villa into a foyer that's decaying and green, and you ask yourself why anyone would choose to live in such a place. The house is bereft of the furnishings that once made it grand, and the air is thick with rot. You move through the foyer to a drawing room, where you hear the tinkling of wind chimes. Beyond a shattered wall of windows you see a flagstone terrace, where sits an aged man in a robe that should be white but has long ago turned yellowish gray.

He beckons to you, and you go. He motions for you to sit at his feet, and you sit. Up close you see that he is even older than you thought, perhaps ninety. His eyelids droop like veils over his rheumy eyes, and the flesh of his cheeks hangs like the comb of a rooster. Each gnarly thumb has a nail that is easily six inches long.

He sits in an ancient wicker chair next to an ancient wicker table. On the table a stumpy candle burns. He asks why you've come, and you see that his mouth is stained red with the juice of betel nut.

'I've come to ask your help, uncle,' you reply. 'I'm told that you have knowledge of very dark things – knowledge from long ago. I have seen a dark thing, but I lack the means to fight it.'

'What have you seen, nephew?'

You tell him about an American with one blue eye and one brown, whose shadow makes a rustling sound when it moves, whose passion is inflicting pain. You relate the things you've seen this man do, and you describe the globe of red crystal through which the man seems to control the forces of chance. You tell him about another man, a young lieutenant in the American Army, who not only opposed the one with mismatched eyes, but tried to kill him.

You've heard the legends about such things. Your own grandfather terrified you with such talk when you were a small boy, but later laughed about it, and you too had laughed when you were older. But you're not laughing now, you say, because you've seen something that defies everything rational.

'Your accent tells me you're from Saigon, nephew. Have you lived all your life in the city?'

'Yes, uncle, near the city – except for the years I spent studying in Europe.'

'You're a man of learning then.'

'Some say so, but I want to learn from you. Universities don't teach the kind of knowledge you possess.'

The old man chuckles demurely. 'No, I don't suppose they do. But let me ask you this: Do you believe in demons?'

Your heartbeat quickens. 'I don't know what to believe, uncle. I'm not Cao Dai or Buddhist. My mother was Roman Catholic, but I've never been religious.'

'Religion has nothing to do with demons, nephew. I've been a priest of the Third Alliance for many years, but the things I speak of are much older than Cao Dai, older even than Buddhism and the Catholics. You understand, don't you, that Cao Dai wisdom comes from our gods, and that we receive this wisdom during seances? This wisdom isn't Cao Dai or Buddhist or Catholic or Communist. It's human, nephew, and it's *old*, older than you can possibly imagine. Can you accept this?'

You nod your head, but then you understand that the old man can barely see, so you say aloud, 'Yes. I can accept that.'

'Then listen to me, nephew. What you have described to me is a thing for which we have no name. It lives not only here in Tay Ninh Province, not only in Vietnam, not only in Indochina. It lives wherever human beings live, and this is as it's been since the beginning of time.'

'What can you tell me about it, uncle?'

'What would you like to know?'

'Everything. Why does it do such evil things? What can we do to fight it? Does it have any weaknesses?'

The old priest grins, exposing black stumps of teeth on cherry-red gums. 'First you must tell me why someone like you, a man who's been abroad, an *educated* man, would believe in demons. Surely you know that the shadow you saw could have been a trick of the eye. As for the man who cast that shadow, he is not so unusual, it seems to me. Every army attracts beasts who crave killing and torture. For that matter, a man with different-colored eyes isn't unheard of, even among our Oriental peoples. Such a trait does not mark a man as evil. Surely you know that.'

Of course you know this. Haven't you told yourself this a thousand times? Patiently you explain what you saw more than five years ago in a firefight near the Michelin rubber plantation. You describe a man whom someone had shot in the face at close range, mortally wounding him. You relate how the dead man got to his feet in the hooch where he'd been killed, just as you were running for cover from exploding mortar rounds. You were sick with terror, having seen too much killing, and you were crazy, yes. But not crazy enough to miss the significance of the man with a hole in his face, a man whose shadow seemed alive, who lived to torture and maim. He grinned at you, this bloody horror, and waded into the brush to retrieve a Chinese-made pistol that you recognized as belonging to your commanding officer, for it had pearl handle grips that some NVA officer had paid dearly to have fashioned. He held it up so that you could see it clearly, then laughed and shouted to you, urging you to give it back to its owner, the man who had killed him with it. He tossed the weapon to you, then bounded toward the rubber plantation like a deer, skimming the ground and vaulting clumps of brush like no mere man could possibly do. Later, using your own methods, you were able to confirm that it was true – your commanding officer had killed this beast, but the beast had not stayed dead.

'So you see, uncle . . .' You swallow heavily, for your throat is on fire. Your eyes are awash in salty tears. 'I'm afraid because the man with a blue eye and a brown one is still alive. I don't know where he is any more than I know *what* he is. I'm afraid for myself, because he knows that I saw him. And I'm afraid for the man who tried to kill him. To be honest with you, uncle, I'm afraid for the world.'

The old man has begun to nod with palsied rhythm, as if he can hear a drumbeat that's beyond the range of your hearing. An afternoon breeze toys with a white wisp of his long mustache, and he looks you straight in the eye. 'You have done well in coming to me, nephew, but I'm afraid you will not like what I have to say. The demon has designs on the man who tried to kill him, of that I have no doubt. These creatures behave according to rigid patterns. If he succeeds in executing those designs, the man who tried to kill him will himself become a demon.'

Your guts tighten. 'What must I do, uncle?'

'You must find the would-be murderer, and you must

watch him. The demon will seek him out, no question about that. When this happens, you must be ready to strike.'

What he tells you next makes you wish that you had never been born, but you listen carefully to every word. You've promised to follow these instructions to the letter, and you're nothing if not a man of your word.

CHAPTER NINE
A Man with Style

i

Rex Caswell kept his three-story floating house moored off the posh shores of the Sellwood Bay Club on the Willamette River. His photography studio, darkroom, and weight room occupied the third floor, while the master suite, a study and a guest room took up most of the second. The main floor, which was for lounging and entertaining, had panoramic windows, two decks, and a gourmet kitchen. The living room boasted as much expensive Japanese sound and video equipment as was humanly possible to cram into it.

Rex Caswell considered himself a man of taste, a connoisseur of life's finer things. He admired style. He wore clothes from Armani, drove a Mercedes 350 SL, and roamed the Willamette on a custom-built cigarette boat with duel V-8s. He worked out ninety minutes a day in his weight room in order to maintain a body that looked thirty instead of the forty-three it really was. He used a tanning lamp to enhance what he considered his 'craggy good looks' and pulled his straight blond hair to the back of his head, where he banded it into a stubby ponytail. He wore a gold bead in the lobe of his right ear, but no other jewelry, except for a simple Piaget watch.

Rex Caswell had more style than anyone he knew.

His photography business was far too small to support his commitment to the finer things, but his cocaine business was more than up to it. For nearly two decades Rex had dealt drugs to young urban professionals west of the Willamette. His 'service area,' as he euphemistically termed it, extended far beyond the Portland city limits. He attributed his success, as well as the fact that he'd never seen the inside of a jail cell, to two things: keeping the business simple, which meant avoiding entanglements with gangs and big-time organized crime, and being ridiculously careful.

On Monday afternoon, September 14, 1992, he picked up a telephone handset, which was the conventional kind with a cord. Rex didn't believe in wireless telephones, because they were too easy to tap.

'Yeah, Mase,' he said when someone answered on the other end, 'I want you to draw ten kilobucks for me and drop it by the house before seven. I've got a game tonight.'

Mason Benoit, who represented a third of Rex's three-man work force, said, 'You got it. I'm on my way.'

The conversation was over. Benoit would fetch ten thousand dollars from a safe in the basement of an apartment building that Rex owned in Maywood Park, which was far away in northeast Portland near the airport. The safe held one of four such stashes of cash that he maintained at widely spaced locations throughout the metro area – 'surplus money' that he couldn't launder simply because he had too much of it. That was one of the little headaches that came with being a successful drug dealer in Portland, Oregon, the City of Roses: you made so much money that you couldn't spend it all, or even bank it, for fear of attracting the attention of narcs and, worse, the Internal Revenue Service. So Rex exercised great care in his use of undocumented cash.

'Are you kidding me?' asked Twyla Boley, having overheard the cryptic conversation. She was his live-in girlfriend of more than two decades. 'You're playing cards again *tonight*?' She punched up the sound on the TV. The local news was on, and the coverage was full of presidential candidate Bill Clinton's visit to Portland today, as well as President Bush's visit to southern Oregon. 'You promised to take me for a boat ride tonight. I was going to make us dinner in the galley, remember?'

'Sweetheart, have you noticed the weather? It's drizzly and cold, and they say it's going to get even worse tonight.'

'I don't care about the damn weather. The boat's got a dodger, and we could eat inside. I just want to get out of this dump, that's all.'

'Twyla, you're whining. You know I don't appreciate whining. If it makes you feel any better, I'll say I'm sorry. I'm sorry. There.' He rose from the red leather sofa and headed for the stairs, needing to go up and change clothes.

'What am I supposed to do all night, while you're out playing poker, for Christ's sake – sit home and watch videos? I'd *planned* to go boating. Maybe just fucking once you could think of somebody besides yourself!'

Rex whirled and glared at her ferociously. He hated hearing a woman use profanity, and Twyla knew this. Back in 1970, when they'd met, while she was pursuing a graduate degree in English and he was struggling to get a career in photography off the ground, he'd thought her the sexiest woman he'd ever seen. She was tall and blonde, a Norse goddess with tempestuous blue eyes and a willingness to be adventuresome. Her cultured upbringing showed in her smooth manners, her refined speech and the way she carried herself. She'd radiated style in those days, and he'd found her irresistible.

Now he shook his head, still staring at her. She'd gone to seed. Her looks were okay for a woman her age – a little mooshy here and there, but acceptable. It was her attitude that stank. She'd become cynical and impossible to please, given to making outrageous demands. She drank too much, coked too much, and no longer cared what she wore. Rex had seen bag ladies with more style.

Had two decades of soft living done this to Twyla? he wondered. Had she become spoiled, having never worked for her living, always getting anything she'd wanted with a snap of her fingers? He wondered now whether he should have insisted years ago that she go out and find a real job instead of sitting around scribbling senseless poetry. Maybe he should have occasionally said no when she demanded new clothes, a new car or a trip to Rome.

'Maybe just once you could wish me luck,' he said. 'Your old boyfriend is going to be in this game.'

Twyla muted the TV again, which showed Bill Clinton before a huge throng of adoring Portlanders, waving his arms as they threw roses to him. 'Oh *brother*!' she exclaimed with a mocking laugh. 'After all these years, and you're *still* trying to beat Lewis Kindred at the poker table! You never learn, do you, Rex? Nobody but *no*body beats Lewis Kindred. I told you that when I first introduced you to him – remember? It was that day in

Tom McCall Park, and you and I were out walking . . .'

Rex remembered, all right. It had happened more than a decade ago. He and Twyla had strolled hand-in-hand along the riverfront on a warm Saturday in July, and they'd unexpectedly come face to face with Lewis as he sat in his wheelchair. Twyla had tried to avoid him, for she'd heard about the grievous wounds he'd suffered, but Lewis's gaze and hers had locked together like a pair of magnets. Lewis had smiled. She'd said hi, having no alternative. She'd clumsily pulled Rex over and introduced him to Lewis, talking about him to Lewis as if he was a champion show dog. It had all been too bizarre.

Meeting the man whose woman he'd stolen years earlier would have been weird in itself, but *this* guy had gotten himself shot to pieces in Vietnam, and Rex had withered under a wave of guilt when he shook Lewis Kindred's hand for the first time. He would have sworn that Lewis sensed his discomfort. *You did this to me, Rex*, the cripple's eyes had said. *If you hadn't lured Twyla away from me, this never would've happened . . .*

Rex hadn't expected to hate the guy. He probably wouldn't have hated him, if Lewis had only acted as Rex expected him to act – a little deferential, a mite embarrassed over the sad state of his body; or better still, a little inferior in the face of the man who'd stolen his girl, a man who stood tall on two strong legs. But Kindred hadn't acted as Rex had expected him to. Kindred had acted like a fucking Brahman, as if the world owed him something. His tone, when talking to Rex, had been the kind you'd use with a parking attendant.

Twyla had asked whether Lewis still played poker, which had caught Rex's interest, because he considered himself a strong player. He'd said so. And Lewis had invited him to a game, though his tone hadn't sounded particularly sincere. Just to piss him off, Rex had accepted, and Twyla had said, *Better be careful, Rex – this guy plays poker like you wouldn't believe*.

Since that fateful day, Rex Caswell had been in hundreds of poker games with Lewis Kindred, and never once had he seen the son of a bitch lose. Dozens of times Lewis had walked away from the table – well, not *walked*, actually; *rolled* – with disproportionate sums of Rex's money. Worse, Lewis had always acted as if this was the natural order of things, that he was *entitled* to Rex's money.

So Rex had taken to studying poker seriously. He'd read books about the game and its myriad permutations. He'd studied positioning and bluffing and betting strategy. He'd read psychology in order to better gauge his opponents. He'd practiced endlessly on his friends, honing his mind to remember the cards and calculate the odds. He'd started driving up to La Center, Washington, on weeknights, where card rooms were still legal, in order to practice on the regular small-timers there. And he'd become very good. But he'd *still* not gotten good enough to beat Lewis Kindred.

iii

'He can be beaten,' insisted Rex through clenched teeth, his hazy blue eyes narrowing with menace. 'There isn't a man in this world who can't be beaten. His day will come, and so will mine.'

'Dream on, big boy,' laughed Twyla. 'The day you beat

Lewis Kindred at poker is the day I fart the *William Tell Overture.*'

'You know I don't appreciate it when you talk like that, sweetheart. I suggest strongly that you clean up your mouth, or I'll clean it up for you. But like I was about to say, I've invested more than ten years of intense study of the game, and I get stronger every time I play. Someday I'm going to take every dime that smug, condescending son of a bitch owns. And when I do . . .' He reached down to where she sat in a leather futon, and cupped her pale chin in his brown hand, a gesture of mock affection. '. . . I'll buy you a half-gallon of refried beans, sweet Twyla, because you'll need them.' He then pinched her nose a bit too hard, bringing a pained cry of protest. 'And I'll expect to hear the *William Tell Overture* as I've never heard it before.'

CHAPTER TEN
The Fanshawe Crowd

i

One reason Lewis Kindred loved the Monday-night game at the Hotel Fanshawe was that the sharpest poker minds in the city were regulars, meaning that the competition was hot, just the way he liked it. Too, there was never a shortage of 'new blood,' which meant fresh money for the taking – a conventioning businessman with a fat wallet, or an itinerant pro who'd blown into town to test the local yokels.

The owner of the Fanshawe was Tommy Iadanza, one of Lewis's best friends, a Vietnam veteran like himself. To those who didn't know him Tommy seemed nervous and maybe a little sour, but this was just his way. Tall and thin and loose-limbed, he had sad basset-hound eyes astride a prominent Roman nose, and a permanent scowl that suggested acute heartburn, which was probably accurate, considering how much linguini with spicy Italian sausage he pushed into his face daily. Lewis couldn't understand how the guy kept the fat off.

Tommy didn't play poker himself, but he loved hosting the Monday-night game, and he went to great lengths to make all the players feel welcome. With help from

Carlotta, his wife, he maintained a steady flow of refreshments from the Huntsman's Bar and Grill downstairs to the playing table. He managed the kitty and administered the bank according to strict rules that every player pledged in writing to honor. He also screened newcomers against infiltration by stoolies, inasmuch as organized poker was illegal in Portland, though Tommy figured the cops knew about the Fanshawe game and just didn't care about it. The game was squeaky clean, after all, and nobody ever got shot or stabbed *here*.

The Hotel Fanshawe stood on Third Avenue Southwest near the intersection with Salmon Street, across the street from a park. The neighborhood had seen better days but might yet see better ones still, given the pace of development in downtown Portland. A tidal wave of prosperity was rushing outward from the center of town, sweeping away decrepit buildings and burying old neighborhoods. Many old hotels like the Fanshawe had suffered the wrecking ball. In 1980, the Iadanzas had saved the Fanshawe from oblivion by buying it, believing that a market existed for clean hotel rooms at reasonable rates, even in booming Portland.

Tommy had dreamed of saving enough to restore the hotel to its original grandeur, envisioning a concierge, a doorman in full brass and braid, and a four-star restaurant to replace the greasy old Huntsman's Bar and Grill adjacent to the lobby. Unfortunately, the market for clean rooms at reasonable rates hadn't been as strong as he'd hoped, and money had become tight. The Iadanzas had managed only to replace the crumbling old marquee over the front entrance and to spot-repair sections of the elaborate terracotta tracery on the façade. As for the interior, they'd settled for installing inexpensive but tastefully neutral contemporary furnishings, rather than the rich art deco they'd dreamed of.

Someday, Tommy still said wistfully to Lewis. *Someday I'm gonna turn this dump into a showplace . . .*

On Monday, September 14, 1992, Lewis arrived at the Fanshawe with Alvin Johnson, who was an affable, rotund man in his late sixties. Known to his poker pals as 'Wisconsin Johnson' in honor of his native state, he wore cheap wool suits even in the hottest weather and dark green sunglasses year round. He owned a Dodge van that was perfect for hauling Lewis and his wheelchair. He was one of the best poker players Lewis had ever known, though he had the distracting habit of eating peanuts without removing them from their shells.

Wisconsin's arch-rival at the poker table was Sidney Gruener, a retired furniture retailer from Lake Havasu City, Arizona, who was as painfully thin as Wisconsin was fat. He had deep, oily eyes that should have belonged to a doctor or a rabbi, for they hinted of a reverent soul that his mouth tried hard to deny. He had a hooked nose and thick white hair that swept straight back from a narrow forehead. The other players called him 'Lake Havasu City Sid.'

A third regular was Connie Wierzbinski, a fiftyish woman who lived on her poker winnings and the dividends from a stock portfolio she'd obtained in accordance with her third divorce decree, some twenty years earlier. Spare and birdlike, she wore Trail Blazers fan clothes and chain-smoked menthol cigarettes. She had light freckles on her slightly sunken cheeks and dull brown hair that she wore short, like a cap.

The card room was on the second floor. A huge circular table, at least eight feet in diameter, stood in the center of the room, covered with green baize and illuminated by incandescent track lights in the ceiling. Ten straight-backed chairs surrounded the table, well padded for comfort and upholstered in a deep blue broadcloth that matched the carpet. When a game was in session, Tommy Iadanza manned a banker's table near the door. He kept the door locked, of course, to prevent any curious hotel guests from blundering in.

Lewis liked most of the people he played cards with. With few exceptions they were honest, down-to-earth folks for whom poker was a sport and a hobby. This level of competition was virtually free of compulsive gamblers, simply because compulsive gamblers lacked the temperament and discipline to compete against players of the quality found in the Fanshawe crowd. To survive with these folks, a player needed complete control of himself. He needed to think logically and unemotionally, to execute complex strategies and tactics, feats beyond the poor powers of gambling addicts. Thus, poker wasn't the game of choice for the vast majority of compulsives, who favored craps, roulette, lotteries, races, and slot machines – games in which pure luck was the overriding factor.

In addition to the regulars, tonight's game included a pair of 'occasionals,' one of whom was an amiable young veterinarian from Beaverton. The other was an intense engineering student from Reed College in Southeast Portland, a blond lad with wire-rim glasses and a loud Hawaiian shirt. New blood came in the body of an electrical contractor from Florida, a well-tanned and immaculately dressed man with a shiny bald head and an engaging smile.

Lewis motored up to the table in his Action Power 9000

and parked in his usual spot. In a ridiculously overdone British accent he said, 'You're probably wondering why I've asked all of you here tonight—'

A wadded napkin bounced off his forehead. 'We *know* why you asked us here,' chuckled Connie Wierzbinski, who'd hurled the napkin. 'You're after our money, like always! Well, I hope you said your prayers last night, slick, because you're in deep shit.' Her chuckle degenerated into a wheezing smoker's cough that made Lewis wince, as it always did.

'Let's not make it easy for him, just this once,' groused Lake Havasu City Sid. 'I've got grandkids who need to go to college.'

Tommy Iadanza carried a chip bucket from player to player, selling red, white and blue chips. Carlotta came behind him with a notepad, taking orders for food and drinks.

'It's Texas hold 'em tonight, same as always,' announced Tommy, dispensing twenty-five hundred dollars' worth of chips to Lewis. 'No limit. If the board wins, everybody splits the pot. Any questions?'

No one had any.

Texas hold 'em was the near-universal choice of serious poker players in America. A variant of seven-card stud, the game was deceptively simple. The dealer gave each player two 'hole' cards, then dealt five communal cards face-down in the center of the table – these were the 'board.' A round of betting occurred immediately after the deal, testing the strength of the players' hole cards. Another round occurred after turning over three of the board cards at once. A fourth and fifth round came after turning over each of the remaining board cards. Players used any combination of their hole cards and the board to make a poker hand. The best hand won.

No-limit Texas hold 'em was popular among real aficionados for several reasons. It accommodated lots of players, unlike seven-card stud, which allowed a maximum of seven with a single deck of cards. Lewis loved the game, especially at a crowded table, where the factor of *position* became vital. This referred to a particular player's place in the betting order, which depended on where he sat with respect to the dealer. Lewis was expert in using his position not only as a bluffing tool, but also as a means of figuring odds. With so many cards left undealt after each deal, playing the odds became extremely important. For this reason, he didn't consider himself a gambler. As Anthony Holden, the great British player, has written, a gambler bets *against* the odds, but a real poker player bets *with* them. Lewis was a real poker player.

'We're still missing somebody,' said Tommy, breaking the seal on a new pack of cards, 'but we may as well get this fiasco under way. You can deal him in when he gets here.'

'Who's the missing man?' asked Lewis.

'Your pal and mine,' answered Tommy with what passed for a grin. 'Rex Caswell.'

To groan aloud would have been bad form, so no one at the table did it. Rex Caswell was arrogant and full of himself. Given to flashing big money, he thought himself a much better poker player than he was. A rumor had circulated that he was mixed up in illegal drugs, but no one had ever presented any proof of this, so the Fanshawe crowd gave him the benefit of the doubt. His faults notwithstanding, the folks at the Fanshawe still put up with Rex after all these years, mainly because he always arrived with money, and he usually left a bunch of it on the table.

ii

Through the closed door of his room Josh heard the telephone ring, heard Kendra pick it up. *Don't let it be for me*, he prayed silently, but no sooner had he breathed the prayer than he heard Kendra's footfalls heading toward his room.

'Your latest Coke bottle is on the phone,' Kendra announced. 'She sounds desperate to talk to you, and more than a little upset. I told her I wasn't sure you were home, but that I'd check.'

Josh shut his eyes and shook his head. He really didn't want to talk to Laurel right now. Having hardly slept last night, he was tired and irritable, and he had a ton of homework. Not to mention a ton of worry.

'So how 'bout it, bud,' pressed Kendra, her green eyes snapping, 'are you home or what?' She glanced around at the clutter of his room. 'God, how can you stand to live in this landfill? Anyway, if I were you, I wouldn't leave this girl twisting in the wind too long. Someone who looks like her isn't going to have any trouble getting dates.' Though only fifteen, Kendra was wise in the ways of the world. She herself was built like a Coke bottle, and the boys at Gavin Dell panted after her like adoring puppies. Josh didn't doubt for a minute that his little sister was more seasoned in romantic matters than *he* was.

'Tell her I'm not home. Tell her I didn't see her after school because I had an editorial board meeting. Say that I'll call her tomorrow.'

'I'll offer to take a message, okay? I don't want to get in the middle of your love life.'

Kendra pulled the door closed after her, and Josh listened to her retreating footfalls, heard her voice from down the hall as she talked to Laurel. He let out a sigh of relief when she hung up the phone.

Leaning back from his desk, he rubbed his eyes through closed lids, then studied the light fixture on the ceiling, trying hopelessly to distract himself from the image that flashed again and again in his mind – the image of Millie with her wonderful mismatched eyes, standing not two feet away from where Josh himself now sat, her hand in his boxer shorts. He felt her breast against his palm, the nipple hardening, and heard her words:

It's very important to me that you do what you agreed to do, Josh . . . Try again . . . Try again . . .

The whole thing seemed absurd. An incredibly sexy young woman wanted badly for him to give a red crystal orb to an old friend – badly enough to sneak into his room at night and give him a handjob when he failed the first time. What was so damned important about the orb, anyway? And why couldn't Millie simply give it to Lewis herself, rather than go through Josh?

He rose from his chair, went to his window and stared down through the dripping foliage of an elm tree to the glistening pavement of Gander Circle, two floors below. Lights shone in the stately old houses on both sides of the street, for it was still early, not yet eight-thirty. A shroud of drizzle hung over downtown Portland, muting the lights of the skyscrapers and bridges, giving the cityscape a dream-like quality. For a crazy moment Josh wondered whether all that happened during the last forty-eight hours had been real. He pulled open the top drawer in his desk, where the orb lay. No doubt about it – this was reality, not a dream. The orb was the proof.

From his window the drop to the yard below was sheer – two floors, at least thirty feet. When craning out the window last night in search of the missing screen, he'd seen no ladder leaning against the house. He'd even gone down this morning to look for marks in the ground, which a ladder would certainly have made, but he'd found none. He tried to imagine how someone would break into his room through this window, lacking a ladder. It was possible, he supposed, that the intruder had shinnied up the column from Lewis Kindred's porch below and swung over the rail onto the Nickersons' deck, which would have been an awesome accomplishment, even without the wind and rain. From the deck, however, the intruder would have needed mountaineering equipment, for Josh's window was at least ten feet away, and he could see no handholds or footholds along the way.

How in the fuck did she do it?

Millie had not only come in through that window, but she'd gone out through it, too, wearing a short shift and stiletto heels. While inside, she hadn't appeared the slightest bit winded or disheveled. It was possible, Josh supposed, that she'd lowered herself on a rope from the roof. She could have climbed onto the roof of the house via the fire escape on the far side of the building, carrying along a length of good strong rope, which she used to gain access to Josh's window. Then, dangling from the rope, she'd managed to take the screen off the window, raise the window itself, and—

Why hadn't he seen a dangling rope when he leaned out to look for the screen?

Shit. Another theory down the tubes.

He went back to the night of Ron Payne's murder,

when he'd seen Millie strolling on the deck of the singer's apartment. Mere seconds later he'd seen her on the ground, as if she'd jumped or, as Lewis Kindred had suggested yesterday, *rappelled* the three-story vertical drop from the deck. Had the police found any climbing equipment in Payne's apartment? Josh wondered. The news coverage had mentioned nothing about climbing equipment or ropes, but this didn't mean anything, he knew. Investigators often withheld such details from the public, not wanting the perpetrator to know just how much they knew.

A coil of fear tightened inside him, the same one that had kept him awake all night after encountering Millie in his room. He was no longer the disinterested observer of the bizarre realities surrounding Ron Payne's death. Having become involved with Millie, Josh had become more than an observer, more than a reporter. He himself was now part of the story.

Decision time. He thrust his hand into the desk drawer and pulled out the orb, then zippered it into a leather fanny pack. He fastened the pack around his waist, threw on a jacket and pounded out his room, headed for the front door.

'Where should I tell Cheryl you are when she gets back from her workout?' Kendra wanted to know. Within the last year, she'd taken to calling her mother by her first name.

'Tell her I had some errands to run. I'll be back soon.'

iii

Rex Caswell parked his Mercedes half a block north of the Hotel Fanshawe in the closest space he could find. He glanced at his Piaget watch and saw that he was more than half an hour late. *Oh well*, he thought. *Business before pleasure*. One of his oldest clients had called just as he was leaving his house, and had begged for a couple of ounces. Mere minutes earlier the guy's boss had told him that he was sending him to a conference in Hawaii for the next two weeks, starting tomorrow, and – well, you know how it is. You can't go to Hawaii without some blow. Rex wasn't very good at saying no.

So here he was at last, armed with cash and feeling strangely lucky. Maybe tonight he would walk out of the Fanshawe a winner, leaving in his wake those poor, misfitted dweebs who had nothing in their lives but poker – chief among them, Lewis Kindred, the King of Dweebs. Then Rex's victory over Lewis would be complete. First he'd taken Twyla from him, and now he would take *this*, the mantle of kingship that Lewis Kindred wore so smugly among his small coterie.

As he entered the lobby he saw an exquisite creature sitting on a divan near the elevator, a light-complected black woman dressed in a mint-green double-breasted jacket with a matching pleated skirt, long and full. She had dramatic, rust-colored dreadlocks and silver earrings that matched the buttons of her jacket. *This woman has style*, he told himself, unable to tear his gaze away from her. She rose suddenly from the divan and approached him, tall and languid in her movements, full in the lips, sinewy. She had one blue eye and one brown.

Rex felt his breath go out of him.

'I'll bet you're Mr Caswell,' she said in a soft Southern contralto. 'I was told I might find you here.'

'Well – I . . . yeah, I mean *yes*, I'm often here on Monday evenings. I don't think I've had the pleasure.'

'No, you haven't, and neither have I. My name is Millie

Carter.' She offered a slim hand, on which the nails were painted the same mint-green as the suit she wore. 'I'm wondering if you might do me a favor, Mr Caswell . . .'

'Call me Rex. All my friends do.'

'Why, thank you, Rex. As I was saying, I would be forever in your debt if you'd let me accompany you to your game tonight as your guest.'

'To the game? As my guest? Why?'

'I'm very interested in poker, and I've been traveling around to various cities, watching games, learning, and even playing now and then. I've been told that this game is *the* game in Portland. Someone gave me your name as the man to see, if I wanted to observe. I do hope you will let me come with you. Who knows? Perhaps I'll be your good-luck charm.' She reached over and smoothed the lapel of his expensive trench coat, which was spotty with raindrops.

Rex stared at her, liking the electric tingle this woman gave him, and his face showed it. He muttered something about this being short notice, something else about the rules prohibiting visitors who hadn't received clearance by the owner of the hotel. Millie smiled dazzlingly, and assured him that she wasn't a police informer. Rex felt a drop of perspiration run down his leg as he laughed with her – of *course* she wasn't an informer. Of *course* she would be welcome upstairs. He would see to that.

iv

At the poker table Lewis was in his element. Here he needed no strong legs or arms; no flawless, unscarred face; he needed only his wits and his nerve. Each game was a world within a world, where the deck of cards represented anything and everything that Fate could dream up to fling at him. Lewis had become adept at maneuvering himself into Fate's small circle of favorites and twisting her cruelty to serve his own ends. At the poker table he possessed something that he lacked in the real world – control.

But it wasn't a soft place, this world within a world. Poker was tough, heartless. Poker demanded your best shot, and sometimes your best wasn't good enough. Sometimes you lost. This was part of the game, and Lewis accepted the good with the bad, knowing that in the end, he would win. This was *faith*, he supposed, or something close to it.

For Lewis the evening had begun well. The electrical contractor from Florida had lost steadily, as had the young veterinarian from Beaverton. Inexplicably, Wisconsin Johnson was also having a bad night, thanks mainly to three big hands that Lewis had won. Already Wisconsin had consumed a half-pound pack of peanuts in the shells, an indicator that he was nervous about his losing streak. The other players were more or less breaking even, while Lewis was more than three thousand dollars ahead.

Then Rex Caswell arrived, strutting his costly clothes, his stubby blond ponytail bouncing comically, a gorgeous racially mixed woman in tow. The instant Lewis laid eyes on her, he knew who she was, for her mismatched eyes gleamed like exquisitely cut gems. She was Millie, who'd starred in the story that Josh Nickerson had told him yesterday. He'd seen eyes like hers before.

Tommy Iadanza was hesitant to admit an observer without prior clearance, but Rex clapped him on the shoulder and said, 'Tom, please. You don't seriously think I'd bring a guest that I hadn't thoroughly vetted –

come *on*, Tommy! I hope you don't think this glorious creature . . .' He pulled Millie close to the table so that all the players could get a good look at her. '. . . could be a cop, do you? I mean, get a grip – can you see a lady like this doing close-order drill at a fucking police academy?'

A gust of laughter went up from all the players except Lewis. He couldn't take his eyes off Millie, and she stared straight back at him, smiling faintly as if he and she shared a strange and precious secret. Lewis felt a stirring in his gut that he'd not felt in a long, long time.

'How about we take a vote right now?' continued Rex. 'All those in favor of letting Millie stay raise your hands . . .' Everybody voted to let her stay. Even Lewis. *Especially* Lewis.

v

Josh drove to Nicole Tran's house and convinced her to come along with him – to where, he couldn't really say. He needed to talk. Nicole, reluctant at first, told him that he wasn't the only one who cared about getting his homework done. But when she got a good look at his face, and saw the tiny spasms of fear and confusion tugging at it, she knew that she couldn't turn him out on his own. She pulled on a hooded rain jacket.

The rain had started coming down in earnest now. Twists of colored light lay on the wet asphalt of downtown Portland, cast there by neon signs and street lamps. Traffic was light. Josh headed along the Willamette, and turned into River Place, where he had no trouble finding a parking place.

'Let's walk,' he said, and they got out of the car, mindless of the rain.

They ambled north along the esplanade, Nicole's arm

hooked into Josh's elbow, alone except for the occasional scurrying couple under an umbrella.

Josh told Nicole everything he'd told Lewis Kindred yesterday – the fact that he'd been outside Ron Payne's apartment on the night the singer died, that he'd seen Millie there, that he'd received newspaper clippings telling of similar murders in other cities across the country. He also related Lewis's own experiences with an orb of red crystal and a man with mismatched eyes, along with Lewis's deep suspicions that those experiences might have been harmless figments of his imagination.

Then Josh told her about last night, what happened in his room. But he stammered and stalled when he got to the part where Millie put her hand into his shorts. Nicole waited for him to finish, silent, expectant, no doubt miffed because he'd withheld so much from her for so long.

Josh forced himself to finish the story, and he felt Nicole's grip tighten on his arm. 'What she did then . . . well, I guess she gave me a handjob, you could say. I wasn't going to say anything about this, but . . .'

'Jesus!' Nicole let go of him and stopped dead in her tracks. '*This* is what you dragged me out on a rainy night to tell me? That Millie gave you a handjob?'

'Nicki, how could I avoid telling you? It's all part of what's been happening to me.'

'Who in the hell do you think I am, anyway – one of the guys? One of those fucking testosterone-poisoned grunge-heads you hang with? You think it's cool to tell me your fucking locker-room stories?'

Josh put his palms to his forehead, shaken by her eruption. 'I thought you'd want to know, that's all.

You're my closest bud, for Christ's sake. If I can't tell you, who can I tell?'

'So, I'm your closest bud, am I? That's great. That's just fucking great.' She whirled on her heels and moved off in the direction from which they'd come. The breeze blew the hood of her jacket back, and her long black hair streamed away from her face. 'Be sure to let me know when you get your next handjob, okay, Nickster? And I'd be especially interested in hearing about Laurel's blow-jobs. I hear she's real good at it. I'll want all the gory details.'

Josh trotted after her. 'Nicki, don't turn your back on me. I need to talk to you. I need your help.' She quickened her pace. Josh had never known a girl who could walk as fast as Nicole without breaking into a run. 'Think about it, okay? Here I am, a normal everyday kid in Portland, Oregon, seventeen years old. I get a wild hair up my ass to write a story about a hometown band. I end up outside the apartment when the lead singer gets killed. I see a mysterious woman. I start getting press clippings in the mail. Then the woman I saw saves me from getting stomped by skinheads and gives me a crystal orb and orders me to give it to someone else. Next thing I know, she's in my fucking room with her hand in my pants, like she's flown in through the window or something—'

He caught hold of Nicole's arm and pulled her around to face him. The rain had drenched her face and hair, but even in the sickly yellow glow of mercury-vapor street-lights she looked great. She also looked pissed off. 'Nicki, don't spazz out on me, okay? This is serious shit. I've gotten mixed up in something very major and very weird. It's wearing me down, eating me up. I need your advice,

and I . . .' He dropped his gaze to the wet cement.
'. . . and I need your friendship.'

When he dared to raise his eyes again he saw that
Nicole's face had softened. Raindrops were running
down her face in rivulets – or were there tears mixed with
the rain? – and her hair clung to her cheeks in damp
bundles. She no longer looked angry, but only a little
hurt.

'What do you want to do, Josh?' she asked, calling him
by his real given name, which she did only when things
were extraordinarily serious.

'I've brought the orb with me. I want to throw it in the
river. I want you to make sure I actually do it, okay?
Don't let me wimp out at the last minute.'

'I think you *should* throw it in the river. I think you
should do exactly as Lewis advised and put this whole
scary business behind you. Forget about Ron Payne and
Demon Beef. Forget about Millie. Get your life back on
track, Josh. Get back to the real world.'

'Good. That's what I want to do.' He nodded over his
shoulder at the Hawthorne Bridge, a graceful lacework of
black metal over the river, rimmed with feeble lights that
looked vaguely like Christmas decorations. 'Up there.
We'll go up there and do the job, okay?'

'Okay, Nickster,' whispered Nicole, smiling bravely.
'We'll go up there and do the job.'

vi

Lewis couldn't concentrate. He'd lost five straight hands
to Rex Caswell – hands in which he should have folded
after the first round of betting. He felt as if his mental
calculator had blown a chip, that his ability to figure odds
had flitted out through his ears.

Rex, on the other hand, was enjoying an unholy blast of luck. Lewis reminded himself that these things sometimes happened, that players occasionally beat the odds several times in succession. A man on a lucky streak was unbeatable, as the pros all knew, and the only way to handle him was to stop playing and give the streak time to fade.

But Lewis couldn't stop tonight, not with Millie watching. She sat in an armchair against the wall, her slim legs crossed and her pretty chin propped on her fist, staring at Lewis with those unsettling eyes of hers. She seemed to be uninterested in everyone else in the room, even Rex, who often turned around to grin at her, celebrating what he probably thought was his great skill at poker.

The first to leave the game was the electrical contractor from Florida, who graciously expressed the hope that they would let him play the next time he came to Portland. Everyone smiled, shook his hand and wished him well.

On the next three hands Lewis lost more than three thousand dollars, all to Rex. He felt as if some toxic vapor had seeped into the room, numbing his synapses and clouding his judgment. The other players obviously saw the writing on the wall and were folding early, but Lewis played each hand to the bitter showdown, trying unsuccessfully to bluff Rex into submission. The problem was that Rex was getting the right cards, and he wouldn't be bluffed.

'Jesus, Mary and Joseph,' muttered Connie Wierzbinski after the latest hand, in which Rex had dealt himself a pair of aces and another pair to the board. 'What you gotta do to get a hand like that?'

'You've got to live right, dear lady,' replied Rex,

grinning in a lopsided way that looked affected.

'Well, I guess my sins have caught up with me,' Connie declared, rising from the table and gathering in her small hoard of chips. 'See you all next time.'

Lewis actually won the next hand, a rather modest haul, inasmuch as Rex folded early and had busied himself with whispering sweet nothings to Millie. Lewis let himself believe that Rex's lucky streak had finally ended, and he resolved silently to take the arrogant asshole apart, piece by piece. This was no-limit Texas hold 'em, right? People had won fortunes playing this game, and had lost them, too, all in a single night. Rex Caswell had plundered Lewis's game reserves, riding a steed named Dumb Luck, and Lewis meant to make him pay. And pay. And pay.

He picked up the deck and shuffled it in his patented one-handed way, since his left hand was good for pushing the option button on a computer keyboard and not much else. The feat was spellbinding to those who'd never seen it before, and Lewis loved doing it, loved the sense of power it gave him. He was the only one he knew who could do this – shuffle, cut the cards and deal without letting the deck touch the table, all with one hand. But suddenly he caught sight of Millie's eyes, and his concentration broke. The deck exploded and cards flew in every direction. Rex Caswell roared with laughter and thumped the table with both hands. No one else laughed.

'God, Lewis, could you do that again, please?' roared Caswell, his eyes tearing. 'It looked like a fucking confetti factory in here!'

Lewis waited for the cards to be collected, grinding his teeth but somehow maintaining his thin poker smile.

Wisconsin Johnson handed the deck to him, and he tried again. The other players waited patiently, riffling their chips as the good players do, keeping their faces down. This time Lewis dealt the cards without a hitch.

Get ready to lose, he said silently to Rex. *Get ready to lose big, you self-consumed bag of shit, because here I come . . .*

vii

They stood at a point midway on the Hawthorne Bridge and leaned against the pedestrians' railing, their shoulders touching. Staring into the black depths of the Willamette River, Josh wondered how many poor souls had slipped over this rail to put an end to whatever tormented them. In his mind he saw human bodies plunging toward the hungry water. He endured a pang of sadness for them, and felt thankful that his problems weren't that bad, that he could end his small torments merely by dropping a red crystal orb into the water.

Or could he?

'Okay, we're here,' said Nicole, her voice betraying a shiver. 'Let's get this over with.'

'Right.' Josh reached down and tugged on the zipper of the fanny pack, which had become stubborn because it had gotten wet. Finally he took out the orb, which gleamed dully red in his palm, its innards swirling like miniature cyclones.

It's very important to me that you do what you agreed to do, Josh . . . Didn't I save your life? Now it's time for you to help me . . .

Josh's eyes went bleary, and he felt as if someone had dropped a chunk of dry ice down his collar. The sound of Millie's voice was as clear in his ears as the whine of the wind and the whoosh of cars on Hawthorne Boulevard. He shuddered radically.

'Are you okay?' Nicole's voice tight with concern. 'You look like you're ready to pass out.'

'I'm okay. It's just that . . .' The orb now grew hot, almost too hot to hold. If it grew much hotter, he would either need to drop it into the Willamette or put it back in the fanny pack.

Try again, Josh. Make him take it, Josh.

He tried to explain to Nicole, but explaining wasn't easy. He didn't know what was happening to him. His mental video screen fluttered to life again, this time with Millie's grinning face, her blue eye and her brown eye blazing forth both promises and threats. Josh's scrotum prickled and the flesh on his back tried to crawl off his bones.

'It's just what, Nickster?'

'Damn it, Nicki, she can get to me, if she wants to. What'll she do to me if I throw this thing in the river, huh?'

'I don't believe this. Not fifteen minutes ago you were straining at the bit to get rid of the damned thing.'

'Maybe I should do what she wants. Maybe I should try one more time to make Lewis take it.'

'Nickster, I swear I don't understand you . . .'

'I'm scared, okay? I'll admit it. I'm scared shitless of the bitch.'

'Then give it to me. *I'll* throw it in. You can tell her I stole it . . .'

'No! Do you really think she's that stupid? She has ways of knowing things, ways of finding things out. She's not like other people, Nicki. Somehow she knew that Lewis hadn't taken the orb when I tried to give it to him.

On top of that – Christ, this sounds weird, I know – but I think she can fly . . .'

'You're raving! You need professional help! If you won't throw that goddamn piece of glass away, or if you won't let me do it, then you'll have to deal with the consequences yourself.'

'Please, Nicki, I want you to understand . . .'

'I understand this,' she spat, planting her fists on her hips. 'You're behaving like a scared little kid. First, you're bound and determined to do one thing, then fifteen minutes later you're bound and determined to do exactly the opposite. Grow up, Josh. Join the world of the big people, and stop looking for monsters in your closet.'

'I'm not looking for monsters . . . !'

For the second time that night Nicole turned her back on him and stomped away, but this time she didn't let him stop her. The hike back to the car was long and silent and wet. Josh kept the orb in the pocket of his jeans, where he could feel its warmth against his leg.

viii

Rex Caswell studied his hole cards, his normally unworried brow furrowed in concentration. The hand had entered the fifth round of betting, 'Fifth Street,' the players called it, and all the other players had folded. It was just Lewis and Rex now.

Lewis had a pair of jacks in the hole, and the board showed a jack, a queen, an ace, a four and a seven. Thus, his hand was three jacks, which was very strong. Keeping his thin poker smile in place, he studied Rex's face, looking for telltale signs of worry or distress, some indicator that the man was bluffing. A bead of sweat. A quick sidelong glance. An involuntary pucker of the lips. Unbelievably he saw all three, and he consciously forced himself to breathe slowly and deeply to hold back a snicker. No doubt about it, the oaf's lucky streak had ended. Better yet, Rex was trying to bluff him, which wasn't altogether stupid, considering the way the cards had fallen tonight.

The betting had been heavy, for neither Rex nor Lewis had passed up a chance to raise. The pot now had more than six thousand dollars in it.

'I guess the bet's to me, isn't it?' said Rex. He glanced at his hole cards one last time, then started counting out blue chips, each of which was worth fifty dollars. He pushed a stack of ten into the pot, and then another stack of ten, and another and another. 'I'll raise you two thousand,' he said.

Lewis's stare passed quickly over his own stack of chips. He had barely enough on the table to see the raise, and he pushed a mound of chips forward. 'Banker,' he called to Tommy Iadanza, who rushed instantly to his side with a bucket of chips in one hand and a ledger book in the other. 'If my credit's good, I'd like an advance of ten thousand dollars.'

Gasps came from several sides, followed by a general hush. This was no ordinary poker hand, the others all knew now. Someone was trying to teach someone else a lesson. The only sound was the purr of Lake Havasu City Sid's chips as he riffled them in perfect arcs from one hand to the other and back again.

'Your credit's good, Lewis,' said Tommy with deep gravity, and he started dispensing piles of blue chips. Lewis withdrew a pen from a pouch in his wheelchair and prepared to sign a note.

'Don't fill in the amount yet,' said Rex, grinning across the table. 'I'll see your ten thousand and raise you fifty – *thousand*, that is.'

Now it was Lewis who gasped, though he didn't mean to. What the hell was going on here? he wondered. Did this dipshit really think he could bluff Lewis Kindred merely by throwing money at him?

'Rex,' said Lake Havasu City Sid, 'there's already a lot of money on the table.' Sid's oily eyes were huge with concern. 'Maybe you should just call, huh?'

'Butt out, Sid. You folded, remember? So how about it, Lewis? Are you going to see my raise? If not, you can forget the note and just write me a check for ten thousand.'

Lewis happened to glance at Millie, who had leaned forward expectantly in her chair. She watched his every move with utter fascination, her blue-brown gaze boring into him as if to seek out all his secrets. He blinked against the intrusion, but those greedy eyes of hers were relentless. They had unnerved him earlier. They unnerved him now.

'What's the matter, Lewis?' asked Rex, tapping his hole cards with a brown finger. 'Has this game gotten a little rich for you?'

'Give me a minute.' For a mad moment Lewis actually forgot what cards he had in the hole. Did he dare steal a peek? A twitchy facial muscle plucked at his poker smile. *Two jacks*, his mind screamed. *Two jacks plus one in the board makes three. That's strong, man, real strong . . .*

Yes, but was it fifty thousand dollars' worth of strong?

'Your minute's up,' declared Rex Caswell, leaning back in his chair and clasping his hands behind his head. 'Let's get on with it, okay?'

Lewis looked up at him and saw trails of sweat running out of his tight blond hairline, streaming down his suntanned face. His hazy eyes were nervous, despite the confident grin. *The asshole's bluffing*, Lewis said to himself. 'I'll see your fifty thousand and raise you another fifty,' he declared, surprising himself with the coolness of his own voice. '*Thousand*, that is – assuming my credit's good.'

Rex's grin fell away, and he quickly looked again at his hole cards. Millie smiled, as if she approved. Her long, slim fingers toyed with some silver bracelets on her wrist, moving them slowly up and down, up and down. Lewis gulped, thinking of a young woman he'd once known all too briefly, for only one night, in fact. Her name had been Thuy Thanh, and she'd been the last woman he'd ever known sexually. He remembered her long, smooth legs, her perky little breasts. Lewis had been a whole man then.

'Another fifty thousand, huh?' repeated Rex Caswell to no one in particular, his brow furrowed again.

'Rex, this is no-limit Texas hold 'em,' Lewis reminded him caustically. 'In this game you can raise any amount you can afford. I'm sure a high roller like you wouldn't have any trouble coming up with that kind of scratch. Hell, fifty grand is walking-around money to you, right?'

Rex glared back at him. 'Okay, asshole. I'll do better than come up with it. I'll see your fucking fifty thousand and raise you a *hundred* thousand. How's that, Lewis? Are we having fun yet?'

'Gentlemen, gentlemen,' said Wisconsin Johnson, rising out of his chair and taking his dark glasses off. 'This has gotten way out of hand. Why don't we . . . ?'

'Shut up, you peanut-eating sack of blubber!' Rex spat.

'This is between Lewis and me. Let's see if he has the stomach to finish what he started. *My* money's green, and if I lose it, I'll fork it over. How about you, Lewis? What color is your money?'

Lewis ground his teeth. He couldn't back down now, not with Millie watching. He could never hope to have her, or any other woman, for that matter, not with his scarred, brutally truncated body. But in this one electric moment he would be a man for her, a man with wits and courage, which was all he needed in this world within a world.

Maybe she would remember him for it. Maybe she would find a place for him in her woman's heart.

'For God's sake, Lewis,' rasped Wisconsin, 'see him and call!'

'Okay,' said Lewis, 'for the sake of everyone's mental health, I'll see your hundred thousand, Rex . . .' There. That much was done. Lewis was on the line for $210,000. '. . . and call.'

Rex blinked sweat off his eyes and reached slowly for his hole cards. Millie didn't bother to follow the movement of his hand, but stared only at Lewis, causing him to wonder for one dazzling moment whether it was admiration, maybe even affection, that he saw in her face. One card came up a ten, and something sucked the air from Lewis's lungs. *No, don't let this be . . . !* And the other came up a king. Rex Caswell had a king-high straight, which beat the shit out of Lewis's three jacks.

An eternity of seconds ground by as Lewis's guts cramped and his throat became hot and tight. The room swam, and the faces of the other players floated and darted in crazy orbits. He felt hands on his shoulder –

Tommy Iadanza's sympathetic hands, he assumed – and heard cryptic declarations of loyalty and good will from the others, their voices echoey as if the walls of the room were made of brass. He saw Rex Caswell's damnably handsome face, craggy and suntanned, sheened with anxious sweat, laughing.

'Hey, all you dweebs, I'm a rich man!' he shouted, and he turned around in his chair to hug Millie. 'This calls for a . . .' Millie was gone, having slipped away like a fading dream. '. . . celebration.' Lewis was glad for it. Defeat was bitter enough fruit without having to eat it in front of her.

'I think the game's over for tonight,' declared Tommy, reaching into his back pocket for the bar tabs. 'I doubt anyone feels like playing anymore.'

'Fuckin' right,' growled Lake Havasu City Sid. 'Lewis, do you have a ride?'

'Let's not get ahead of ourselves,' said Rex, standing and leaning forward on his palms. 'There's the small matter of two hundred and ten thousand dollars.'

Lewis stared up at him, feeling weak and small in his wheelchair. He started to speak, but his throat was full of mucus. He coughed, swallowed, tried again. 'It'll take me a while to raise that much.'

'I don't understand. You're not telling me you played poker with money you don't have, are you? Is that what you're telling me, Lewis?'

'You said my credit was good.'

'Yes, indeed. I *did* say that, didn't I? I said it as a businessman, Lewis, assuming that you, as a decent, honest citizen – a businessman yourself – would know how fucking much you're good for.'

Lewis forced himself to breathe. 'I'm good for the

money, Rex. But I can't give it to you now. Like I said, it'll take a while to raise it.'

'A *while*? How long is a *while*?'

'I don't know. I need to sell my mutual funds and my bonds. I need to borrow some money. Talking to bankers, brokers – three weeks, a month . . .'

'You've got a week. Seven days. Bring the money with you to next week's game.'

'Wait just a damn minute!' raged Tommy Iadanza. 'You're not talking to some deadbeat here, you're talking to Lewis Kindred. He said he's good for the money, and he needs a little time to raise it. The least you can do is—'

'Shut up, Tommy,' warned Rex smoothly. 'This is none of your affair.'

'The hell it isn't! Lewis is a friend of mine, and I'm *making* it my affair.'

'Back off,' said Rex with real menace this time, turning to face the tall, gangly Italian. 'I'm in no mood for this.'

'Maybe you're in the mood to get your ass thrown out the window!' Tommy roared, and he started forward. Wisconsin and Sid just managed to catch him and hold him back, one on each arm.

'Tommy, I can handle this!' shouted Lewis. 'I got myself into it, and I'll get myself out.'

'Hey now, that's the spirit,' Rex replied, sneering. 'The King of the Dweebs is owning up to his responsibilities. I like that.' He came around the table and put his face close to Lewis's, smelling of sweat and expensive cologne. Lewis nearly gagged. 'There's no need to be down on yourself, your majesty. You just got yourself bluffed by a master, that's all. I've been waiting ten years for this night, reading, studying, practicing – ten long years. I plan to enjoy it, to savor the victory. That's why I gave you a whole week to come up with the money. I need a week to let the glory of this night sink in properly.' He rose to his full height and stood like a giant over Lewis, a blond Paul Bunyon in an Armani sport coat. 'Don't forget, Lewis – bring the money to the next game. All of it. In cash. I don't even want to think about what will happen if you don't.'

He turned and gave a mocking salute to the others, who had clustered in a corner around Tommy in order to keep him back. 'Have a nice evening, all you pathetic rat-fucks. See you next time.' He draped his expensive raincoat over one arm and walked out of the room, whistling. A moment later Lewis heard his laughter echoing down the corridor.

CHAPTER ELEVEN
Young Crows

i

Tuesday dawned wet and wild. Thanks to summer road film that became slime with the arrival of rain, the morning rush in the Portland metro area was like a bumper-cars event.

'Be careful driving to school, Josh,' his mother told him as she headed out the door to work. She wore a gray-flannel suit, a pink dress shirt with a button-down collar and a flouncy floral-print scarf – very businesslike, Josh thought, but not particularly alluring. He wished that Kendra would give their mother some fashion tips.

'You be careful, too, Mom,' he said.

He and Kendra left for school at 7:30, which gave them half an hour. In order to avoid freeways, Josh drove to the top of Gander Ridge on Montgomery and turned downhill toward Burnside. Unfortunately, a legion of other westbound commuters had gotten the same idea, and a long line of cars inched toward the intersection with Burnside, bumper to bumper, left turn signals all flashing blearily. Josh fell into line, swearing under his breath.

'Oh, this is really special,' griped Kendra, gnawing a carefully painted fingernail. 'I'm going to be late for my chemistry lab. I *told* you we should've taken the Sunset Highway, you dolt. But noooooooo . . .'

'Blather on, stupid one,' said Josh, grateful for the distraction from the worry that had festered in his brain since Saturday night. 'The freeway's a hair ball in all this rain, which you'd know if you listened to the radio. Leave the driving to someone with a fully developed frontal lobe, okay?'

They arrived at Gavin Dell with minutes to spare, but Josh didn't turn into the student parking lot. He pulled into the front drive and halted to let Kendra out. 'So what's the deal?' his sister wanted to know. 'Are you cutting school today, or what?'

'I've gotten an upset stomach. I think I had too much pizza last night. Don't worry, I'll be okay.' This wasn't a total lie, because he did indeed have an upset stomach, though he'd eaten no pizza last night.

'I'm not worrying, believe me,' replied Kendra. 'I hope you know what you're doing, that's all. Just remember to pick me up at three-forty-five.'

'I, too, hope I know what I'm doing. And yes, I'll pick you up at three-forty-five. Keep a tight butt, okay?'

'Spare me your adolescent crudities.' She slid out the door and slammed it behind her.

ii

He returned home and went immediately to his room, opened his desk drawer and took out the orb. In the gray light of morning it didn't look particularly special, even when he held it up to the window. It was a ball of crystal, he told himself, and that was all – some sort of glass bauble that caught light in strange ways and gave the impression of movement inside it. No way could he make himself believe that the thing was actually alive, even though it was warm to the touch much of the time. Some kind of chemical effect, probably. Anyhow, he'd decided not to concern himself with the nature of the thing, what it was or what it wasn't. He'd decided to concern himself with giving it to Lewis, as he should have done in the first place.

He used the circular staircase that descended to the front foyer. Leaded glass windows above the front door transformed the gloom of the morning into shafts of gold, red and amber, but the artificial cheeriness did nothing for Josh's mood. Turning right on the landing, he entered a short corridor that led to Lewis Kindred's apartment. Two steps away from the door he halted, hearing voices from within. Creeping a step closer, he noticed that the door was ajar. He heard a woman's voice that he recognized instantly as that of Juliet Kindred, Lewis's spinster aunt and the owner of Sloan House.

'. . . and if I were to give you money, I would be interfering with the work of the Holy Spirit – can't you see that, Lewis? I fully believe that the Holy Spirit has decided to bring you down a peg or two, just to show you once and for all how much you need the Lord in your life.'

Josh took a step back from the door, cringing. He knew how Lewis detested his aunt's blind religiosity and her strident right-wing views.

'Juliet, please don't make this any tougher than it already is,' pleaded Lewis, his voice strained. He sounded as if he'd been drinking. 'You know I wouldn't dream of asking you if it wasn't an emergency . . .'

'Oh, I can just imagine what kind of emergency it is. You've gambled away everything you own, haven't you?

Don't lie to me, Lewis. I've always known this would happen. I knew it years ago when your father taught you those horrible, Satanic card games. I begged the Lord to forgive him for polluting an innocent child's mind with the devil's knowledge, and I prayed for you, too, Lewis, that you would turn your back on that filth and give your life to Christ. But you did just the opposite. You immersed yourself in sin, and gave yourself to the secular humanists and philosophers who deny the Lord with every breath. You took to cards and gambling, and when the Holy Spirit intervened, taking your legs from you, even then you hardened your heart . . .'

'Damn it, Juliet – will you *please* stop preaching?'

Josh pressed his back against the wall of the hallway, half expecting Juliet Kindred to storm out of Lewis's apartment. He envisioned her standing before Lewis's wheelchair, ramrod straight with militant conviction, her long face heavily powdered and rouged, her gray hair perfectly coifed, her eyes fiery with zeal. He imagined her wearing lots of expensive jewelry, for she believed that Christ wanted his born-again flock to wear their riches as a testimony to his beneficence.

'I preach to you because I love you, Lewis, just as the Savior loves you. He wants you to come back to him. That's why he let you lose your legs, and that's why he's allowed you to lose your money, to show you how hopeless life is without him . . .'

'Do you have any idea how ridiculous that sounds – that God loves me so much that he took my legs and wiped me out financially? Crimony, Juliet, I need help! If you can't help me, or *won't* help me, just say so, but spare me the bullshit about how God loved me so much that he made a paraplegic out of me.'

'I'll thank you not to use that kind of language in my house, Lewis Kindred. And if you refuse to let your heart be softened, I suggest you pray to the humanistic philosophers whose books line your shelves, and see whether *they* come rushing to your aid.'

Josh sensed that this was the moment to retreat from the door. He darted back into the foyer, where he pretended to be fetching the morning *Oregonian* from the row of tubes next to the tenants' mailboxes. Juliet Kindred did indeed rush out of Lewis's apartment, her sharp chin thrust out and her twiggy limbs pumping, her necklaces swinging and her eyes focused straight ahead. She paid him no attention as she swept into the elevator, which stood open. The doors whooshed shut, and she was gone.

iii

'Lewis, are you alone? It's me.' Josh knocked gently on the door frame for the sake of common courtesy, though he didn't need to. Lewis kept his door unlocked in the event that a neighbor needed to rush in to help with an emergency. He'd often said that he had no secrets to keep from Josh.

'Come on in, mahatma. There's a pot of coffee made, if you're interested.'

The apartment smelled both of brewing coffee and stale beer. Josh fetched himself a cup from the kitchen and went to the living room where Lewis sat in his Action Power 9000, staring through a rain-spattered window at the gray morning.

'Why aren't you in school?'

'I need to talk to you. Missing a day of school won't wreck my life.' Josh saw that the pouches below his friend's weary eyes looked like bruises. The wrinkles in his sweatshirt and corduroy jeans suggested that he hadn't bothered to undress last night. He seemed fragile. 'Lewis, are you okay? You look . . . well, I mean . . .'

'I look like shit, right? Don't worry about insulting me, mahatma – I'm beyond that. Besides, looks aren't everything. In *my* case . . .' He chuckled miserably, and glanced down at his stumps. '. . . looks aren't anything.'

Josh thought, *I've never seen him like this . . .*

'I met Millie last night,' Lewis announced matter-of-factly. 'Her full name is Millie Carter, or maybe you knew that. She sat in as a spectator at the Fanshawe game. You were right – she's world-class gorgeous. She showed up with a guy named Rex Caswell, a real – *winner*, I guess you could say. I don't think I've ever met a woman quite like Millie. I put on quite a show for her. I was in rare form.' He reached into a pouch of his wheelchair and took out a bottle of Beck's beer, which he tipped to his lips.

'Lewis, what's wrong?'

'Nothing's wrong. Everything's hunky-dory. I lost two hundred and ten kilobucks, that's all. Did it all by myself, too, just me and my trusty ego.' He took another long pull from the bottle. 'Want to hear about it? It's not very uplifting.'

Josh nodded. He tried hard to forget about the red orb in his side pocket, which every now and then seemed to throb.

iv

The intercom in Rex Caswell's study bleeped, notifying him that his underlings had reached the security gate in the parking lot of the Sellwood Bay Club. He punched a button that electronically unlocked the gate, then glanced out the wide window of his study toward the misty shore. He watched the two men amble down the inclined ramp to the docks, shoulders hunched against the drizzle, hands pocketed in their breakers – Tweedledum and Tweedledee, though they were nothing alike. Rex never called them this to their faces, of course. Good help was hard to find in this business.

Rex was naked, having just showered after his workout in the weight room upstairs. He often padded around the house with nothing on, liking the unfettered feeling it gave him, liking even more the twitchy glances he drew from Twyla. Her body didn't compare with his, and they both knew it. Though Rex had often urged her to start working out, and had even offered to coach her himself, she'd opted for the life of a couch potato. *One of these days*, he said to himself, *I'm going to bounce her out on her rosy ass and go after someone with style. I'll find someone who knows how to make herself up, how to wear her clothes, how to talk to a man – someone like Millie Carter . . .*

Yeah, right. Millie's interest in him had been remarkably short lived, given that she'd slipped away at the moment of his victory over Lewis Kindred without so much as blowing him a good-bye kiss. More to the point, he knew that he could never trust Twyla to keep her mouth shut about his business, especially if he tossed her into the street. Thus he kept his extracurricular sexing covert in order to avoid making an enemy of her. He'd been reduced to slinking around like an old married guy in the suburbs. He invented business trips in order to free up his nights and evenings, badgered friends into covering for him, constantly maneuvered through a labyrinth of lies. Much as he hated the deception, he had no alternative. He loved beautiful women, and with Twyla around, he needed to slink and badger and maneuver.

The doorbell chimed downstairs, and he pulled on a plush terry-cloth robe that reached to the floor. He went down in his bare feet.

Twyla had opened the door for Mason Benoit and Lester Pittman, two of Rex's employees, and had seated them in the living room. Rex's third employee was a part-time landscaping worker who did nothing but mule drugs for him.

Benoit was an athletic black man of twenty-five who looked as if he could bench-press a Fiat. He dressed conservatively, often in expensive wool slacks and dark cotton shirts like those he wore today. He spoke in low, polite tones, which, together with his choirboy's face, suggested that he couldn't harm a flea. But the fact was, Benoit would pull the fingernails off a nun, if the pay was right. Smart, reliable and discreet in his drug life, he was Rex's most valued employee, and Rex paid him well.

Les Pittman – 'Spit' to those who knew him – was even bigger than Benoit, and approximately the same age. He looked as if he could press a Fiat full of wet cement. Unlike Benoit, he was white, balding, slovenly and stupid. He had tiny colorless eyes that looked like ball-bearings imbedded in an oversized cantaloupe. Spit wouldn't harm someone for money or drugs. He would do it because he *enjoyed* it.

Rex regretted the need to employ people like Benoit and Pittman, but these graceless times required it. The Crips and Bloods had moved into Portland, bringing with them their penchant for setting boundaries and markets, for taking over or 'smokin'' the competition. Fortunately few of his clients would deign to visit a drug house on the mean streets of Inner Northeast or Albina, where the gangs ruled, to score an ounce or two of blow. They much preferred dealing with someone like Rex – white, yuppie-ish and less intimidating than a militant black man armed with a Hechler and Koch submachine pistol. So Rex's action didn't intrude on the Crips' or the Bloods' markets. But Rex still needed 'beef' like Benoit and Spit to guard his stashes from raids by the gangs and to keep his own middlemen from turning on him. Rarely had he needed to commission the breaking of a head or an arm or a leg, but when the need had arisen, Benoit and Spit had proved themselves worth their combined weight in platinum.

'Don't get up, guys,' said Rex, lowering himself into a huge leather recliner. 'I won't keep you long. The reason I have this shit-eating grin on my face is that last night I won two hundred and ten large at the poker table.'

'The rich get richer,' said Mason Benoit, giving a fist salute and beaming.

'That's unreal,' breathed Spit. 'I've never heard of anyone winning that much in a poker game.'

'Oh, it's real, all right,' said Twyla, delivering a tray of screwdrivers in frosted glasses from the kitchen. 'He's been walking on air ever since he came home last night. He's been acting like a little kid on Christmas morning.'

'Thank you, sweetheart,' said Rex, accepting his drink. He always enjoyed a screwdriver after working out. 'She's right, I'm happier than a worm in a cream puff, but there's one small concern. The geek I won it from hasn't raised the money yet. Says he needs time to sell stocks and bonds, get loans, all the usual excuses. I gave him seven days. I feel it would be appropriate to remind him gently of his obligation.'

'You want us to twist his crank a little?' asked Spit, looking eager. 'Maybe put a notch in his ear or some-thin'?'

'Let the man finish, Spit,' said Benoit.

'I said *gently*,' Rex reiterated. 'Don't give him any pain at this early stage. Just scare the living dog-fuck out of him, okay? The pain will come later, if need be.'

'Good,' said Spit, his tiny eyes dancing.

Rex picked up a notepad, jotted Lewis Kindred's name on it and handed it to Benoit. 'He's in the phone book. You may want to scope out his habits for a day or two before making contact in order to decide on the right time and place. When you do it, make it good. Make sure he understands that we take a *very* dim view of people who don't pay poker debts on time – even guys with no legs.'

'The man's got no legs?' asked Benoit.

'Nothing but stumps. Any problem with that?'

'Me? I have no problem with that. You know me, Rex – I do what needs to be done. The same goes for Spit.'

'Good. Now finish your screwdrivers and get out of here.'

v

'. . . So that's what happened, mahatma. I lost control. My concentration went south. I knew better than to try to bluff that fuck-stick, but I did it anyway. He had the right cards, and I didn't.'

'And now you owe him two hundred and ten thousand dollars?' Josh was incredulous. He tried to imagine what a person could buy with that much money. A pair of Ferraris sprang to mind. Or two hundred entry-level

Macintosh computers. Or an education at Northwestern University in Chicago – replete with an advanced degree or two, including books and living expenses. The sum boggled his mind, especially when he considered that Lewis had lost that much in *one* hand of poker.

Lewis nodded as if he himself didn't quite believe it. He drained his Beck's and pulled a fresh one from the pouch on the side of his wheelchair. Using his good hand, he prized the lid off and it clattered onto a nearby coffee table. As he poured beer down his throat, a gust of wind huffed at the window, pressing veined spirea leaves against the pane. He lowered the bottle and belched softly. 'Before you got here I made the mistake of asking my aunt to help me out . . .'

'I know. Your door was open, and I overheard you talking, but I had no idea how much money you were talking about.'

'Funny thing is, Aunt Juliet has a ton of money socked away, probably enough to pay off Rex Caswell and not notice it. But will she lend me any? Not on your life – *unless*, that is, I accept Christ as my personal savior and promise to stop playing poker. Don't you love that? My aunt tried to bribe me into becoming a born-again Christian!' He chuckled bitterly and toyed with the joystick on his wheelchair console.

'What you're saying is, you don't have enough to pay off this Rex guy, is that it?'

Lewis leveled a bloodshot stare at him. 'If I sell everything I own, mahatma, and cash in all my equity stocks and bonds – plunder my retirement fund, in other words – I'll still be about fifty thousand short. With my veteran's pension and my small outside income, I don't have the faintest hope of ever paying him off.'

Josh suddenly hated Rex Caswell, intensely, even though he'd never met the bastard. Based on what Lewis had told him, Caswell wasn't even a very good player, but only lucky. And luck didn't care about justice, who's deserving and who's not, whether you're a saint or a fuck-stick.

Years ago Lewis had taught him how to play poker, and he enjoyed the game, but he wasn't in Lewis's league and never would be. He was good at figuring odds and he could remember the cards as well as anyone, but he lacked the go-for-the-jugular aggressiveness needed to become a first-rate player. He understood this and didn't let it bother him, for poker wasn't the only joy in life, not by a long shot. Lewis himself had taught him to avoid becoming obsessed with only one thing. It seemed unthinkable that Lewis would let himself be ruined by an obsession.

'*Why*, Lewis?' Josh demanded. 'Is it *that* much fun? I mean, it's a *game*, man – a fucking game, that's all.' He was out of the chair now, gesturing. 'You sit around with a bunch of old smart-asses and compare combinations of cards that someone passes out at random. How could you have let it get so out of hand that you lost everything you have? Will you tell me that, Lewis? *Please?* I've got an inquiring mind, man, and I want to know.'

Lewis's shoulders sagged. 'Don't you think I haven't asked myself the same thing a thousand times since last night?' He touched the joystick of the wheelchair, and the contraption hissed to life, moving in the direction of his bedroom. 'You'll have to excuse me, mahatma. I've got an appointment with my broker in an hour. I need to take a shower and put on some clean clothes.' He halted the chair abruptly and executed a smooth one-eighty, his

230

face twisting. 'Okay, damn it, I'll tell you why it happened. When I play poker, I'm as good as anyone at the table. I don't need arms or legs, and I don't need to be pretty. When I play poker, I've got everything I need up here.' He tapped his temple with a fingertip. 'But last night was different, mahatma. Last night I tried to be something more than I needed to be . . .'

'For Millie?'

'How did you know that?' Lewis nosed the chair right up to Josh's knees, and glared up at him. 'How in the hell did you know that?'

'I know what she's like, Lewis.' The wind gusted again, and the patter of rain at the window intensified briefly. 'She's responsible for what happened to you last night. *She* did it to you. Somehow she fixed it so you would lose.'

'Don't try to turn this thing into something it isn't, Josh. What happened to me was my fault, no one else's. I took stupid risks, that's all. Now I've got to pay the price.'

'Man, you don't know what she's capable of . . .' Josh cut himself off in order to let his brain catch up with his mouth. Could he really say what Millie Carter was capable of? He'd seen her in action against a pack of skinheads, and having seen that, he was no longer so sure that she hadn't killed Ron Payne. Whoever had ripped Ron Payne to pieces was physically strong, no doubt about it – and maybe Millie was that strong. And maybe she'd exited Payne's apartment in the same manner she'd exited Josh's bedroom on Sunday night, riding a moonbeam or levitating or whatever. But was he ready to voice these crazy suspicions? *Not now*, he decided.

'Hey, don't worry about me, mahatma,' said Lewis,

reaching up to clamp his hand on the kid's shoulder. 'Things will work out. It's not the end of the world. You'll see.'

Josh blinked away tears, embarrassed by them. He needed to get out of here, and he needed to do it right this minute. 'I've got to go.' He gripped Lewis's hand in both of his, then whirled away toward the door.

vi

He watched from his rain-streaked window as Lewis, aided by Tommy Iadanza, left Sloan House for his appointment with his broker. Tommy held an umbrella overhead and steadied the wheelchair while Lewis skillfully maneuvered himself into the passenger's seat of the Iadanzas' Taurus, no small feat for a man with mere stumps for legs and only one strong arm. Once Lewis was safely ensconced, Tommy quickly dismantled the Action Power 9000 and put the pieces in the trunk of the car. Then they were off, the tires of the Taurus whispering on the wet asphalt of Gander Circle. The mist closed behind them like a stage curtain.

Josh watched them go, feeling useless and left behind. He stayed at the window long after they were out of sight, his gaze wandering over the other houses on Gander Circle, all of them old like Sloan House but of different styles, all appearing to harbor unhappy secrets.

Staring at the houses, reading their faces one by one, Josh came to a fresh conclusion about what he must do. He dug the orb from his pocket and studied it a final time. He saw himself driving down to Front Street, parking under the Hawthorne Bridge and walking to the spot on the bridge where he and Nicole had stood last night. This time he didn't hesitate or waver. He saw himself hurl the damned orb toward the center of the Willamette River, and he didn't stop following it with his eyes until it struck the water and disappeared in a tiny explosion of red.

Yes, that would be the best course of action. He damned himself for not doing it earlier, when both Lewis and Nicole had urged him to. His life had been hell from the moment he'd first laid eyes on the orb, but he now understood that it had touched Lewis, too, and deeply. Josh felt certain that by throwing it into the river, he could rid himself and Lewis of its influence and of Millie, too.

He couldn't explain how he knew these things – he just *knew* them, even though they contradicted all the sane and sensible views he'd derived through his liberal, up-to-the-minute education. Magic. Levitation. Second sight. Lewis himself had warned him away from such blather, but Josh had seen what he'd seen and knew what he knew. Or thought he did.

Having made the decision, he felt better, and the world seemed a little friendlier. Hunger rumbled in his stomach. He went to the kitchen, found a loaf of whole-wheat bread in the freezer and slipped a slice into the toaster. He found margarine and marmalade in the refrigerator, slathered them on the hot toast and poured himself a glass of cold milk. He carried the food into the living room and sat on the sofa, intending to eat his toast, drink his milk and rest a moment before embarking on his mission to the Hawthorne Bridge.

He bolted awake suddenly, blinked, and jerked his wrist up to look at his watch. He'd slept more than two hours. It was almost noon.

A squawking drew his attention to the window. Outside a pair of young crows played in the branches of a

Pacific dogwood, their feathers shining blue-black in the sunlight. *Sunlight?* He rose from the sofa and moved to the living room window, where he saw ragged patches of blue between gray boulders of clouds. The sun peeked from behind one of them and poured its yellow warmth onto his face. The rain had passed, at least temporarily.

He heard something, or *almost* heard it. A shallow breath, drawn and held, perhaps. The faint shush of a shoe over carpet. The shifting of a garment over skin as its wearer moved but held up, not wanting to be heard. He turned and surveyed the living room, which in the space of seconds brightened, darkened, then brightened again as clouds toyed with the sun. His mother's heirloom clock sat in its place on the mantel, faithfully tick-tocking away the seconds, its short pendulum swinging. The rounded Scandinavian furniture squatted in its tasteful groupings, guarded by the expensive lamps and carved teakwood tables that his mother so prized.

All seemed as it should be: quiet, ordered, clean. Except for a drinking glass that was a third-full of milk and a plate with a few bread crumbs on it, nothing appeared out of place in the living room. The young crows chattered boisterously in the dogwood. A car whispered past on the street below, and an airplane droned overhead – sounds barely heard, but *needed*. Josh told himself that he'd heard no threat and almost believed it.

His hand went to the side pocket of his oversized flannel shirt, where hung the orb, heavy and warm. He'd made a decision, and the time had come to carry it out. No more vacillation. He would go to the Hawthorne Bridge right *now*, and do what he needed to do. He started toward the foyer but he saw something out of the corner of his eye, a smear of movement like the tip of someone's elbow disappearing around a door sill, not really seen at all, but inferred, perhaps falsely, because it could have been nothing more than a mote floating across the corner of his cornea.

He froze.

Had it gone into the kitchen? The dining room? Had it entered the hallway that led to the bedrooms? Josh searched the patterns of shifting light and shadows for some new clue, but found nothing. His eyes were playing tricks on him, surely. He inched toward the dining room, drawn by the tingling need to verify that nothing was hiding there.

In the dining room he found only the glossy teakwood table, the china hutch, the clusters of family photos on the wall – all innocent and still. He went to the French doors that gave onto the deck and stepped into the blazing sunshine. He filled himself with the clean smell of rainy trees, then walked to the rail, which overlooked the street and the circular drive that accessed the service entrance to Sloan House. Beneath a spreading elm sat a sinfully black Jaguar convertible.

A thread of terror wrapped itself around Josh's spine. He wanted to believe that the car belonged to anyone but Millie Carter, but he couldn't convince himself.

Was she inside the apartment? If so, how had she gotten into the building without a key? *Stupid questions*, he muttered under his breath. Why in the hell would she need a key, when locked windows and doors apparently meant nothing to her? Of *course* she was in the apartment.

He turned and made for the French doors. Stepping across the threshold, he became conscious of the structure of the apartment and the house itself, the confining walls and channeling hallways, the inhibiting doors. Here she could easily corner him, given her dexterity and speed, but his only other option was to go over the rail of the deck and risk death in a two-story plunge to the cement patio below. He edged around the dining-room table, away from the door into the kitchen, listening. The silence crowded him, felt massive and palpable. The door between the kitchen and dining room stood open, as it normally did, admitting a wedge of yellow sunlight from the kitchen window on to the beige carpet. Then a large section of the wedge went black, as if someone, something, passed in front of the kitchen window – not black, exactly, but deep *blue*. The darkness of the thing was so vivid that the texture of the beige carpet disappeared in its bulk, obliterated by a hissing swarm of living beads that were too small to see. A profile took shape in the mass: a strong cheek and jaw, a slender neck, a mass of dreadlocks tumbling from the crown on to the shoulders.

Josh's breath deserted him as terror clawed at his throat. Somehow he forced his legs into action, and charged through a thickening dream-web into the hallway from the dining room, the web grabbing at his head and limbs, snagging him, trying to hold him back. His footfalls sounded like a cannon on the carpet, and for a hellish moment he heard the rustle of the shadow moving over the carpet behind him and over the walls, chasing him. He found the front door and plunged through it. His feet pounded on to the second-floor landing, then down the curving staircase into the main foyer.

He aimed for the front door of Sloan House, beyond which sunlight ruled, but something steered him to his right, into the gloomy hallway that led to Lewis Kindred's apartment. The door was unlocked, as always, and he dived through it, pulled it closed behind him and threw home the dead bolt. Knowing the apartment like the back of his hand, he went straight to Lewis's bedroom and the bed table where Lewis kept his .45. How many times had Lewis showed him the weapon, warned him about it, demonstrated how to load and unload it? How many times had Lewis said, *Never touch this thing, mahatma, unless you plan to kill someone* . . .

Josh whipped it out of the drawer and switched off the safety. After certifying that it had a full magazine, he cocked it, which put a round in the chamber, then carefully eased the hammer into the half-cocked position. He went into the study and sank into an armchair that squatted in the corner next to Lewis's computer desk. Scarcely breathing, he listened to the sounds of Sloan House – the faraway whisper of air rushing through the ventilation system, the electrical buzz of Lewis's refrigerator, the ticks and snaps of old timbers shifting gradually, settling. Above him he heard a creak of floorboards beneath a thick carpet, which could only mean that someone was moving around in the Nickersons' apartment.

His flesh crawled, but he forced himself to breathe normally, fearing that he might otherwise start to hyperventilate. Josh wasn't certain that he was safe here, but he was certain of this: If Millie Carter came for him, he would put nine .45-caliber slugs into her.

vii

Lewis Kindred's stockbroker had his offices in the PacWest Center, a tall tower with rounded corners, blacked-out windows and a dull metallic finish that fit the cold, calculating image of its tenants – brokerages, law firms and accounting firms, mostly. Tommy Iadanza waited in the reception area and thumbed through a *Forbes* magazine while Lewis met with his broker in an inner office on the twenty-fourth floor.

The session lasted longer than absolutely necessary, since the broker was understandably chagrined upon receiving instructions to sell virtually all the mutual fund shares and bonds owned by one of his favorite clients, investments that represented a lifetime of savings and the hope of a dignified retirement. He asked for an explanation, for some assurance that Lewis knew what the hell he was doing. Lewis candidly laid out his reason for the move, which caused the man merely to shake his salt-and-pepper mane and stare out his window for a long moment. They talked at length about alternatives, but reached the unhappy conclusion that Lewis didn't really have any – not if he wanted to pay the debt in accordance with Rex Caswell's demands. The proceeds from the sale of the shares and bonds wouldn't come close to doing the job, unfortunately. Knowing what he knew about banks and commercial lenders, the broker could offer no encouragement about the prospect of getting a loan to cover the balance of the debt. The session ended with grim smiles and a long handshake.

Afterward, Lewis and Tommy Iadanza went to the Huntsman's Bar and Grill in the Fanshawe, which had already filled to near-capacity. They sat in a booth near the rear, where the wheelchair wouldn't block traffic. The lunch crowd was mostly office workers and young professionals. The women wore summer clothes and tans, despite the damp and nippy weather, and the men wore brightly patterned ties to offset their sober business suits.

Lewis loved this place. He loved the enormous back bar with its glossy wood, its long column of booze bottles and arching mirror. He loved the ceiling fans and the mounted sailfish above the front door, the scruffy animal heads that gazed down from the high walls, the ancient ceramic-tiled floor and the brass foot rail that spanned the length of the bar. In every booth hung photos taken here around the turn of the century, when the Fanshawe was new and its proprietor wore a handlebar mustache.

The Huntsman's was comfortable – worn but not worn out, free of artifice and pretense. Lewis remembered the era before the Iadanzas bought the hotel. In those days there was a public card room in the rear, where a serious poker player could always find a friendly game of dealer's choice. His own father had played cards here countless times, as had Lewis himself as a teenager.

He stared at the menu and wished he was hungry. When Carlotta Iadanza came to take their orders, Lewis asked for a pint of Full Sail Golden.

'That's not much of a lunch,' Carlotta chided, her eyes flashing under her dark eyebrows. 'You really should have something substantial, Lewis.'

'She's right,' said Tommy. 'You can't live on beer. Whatever you want, it's on the house.'

'Thanks, guys – I'm really not very hungry . . .' Lewis happened to glance toward the front of the café, where a trio of video poker machines stood against a plate-glass window. A middle-aged man in an expensive suit sat at one of the machines, a cigar in his mouth and a long-neck Budweiser in his fist, punching quarters into the machine as fast as it would take them. On the other side of the window stood another man, slight of build and short, dark-haired, his face obscured by shadow and fronds of potted palms. He stared into the Huntsman's Bar and Grill as if searching for someone.

Lewis felt his heart quicken as a familiar old fear wrapped its fingers around his throat. Before he could draw his next breath, the man darted away, as though his gaze had found Lewis's face and this was all he'd needed.

Numbah one chop-chop . . .

'Lewis, are you okay?' Tommy asked.

'Me? Yeah, I'm great. Why?'

Tommy and Carlotta traded glances. 'You look anemic,' offered Carlotta. 'Maybe I should bring you the liver and onions, get some iron into your system.'

Numbah one chop-chop, okay . . . ? Lewis struggled to control his rebelling gut. His phantom feet itched furiously, and he longed to pull the cuffs of his pants up and scratch his stumps raw. 'Look, there's nothing wrong with me that two hundred and ten thousand tax-free dollars wouldn't cure. And with all due respect, Carlotta my love, I'd rather have a spinal tap than a plate of liver and onions.'

'Then at least have a cheeseburger. Will you do that much for me?'

With his heart still pounding and his neck cold with sweat, Lewis agreed. But he insisted on a pint of Full Sail to wash it down, hoping the alcohol would douse the fear in his throat. *It wasn't No Bick, you silly son of a bitch. No Bick belongs to another time, another place . . .*

During lunch Tommy talked about last night's football game between the Dolphins and the Browns, which he'd taped on his VCR and watched in the wee hours of the morning. Lewis listened quietly to his chatter, taking an obligatory bite of cheeseburger now and then, knowing that Tommy was trying to distract him from the ugly reality of $210,000 owed to one Rex Caswell. But he couldn't suppress his awareness of the minutes and hours ticking by, of the fact that already he had less than a week before the moment of truth. By tomorrow morning he would have only five days left.

Tommy was mopping up the last of his red sauce when three old friends approached the booth and slid in on either side of Lewis – Wisconsin Johnson, Connie Wierzbinski and Lake Havasu City Sid. They all smiled at him, asked how he was doing and generally tried to act as if this wasn't a prearranged meeting. For expert poker players, they weren't particularly good at keeping the telltale signs of conspiracy off their faces.

'I suppose you're wondering what's going on, Lewis,' said Lake Havasu City Sid finally, his thin face twitching here and there. 'In a nutshell, we think you got shafted last night – we don't know exactly how it happened, but regardless of how it happened we think it stinks. Maybe Rex was just lucky . . .'

'If he wasn't lucky, he was cheating,' Lewis said flatly. 'And to tell you the truth, I don't think he's smart enough to cheat that well.'

'We agree. But regardless of how he did it, we don't think it was your fault, Lewis. You don't deserve this. You're too good a player, and – well – you're too good a person. We've gotten together and decided we want to help you out.'

'Help me out? I don't understand. Help me out *how*?'

Sid took an immaculate white handkerchief from the breast pocket of his navy sport coat and dabbed his oily eyes, then blew his nose and tucked the handkerchief away. He adjusted his yellow tie, needing to get it perfect before going on. 'The four of us – Wisconsin, Connie,

Tommy and I – figure we can help you cover your loss to Caswell,' he said. 'If you can kick in twenty percent, say – that's in the neighborhood of . . .'

'It's exactly forty-two thousand dollars,' Lewis said, his voice betraying his annoyance.

'Well, yes – forty-two thousand. That leaves a balance of something like . . .'

'A hundred sixty-eight thousand.'

'Yes, right around that number.' Sid ran a hand through his thick white hair and glanced around at the others, all of whom kept their stares glued to the vinyl tablecloth, obviously happy to let him handle this. 'Lewis, we've all known you a long time. Each of us considers you a friend. What happened to you last night was an accident, like getting hit by a bus. We all saw it, and we all felt it—'

'It wasn't like that at all,' Lewis interrupted. 'Rex Caswell was lucky last night, and being lucky is no sin in poker. He beat me fair and square.'

'*His* kind of luck isn't right, Lewis,' wheezed Connie Wierzbinski, looking as if she desperately needed a cigarette. 'It isn't – *natural*.'

'Bullshit,' said Lewis, his phantom toes itching. 'A man wins at poker, he's entitled to get paid by the loser.'

'Lewis, if this had happened to any one of us, you'd feel the same as we do,' said Wisconsin Johnson, his triple chin gleaming, his eyes hidden behind dark glasses. 'You'd want to do something to help. None of us is what you'd call rich, but we're all capable of digging up some cash, and we're willing . . .'

'Forget it!' blurted Lewis loudly enough to attract attention from the surrounding tables. 'Poker isn't a team sport, folks. It's every man for himself, in case you've forgotten, and it's plain unethical to gang up against one player, even if he happens to be a reprobate like Rex Caswell.'

'Will you stop with the ethics?' pleaded Sid. 'We're not trying to gang up on anyone. Our purpose is to keep you from being ruined, Lewis. We care about you, that's all.'

'No, that isn't *all*. You also feel sorry for me, right? Poor old Lewis Kindred, trapped for life in a fucking wheelchair – pretty pathetic, isn't it? Save the women and children and cripples – isn't that what you mean? Well, here's a flash for you: I lost to Rex Caswell because I played stupid cards, and I deserved to lose. I plan to face the consequences like a man, to stand up on my own two feet, if you'll pardon the expression. I don't need your pity, and I don't need your money.' He pulled the joystick and backed his wheelchair away from the table, then made for the front door as fast as his electric motor would take him.

viii

Tommy Iadanza parked his Taurus in the front drive of Sloan House, and hurriedly assembled the Action Power 9000. Watching through the passenger's window, Lewis felt burdensome and worthless and regretted his explosion of rage in the Huntsman's. Tommy had caught him outside on the sidewalk, and had insisted on driving him home, which was fortunate, because minutes later the sun had disappeared and the rain had begun anew.

'I'm sorry I was such a prick,' Lewis said as Tommy helped him into the chair.

'Don't sweat it. Anyone who loses two hundred thousand bucks is entitled to be a little owly.' Tommy walked alongside the chair, his long arms swinging awkwardly, as

Lewis motored to the entryway of Sloan House. The rain was falling hard now, and both of them were getting soaked.

'I appreciate what you and the others wanted to do,' said Lewis, pushing his key into the lock, 'but I hope you can understand why I can't let you do it. My old man taught me that a poker player doesn't do certain things, one of which is pool money against another player. I don't think I could live with myself if I . . .'

'Lewis, don't kid yourself, and don't kid me, okay? This isn't about your old man's ethics – you know that and so do I.' The rain had matted Tommy's dark, thinning hair, and a single droplet dangled from the tip of his aquiline nose. 'It's about your pride,' he went on. 'You don't want to feel dependent, which is understandable. You don't want to be a taker. I can relate to that, and so can the others. Just don't hold it against us for trying to be here for you.' He held out his hand, and Lewis gripped it eagerly.

'I don't hold it against you, Tommy.' He wanted to say more, but he didn't trust his vocal cords right now. 'We'll talk about this later.'

'Right. Better go in before we both drown. Do you plan to put in a shift at the Center tomorrow?' He referred to the VIP Center, which stood for Veterans In Progress, a private relief organization that provided counseling and direct aid to homeless veterans. For the past decade both Lewis and Tommy had worked as volunteers one morning a week.

'Sure, why not? I'm not the only guy in the world with problems, right?'

'Now *that's* the Lewis Kindred we all know and love. Pick you up at nine.'

Tommy loped back to his car, and Lewis let himself into the welcome dryness and warmth of Sloan House. He paused to gaze through the glass pane as the Taurus swung out of the drive.

Tommy Iadanza was as good a friend as anyone could hope to find. It was Tommy, no doubt, who'd come up with the idea of the Fanshawe crowd pooling its resources to cover the loss to Rex Caswell. The other members of the Fanshawe crowd – Wisconsin and Sid and Connie – were also good friends, but none was as close to him as Tommy, a fellow Vietnam vet.

Lewis worried that he didn't deserve friends of this magnitude. He'd been a burden to them, he supposed, especially to Tommy, who had countless times chauffeured him to wherever he'd needed to go, taken apart his wheelchair and put it back together again, carried him up and down flights of stairs, and done all the other small chores that aren't small to someone with no legs.

As he often did when he was depressed, he wondered how his life would have turned out if he hadn't lost his legs. A two-legged Lewis Kindred would not have retreated to the shadows, but would probably have gone on to graduate school and a career in academe. Or he might have shifted gears completely and gone into business or law. He might have become a writer of philosophy or even novels. Hell, he might have become rich. It was likely that a two-legged Lewis Kindred would have considered himself superior to someone like Tommy Iadanza, who lacked a college education and wore his coarseness like a favorite Hawaiian shirt. A two-legged Lewis would have acquired sophisticated friends who never talked with their mouths full, who attended charity events and gave receptions for visiting lecturers. And, legs or no legs, Lewis would have been the poorer man without Tommy Iadanza's friendship.

He aimed his chair toward the dusky passage that led to his apartment. He found the door to his apartment locked, which was strange, because he never locked it. A man with no legs, he believed, was likely to need a neighbor's help one day.

He was totally unprepared to find Josh Nickerson in his studio, sprawled in an armchair with the stereo headphones on his head, a can of Diet Rite in one hand and Lewis's old .45 in the other.

The kid's eyes were closed, but he wasn't asleep, for his head was nodding to the rhythm of the Eagles' 'Hotel California.' Lewis motored to the armchair and tapped Josh's knee, and Josh jolted upright as if he'd suffered an electrical shock. For a harrowing fraction of a second Lewis feared that he would shoot him, so wide and round and full of fright were his eyes.

'Wow, I didn't hear you come in, man,' breathed Josh, pulling off the headphones and setting aside the pistol. 'This looks pretty weird, I'll bet.'

'You've got that right. What's with the bullet-launcher?'

'This . . . uh . . . is a little hard to explain, Lewis . . .' He stared guiltily at the weapon on the table next to him, then studied his own hands as he cracked his knuckles. 'I was upstairs in our place, and I fell asleep on the sofa in the living room. When I woke up, someone was in our apartment. I got scared and ran downstairs, and when I saw your door was open, I came here, thinking it was probably the safest place I could be. I locked myself in and got the gun out, in case she . . .'

'*She?*'

'It was Millie Carter. I don't know how she got in – the place was locked. But this babe doesn't need keys, I guess.'

'Did she say what she wanted?'

'I only saw her shadow, and I got out of the apartment before she could get me. I've never been that scared in all my life, Lewis. I figured I would have a better chance against her down here, using your gun. I swear to God I would've shot her if she came after me.'

If he only saw a shadow, Lewis wanted to know, how did Josh know whose it was? Shadows didn't wear name tags, last time he looked. The boy's answer dredged up old memories and old fears, like drawing water from an abandoned well and finding something dead floating in the bucket. The shadow that Josh had seen was of a kind that Lewis himself had described when telling the story of Gamaliel, a shadow that rustled and swarmed with bits of living matter. And its color wasn't black but a deep blue.

Lewis felt no onslaught of paralyzing fear, which surprised him. The rational compartment of his mind was in high gear. Josh had fixated on the beautiful Millie Carter and had subconsciously attached to her certain traits that fit Lewis's own description of another racially mixed person who had one blue eye and one brown. One of these traits was a deep blue shadow. There were no doubt others.

'She's been in the apartment before, Lewis,' said the boy, running a finger around the circle edge of his soda can. 'She was there Sunday night, in my bedroom, actually.' He described what had happened that night, even the part about the handjob, while Lewis sat mesmerized. Lewis's face whitened when he heard how urgently Millie had charged Josh to give the red orb to him. 'I wasn't going to tell you about this, especially after you lost all that money. I figured you had enough to deal with right now. I was going to do what you said I should do in the first place, and that's throw the fucking thing in the river, but I fell asleep in the living room, and – well, you know the rest.'

Lewis dug his fingers into his still-damp hair, feeling eerily connected to another place and another time, a realm where roamed a mysterious black-white man who carried an orb of red crystal and sported an affinity for poker. That creature, too, had tried hard to give the orb to Lewis for some unknown reason, and had eventually succeeded – in a way. 'Did you do it?' he asked Josh, struggling not to betray the fear rising inside him. 'Did you throw it in the river?'

'Not yet. I've stayed right here, hiding. I heard Millie's car leave a while ago, but I stayed anyway, because I wanted to talk to you. I hope it was okay if I listened to some of your CDs.' He noticed Lewis's damp clothes and the droplets clinging to the chrome surfaces of the wheelchair. 'So, why are you all wet? Did you drive that thing through a car wash?'

'I think you should do what you planned to do, mahatma. Take it to the river. Throw it away and forget you ever heard of Millie Carter.'

'Lewis, I've been doing some thinking.' He reached into the pocket of his bulky flannel shirt and took out the orb, which caused Lewis to squirm. 'In Vietnam you and Gamaliel did an experiment with the orb. He put it on your side of the table while you were playing cards and it made you win, right?'

'He didn't give it to me – not then. I wouldn't let him.'

'But it was *with* you when you did the experiment. It

was near enough to you that it gave you the power to win.'

'That's what he wanted me to believe. What really happened is that he played some kind of trick on me.'

'Get real, Lewis – he didn't play any kind of trick on you. The orb has power – you can see that just by looking at it. You yourself used it at the vets' hospital here in Portland, when you beat the guy from New York at cards. You couldn't lose unless you consciously tried to.'

'I don't know if that's the way it really was. Just because I remember it that way doesn't mean it actually happened that way.'

'Then what about Gamaliel's shadow, and Millie's shadow? And what about the monster he became when he killed the girl in the whorehouse back in Vietnam? You've seen all these things with your own two eyes . . .'

'It's only what my mind *tells* me I saw. There's a part of my mind that's sick. It's what Vietnam did to some people . . .'

'Bullshit! You're not sick, and neither am I! We've both seen what we've seen! You've told me dozens of times not to believe in anything I can't see and touch, Lewis. Well, I've *seen* Millie's shadow, and I've *seen* what she's capable of. And I can *touch* this orb and hold it in my hand. I can *feel* how warm it is, and so can you.' He pushed it toward Lewis, causing him to shrink back in his chair.

'Keep that fucking thing away from me!'

'Lewis, listen. You can use it to win your money back from Rex Caswell, to get your life back on track.'

'Jesus Christ, are you out of your . . . ?' Lewis grimaced as a wave of nausea flowed through him, as if someone had suggested that he cuddle up in bed with a dead cat. 'No way in hell I'll ever touch that thing again! I told you to get it out of here.'

'And what happens if I do that? What happens when Rex Caswell comes knocking at your door, wanting his two hundred and ten thousand bucks? How are you going to pay him, Lewis – with a smile? Or are you going to sit still and let him take everything you have?' Josh suddenly seemed much older than his seventeen years, harder and more callused. 'You don't deserve to spend the rest of your life scraping along with nothing. You've worked too hard to let him turn your whole life to shit. All you need to do is challenge him to another game, a rematch. Tell him you've got the money you owe him, and that you want to go double or nothing. Then you can . . .'

'Shut up! I've told you I can't touch that thing!'

'Not even to save your own future?'

Lewis struggled to keep his voice from quivering. 'I may not be much, mahatma, but I'm not a liar or a cheat. It's true, I used the orb once to win at cards, and it made me feel dirty inside. I won't do it again. My old man taught me that your life isn't worth a gob of spit if you're not honest, and I've tried to teach that to you, too . . .'

'You *have* taught me, Lewis.'

'So, what kind of an example would I be to you if I used that – *thing* to beat Rex Caswell out of his money? Do I need to spell it out for you? My old man would roll over in his grave.'

'But these are special circumstances, Lewis. You lost to Caswell because of Millie Carter. You were a *victim*, and you're entitled to even things up.'

'I wasn't a victim, mahatma – I was stupid. I lost at cards because I lost control of myself. There's a price to pay when you let yourself get out of hand like that, and I intend to pay it.' He leaned forward in his wheelchair and took hold of Josh's arm. 'I want you to learn from this,' he said. 'Watch what happens to me, and make sure it never happens to you. Keep control of yourself, and don't get carried away trying to teach someone a lesson, not even if he's a human slug like Rex Caswell.' Lewis let go of Josh's arm, then wheeled around and headed for his bedroom. Before closing the door behind him, he turned the chair to face the boy a final time, his eyes brimming. 'Take the orb to the river, Josh. Go *now* while the sun's still shining and there're lots of people around. Go to the river and throw it in, for Christ's sake.'

CHAPTER TWELVE
A Small Reality

i

The next morning Lewis rose well before dawn, unable to sleep. Through his window he could see tongues of mist swirling in the purplish aura of the streetlights on Gander Circle, portending a gray and drizzly dawn. He took a shower, using a specially designed sling that allowed him to hoist himself out of his chair and suspend himself in the shower stall. Later he toasted an English muffin and switched on his computer, needing to catch up on work that he'd neglected yesterday.

He was tired, for he'd tossed and turned throughout the night. Shortly after midnight he'd imagined that he heard No Bick rattling a window to test whether it was locked, and he'd flicked off the safety of his service .45 only to spend an hour listening to his own heartbeat. Time and again he'd forced his eyes shut in a determined attempt to sleep, only to see the grinning face of Gamaliel Cartee with its mismatched eyes staring hungrily at him across an expanse of green baize. As a grand finale he'd dreamed that the crystalline orb had somehow gotten into his mouth and he couldn't open his jaws wide enough to expel it. He'd bolted upright in bed, gagging and heaving, feeling as if he was choking to death even after he was fully awake.

Now he stared at his computer for long moments, seeing nothing of the sales brochure displayed by the page-layout program on the screen. Rather, he saw Josh Nickerson's earnest face and heard his pleading voice: *You were a victim, and you're entitled to even things up . . .*

What must the kid think of him, Lewis agonized, having seen him at his absolute worst – beaten, humiliated and scraping for money? He hoped desperately that Josh hadn't come to pity him, for Lewis doubted he could endure that.

He clenched his good hand into a fist and pounded it hard on the desk. Starting this moment, he resolved, he would behave in a way that would make Josh proud of him. No more cowering from old memories and harmless baubles of red crystal. Somehow he would dispose of the crisis with Rex Caswell, and he would do it like a man. If lean times lay ahead, so be it – he would survive. And thrive again, damn it.

Turning away from his computer, he scanned the ranks of books that lined his walls, the philosophers' treatises on creation and each man's place in it. He smiled to himself. For all he'd read about the nature of the universe during the course of his adult life, he'd learned something new just within the past few days. He'd learned that each man generates his own small reality independent of the grand workings of the cosmos, and that what matters is the role he defines for himself within the confines of that small reality.

The time had come for Lewis Kindred to play a new role. From this moment on, he vowed, he would conduct himself as if he were a whole man.

ii

Tommy Iadanza arrived on the stroke of nine to drive Lewis to the VIP Center. After installing him in the passenger seat of his car, he slid in behind the wheel and said, 'I hate to say this, bud, but you look like shit. Your eyes look like a couple of assholes, and I mean that in the most positive sense, of course.'

Lewis chuckled. 'I didn't sleep much last night. What's your excuse?'

'Well, now that you asked, I stayed up till two-fifteen watching videos, so naturally I was tired as hell by the time my head finally hit the pillow. Then – wouldn't you know it? – Carlotta wakes up, and she's hungry for my alabaster body. It's like she's been eating ginseng by the loaf – she wants it twice, three times, four times. When I rolled out of the sack this morning I felt like I'd been hooked up to a damn milking machine.'

'Poor baby. We should all suffer such plagues.'

The VIP Center on SW Second Avenue was sandwiched between a Greek restaurant called Berbati and a Persian one called the Green Onion. Its shabby exterior belied an immaculate reception area, where waited a dozen or so men who ranged in age from twenty to seventy. They sat in brightly colored resin chairs, drinking the coffee and eating the doughnuts that the Center provided free of charge, leafing through magazines and staring at an old black-and-white television set bolted to the ceiling. Most wore drab, dingy clothes, though several were neatly groomed and dressed, having spruced themselves up for their appointments with the VIP counselors. One man, a World War II-era vet, from the look of him, sat in an old wheelchair with a bent frame, while a younger man with one leg dozed in a corner, leaning precariously on his crutches.

Lewis felt an aching compassion toward all these down-and-out veterans, but his heart went out in a special way to the disabled ones, for he understood firsthand the torments they suffered. He had walked in their shoes, so to speak, and he couldn't look at one of them without thinking, *There but for the grace of God . . .*

He and Tommy threaded their way through the waiting room. At the rear was a closed office with a door plaque that said EXECUTIVE OFFICES. Suddenly the door burst open, and out dashed a fast-talking, fast-walking woman who weighed probably three hundred pounds, wearing a huge designer sweatshirt embroidered with a red rose and the phrase, 'Rose City Mama.' She had short gray hair cut like a Benedictine monk's but lacking the tonsure. She was Audra Fallon, the assistant director of VIP, and the owner of one of the sweetest smiles Lewis had ever known.

This morning she was not smiling, however. Behind her trooped a pair of middle-aged men in crisply laundered army field jackets and expensive haircuts. Neither of them was smiling, either. Lewis noticed that each man wore a pin that said, 'Veterans for Bush/Quayle '92.'

'One thing we don't need around here is politics,' said Audra as she moved past Lewis. 'We're here to help veterans, not to campaign for George Bush or anyone else.' She halted, pulled open the door to the reception area and held it wide. 'At the risk of being rude, I'm afraid I'll ask you gentlemen to leave.'

The taller of the two men held up suddenly. Smiling like an insurance salesman, he said, 'Miss Fallon, I'm afraid I haven't done a very good job of communicating with you.' He sported a tanning-booth complexion and a build that implied regular workouts in a weight room. 'We're not trying to politicize your organization – far from it. All we want to do is talk with some of your clients and enlist three or four of them to participate in a public-relations project on behalf of the president.'

'It'd really help us out, Miss Fallon,' added the shorter one. 'The president can use all the support he can get. We're putting together some brochures and newspaper ads targeted at veterans, Vietnam veterans in particular, stressing the president's war record and the fact that his opponent doesn't even have one. We need some bona fide vets in the photos – guys who're clearly disabled . . .'

'Guys in wheelchairs, on crutches, that sort of thing.'

'Right. They'd lend authenticity and generate sympathy among other vets.'

'This isn't an advertising agency,' Audra declared with a scowl so ferocious that it made Lewis cringe. 'This is a charitable institution. Most of our clients are desperate by the time they get here. Many are homeless, jobless and addicted. They need help, not—'

'*Not* Bill Clinton,' interrupted the taller of the Bush men, still smiling. *An alligator's smile*, thought Lewis. 'They don't need a lying, womanizing draft-dodger as their president, Miss Fallon . . .'

'It's *Missus* Fallon,' Audra corrected him. 'I'd appreciate it if you'd get it right.'

'I'm sorry – *Missus* Fallon. I'm just trying to make the point that it would be an affront to the men you serve if Bill Clinton got elected president. Here's a guy who maneuvered, schemed and lied to get out of serving his country in the military, while men like your clients put their lives and limbs on the line. While we were over in Vietnam getting shot at, pukes like Clinton were organizing protests against the war, calling us baby-killers and . . .'

A man's voice rolled forth like thunder from behind them, a dark voice that commanded undivided attention. 'The lady asked you gentlemen to leave, and I think it would be wise of you to do just that.'

He was a burly man with silvering eyebrows that stood out vividly from his forehead and a round face that was as black as dreamless sleep. His huge hands looked well accustomed to gripping the wheels of the unmotorized wheelchair in which he sat, and his legs dangled at troubling angles. A monstrous yellow cat curled in his lap, its eyes slitted. 'I'm sure you gentlemen have the decency not to stay where you're not wanted.'

The taller of the Bush men took a step toward the man in the wheelchair. 'Excuse me? Are you talking to us?'

The eyes beneath the silver eyebrows became hard as black diamonds, and the leathered hands coiled into fists. 'You *know* who I'm talking to. Do yourself a favor and get your sorry asses out of here while you still can.'

The tall man blanched through his store-bought tan and gazed for a few seconds at the ceiling. He turned back to Audra. 'Is this guy supposed to be your bouncer, or what?'

'He's a man who served his country,' Audra replied, framing each syllable with great precision. 'He suffered a bullet in the spine and total paralysis of his legs. He has no job, no home and no health insurance . . .'

'And I drink a fifth of bourbon every day, mixed with milk to keep my stomach from being eaten away,' added the man in the wheelchair. 'It helps the pain.'

By now everyone in the room had paused to listen, perhaps two dozen people, including counselors, clients and clericals. Lewis could plainly hear the purring of the giant yellow cat in the black man's lap.

'If he's a veteran, he's entitled to help from the government,' said the smaller Bush man, his voice quivering. 'He should be in a veterans' hospital somewhere . . .'

'I've been in most of the veterans' hospitals on the West Coast, and I can tell you, mister, that I won't go back to any of them,' said the black man, 'not that it's any of your business. If the current president cared about me, I wouldn't be here. Now, I'm only going to say this one more time: Get out of here, and get out of here *now*.'

The shorter of the Bush men sidled past his partner and made for the front door, muttering something under his breath about wanting no trouble. The taller one stuck his nose into Audra's face and glared at her. 'If I were you, *Missus* Fallon, I'd hit the fund-raising circuit, and I'd hit it hard. Federal help might be hard for you to come by, from now on . . .'

'We're a private, nonprofit relief organization, Mr Frobisher. Our federal money dried up during the Reagan administration, so it won't do you any good to threaten us.'

The man trembled, he was so angry. Lewis thought for a moment that he might actually stamp his feet. 'I assure you, Mrs Fallon, that the president's people in Washington will hear about this. You're not dealing with a nobody here . . .' Tommy Iadanza sniggered aloud, and a sprinkle of laughter went through the room. The Bush man cast poisonous glances all around, then fled through the door.

Suddenly the black man in the wheelchair started to laugh uproariously, and everyone in the room laughed along with him, including Audra Fallon. She planted a kiss on his forehead, which only made him laugh all the harder. 'Dewey, you're a treasure!' she exclaimed. 'I thought I was going to have to wrestle that guy to get rid of him.'

'Hey, woman, have I still got what it takes, or what?' shouted Dewey, starting to wheeze. 'Once a drill sergeant, always a drill sergeant, I guess. It's all in the voice, hear what I'm sayin'?'

Lewis maneuvered his wheelchair next to Dewey's in order to catch his hand and shake it. 'What you did warmed my heart, brother. You made us proud!'

'Want to know somethin'?' asked Dewey. 'I was actually hopin' he would try to muscle me, 'cause if he did, I was planning to let him have some of this.' He pulled an eighteen-inch-long length of pipe from inside his verminous army-surplus trench coat. 'And if that didn't work, I was planning to feed him to Big Sister here.' At the mention of her name, the huge yellow cat opened her eyes ever so slightly, but quickly closed them again.

'What you've just seen, ladies and gentlemen,' said Tommy Iadanza, drawing a cup of coffee from the urn near the door, 'was a couple of *professional* vets, the kind who join organizations and march in parades, carrying banners that say things like, "Don't forget us." They're always trying to get on the nightly news and in the newspapers. They tell a lot of war stories and generally act superior to anyone who had the good sense to avoid going to Vietnam.'

'And most of their war stories are bullshit,' said

Dewey. 'I'll bet that those two Bush assholes were REMFs, if they were even in Vietnam at all.'

'The odds are good that they didn't see any action,' Lewis agreed. 'Only fifteen percent of all the guys in 'Nam actually got out in the field and mixed it up with the VC and the NVA.'

'And it was the other eighty-five percent in the rear who bitched the loudest about being in the army, not to mention being in the 'Nam,' added Tommy, smirking. 'Those were the guys who got into trouble with MPs, or became alcoholics, or got hooked on drugs. I should know – I was a REMF myself, and I was one of the worst.'

This brought a guffaw from Dewey. 'Hell, that's nothing to be ashamed of, soldier. In my unit we considered the REMFs the smart ones. We were *all* tryin' to figure out how to become REMFs!'

Audra clapped her hands together to still the laughter. 'Folks, I hate to put an end to this unbridled hilarity, but we all have jobs to do. Let's get this train back on the tracks, okay?' She lowered her voice. 'Lewis and Tommy, thanks for showing up. I've got three guys for each of you to talk to, all homeless, all detoxed. One of your guys, Lewis, is missing a leg, so I thought it would be best to steer him your way.' She led them back to her office, where she presented them with folders on each of the men to be counseled. 'Do what you can to motivate these guys, okay? I think they're all good prospects . . .' Which meant that Audra hoped desperately that with a little help and compassion these men could kick their habits, find jobs, and slay the demons that had driven them to the oblivion of the streets.

iii

No one at the VIP Center knew Dewey's full name, his real name, or even whether Dewey was his first, middle or last name. No one knew where he came from, whether he had living relatives, or even whether he was really a veteran. He was 'undocumented,' in the parlance of the relief and welfare community, meaning that he could produce no military discharge papers, birth certificate, passport, social security number or any other document to prove who or what he was. Consequently, nobody could establish whether he was eligible for any public or private assistance programs.

He slept in alleys and doorways, or wherever his wheelchair would fit, meaning that he sometimes slept in the open. On winter nights he slipped Big Sister into his shirt where she slept next to his skin, no matter that she was infested with fleas, because both of them needed the warmth. More than once Big Sister had kept him from freezing to death, he'd boasted.

On every Wednesday for the past decade, Lewis had taken Dewey to lunch, usually to one of the take-out places in the outdoor arcade of the New Market Theater, since indoor restaurants had rules about cats and Dewey wouldn't go anywhere without Big Sister. The arcade was partially enclosed in glass like a greenhouse, so they could eat without getting wet even on rainy days. Over lunch they talked politics, religion, philosophy and even poker. Sometimes they talked of the army and Vietnam, but not often.

Lewis had learned little about why Dewey had ended up on the street, homeless and alcoholic, undocumented and adamantly opposed to entering the system. He could only guess that Dewey had suffered some deep, unquenchable pain that had become so much a part of him that he could not give it up for fear of forfeiting a piece of himself. Lewis had seen it happen before: the pain of a wound becomes the anchor-point of a man's life. Take it away and you set him emotionally adrift. To cope with the pain, Dewey drank enough to kill a lesser man at least three times over. Within the past several years, the effects of the booze had deepened the lines of his face. He'd developed a yellowish cast in the whites of his eyes and a slight trembling of his hands.

Despite his alcoholism, Lewis had found Dewey to be a decent and interesting man who cared about the world around him and had worthwhile things to say. Lewis enjoyed spending time with him and had often invited him into his home. But Dewey had never accepted the invitation, not even on Christmas when Lewis customarily served dinner to three or four homeless vets. Seemingly, Dewey felt as though he'd made his choices about how to live, and having chosen an unwashed life in the streets, was loathe to intrude into the clean and warm confines of another man's home. Maybe he feared that he might come to crave cleanliness and warmth once again.

iv

Lewis and Dewey had lunch at Mai Ly's Oriental Kitchen in the outdoor arcade of the New Market Theater, their wheelchairs parked next to an ancient bench made of wrought iron. A mounted cop waved casually to Dewey, for Dewey was a fixture in Old Town. Most of the pedestrians who passed the bench, however, lowered their eyes and pretended not to notice the pair of men in wheelchairs. Lewis and Dewey were well accustomed to this practice among the able-bodied.

Dewey shared his chicken and pea pods with Big Sister, who ate greedily, while Lewis picked at an order of Szechwan shrimp. The morning's activity had distracted Lewis from his own personal woes, but now, with an hour of free time on his hands, he couldn't help grappling with the ugly reality of his debt to Rex Caswell. Dewey asked what was wrong, but Lewis shook off the question and talked instead of a man he'd counseled this morning who had lost a leg to a booby trap in the Mekong Delta.

'Doug would have a lot going for him if he could only get his head on straight,' said Lewis, glad for the diversion. 'He's smart. He's got a couple years of college under his belt. There's no reason he can't make a good living for himself if he stays clean and sober.'

'So, what's his problem?'

'Self-image, I think, like most of the others. The fact that he's minus a leg is only a part of it. Being a Vietnam vet is the real problem, because he sees vets as a pack of losers. If you're a vet, you've got two strikes against you.'

'Almost like being black, uh?' Dewey chuckled deeply. 'I hope you told him that's a load of bullshit.'

'Oh, I told him. And I told him about my old bud, Jesse Burton, who went home from the 'Nam and wrestled with drugs and booze and won. Then he went on to school and got himself a doctorate in education. Now he's holding down a big important job with the National Education Association.'

'I remember you talking about him before. Black man, right?'

'Right. I tried to make Doug understand that being a Vietnam vet isn't a blot on your life. Very few of us got hooked on booze or drugs. The overwhelming majority of vets haven't let the war keep them from living good lives. The guys who've ended up on the street, carrying around habits, have more than Vietnam to blame.'

'Don't I know it? Hell, I could've gotten these dead legs by crackin' up a car or getting hit by a bus. It could've happened even if I hadn't gone to Vietnam, and I would've *still* been drinkin' a fifth of bourbon every day.' For some reason Dewey found this funny, and he laughed in his infectious way.

'What time is it?' he asked suddenly.

'Quarter to one.'

'Time for confession. Want to come along?'

Lewis nodded, and they set out west across the square, their wheelchairs jouncing slowly over the paving stones. They went half a block up Ankeny Avenue until coming to the '24-Hour Church of Elvis,' a narrow storefront with a musty display window. The 'church' was actually a sidewalk console with a coin slot and push-buttons. It dispensed an off-brand religion that glorified shabby plastic images – not so different, really, than most other religions, in Lewis's view. Behind the glass lay the 'altar,' a dizzying array of photos, figurines, souvenirs and doodads, most of which concerned Elvis Presley. A video screen mounted inside the window urged the visitor to deposit twenty-five cents into the coin slot, and then to press the appropriate button to specify a wedding, a confession or a sermon.

Yes, people could actually have a 'church wedding' right here on the sidewalk, providing someone in the wedding party could come up with a quarter. It had happened more than once.

'Hit me with a quarter, Lewis,' said Dewey, holding out his palm. Lewis did so, and Dewey pushed the coin into the slot. He selected CONFESSION, then leaned close to the microphone and muttered something that Lewis couldn't hear. A few moments later the computer screen flashed a message of absolution, and Dewey backed away from the window, looking cleansed of his sins.

'I feel like a new man,' he said, beaming. 'Nothin' like a little forgiveness to brighten up your day. Now if I could just talk this thing into giving me a new pair of legs . . . !'

Lewis laughed. 'Get a pair for me, while you're at it!'

'I guess it's time to go our separate ways, brother,' said Dewey, pain glittering in his eyes. 'I need to buy a quart of milk.'

Lewis winced. This was Dewey's way of saying that it was time to hit the bottle in earnest, for the pain had flared, and it would continue to flare until he doused it with bourbon.

'I'll walk you to the store,' Lewis said, reluctant to leave him alone.

'That's not necessary. You've got troubles of your own – anybody can see that. Go back to the Center, Lewis. Tommy will be waiting to take you home.'

'I don't want to go home just yet. I need some company, and . . .' Before he could finish the thought, a shadow fell across his face, and he turned to see who or what had eclipsed the sun. Standing over him was a very large man in his mid-twenties, with massive shoulders and a surprisingly small head. He had tiny, washed-out eyes that looked devoid of humanity. Lewis felt a jolt of fear.

Suddenly the world went topsy-turvy as someone tilted Lewis's wheelchair backward, and he was looking straight into the blinding sun. He heard Dewey scream his name. Someone caught a fistful of his hair, igniting a rash of pain across his scalp. The balding man pushed his face close to Lewis's and grinned wildly. 'How's it goin', stumpy?' His gamey breath flooded Lewis's nostrils.

Lewis caught sight of another man off to his left, slick-looking, dressed in an expensive anorak and tailored slacks. He was as black and clean as the bald one was white and slovenly, but not as massive. His smooth face could have belonged to a choirboy.

'Let's not be disrespectful, Spit,' said Mason Benoit, moving toward Lewis with something in his hand. 'This gentleman is a Vietnam veteran, after all, and the second-best poker player in Portland.' He flicked a switch on the thing in his hand, and it issued an electrical buzz. It was a battery-powered hair clipper. 'He's a man of great dignity, can't you see that?'

'How come he's got so fuckin' much hair, and I don't?' asked the balding man and Lewis knew immediately who had sent them and what they meant to do.

'Luck of the draw,' answered Benoit, grinning malevolently. 'How about we take some of his and give it to you? Would that make you happy, Spit? Would that satisfy your highly developed sense of justice?'

Spit grinned stupidly. 'It sure would.'

Lewis's mind raced. The thought of getting his head shaved didn't gall him as much as the prospect of playing the victim to these maniacs. He didn't doubt for a minute that Caswell had sent these pillars of the community to deliver a 'reminder' about the poker debt he owed, as if he needed one. Acting on impulse, he jerked back the joystick of his wheelchair, throwing it into reverse and catching Spit by surprise. The chair slipped from Spit's grip and abruptly righted itself, causing Lewis to bite his tongue as the front wheels slapped down onto the sidewalk. Then he shoved the joystick forward and plowed hard into the black man, the motor whining. Benoit careened against the glass of the 24-Hour Church of Elvis and landed on his ass, dropping the battery-powered clipper.

Suddenly Dewey joined the fray, wheeling into the path of Spit, who'd lunged forward to make a grab at Lewis. Spit tumbled over Dewey and sprawled onto the sidewalk, painfully bruising his elbows. Big Sister squealed and leapt out of Dewey's lap, but Spit caught her by the scruff of her neck as he scrambled to his feet. The cat bit and scratched, leaving a bleeding wound on his hand and angry tracks of red across his cheek.

'Son of a bitch!' Spit screamed, and Lewis whirled his chair around, looking for help from passersby. A knot of yuppie-types strolled down the opposite side of the street. They'd heard the commotion, but they just stood and watched.

'Forget the fuckin' cat!' shouted Benoit, having righted himself. He moved toward Lewis again, his smooth face no longer looking like a choirboy's. 'I said, throw the fuckin' cat away, Spit! Let's do our fuckin' job and get out of here.'

Spit grabbed Big Sister's tail with his free hand and swung the screeching animal brutally against the display window of the 24-Hour Church of Elvis – twice, three times, leaving smears of blood on the glass. He tossed the twitching corpse into the gutter and rounded on Lewis again.

Dewey had a length of pipe in his hand and fury in his eyes. Approaching from behind, he jammed the pipe hard between Spit's legs, causing him to howl and double up, then crumble to the sidewalk. Dewey whipped the pipe hard against the bridge of Spit's nose, which spewed blood as if someone had turned on a spigot.

'What the hell—?' shouted Benoit, groping inside his anorak for a gun. Lewis drove his wheelchair into him at full throttle, and Benoit fell across the armrests, arms and legs flailing. Lewis caught Benoit's wrist in his good hand and twisted, causing the black man to shriek in agony and drop the gun. As Benoit flailed to regain his feet, Lewis snatched up the gun from the sidewalk and thrust its muzzle hard against his cheek.

'Make one more move, fuck-stick, and you're dead,' he hissed through clenched teeth. Benoit slid slowly to his knees.

By this time Dewey had rained at least a dozen blows with the pipe on Spit's head and shoulders, and Spit had collapsed in a bloody mess on the dirty cement. He wouldn't have stopped if two mounted policemen hadn't galloped to the curb and rushed in to grab the length of pipe. Dewey would have beaten Spit to death, Lewis was certain.

v

Later, they sat together in the shade of the neoclassical colonnades in the Market Block, neither doing much talking. Having given statements to the cops, they'd gone to the little neighborhood grocery on the corner of Burnside and Third, where Lewis had bought a fresh quart of milk for Dewey.

For the first time ever, Lewis was able to detect signs of inebriation in his friend, who had methodically polished off a third of a fifth of bourbon within an hour, sipping first from the bottle in the brown paper sack and then from the milk carton. Occasionally he paused to stare at the bundle wrapped in plastic beside his wheelchair, the remains of his longtime companion, Big Sister. Lewis saw no tears in his eyes, heard no quiver in his voice. Decades of suffering had drained him of tears, Lewis figured.

'Dewey, I want you to come home with me tonight. The living room sofa folds out into a bed. I'll heat up some chili and we can listen to some good music, maybe watch a little tube.'

'Forget it. I don't need any sofa that folds out into a bed, and I don't need any chili. I only need to be alone, okay?' His speech was slurred, his eyelids heavy. Lewis worried that he might fall out of his wheelchair.

'Dewey, we're both hurting. Neither of us should be alone tonight.'

'Not true. *I* should be alone, because that's what I deserve.' He stole another look at the bundle on the ground. 'What'll happen to those motherfuckers, Lewis? Will they go to the joint?'

'I hope so. I hope they'll go to the joint for a long, long time.' Lewis didn't believe that this would happen, of course. He'd heard the story that the one named Benoit told the cops after the ambulance had sped away with Spit. They'd been walking quietly along the street, minding their own business, when the black man in the wheelchair suddenly attacked his friend with a length of pipe for no reason. More incredible, the man's *cat* had also attacked, and Benoit had drawn his gun only to scare the cripples and break up the ruckus. But the white one had slammed his wheelchair into him and taken his gun away, then threatened to kill him. Benoit was glad the cops had arrived when they had, or God only knows . . .

'Know what I think, Lewis? I think they'll both be out on the street before it gets dark. The cops won't believe their story, but you and I aren't hurt, so the only real charge is carrying a gun. Unless one of them is on probation or has a warrant out for him, they'll both be free and walking around tonight.'

'You may be right,' Lewis agreed, sighing. 'On the other hand, you might've hit the big one hard enough with that damned pipe to keep him in the hospital for a while.'

Dewey shook his head and said he hadn't managed to crack the bastard's skull, though he'd tried. God knows he'd tried. He looked up at Lewis with hopeless eyes. 'What am I gonna do without Big Sister, man?'

'I don't know. I wish I could . . .' He saw Tommy Iadanza jaywalking across Second Avenue from the VIP Center, coming to fetch Lewis and drive him home. 'Please come home with me, Dewey. You're in no shape to take care of yourself tonight.'

'Hey, I've survived out here this long. Nothing's gonna happen to me. If you want to help, lay ten bucks on me so I can buy a bottle of decent whiskey.'

'I'll give you twenty if you promise to get a roof over your head. I mean it, Dewey. You can buy yourself another bottle, but I want you to get inside somewhere. Is it a deal?'

'It's a deal.'

Lewis dug out his wallet and gave him the last twenty-dollar bill he had.

CHAPTER THIRTEEN
A Change of Heart

i

When he arrived home from school on Wednesday afternoon, Josh found Nicole Tran in the gazebo behind Sloan House, eating an apple, her nose buried in Camus's *The Plague*. He eased himself into the vacant side of the wicker love seat in which she sat.

Without looking up, Nicole said, 'So, you're alive, after all. Some of us were beginning to wonder.'

'It's been what? – two days since we talked?'

'I haven't been counting, actually.'

'Nicki, let's dispense with the attitude, okay? You sound like Laurel, for Christ's sake.'

She wrinkled her nose and crossed her eyes in a way that had always made Josh laugh, and it made him laugh now. 'Check me into the nearest personality-transplant center.'

'It's all right for me to insult my girlfriend, but not for *you*. Give me a bite of your apple, damn it. I skipped lunch today to do homework I should've done last night.' Nicole handed over the apple and Josh sunk his teeth into it. 'Actually, Laurel's not so bad when you get to know her,' he said with his mouth full.

273

'You're the only one I know who doesn't like her.'

'It's not that I don't like her, I just can't understand what you see in her.'

'Aside from the fact that she looks like she just stepped out of a beer commercial, you mean?'

'Aside from that, yes – not to mention the fact that she lets you do anything you want to her.'

Josh gave her a playful punch on the shoulder. 'What else do I need?'

'If you don't know by now, I'm certainly not going to tell you.' She rose from the wicker love seat and leaned against the railing that ran around the edge of the gazebo. The sun had begun to slip behind the rim of Gander Ridge, and deep afternoon shadows stretched across the lawn.

'Can I assume that you've forgiven me for the way I acted on the bridge Monday night?' Josh asked.

'There's nothing to forgive.'

'You seemed pretty mad when I told you about Millie Carter coming into my room and what she . . .'

'Let's not dredge that up again, okay? When it comes right down to it, I'm the one who should apologize.'

'Why is that?'

'Because I don't have any reason to be mad at you for telling me . . .' She paused a long moment, seeking precisely the right words. '. . . for *divulging* certain intimate details of your sex life. You and I certainly aren't romantically involved with each other – never have been and never will be. I don't have any basis for being offended. I see that now.'

'I've always figured that you and Lewis are the two people in the world who I can talk about *anything* with, no matter how embarrassing it might be. As for my sex life, please don't assume that Millie Carter is part of it. The only thing I feel toward her is . . .'

'Nickster, let's drop it, okay? You forgive me, I forgive you. Can we let it go at that?'

'You got it. Consider it dropped.'

She turned toward him again, her delicate Asian face dark with worry. 'There's still the matter of the orb, though. Did you get rid of it?'

Josh felt a pit develop in his stomach. He'd carried the orb with him today in his nylon rucksack along with his books and notebooks, having promised himself that he would get rid of it as soon as possible. But he knew that he couldn't throw it away, at least not yet, because it represented *hope*. It was Lewis Kindred's only means of disposing of his debt to Rex Caswell and regaining control of his life. How could he tell Nicole all this, he worried, without leading her to conclude that he was certifiably one banana short of a bunch?

'You didn't do it, did you?' said Nicole, reading his face. 'You still have it, don't you?'

He nodded. Something moved inside his rucksack, which he'd slung over his knee, but he decided that it had only been the shifting of his cargo of books. 'Nicki, something has happened, something really bad. Lewis was playing cards at the Fanshawe, like he does every Monday night, and there was this guy named Rex Caswell, a real slug . . .'

He told her about Lewis's loss of $210,000 to Rex Caswell. He told her about Millie's second visit to the Nickersons' apartment yesterday. And he told her about his strong suspicion that Millie was behind Lewis's recent blast of bad luck at the poker table. The telling went remarkably smoothly. Not once did Nicole interrupt him.

275

'So, I'm hoping Lewis will come to his senses and use the orb to get out of this mess,' he concluded. 'I've tried to convince him he should challenge Rex Caswell to a rematch, then use the orb to win back the money.'

'What did he say to that?'

'He threw a shit-fit. Told me he would never touch the damn thing again. Said that he'd once used the orb to win at poker, and afterwards he felt all dirty inside. He thinks that using it against Caswell would be the same as cheating.'

Nicole said nothing for a long time, but only gazed across the lawn of Sloan House, her brow furrowed. When she spoke again, it was hardly above a whisper. 'Nickster, this is scary stuff, and I don't like it. I've never believed in the supernatural before—'

'Neither have I. But you've seen the orb and touched it. It doesn't take a rocket scientist to know that it has some kind of power.'

'Which is exactly my point. What we're dealing with here defies all reason. The orb is doing something to you, Nickster. It's creating conflict between you and your friends.'

'Between you and me?'

'You and Lewis, too. You're pressuring him to use its power to get his money back, which he considers cheating. He can't do what you want without sacrificing his principles. Don't you see the implications of that?'

'What choice does he have?'

'I don't know. I wish I did.'

Josh, too, wished he could think of other alternatives – neat ones, happy ones. Lewis couldn't simply run out on his debt to Caswell. And killing Rex Caswell was out of the question, if for no other reason than neither Josh nor Lewis endorsed the killing of human beings. Josh couldn't even stomach fishing with live bait. So what was left, except to use the orb to erase the debt, and thus right the injustice that Josh was certain had come at the hand of Millie Carter?

Again he thought he felt something move inside the rucksack, but again he told himself that it had been his books shifting.

ii

He walked with Nicole as far as the front drive of Sloan House. 'Nicki, I'm sorry about all this,' he told her. 'I'm sorry I didn't get rid of the orb when you wanted me to.'

'From what you've told me, I'm not so sure that getting rid of it would've solved anything. You still would've had Millie to deal with.' She stopped walking and tapped a front tooth with her fingernail, thinking. 'I wonder who she is and what she wants.'

'I worry more about *what* she is.' He shuddered, remembering Millie's shadow on the carpet of the dining room. 'Hey, why don't you come and split a pizza with me? I'm not wild about the idea of being alone right now.'

'I'd like to, but I shouldn't. Things aren't so good at home right now . . .' Her eyes filled with worry. 'It's my dad. He's been acting kind of strange again, and I can tell that my mom is worried sick about him. I really should get home.'

'Has he started going out at night again?'

Nicole nodded. Over the years her family had suffered periods when Mr Tran came and went at all hours, missed meals, broke appointments and generally lived a secret life apart from his wife and daughter. Mrs Tran had assumed that he was seeing another woman, but Nicole had never believed this, for she'd seen a torment in her father's face that didn't fit a man who was cheating on his wife. It had seemed more like *desperation*. More than once she'd expressed to Josh the fear that her father was mentally ill, that he may even have suffered hallucinations.

'I'm sorry,' said Josh, patting her shoulder. 'Go be with your mom. I'll call you later.'

'Thanks for understanding,' she said, smiling thinly. She headed down the hill toward the Tran family's house.

Josh watched her for a moment and suddenly a new worry seized him. He and Nicole were seniors in high school, which meant that next year they would each head to college, probably in different directions. If things went as hoped, Josh would study journalism at Northwestern in Chicago while Nicole would attend Stanford near San Francisco, seeking a degree in literature. Would they also drift apart, he wondered, displacing each other with new friends? The thought generated a pang. *No!* he said, startling himself, because he'd said it out loud. *I won't let it happen.*

He slung his rucksack over his shoulder and let himself in. The elevator in the foyer stood open, and though he usually bounded up the stairs four at a time, he felt tired today – bone-tired, in fact. The stress of the past four days had worn him down, so the elevator was a temptation he couldn't resist. He'd taken three steps toward it when Lewis Kindred's voice stopped him.

iii

'It's about time you got home, mahatma.' Lewis sat in the deep shadow of the corridor that led to his apartment, clutching a bottle of Full Sail Golden in his fist. The crystal chandelier in the foyer reflected tiny shards of sunlight that danced along the chromed surfaces of his Action Power 9000. 'Got a minute?'

'I do if you've got a Diet Rite in your fridge.'

Lewis waved him inside. Sitting across from each other, they traded small talk. Josh tried not to show his worry over how Lewis looked – wrung-out, bleary-eyed, and half-drunk. The woven wastebasket next to the computer desk held at least four empty beer bottles.

'Enough of the happy horseshit, mahatma,' said Lewis after an uncomfortable pause and a long pull from his beer bottle. 'You're probably wondering why I'm drunk at four in the afternoon.'

'It had crossed my mind.'

'You'll know soon enough. Did you get rid of the orb?'

Josh took a deep breath before answering, lowering his eyes. 'Lewis, I couldn't do it. I wanted to, believe me—'

'Good. Because I need it.'

Josh glanced up. 'You *what*?'

'I've thought about your suggestion that I use it to win back my money from Caswell. I've decided you were right.'

'You *have*? Lew, that's great! I've got it right here.' He hoisted his rucksack onto his lap and pawed through it. For a few frantic seconds he worried that he might've lost the thing, but then his fingers found its smooth, warm curvature, and he pulled it out. He held it up before Lewis, who stiffened at the sight of it. The orb gleamed uncannily in the weakening light.

Lewis wedged his beer bottle between the stumps of his legs and reached out unsteadily, his hand trembling. The instant his fingers made contact with the orb, his face paled, and Josh nearly jerked it away, fearing that Lewis was suffering some kind of attack.

'I want you to know something, mahatma. I'm not doing this only for myself. Today, something ugly happened to someone I care about, a man who lives in a wheelchair like I do. Rex Caswell sent two of his no-necks to *remind* me of the money I owe him, and while they were *reminding* me, they killed an old flea-bitten cat. That cat was the only real family my friend had left, and she was worth more to him than a million bucks would be to you or me. He lost her because of *me*. After it happened, I suddenly understood that I had to do something . . .' His eyes moistened. He coughed and went on. 'I can't let Caswell get away with it. Let's face it – I don't have a prayer of raising all the money I owe him. I can raise two-thirds or maybe even three-quarters of it, but no matter what I do, I'm going to be at least fifty thousand short. Caswell will lean on me any way he can to force me to come up with the rest of the money. It'll occur to him that the best way to do this would be to hurt the people I love, and that's what he'll do. Do you know what *that* would mean, mahatma?'

Josh swallowed. 'What?'

'I'd have to kill him.'

Josh's neck went prickly and cold. 'You don't mean that, man.'

'I *do* mean it. If Caswell were to hurt you or one of your family, or Tommy Iadanza or Carlotta or one of their kids, I'd load up my old Colt .45 and I'd find the son of a bitch, and I'd pump a full clip into him.'

280

Josh wanted to be sick. 'You can't do that, Lewis. You can't even think it.'

'You're right,' said Lewis, placing the crystalline orb next to his cheek. The thing no longer repelled him, apparently. He stared blindly as he talked, and a tear splashed down the side of his nose, vanishing between his dry lips. 'That's why I've decided to take your advice. I need to challenge Rex to a rematch. We'll play five-card draw, one on one, and if I have this thing with me . . .' His fingers caressed the orb, causing Josh to squirm. '. . . I won't lose. I'll get rid of the debt, mahatma, and I'll spare myself the unwholesome chore of killing that slimy son of a bitch.' He pulled the cuff of his sweatshirt across his eyes, drying them. 'So you see, it's not just for myself that I'm doing this. I'll get my life back, sure, and I'll be able to face the future without worrying about living under a bridge after I retire. But it's not just for myself.'

'I understand.'

Lewis looked up abruptly, letting his hand and the orb go to his lap. '*Do* you, mahatma?' He leaned forward on his stumps, and Josh caught a blast of his beery breath. 'Do you understand how it feels to try to stand up to someone when you don't have any legs? Do you understand what it's like to see women all around you – pretty ones, ugly ones, fat ones, skinny ones – and you want them all, or you want just one, it doesn't matter which one, you just want *one* woman to love you but you know that it'll never happen, because you've got no legs?' He ran his tongue over his dry lips, which looked ready to crack and bleed. His gray eyes were wells of anger. 'Do you understand what it's like to give up everything you've ever dreamed of being,

281

because you can't hack it without legs?'

Josh shook his head miserably.

'Well, it doesn't matter whether you understand or not.' He chugged the rest of his beer. 'I made a resolution today. I was sitting right there in front of the computer . . .' He waved his hand toward the desk. '. . . and I decided to start acting like a *whole* man, mahatma. I'm tired of being the victim, tired of being the guy everybody feels sorry for. From now on I'm the guy who stands tall . . .' He actually raised himself on his stumps, his butt braced against the back of the wheelchair, *standing*. The feat produced pain, and his face showed it. 'I'm going to stand up against Rex Caswell, mahatma. I'm going to beat him any way I can.'

CHAPTER FOURTEEN
Between Hell and Heaven

i

Twenty-four hours after Josh Nickerson handed over the orb to Lewis Kindred, a stiletto-shaped powerboat eased into a slip outside a posh floating home at the Sellwood Bay Club on the Willamette River. Mason Benoit hopped from the deck onto the dock and tied her next to the monstrous cigarette boat already in residence. Benoit's partner, Spit Pittman, clambered after him, his head a mass of white bandages, his face a hodgepodge of purple and green bruises. Spit moved unsteadily as if his balance was in doubt, which it probably was, considering the beating he'd taken from an ageing black man in a wheelchair the previous day.

They made their way to the lower deck of the house, where Twyla Boley leaned at the railing with a vodka tonic in one hand and a cigarette in the other. 'Rex is waiting for you guys inside,' she said with an impish grin. 'I think he's mad enough to cut you both into little pieces and feed you to the seagulls.' As though on cue, a gull screamed overhead and wheeled toward the far shore.

'Thanks for the warning,' said Spit, and he walked on dizzily, like a tipsy gorilla.

Twyla spied the elastic wrist brace that Benoit wore on his left arm. 'What happened to your hand, Mase?' As if she didn't know. Benoit only glared at her as he walked into the house.

Inside they found Rex Caswell nervously pacing the living room. He wore a silk shirt and well-tailored slacks, which was normal attire for him on a weekday afternoon. But he wore something else that immediately gave his underlings cause to cringe – a shoulder holster with a Glock nine-millimeter pistol in it.

'Sit down,' he ordered, his eyes hazy with anger. He stared at each of them in turn, Spit with his masses of bandages and bruises, then Benoit with his wrist brace. 'Look at you guys – supposedly the best muscle available on the West Coast. Steel men, I was told. Knowledgeable about weapons. Reliable. I believed every word of it, and I put out major bucks to get you and keep you in the manner to which you've become accustomed. But what happens when I send you to do a simple little job like laying some tough talk on a guy with no legs?' He needn't have spelled it out, but he did, his tan face pinkening as his blood pressure climbed. 'One of you ends up being hauled off in an ambulance! The other gets his *wrist* sprained . . .'

'Kindred has a strong right hand, Rex,' protested Benoit, massaging his injured limb.

'Shut up!' The muscles in Rex's neck bulged like towing cables. 'Right now I'm trying to figure out what the future holds for two dip-shits who attack a pair of disabled veterans in wheelchairs, in downtown Portland over the fucking noon hour, yet, and not only get themselves beaten up, but arrested! What am I supposed to think of guys like that?'

'Rex, what happened yesterday was a fluke,' pleaded Benoit, swiping perspiration from his upper lip. 'We're not even going to be prosecuted, wait and see. They confiscated my pistol – so what? Nobody got hurt except Spit, and the D. A. doesn't have the time or resources to . . .'

'I said shut the fuck up!' Rex's right hand darted to the shoulder holster, and his fingers played over the handle of the Glock, but he didn't pull it out. He watched the effect of the gesture on his underlings, who sucked deep breaths and slowly exhaled. 'Neither one of you should've been carrying a piece in the first place, because the job didn't call for it. Even Spit knew that much, for Christ's sake. I would've expected a little more from you, Mase. Don't I pay you enough to get better than this? How in the fuck do you afford that boat tied up out there, huh? Or that townhouse of yours in Northwest? Or that BMW you drive? Where does the money come from, Mase – from your nine-to-five job designing computers in Beaverton? Or from your brain-surgery practice? I'll tell you where it comes from . . . !'

'It comes from you, Rex. I know that, and I appreciate it.'

'You're damn right it comes from me!'

The telephone bleeped, interrupting the tirade. Rex shouted for Twyla to pick it up, but it continued to bleep. He swore when he caught sight of her through the glass doors beyond the kitchen, contentedly smoking and drinking on the sunlit deck, oblivious to the phone. 'Fucking graceless cow,' he muttered. Grinding his teeth, he answered it himself.

ii

Lewis clutched the handset in his sweaty fist. All day he'd rehearsed for this moment, having actually written out his lines and read them aloud repeatedly. He'd edited and redrafted them at least half a dozen times and had tested varying inflections in his delivery, determined to get it perfect. He'd even written contingency responses to different things that Rex Caswell might say.

Now, gazing at the red crystal orb that lay on the table next to his telephone, feeling as if it was a living eye through which some creature of hell was watching him, he waited for Rex to answer the telephone. What are the odds, he wondered nervously, that Rex would actually take the bait?

'Hello!'

He sounds angry, Lewis thought. *Good or bad?* 'Rex, this is Lewis Kindred. Remember me?'

A long, dumbfounded silence. Finally: 'Uh, yeah. Lewis. Of course I remember you. Think I'd forget somebody who owes me a couple hundred large? To what do I owe the pleasure of a call from the Stumpmeister himself?'

Lewis forced himself to stick to the script. 'Just thought I'd call to tell you that I've the raised the money I owe you.'

Another dumbfounded silence. 'You *have*?' Lewis smiled, because Rex sounded terribly deflated. 'You raised two hundred and ten K in three days? No way.'

'*Yes* way. I'm sitting here looking at it, actually.' In truth, he was staring at the orb, telling himself that he'd not seen it move a few seconds earlier.

'No shit. I gotta say it, Lewis – I didn't expect you to

pull it off. What did you do – blackmail somebody or maybe grease a rich uncle?'

'None of your business, Rex. You should take the money and thank the gods of poker that they gave you one night of pure, unmitigated luck.'

Rex laughed loudly. *Too* loudly. 'Is that what you're telling people, big guy? That I had a lucky streak?'

'I don't need to tell anybody anything. People were there. They saw what happened, and they talk.'

'Are you saying that people think I didn't really beat you, that I just had a wild spin of luck? Is that what you're saying?'

'Jesus Christ, what do you expect? We've been playing poker together for something like ten years, and every night until last Monday you've left money on the table, *big* money often as not. Then suddenly you're unstoppable – not to mention that I get an attack of the stupids and play the worst cards I've played since I was thirteen. You ended up winning big. These things aren't unheard of, you know. Every hack gets at least one lucky streak in his life, and you've had yours. Nice for you, too bad for me. Still, it's not the end of the world. I'll survive, maybe even prosper.'

Lewis listened to heavy breathing over the line, the slow ventilation of rage. Rex labored to get his voice under control. 'You're really something, Lewis. For a guy who's lost his legs, his woman and more than two hundred thousand dollars, you talk awfully big.'

'Oh, but I do more than talk, Rex.'

'Yeah? What's that supposed to mean?'

'I'll give you a chance to show what you're really made of, my friend. I'll take a rematch, if you're up for it. We'll play draw poker, just you and I, with an ante of, say, fifty thousand dollars. We'll each put up another hundred large as a side bet. The game will stop when one of us gets scared or tired. What do you say?'

'You've got to be out of your goddamn mind. Why would I do that when I'm more than two hundred thousand up? Sounds to me like you're chasing bad money, Lewis.'

What the hell is this? Lewis worried, his guts turning. *Is Rex Caswell getting smart?* 'You would do it, Rex, because you need to prove that you're good. I say you were lucky Monday night. I say you couldn't do it again in a million years.' *Careful. Don't lay it on too thick.*

'So why should I give a rusty fuck what you say? Who listens to you these days? You've been beaten, remember?'

'Hell, you're right. Nobody listens to me. Forget I mentioned it. Give me your address, and I'll bring the money to you tomorrow. Or if it's more convenient, I can meet you at a bank or something.'

Silence, long and deathly. *His wheels are going around*, thought Lewis. *What he decides will determine whether I have a life left.* Lewis's gaze wandered to the photographs that lined one wall of his studio, and he caught sight of his parents' wedding portrait. His father stared down at him with an honest smile on his face. Lyle Kindred had been the most honest man Lewis had ever known. A breeze moved branches outside the window, casting alternating shadows and bursts of sunlight across the orb. The orb diffused the shifting light and threw out a shard of red that traversed the face of Lyle Kindred, causing his eyes to change fearsomely. They became red and penetrating, accusing. A demon's eyes. Lewis blinked and looked quickly away, his heart in his throat.

'Wait a minute,' said Rex. 'I'm not afraid to go another round with you, not even for high stakes. If that's what you want, Lewis, I'm game. Bring enough money to play poker this time, you son of a bitch, because I'm not taking any more IOUs.'

'How about next Monday night at the usual time and place? Just don't drag along those no-necks who jumped my friend and me yesterday in Old Town. If I see one of them, I'll rip his leg off and beat him to death with it.'

'I'll be there, and I'll be alone. Remember what I said, though – bring the fuckin' money. I want to see it before we start.'

'Don't worry,' Lewis assured him, his throat feeling suddenly parched. 'I'll bring plenty of money.' His stare wandered to the orb, which sat in its place, its innards swirling. *And I'll bring something else, too*, he thought.

iii

Shortly after midnight, Nicole Tran laid a blanket over her mother, who'd finally fallen asleep on the living room sofa, exhausted after three consecutive nights of sleepless worry. Nicole had kept the vigil with her, sitting in an Ethan Allen swivel chair for hours on end, listening to classical music and reading her school assignments. Once again her father hadn't come home, but had left his downtown office promptly at five and gone out without leaving a message for his wife or daughter.

During past periods of such strange behavior, he'd sometimes returned in the small hours of the morning, going straight up the back stairs to his den and locking himself in. Nicole had learned the uselessness of knocking on his door, for at times like these he wouldn't talk to either his wife or daughter.

Only in recent years had her mother begun to confide in Nicole, disclosing her suspicions about the possibility of another woman. In many ways Nicole's mother was the traditional Vietnamese *ba*, the dutiful wife who wouldn't dream of questioning anything her husband did, but she'd lived in America long enough to acquire some rudimentary Western feelings about a wife's personal rights and entitlements. Her Vietnamese nature tugged her in the direction of quiet forbearance, while her American side insisted on confrontation and resolution. Nicole hated seeing her mother torn like this but she couldn't hate her father for causing the pain. She simply couldn't believe that his behavior had anything whatever to do with another woman, for he too was the picture of torment, not of a man sneaking out to cheat on his wife.

Nicole stood over her mother a long moment, listening to her regular breathing and feeling glad for one small blessing – that she'd finally fallen asleep. As the final strains of Mozart's Symphony No. 26 came over the speakers of the stereo, Nicole heard a light thump and a squeak at the rear of the house and knew that her father had come home.

She climbed the front staircase to her room, which was on the second floor at the front of the house, unlike her father's den, which was at the rear. She collapsed onto her four-poster bed and lay silent a moment, eager for sleep but afraid that it would not come.

The *sound* came again, a rapid-fire thumping that she couldn't define, almost like the drumming of human fingers on a wooden surface, except it couldn't have a human source, because the rhythm was too fast and too prolonged. It was too *machine*-like. She'd heard the sound often in the past, always in the late-night or early-morning hours when the household should have been deeply asleep, and several times she'd followed the sound until coming to the locked door of her father's den. Pressing her ear against the door, she'd heard another sound beneath the beating: her father's voice, moaning in Vietnamese, of which Nicole knew only a few words. His tone sounded fearful, almost panicky, as though he was suffering some horrible dream or hallucination.

Knowing the futility of doing so but desperately needing to do something, she left her room and entered the dark hallway that led to the rear of the beautiful old Queen Anne house. Her father was intensely proud of this house, which he'd bought and presented to his family twelve years earlier, after his janitorial business had started to net decent money. He'd furnished it in expensive Early American trappings, a statement that he and his family had fully embraced their new land – except for his den, which at first glance seemed to have been lifted intact from a little corner of Saigon. It contained a multitude of old books that dated to Vietnam's colonial past, many in French and Vietnamese; authentic statues of the Buddha, photos of departed ancestors mounted in ceremonial frames, a little altar with joss sticks, and icons that Nicole had learned were artifacts of the mysterious Cao Dai faith; and finally, old trunks full of bizarre objects that her father had arranged to have sent by friends in Vietnam, or things he'd scrounged from other Vietnamese immigrants – inscriptions from gravestones, stolen offerings to the dead, stumps of candles taken from the prayer altars of Roman Catholic churches in and around Saigon. Why her father would collect such things, she had no idea.

Once again she came to the door of his den, tested the

handle, and found it locked. Once again she heard the soft sounds of a man sobbing and moaning from within. Nicole longed to go to him and offer a daughter's comfort but the locked door kept her out as it always had before.

iv

Despite the fact that Lewis Kindred had the orb in his possession, the earth continued to revolve on its axis, birds sang, and human beings went about their daily business, all of which he took some small reassurance from. He told himself that he hadn't entered into any kind of Faustian bargain, that using the orb would not damn him to eternal agony or cause the downfall of Western civilization. He would do what needed to be done, then dispose of the orb forever. Life would be good again.

On Friday morning he motored into his studio where a desk calendar told him that it was September 18, 1992. Only three more days until the rematch with Rex Caswell.

Three days to-day, between Hell and Heaven!

He smiled. The line was from Dante Gabriel Rossetti's dark and unnerving poem, 'Sister Helen,' an artifact of his courtship of Twyla Boley, who'd been an ardent worshipper of the Pre-Raphaelite poets of the mid-nineteenth century. Lewis had spent many an hour pretending to listen raptly to Twyla's reading of George Meredith, Algernon Charles Swinburne and the Rossettis, though he himself found little to love in the Pre-Raphaelites' devotion to heavy-duty moralizing. Such was Twyla's fascination with them that she'd even attempted to imitate their style in her own poetry, employing the archaic language and medieval subject matter that so put Lewis off. He'd considered her poems downright laughable, but he'd never laughed aloud, of course. What Twyla had lacked as a poet she'd made up for in other ways, not the least of which were pleasures of the flesh.

Throughout the weekend he tackled his contract work, keeping his nose to the computer screen. With the television providing the needed background noise, he managed to finish several projects and start another. Newscasts came and went, together with football games, sitcoms, movies, and ads. The world spun on. Throughout the Portland metro area preparations were under way for Oktoberfest, with celebrations planned in countless parks, pubs and restaurants. Local churches were buzzing about next week's Billy Graham Crusade, which would take place at Civic Stadium mere blocks from Sloan House. In France, voters were deciding whether they liked the Maastricht Treaty. George Bush and Bill Clinton went at each other tooth and nail.

While waiting for Monday night and the Big Event, Lewis kept mostly to himself. Several poker associates called with invitations to games but he declined. He wanted no poker until he next cut the cards with Rex Caswell.

Josh visited late Sunday night. 'What's with the locked door?' the boy wanted to know as Lewis backed his wheelchair to let him in.

'I've been a little jumpy after what happened in Old Town. I've got a spare key you can have.' Lewis locked the door again and led the way into the studio, where Josh plunked his lanky frame into his usual spot, the cushy armchair next to the computer table. Lewis pawed through a drawer and took out a spare key, which he flipped to Josh.

'All set for the big showdown tomorrow night?' the kid asked.

'I'm ready. I'm not looking forward to it, mind you, but I'm ready.' Lewis had related in great detail how he'd issued the challenge to Caswell, how Caswell had snapped it up like a hungry dog after a T-bone. 'See how steady I am?' He held his hand out flat, and it was as stable as the hand of a statue. 'I haven't had so much as a beer since Wednesday.'

'Can I come along with you tomorrow night?'

'No way.'

'Lewis, I want to come along.'

'I've just told you, mahatma, you can't.'

'Why?'

'Because it won't be clean, wholesome fun, that's why.'

'I'm not after clean, wholesome fun. I just want to be there.'

'Forget it.'

'But you'll need the moral support, Lewis. You'll need a friend, right?'

'Wrong. Tommy will be there, and most of the others, too, I think. My cheering section will be more than adequate.'

'Lewis, I *need* to come along,' pleaded Josh, suddenly sitting up straight in the chair, his face grave. 'I'm thinking of writing about all this someday. I need to see it happen with my own eyes. It wouldn't be the same to get it second hand. You can understand that, can't you?'

'You're only seventeen, mahatma. This is going to be an adults-only affair.' Lewis avoided looking at him and studied the joystick on his wheelchair. 'It won't be the sort of display that's suitable for kids.'

'Why? Because there'll be strong language? Because there'll be adult themes? I was old enough to save the orb for you, wasn't I – old enough not to throw it away, like you kept telling me I should?'

Lewis visualized the scene in the upstairs cardroom of the Hotel Fanshawe and asked himself what could happen there that would be too lurid for the tender eyes of a seventeen-year-old, especially if that seventeen-year-old was Josh Nickerson. He could think of nothing. Moreover, if Josh hadn't kept the orb, Lewis would now have no hope of regaining control of his life. So Lewis owed him something. In fact, Lewis owed him a *lot*.

'Okay, goddamn it, you can come along. But don't tell your mother about this, okay?'

'Mom wouldn't be a problem even if she knew about it. But, if you don't want me to tell her, I won't.' He got up from the chair and stuck out his hand. 'Thanks, Lewis. You won't be sorry.'

Lewis shook his hand and thought that Josh's grip was noticeably firmer than he remembered it.

v

Rex Caswell strode briskly into the lobby of the Fanshawe, his custom-made eel-skin attaché case hitting his thigh with every stride. He patted the breast pocket of his Armani blazer to certify that he'd brought his cellular phone. His own pistol bulged comfortably in his armpit. He was ready for anything, and he felt good.

Throughout most of the weekend Twyla had pleaded with him to call Lewis Kindred and cancel tonight's game. 'He's setting you up, Rex. This is so like him! He'll take every cent of your money and make a laughingstock out of you!'

Rex had laughed and thanked her sarcastically for her pure, unbounded faith in him. Then he'd told her not to worry. 'I've beaten this son of a bitch before. I'll beat him again.'

When he saw Millie Carter rise from the sofa near the elevators, he nearly swallowed his tongue. She wore a burgundy silk jumpsuit that left her brown shoulders bare, a massive emerald necklace and lipstick that looked like liquid pearls. She was even more gorgeous than when he'd last seen her. She smiled dazzlingly as he approached, her teeth a storm of white against her dark complexion. His knees went weak.

'Rex! It's good to see you again. How *are* you?' She offered her hand with a decidedly old-fashioned Southern flourish, and he took it, found it cool and smooth. She leaned close to him, and he caught the faintest whiff of citrus-flavored perfume. 'I assume there'll be another game tonight. Would you be interested in having a tag-along again?'

Rex cleared his throat, making sure his voice was ready. No other woman had ever affected him like this. 'Well, Millie – it *is* Millie, isn't it?' He knew damned well what her name was. Her exotic, mismatched eyes had haunted his dreams every night for the past week. 'I don't quite know what to say. You see, I'd thought you'd abandoned me last week. One minute you're with me at the poker table, and the next minute – poof! – you're gone. I really didn't know what to think.'

She giggled and shook her head girlishly. 'I am sorry about that, Rex, but something came up, something of a – uh – shall we say, *feminine* nature. By the time I got back from the little girls' room, you were long gone.'

Rex lowered his face and regarded her through his blond eyebrows, like a schoolteacher having heard the most outrageous story from a student who hadn't done her homework. 'Sweetheart, I've been around the block a few times. Give me some credit.'

'Another tack then.' She wetted her lips with her tongue, smiling lasciviously. 'You've got to admit that I brought you luck last week.' *Luck.* That word again. 'In fact, I don't think I've ever brought anyone quite as much luck as I brought *you*, Rex. Think of me as your talisman, your walking-talking, good-luck charm.'

'How do I know that you were the charm, eh? How do I know it wasn't the new pair of socks I put on before leaving the house?'

'Really, Rex. Have you ever won like that before? You don't actually think a little old pair of socks could bring you two hundred and ten thousand dollars from one of the best poker players in the country?'

He ground his teeth, but he couldn't bring himself to be angry at her. Suppose it *had* been pure luck that produced his big win over Kindred? If Millie had been the source of it, he would be crazy not to have her by his side tonight. 'You've talked me into it, Millie. But I warn you: If I win again tonight, I'm afraid I'll have to keep you.'

vi

During the few minutes before the game started, Josh made mental notes about the room and the people in it, for he'd been serious when telling Lewis that he meant to write about this night. He meant to remember the details. If Tommy Iadanza had let him, he would have taken real notes in the spiral notebook he'd brought along, but

Tommy had worried that some of the people in attendance would feel uneasy if someone sat in a corner and wrote things down.

The room was lighted by cans on tracks in the ceiling, furnished with blue-upholstered chairs and a huge round table covered with green baize. Tommy's wife, a pretty brunette of forty, bustled around the table taking orders for food and drinks. The rest of the Fanshawe crowd were as Lewis had often described them: the rotund Wisconsin Johnson, wearing a cheap wool suit, popping peanuts into his mouth with the shells still on them; the immaculate Lake Havasu City Sid with his thin face, white mane and solemn eyes; the freckled Connie Wierzbinski in her Trail Blazers sweatshirt and baseball cap, whose smoker's hack rattled her spare frame and left her gasping.

Lewis wore a crisply laundered button-down shirt and corduroy jeans with the cuffs tucked under his stumps, his hand clamped around the handle of a battered briefcase that sat on the floor next to his Action Power 9000. The briefcase contained a thousand hundred-dollar bills, which represented a good portion of Lewis's liquidated retirement fund, neatly bundled into stacks of fifty. Earlier in the day, Tommy had arranged for him to cash his broker's check at the U.S. Bank branch down the street.

Watching Lewis, Josh thought, *He's on autopilot. He's functioning, but he's a million miles away*. Josh had seen the look many times.

Where was the infamous Rex Caswell? he wondered. And would Rex have Millie Carter in tow, as he had last week? The thought of seeing Millie again generated a low-grade panic, but more urgent than this was his curiosity over her connection to Rex. Were they partners, maybe even lovers? Or was Millie using Rex to serve some dark purpose, just as she'd used the skinheads who'd attacked Josh and Nicole in an alley? Josh wondered, too, if she'd even used Ron Payne in some unholy way, having profited from his gruesome murder.

He didn't expect to get answers to all his questions tonight, but he did expect something extraordinary to happen, something that would go far beyond the mere fact of Lewis winning his money back. He had no clear idea of what that *something* was – only a rock-solid certainty that it would indeed happen. And he would be here to see it.

vii

While waiting for Rex Caswell to arrive, Lewis pondered whether death was a process or a dismantling – a philosopher's problem that had fascinated him since his freshman year in college. The answer, he supposed, depended on what life was.

Wisconsin Johnson said something to him, and he replied with something witty, or at least he assumed it'd been witty, because Wisconsin gave out a belly laugh and tossed another peanut into his mouth. Lewis's eyes and mouth and hands went about their business without him, keeping up appearances.

The door opened, and Rex Caswell made his entrance, his butter-soft briefcase in his hand. Behind him – tall and elegant – came Millie Carter, moving languidly like a swan. She smiled broadly at Lewis through the haze of Connie Wierzbinski's cigarette smoke, then smiled in turn at everyone in the room, including Josh Nickerson, who, when he saw her, instantly looked anemic. Lewis worried that he might actually faint. Rex noticed the effect she had on the boy and laughed loudly. Millie took a seat along the wall, not directly behind Rex but off to his right, which gave her a clear view of Lewis.

Her hour at last, between Hell and Heaven!

Tommy Iadanza, assuming the role of emcee and referee, explained what would happen tonight. Lewis and Rex would play a private one-on-one game of no-limit five card draw, the ante being $50,000. The players would make a side bet of $100,000. They would cut for the deal, and the winner of each hand would deal the next one. A game with stakes like these wasn't likely to last long, so everyone present was welcome to play Texas hold 'em after it had concluded. As always, drinks and eats were available from the Huntsman's Bar and Grill.

Wisconsin Johnson, Lake Havasu City Sid, and Connie Wierzbinski sat next to each other on Lewis's right, all eyeing him confidently and nodding their encouragement. For some absurd reason they reminded him of the chorus in a Greek tragedy, positioned at the edge of the stage – in this case, the table, from which they would offer their comments on the action. He wondered who the hero would be, recalling that heroes don't fare well in Greek tragedy. And nestled in the front pocket of his jeans, unnaturally warm and vibrating slightly, was the orb – the deus ex machina, the divine solution. It wouldn't swoop down onto the stage, as in actual Greek tragedy, but would stay hidden in Lewis's pocket.

Tommy Iadanza produced a new deck of cards still in the wrapper and passed it to each player for his examination. Then he broke the seal and placed the deck on the table.

'Before we cut the cards, I want to see the money,' Rex

declared. 'I want to make sure you brought enough to pay me what you owe me.'

Lewis hoisted his battered old attaché case onto the table, pressed the lock buttons and lifted the lid. The money shone greenly under the track lights, and the chorus murmured. 'There's more than enough here, Rex,' he lied. 'By the way, I assume that *you* brought cash.' Rex stared at the open case and chewed on his tongue, obviously weighing whether to insist that the money be counted. 'I won't demand that you show me your money,' added Lewis. 'If you say you have it, I'll take your word for it.'

'All right, let's ante up and get this fucking show on the road.'

Lewis and Rex cut the cards, and Rex won the deal. Balancing the attaché case on his stumps, Lewis took out ten packets of hundred-dollar bills and flipped them into the center of the table, one by one, staring Rex in the face while doing so and smiling his poker smile. In the corner of his eye he could see Millie, perched on the edge of her chair with her legs crossed, her chin resting on a fist, riveting him with her two-colored gaze. He concentrated on watching Rex shuffle the cards, keeping his gaze away from Millie's, but this didn't prevent a return of the feelings he'd suffered a week ago at this very table – a craving to look good in her eyes, a need to prove himself the equal of a whole man. Rex finished shuffling and slapped the deck down in the center of the table so that Lewis could cut the cards a final time, which he did. Rex then started to deal.

As the cards slid softly from the deck over the baize, Lewis involuntarily glanced at Millie, his attention inexplicably drawn to her despite his best efforts to shut her out. He absorbed a full blast of her heat and cold, her brown and blue, her love and hate, her incomprehensible duality. He felt both repulsed and attracted, but this didn't matter, for he immediately plunged into a vivid dream-scenario that featured him in bed with her, his hands running over her breasts and pulling away the layers of her clothing, her lips on his, her tongue against his, her legs entwined with *his* legs—

'Are you going to pick up your cards, or what?' Rex Caswell demanded.

Lewis found that his eyes were open wide and stinging, because he hadn't blinked them in God-only-knew how long. He blinked them now, and tears formed. A bead of saliva ran from the corner of his mouth as his orgasm pounded, and he was barely able to hold himself motionless lest everyone in the room detect what was happening to him. The orb, warm and wet in the front pocket of his corduroy jeans, pressed against his stiff cock, and Millie smiled faintly as she rocked back and forth in her chair with only a hint of motion, unnoticed by anyone but Lewis.

'What's the matter with you, Stumpmeister – are you having some kind of damn seizure?' Rex glared at him now with undisguised contempt. 'Pick up your cards and play poker, okay?'

Lewis picked up his cards, but when he saw them, he felt immediately sick. Rex had dealt him a potential double-ended straight – the deuce of clubs, three of hearts, four of diamonds, five of hearts, and jack of spades. The odds were five to one against his drawing either an ace or six to complete a strong hand. What sickened him was the fact that he'd seen this hand before, in another life, in a dark and dirty Quonset building in a vile place called Cu Chi Base Camp. His opponent had been a man named Gamaliel.

Pinheads of sweat popped out on his forehead as the orb again pressed into his groin, a thing alive. He dared another glance at Millie, who sat with her eyes closed, her full lips undulating and contorting ever so slightly as if they controlled the movements of the crystal. The dream seized him again. He saw himself push his face into the tender mound between her legs, inhaling the spiciness of her vagina, and he felt her mouth close over his cock, her tongue thrashing its head and stirring him to a frenzy.

'The bet's to you, Stumpmeister. I'd like to finish this hand before I reach retirement age, if you don't mind.'

One of the chorus said, 'Don't let him rush you, Lewis. You're entitled to think things over.'

Lewis heard himself say, 'Five hundred dollars.' He saw the fingers of his right hand cull out the jack and set it aside, meaning to discard it.

'Five hundred dollars,' repeated Rex, scowling at his cards. 'Where're your balls, Lewis? Don't you have any more faith in your cards than that?'

Lewis's balls were busy right now, as was his tongue. The dream was as actual to him as this poker game. He had another orgasm, this one even more wrenching than the first. He felt it down to his *toes*.

'I *said*, I raise you ten thousand dollars,' barked Rex, repeating what he'd said thirty seconds earlier. 'Are you sure you're capable of playing this game, Stumpmeister? You're acting like you've dosed up on Quaaludes or something.'

'I'm okay,' said Lewis, staring at Millie. She opened her eyes and rolled them at him dreamily, as if to say, *That was good, Lewis. But I'm not finished with you, lover – not by a long shot*. 'I'll see you and call.'

Rex dealt him another card, then dealt himself one. The sneer on Rex's face suggested that he felt certain of winning, meaning that he had strong cards. Lewis was on his back now, and Millie was astride him, her willowy body slick with sweat, and she was working his cock into her, mewling sweetly. She started pumping him furiously, her sweet breasts jouncing, and he could see that she too was on the verge of orgasm. She screamed loudly enough to shatter windows throughout the city, and Lewis howled as he came, causing earthquakes and tidal waves. His hands and arms tingled; his legs and feet tingled. *He was whole again* . . .

He glanced at his new card, though he needn't have, for he knew what it was – a six, which gave him a six-high straight.

'What do you say we wrap this up right now?' Rex suggested. 'It's clear you're not having a good time, Lewis. Tell you what we'll do: Let's skip the last round of betting and call. We'll keep the bets we have on the table, but let's up our side bet from a hundred thousand to double or nothing what you already owe me. That would bring the total pot to . . . let's see . . .'

'Five hundred and forty-one thousand dollars,' said Lewis, suddenly energized. His poker smile came back. Though his clothes were damp with sweat, the effect of sweltering in Millie's heat, he felt virile and strong. He almost believed that he could rise out of the wheelchair, climb onto the table, and walk across it on his own two feet. He felt as if he could kick Rex Caswell squarely in the teeth and then dance on the ratfucker's head. 'Sounds like a good bet to me, Rex. Let's do it.'

Taken aback by Lewis's sudden transformation, Rex

hesitated, then glanced again at his cards. He breathed heavily and loudly through his mouth, as if he were lifting weights. 'Half a million bucks and change,' he said aloud to himself. He turned to glance at Millie, saw that her eyes were closed, and turned back to the table. 'Did you bring enough to cover a bet as big as this?' he asked, his blond eyebrows twitching.

'Immaterial,' answered Lewis. 'I'm not going to lose. I don't have the money here, Rex, but I'm good for it.'

'You cocksucker! Didn't I tell you to show up with enough cash to play the game? How do I know you can cover the bet and still pay me what you owe me?'

'Let's watch our language here,' Wisconsin Johnson protested. 'We've got ladies in the room, for Christ's sake.'

Movement from Rex's right caught Lewis's eye, Millie's hand reaching toward Rex and settling on his arm, causing him to start as if jolted with a cattle prod. Millie leaned close to him, her emerald necklace glittering. 'I'll cover him if he's short, Rex. If you win, I'll have the money for you within the hour.' Rex gaped at her for a full ten seconds, and Lewis noticed dark circles in the armpits of his Armani sport coat.

'Okay. That's good enough for me.' Rex turned his cards over one by one, revealing what Lewis knew would be there – a full house, jacks over nines, the same hand that Gamaliel Cartee had turned over in Cu Chi. Another miracle beyond the bounds of mathematical probability. Anguished sighs came from the chorus, along with a gasp from Josh Nickerson and a groan from Tommy Iadanza.

'Sorry about this, asshole,' said Rex, a grin stretching across his handsome face. 'Seems like the poker fairy hit you with the loser-stick. Second time in a row, you pathetic cretin! That's almost three-quarters of a million dollars you owe me! When are you going to learn, Lewis? You're history, man! *Le roi est mort, vive le roi!*' He pounded the table with a manicured fist, wiped his tearing eyes with a linen handkerchief, and then laughed some more. He didn't stop until he noticed that Lewis was laughing along with him, which made him instantly sober.

'I hate to be a wet blanket,' Lewis said, 'but you've just made an incredible ass of yourself.' He reached down to turn over his own hand, which only moments ago had been a six-high straight, a loser to Rex's full house. First card: a six. Second card: a six. Third card and fourth card: both sixes. The orb had worked its magic, and, having done so, lay inert and cold in Lewis's pocket like the lifeless crystal bauble it was supposed to be.

Millie's laughter cut through the air as Rex Caswell stared stupidly at Lewis's four sixes – laughter that was husky and full, not totally feminine. Lewis cringed. *Why laughs she thus, between Hell and Heaven?*

'You cheating cocksucker!' hissed Rex, his face hardening like stone. 'You set me up! You knew this would happen . . . !'

'Wrong. You set yourself up. You dealt the cards. You suggested the double-or-nothing side bet.'

'We've only played one hand!' bawled Rex. 'We can't quit after only one hand. This doesn't prove any-fucking-thing. It doesn't prove you're a better player than me.'

'You're probably right about that, Rex. It only proves I'm richer, at least for the time being. Well, I'm tired, folks. I think I'll get out of here while I'm ahead, go home, and make myself some hot chocolate.'

The others finally came out of their collective shock

and jumped up from the table, pushing back their chairs and crowding around Lewis. They slapped him on the back, cheered and whistled. They called for drinks from the Huntsman's, and Tommy Iadanza declared that drinks were on the house.

'I assume you brought enough money,' said Lewis to Rex, 'to cover your loss. In addition to what's on the table, you owe me four hundred and twenty thousand dollars. If you don't mind, I'll take it now.'

Rex trembled with rage, his nostrils flaring and his jaw muscles rippling. He clenched his hands into fists, then carefully unclenched them. Lewis wouldn't have been surprised if he pulled a gun out of his coat and started shooting. 'I only brought three hundred thousand. I can give you the rest tomorrow.'

'I don't understand. You're not telling me you played poker with money you don't have, are you? Is that what you're telling me, Rex?'

'I *said*, I can give you the rest tomorrow. What the hell do you want from me?'

'You've got an hour,' said Lewis, savoring this turn-about. 'Bring the money here and give it to Tommy. I'm making him my representative.'

'I can't get it in an hour, asshole! I have to drive clear across town, then back again. It's humanly impossible . . .'

'An hour,' Lewis repeated. 'Have the money here in an hour, or I'll come for you.' He backed his Action Power 9000 away from the table and drove it around to where Rex sat. He leaned forward in the chair so that he and Rex confronted each other chin to chin. 'Don't disappoint me, Rex. If you disappoint me, I'll do something horrible to you, I promise, something so bad I can't even say it. Do we understand each other?'

Rex nodded, his blue eyes misting with hatred, sweat streaming down his face as he trembled.

'I suggest you call one of your muscle-heads and get the ball rolling,' said Lewis. 'Time's a-wasting. You now have . . .' – he glanced at his watch – '. . . fifty-eight minutes and forty-three seconds.' He then pulled the orb from his pocket and spun his chair around to confront Millie Carter. He tossed the orb into the air twice, three times, then held it tightly in his fist. It no longer seemed warm, but he didn't study it closely, so he didn't know whether its innards still swirled with crimson life. He didn't want to know. He wanted only to get rid of the thing, for despite the victory it had just given him, he felt defiled, sullied. 'I'm glad you came tonight,' he said to Millie. 'I hope you found it entertaining.'

'I could say the same to you,' she answered, eyeing the orb. 'I'd say your good-luck charm performed admirably.'

Lewis tossed it to her, and she caught it smoothly, not taking her gaze from his. 'This isn't mine,' he said. 'Give it back to its rightful owner, whoever that is.'

'But *you're* its rightful owner.'

'No! Not now, not ever.' Lewis looked around for Josh, who leaned against the far wall of the room, looking peaked. 'Let's go, Josh. It's been a long night, and you've got school tomorrow.'

Tommy Iadanza stepped forward, dug into his pocket for his keys, and handed them to Josh. 'Take my car. When you get him home, stay with him. I'll call when this son of a bitch delivers the money.' He nodded to indicate Rex, upon which Rex got to his feet and strode from the room, slamming the door rudely behind him and leaving in his wake the scent of nervous sweat and expensive cologne.

Lake Havasu City Sid had gathered up the cash and had stuffed it into Lewis's attaché case, which he now handed over to Tommy. 'Better put this in your safe for tonight. I'll arrange for an armored car to pick it up and take it to the bank in the morning. Is that okay with you, Lewis?'

It was. Lewis thanked Sid, thanked them all for showing up tonight, for offering him their help and comfort when he needed it. He pledged that from now on he would try to be as good a friend to them as they'd been to him.

Millie rose from her chair, still holding the orb in her hand, and walked over to Lewis. She smiled with her snowy teeth, and a hush fell over the room. 'I'd be happy to buy you a drink, Lewis – my way of saying congratulations. You name the place.'

'I don't deserve congratulations. I'm not proud of what I did tonight.'

'Oh, but you should be. You've taken a major step toward a new life, toward freedom and power. You should revel in it.' She put the orb to her lips and kissed it.

Lewis figured that he was the only one in the room – with the possible exception of Josh – who knew that she wasn't talking about the wonderful things that his newly won money could bring. A voice came to him across decades past, across an ocean, the voice of Gamaliel Cartee, and it chilled him. *'You've seen what this little bauble can do,'* Gamaliel had said. *'The possibilities are limitless, and they're all yours. In the hands of someone like you –* well, *you can just imagine what you could accomplish. All you have to do is* accept.' Lewis had resisted the attempt at seduction then, and he meant to resist it now.

'I'm afraid I can never go anywhere with you,' he said. He motioned Josh forward and pushed hard on the joystick of his wheelchair, and the chair carried him quickly from the room.

CHAPTER FIFTEEN
As the Night Deepens

i

Upon arriving home with Josh, Lewis locked himself in the bathroom, stripped off his clothes and climbed into the hoist. He lingered under the jets of water for nearly forty-five minutes, making it as hot as he could stand it, acting out an urge to cleanse himself, he supposed. He lathered and washed vigorously, rinsed and lathered again, but he couldn't wash away the crawling sensation of having wallowed in a nest of maggots.

While riding home, it had occurred to him that he hadn't resisted the seduction of the orb after all, for he'd used it to win back his money from Rex Caswell, hadn't he? This wasn't the first time he'd used it in this way – he'd done the same thing at the Veterans Affairs Medical Center on Marquam Hill, teaching a lesson to a braggart who thought he was the Muhammad Ali of poker. The fact that Lewis had given the orb back to Millie Carter was no comfort, because a man can't undo something he's already done, or so his father had always taught him.

He pulled on a clean pair of underwear (the ones he'd worn earlier were semen-soaked), a freshly laundered sweatshirt and a pair of gym trunks, not caring whether

Josh saw his naked stumps, for Josh had seen them many times and didn't think them particularly gross. Then he maneuvered himself into his wheelchair and motored into the kitchen to fetch himself a beer.

When the telephone rang, Josh picked it up. Lewis surmised from the relieved expression on the boy's face that the caller was Tommy Iadanza, and that the news was good. Rex Caswell had delivered the money.

Lewis and Josh sat across from each other in the studio, neither saying much, though each sensed that the other had quite a lot to say. Lewis knew that the boy's head swarmed with questions about what had happened tonight, and although Lewis felt obliged to explain certain things to him, he doubted whether he could reveal all he knew or all he'd felt. A man simply can't share some things.

Finally Josh spoke up. 'It was scary, wasn't it?'

'Yeah. I guess it was.'

'But there's nothing to be scared of now, is there? Everything came out okay.'

'I don't know if that's true, mahatma. Who can say whether it's over yet?' Lewis couldn't bring himself to lie, not here beneath the portrait of Lyle Kindred, an honest man who'd tried so hard to raise an honest son.

'You don't think Rex will try to get back at you somehow, do you? The guy's got to be too smart to hurt you now, not after what happened in front of half a dozen witnesses. If he came after you, the cops would know exactly who to nail, right?'

'It's not Rex I'm worried about.'

Josh fell silent for a long time, his anemic-looking face showing whitely under his thatch of reddish hair. His hands worried the fabric of his bleached denims as the gears of his mind ground round and round. 'It's Millie, isn't it? You're afraid we haven't seen the last of her.'

'Josh, I don't know what to think.'

'I don't either. Some things just aren't supposed to happen, are they? Good-luck charms aren't supposed to work, and shadows aren't supposed to be alive. The problem is that we've both seen stuff like this, Lewis. If you're out of your gourd, then so am I.'

A nut of pain took root behind Lewis's eyes, and he massaged his eyeballs with his good hand for a long moment. Then he took a deep swig of his beer. 'What I did tonight wasn't right. I got dirty, contaminated. I would've gotten less dirty if I'd called up my aunt Juliet and told her that I'd accepted Jesus as my personal savior, just so I could get my hooks on her money.'

'You don't really think she would've given it to you, do you? Not two hundred thousand dollars . . .'

'You're right – she probably wouldn't have given it to me. She would've thought up some reason why God wants me to suffer for my own good. But that's not the point. By using the orb, I let somebody touch me, mahatma . . .' – if the kid only knew – 'somebody filthy. Now I've got the filth on me, and I don't know if I can get it off.'

'But you gave the orb back to her. And she accepted it, didn't she? Shouldn't that count for something?'

Lewis let his head fall against the back of his wheelchair and stared at the ceiling, wondering how he might explain how he and Millie had connected tonight, how their souls had locked together in sexual fury while their bodies sat quietly at a poker table. How could he ever describe the hellish exhilaration he'd felt in her embrace, when at the moment of orgasm he discovered that he had two strong legs? He'd been whole again, damn it! Somehow Millie and the orb had done that to him, *for* him.

No, he couldn't tell Josh such things.

Josh stood up and stretched wearily, though it wasn't really late. In his baggy jeans and flannel shirt, he looked gawky and painfully thin, almost frail. He moved to Lewis's side and put a hand on his shoulder. 'This could be the end of it, you know,' he said. 'For whatever it's worth, Lew, I think you did the right thing. But if it wasn't the right thing, then I'm as much to blame as you are, because I talked you into it.'

Lewis smiled at the absurdity of laying a portion of his guilt on a seventeen-year-old boy. 'Mahatma, you didn't talk me into anything. I made my own choices. I pay my own way.'

'I knew you'd say that, and I don't care, because we're in this thing together. Whatever happens, I'm going to be here for you. You won't be alone. Count on that.'

At this moment Lewis couldn't have loved this kid any more intensely if he'd been his own son.

ii

Sloan House was silent but for the faraway sounds of the city – an occasional siren, the passage of a jet across the sky, the bonging of a bell in a distant steeple. Now and again a breeze stirred the spirea outside Lewis's window, producing the tiny squeak of twigs against his windowpanes, or radiator pipes snapped and groaned as they expanded and contracted. Every hour or so, the motor in Lewis's refrigerator kicked on.

Lewis sat upright on his bed, propped with pillows, his eyes wide against the dark. At his side lay his old service .45, locked and loaded with the safety switch engaged.

No Bick was on the veranda outside his window, a skulking man-shape that several times had slipped past the bedroom to try windows elsewhere in the house, to test the outer doors front and back, to seek a trellis, perhaps, by which he could climb to windows not accessible from the fire escape on the west wall. Lewis had recognized the shape of the little man's head, a silhouette against the purple haze of the street lamps on Gander Circle. Here, in the nonrational compartment of his brain – the one in which Lewis had earlier tasted Millie Carter's sweet body – he'd even noted that No Bick had become slightly stooped and less angular as middle age came on, making the vision more real than a harmless hallucination, for surely a mere hallucination would've depicted No Bick as Lewis had last seen him – young and robust and quick, not a man wearing down with time. Too, Lewis sensed desperation in his movements, an urgency to find a way in and finish what he'd begun more than twenty years earlier: the devouring of Lewis Kindred.

The man-shape rose before the window once again, and Lewis's wide eyes caught the dull gleam of lamplight reflected from something metallic, the blade of a knife or the barrel of a gun. His hand found the .45, and he thumbed the safety off. As he raised the pistol, his head ached with questions that he feared he could never answer, except to say that Vietnam had found him at last and had come to claim him. In a sense, he'd never left Vietnam at all, for a part of him was still there – not only his severed legs, but also his soul, or at least the portion of it that he'd given to the Black Virgin, and a portion, too, that he'd left with a beautiful whore named Thuy Thanh. Vietnam had followed him home, haunted him in dreams, twisted his mind through the powers of the orb and sought his complicity in evils that he couldn't begin to understand. No Bick was part of it, certainly. And Millie, too. Lewis Kindred and Vietnam were one.

He leveled the pistol at the shape beyond the window, his heartbeat thumping in his ears and his gut twisting. Whatever might happen tonight, he meant to go down fighting, for this would prove that he still had some of his father in him. Lyle Kindred would never have surrendered to that which he knew was wrong, but would've fought the evil until his last calorie of strength was spent. Lewis meant to do the same.

The man-shape took something from a bag he carried, a tire iron or a crowbar – Lewis couldn't quite make it out – and reared back to shatter the window. Lewis decided to hold his fire and let him come crashing in, to wait until he'd drawn so close that Lewis couldn't possibly miss. Fractions of a second elapsed with glacial slowness, the man-shape's arm raised with the tire iron or crowbar in one fist, the knife or pistol in the other, while Lewis struggled to breathe.

What happened next convinced Lewis that he was dreaming. Red light spilled through the window from a source somewhere behind the man-shape, like a star cluster popping on the Fourth of July, except this source of light wasn't falling to earth. The man-shape whirled around, startled, and the orb came into view, orbiting his head slowly and flinging out its crimson strands of light. It halted near the windowpane, as if to bar No Bick's way, and Lewis's chest constricted when he saw that the man-shape was indeed No Bick, wearing not jungle fatigues but dark golfing slacks and a modern anorak. The little man's mouth was agape in terror, his eyes stupidly wide and unblinking. The orb hung in the air mere inches from his face, unsupported by any manmade device, bobbing slowly as if riding an invisible wave on an invisible sea.

'Don't worry, Lewis,' whispered someone close, and he felt her breath on his cheek. His eyes darted to his left, and he saw her crouch next to his bed, having slipped in soundlessly, like a wraith. 'He can't hurt you now. He'll never try to hurt you again, I promise.'

The red aura shifted and brightened as the orb moved toward No Bick's head, and the instant it touched his skin, it flashed white like a tiny nova, sending a shower of sparks onto the veranda. No Bick's hands flew to his forehead and his mouth yawned in silent agony. He flailed and gyrated like a man possessed, twitched as though electrocuted, and collapsed to his knees. Lewis scrambled toward the foot of his bed, half-sick with the horror of finding Millie Carter next to him in his room, but needing to see what was happening to No Bick. Seconds later the orb wheeled in the air and sailed out of view, leaving No Bick to flee into the night, lurching and bucking like a wounded animal.

Lewis turned back to Millie, who stood upright now, tall and beautiful in the quarter-light of the street lamps on Gander Circle. He opened his mouth to challenge her, but his voice was gone. He raised his pistol and pointed it at her.

She giggled insouciantly, tossing her rusty dreadlocks in an almost playful way. 'You're not really going to shoot me, are you, Lewis? After what we've been to each other?'

Her hand snaked around to her back, where it found the snaps that held her silk jumpsuit in place. The garment fell away, and she stepped out of it, wearing only a tiny bra of black lace and matching panties. Lewis forced a dry swallow, his eyes wandering over her full breasts, her belly, the curve of her hips. He tasted sweat dripping into his mouth from his upper lip, and his hand suddenly couldn't hold the pistol steady. Millie unsnapped the bra, and it too fell, freeing her proud breasts. Her hands slipped deep beneath the lace band of her panties, pushing them down, and then she was free of them, naked and long-limbed, grinning whitely in the night.

'What we had was wonderful, Lewis,' she whispered, her eyes gleaming blue and brown. 'But it wasn't enough. It wasn't enough for you, and it certainly wasn't enough for me.'

Lewis let the pistol drop to the mattress.

PART III

'Come away, O human child! . . .
For the world's more full of weeping than you can
understand.'

William Butler Yeats
'The Stolen Child'

CHAPTER SIXTEEN
The Weakening Eye of Day

i

As a red sun settles into the hills that lie between Cu Chi and the Cambodian border, your heart breaks – not because of the sunset, which is indeed beautiful, but because you hear the choking cries of your infant daughter in the dusky room behind you, and you become aware that she will never know the beauty of this land. Your wife quiets her with cooing words and gives her a breast, but what can you give her except uncertainty?

You turn back to the second-floor window where you've sat silent for the past hour, laboring to imprint the sights, sounds and smells of Cu Chi City onto as many brain cells as possible, for soon you'll have nothing left of this place but your memories, a thought that ignites sorrow in your throat. You've gazed into the torrent of human life in the streets below, listened to the chatter of voices and the whine of small motorcycles, breathed the smells of cooking and livestock and engine exhaust. Above the clutter of roofs and television antennas, palm trees tower black against the fiery horizon, and a rain-smelling breeze stirs the bougainvillea that grows along the shrapnel-pocked walls of this old apartment house.

The shadows of evening deepen, and night spills over the horizon to flood the warrens and alleyways of Cu Chi.

Despite your education in the West you are every bit an Asian, a Vietnamese. The bonds are strong that tie you to your home and the graves of your father and mother. To leave this place, knowing that you can never return, generates a grief that's almost blinding, not unlike the grief a man would suffer over the death of his wife or baby.

The Americans have been gone from Vietnam for nearly four months, longer than that from Cu Chi, and you've found the silence they left in their wake almost overpowering. The *whup-whup* of helicopters no longer overlays every aspect of life here, and the ground no longer shudders with the eruptions of mortars and artillery. The whores have all gone – to where nobody seems to know. The sprawling American base camp at the edge of town has become a slum peopled by civilian refugees who scattered before the onslaught of the North Vietnamese Army, only to have the invading tide overtake and surround them. The North Vietnamese have converted part of the base camp into a 're-education center,' where people either die or learn to talk like Marxists. They eat and sleep where GIs once ate and slept, but unlike GIs they don't scrub the floors, line the sidewalks with painted stones, or kill the rats.

You tell yourself to savor the quietude while you can, for the days ahead will be harrowing ones. Escaping Vietnam is no easy matter. Fleeing to the south coast is a dangerous undertaking with a woman and an infant in tow, more so when you lack authorization to travel or identity papers to show that you're a legitimate 'soldier of the emancipation' (which you're not). To be found out would mean, at the very least, being clapped into a re-education center for an indefinite period. If the authorities catch you and discover that you're a traitorous *Hoi Chanh* who helped the Americans kill soldiers of the National Liberation Front and the NVA, they will cut off your testicles and hang you in a tree to die.

But reaching the coast and boarding the boat are only the beginning. Next comes surviving the voyage itself. You've heard the stories about disease aboard boats which are crammed to the gunnels with humanity, so that sickness spreads like fire in dry bamboo, once it starts. You've heard about the raging storms, the Vietnamese patrol boats, the Malay and Thai pirates who sink freedom ships with all aboard after stealing everything of value. You've heard about refugees who have reached foreign shores only to end up in sweltering camps where they languish until the natives find the means to ship them somewhere else.

Is this what you will give your infant daughter – uncertainty, sickness, maybe even bloody death?

You've marveled at how many of your countrymen have undertaken the challenge of escape, driven by a thirst for something you've come to believe is illusory – freedom. You too must accept the challenge, but not because you harbor any romantic notions about life in the West. After all, you've been there. You've endured the racism, the disapproving sidelong glances on the street, the barely whispered references to a 'gook,' a 'chink,' or a 'slope.' You must go to the West not because you want to build a new life, though you suppose that this is what you'll do, but because you have something you've yearned for all your life – a truly just cause.

ii

Your parents were teachers and vociferous foes of socialism who fled Hanoi in the early fifties to settle here on the fringe of Saigon, bringing with them their children, your grandfather, an aunt and an uncle. Because your parents were teachers, you and your siblings learned early how to study, and your marks were especially good – so good, in fact, that you won scholarships to study in Paris and London. You've often smiled at the irony of having learned your social and economic radicalism in the great universities of the capitalist West, a radicalism that drove you to join the National Liberation Front when you returned home. Somehow you managed to keep from your parents the fact that you had become one of the enemy, whom they called Viet Cong, a vulgar term that until the war no one ever used in polite company. Like so many others you wanted only justice for your people, which you equated with throwing out the Westerners.

Years of soldiering, however, did not harden your political beliefs, despite the endless indoctrination sessions, the forced reading of Ho Chi Minh and Marx and Mao, the sloganeering and the drills. Speaking with escapees from Ho's north, you learned that life under socialism is a cruel joke, a mere permutation of the tyranny that the people of Indochina have endured in one form or another for a thousand years. You came to believe that the village society of Vietnam is ill-suited to any political ideology born in the West, and though you acquired no love for the corrupt puppet government in Saigon, which plundered the public wealth and transported it to private bank accounts in Switzerland, you failed to maintain any enthusiasm for the NLF. You saw that your own NLF comrades were not above committing atrocities that rivaled and surpassed anything dreamed up by the murderous president Duong Van Thieu or his lieutenant, Nguyen Cao Ky. War is war, you learned, and anyone who ascribes virtue to it is a liar.

After the disastrous Tet offensive of 1968, which the NLF cadre had staged as a 'final battle' to bring about the collapse of the Saigon government, you decided to switch sides. The Americans had largely destroyed the NLF as a viable combat organization, and the NVA had become the principal vehicle for the national cause espoused by Ho Chi Minh. The Americans, you figured, represented the best hope of ending the war soon, and that was all you wanted – to *end* it. To stop the butchery. To let the tears dry.

You marvel now over your own stupidity. You, with your Western academic degrees and your knowledge of the outside world, should have understood the geopolitical realities that barred the Americans from launching an all-out military effort to defeat the NVA. Having read Western magazines and newspapers, you should have grasped that the war had deeply divided the Americans themselves on moral grounds. But no, you *didn't* understand and you *didn't* grasp. You turned your back on your comrades to join the Saigon government's 'Open Arms' program, which welcomed disgruntled Viet Cong into the fold, placed them in an elite branch of the ARVN, and sent them back to the battlefield to kill their former comrades.

You became a Kit Carson, which meant that you were assigned to an American unit to serve as a special combat advisor, one who knew firsthand the tactics of the Viet Cong and the NVA. Your role was to prevent the GIs from blundering into booby traps, mines, and ambushes, but you never played that role very successfully. Seeing the destruction and hardship that the GIs inflicted on the civilian population – some of it unintentional, some of it not – you couldn't muster any sympathy for these brutes. You became silent as stone, responding to Americans' questions with 'No bick,' which was pidgin English for, 'I don't understand.' The Americans even took to calling you No Bick, ignoring your real name, not dreaming that you spoke better English than most of *them* did.

You drifted into a fog that enveloped your brain and your heart. You ate, slept and survived. Your life became an unfeeling dream in which little mattered, not causes, not justice, not even your own existence.

The fog lifted, however, on a scorching autumn afternoon in 1970, as you witnessed a spectacle of cruelty inflicted by a creature who wore the uniform of an American sergeant and cast a shadow that seemed like a living thing, a mixture of indigo and midnight. The sight awakened boyhood memories of old folks' tales of creatures whose shadows rustled and whose mismatched eyes could freeze the blood in your veins. Only one of the Americans had the nerve to oppose the creature. Only this young lieutenant had the guts to believe his own eyes and stop the torture of an innocent young girl. Not until later did you learn that the beast would wreak horrendous revenge upon that young lieutenant. And not until later did you understand your own obligation to thwart the creature's craving to create more of its kind. Having learned these things, your course became clear to you. At long last you had a cause you could believe in with all your heart.

iii

The old *ba* is a long-time friend of your family and the owner of a small apartment house near the center of Cu Chi where you have hidden for the past week. The war has taken her husband and two sons, leaving her only a daughter-in-law to help manage the business, but this is hardly a matter of concern to her anymore, for an official arrived yesterday from Saigon and informed her that the government plans to 'requisition' the building within the next ten days. She may or may not be allowed to live in one of the rooms after the takeover, depending on how much space the new government needs.

Long before the sun is up, she steals into your room and shakes you awake, then shakes your wife, too, gently, taking care not to stir the baby. The time has come, she whispers. You must start your journey before the guards at the checkpoints are awake. After a short, silent breakfast, you hug the old *ba* and touch her brown face, not knowing what you can possibly say to her. She squeezes your hand. She presents your wife with a bundle of food that she has prepared for your journey, portions of boiled rice tied into small cotton sacks, a bunch of bananas, three tins of Norwegian sardines bought on the black market. Your wife shoulders the bundle of food, you shoulder your sleeping daughter, and together you slip out through the alley, while the old *ba* weeps in the doorway of the kitchen and waves a silent farewell. Darkness closes around you. Far away a rooster crows. A dog barks.

The journey has begun.

You will walk most of the way to the coast, keeping away from the main roads as much as possible, skirting the checkpoints by slogging through rice paddies and orchards. You will go south past the towns of My Tho and Ben Tre, giving a wide berth to the major city of Can Tho, heading into the flat delta region that in a good year can grow enough rice to feed all of Indochina. You will cross five separate branches of the mighty Mekong River. You will beg rides in carts and cyclos whenever you think it safe to do so. You can't know this now, but you will ride many miles in a salvaged American army truck driven by an NVA soldier who doesn't care about your politics, who you are, or where you're going – only that you and your family get to safety. The soldiers at the checkpoints will poke their faces into the rear of the truck, and they will see you, of course, but they will wave you through, for they are tired of war and suffering and terror. Hardly anyone, it seems, wants to make trouble.

Again and again on your journey, whether trudging along a dusty road or jouncing along in the rear of a cyclo, you relive moments that time can never soften, much less erase. You see yourself on a misty afternoon more than five years ago, standing outside a makeshift hooch in the Ho Bo Woods while a firefight rages around you. You're talking to a man you know is dead, for he has a bullet hole in his face, and his flesh is the flat, washed-out gray that comes with death. He retrieves a pearl-handled pistol from the bushes, flips it to you, and tells you to give it back to the man who shot him – Lieutenant Lewis Kindred. 'Tell him who brought it to you,' he commands in perfect Vietnamese. 'Tell him our dealings are far from ended. We have much to do together, he and I – much to do!' Then he bolts away, moving over the ground like no mortal man can move, whether dead or alive.

You see yourself hiding out in the Ho Bos for the next

few days, scuttling along the ground like a frightened animal, living in holes and uprooted tree trunks, avoiding both the Americans and the NVA. Eventually hunger drives you back to Cu Chi City. Within a few more days you enter the base camp and go to the Triple Deuce battalion area, where you report in. You tell the command sergeant major that you became separated from the scout platoon during the battle, and only with great difficulty have made your way back. The command sergeant major believes you, and Triple Deuce takes you off its missing-in-action list.

In your mind, you see yourself sneaking into the Twelfth Evac that night, finding Lewis Kindred on a white-sheeted bed, his face eerily lit by moonlight streaming through a window. Hideously wounded, delirious with pain and drugs, he talks to you, thinking you're his father who you surmise has died some time ago. Lewis describes how and why he needed to kill a man named Gamaliel Cartee, and he begs your fatherly understanding, your forgiveness. You try to assure him, but he doesn't hear your voice, only the voice of his long-dead father who cannot forgive him for reasons that you can't learn. You comprehend now that what the blue-brown-eyed man told you days earlier in the Ho Bos was true – Lewis Kindred had indeed shot him, and your heart goes out to Lewis, because like him you believe strongly that Gamaliel desperately needs killing, that creatures like him cannot be allowed to live. Years will pass, though, before you discover in your heart what you must do. The message won't crystallize in your brain until you go to the jungle north of Tay Ninh, to a tumble-down colonial villa where an aged renegade priest lives. But this is another scene.

iv

Forty miles south of the Mekong Delta lies the town of
Bac Lieu, surrounded by farming hamlets and checker-
squared rice paddies of varying shades of green. The
town itself is a hodgepodge of architecture strewn with
tangles of concertina wire and crumbling sandbag bunkers that no one has yet seen fit to cart away. A few miles
further east lies the South China Sea, a flat expanse of
hazy blue under a blast-furnace sky, bordered by a beach
dotted here and there with disused pagodas.

Along this coast countless thousands of Vietnamese
have embarked upon the unknown, chugging away from
the tan beaches in leaky tugs and river barges to rendezvous on the high sea with cargo ships or fishing trawlers
or converted oil tankers, hoping to reach a world they
perceive to be more sane and more forgiving than the one
now ruled by Hanoi. You and your family seek to join
their number.

You meet your contact man in the village of Vinh Loi
on the outskirts of Bac Lieu, and he confirms that the
escape network is ready for you. You pay him virtually all
the money you have left, and he counts it before folding it
away. But then you give him one thing more – the
pearl-handled K-54 pistol that you've kept these past five
years, together with a letter that contains the name and
address of your brother, who months ago escaped to
Thailand. Your contact man swears that he will send the
weapon to your brother in accordance with your wishes.
Your brother will later send it to you in America, if
you're lucky enough to get that far, for you wouldn't be
able to bring a firearm through customs in any foreign
country, least of all the United States.

You hope intensely that the contact man is honest, that

he won't simply keep the pistol for himself or sell it and pocket the money. But his eyes are clear and steady, which you find reassuring. The weapon is important to you not because you may actually need it to kill Lewis Kindred (America is full of guns that any fool can buy on almost any street corner), but because it's a hard, cold artifact of the private war you have joined. Gamaliel Cartee gave it to you with his own hand, a dead hand. It had belonged to Lewis himself. It's a piece of material evidence that helps you convince yourself that you aren't insane, whenever doubts arise, which is often.

'And what will you do in America?' asks the contact man with a hint of reproach in his voice. 'Are you skilled? Do you speak English? I hope you aren't thinking of opening a restaurant, because I'm told that America already has three times as many Vietnamese restaurants as it needs.'

You force a smile. 'I'm a scholar, an economist. Perhaps I'll teach.' Actually, you'll take whatever work you can find in Portland, Oregon, for this is where you must go, the city in which Lewis Kindred lives. You learned this at the Twelfth Evac, under the pretext of wanting to correspond with your former platoon leader after he'd gone home.

The contact man laughs. 'Do you really think that the Americans would let a Vietnamese teach in one of their schools? I hope for your sake they will, but I have trouble imagining it.'

'Not all Americans are GIs. There are many who admire learning, and their schools have teachers of all races. Perhaps I will be one of them.'

Perhaps. A frightening word. The fact is, you have no idea what lies ahead.

CHAPTER SEVENTEEN
Curtains of Rain

i

The weather on Wednesday morning, September 23, was in keeping with Rex Caswell's mood – foul. Gray curtains of rain swept across the wide Willamette, driven by gusts that roused a chop on the river and set the floating house to jiggling. A solitary seagull stood on the railing of the deck, bedraggled and miserable-looking in the downpour, taking solitary refuge in the lee of the house.

Having lain awake since well before dawn, Rex got up and put in a half-hearted workout in his weight room, then soaked himself in the hot tub while rain thrummed against the skylight above him. He went downstairs shortly after eight-thirty, drawn by the aroma of coffee.

Twyla sat across the table from him as he ate his breakfast, saying nothing. Her eyes said plenty, though, and Rex had caught their meaning a dozen times since the debacle at the Hotel Fanshawe. *Didn't I tell you what would happen?* her eyes taunted as she munched a slice of toast. *Didn't I warn you that Lewis was setting you up?*

Suddenly he'd had enough. He picked up his bowl and slammed it full-force into her face, hard enough to drive her back against the sliding glass door that gave onto a deck. Cream of Wheat flew in all directions, spattering the walls, the ceiling, and the expensive sideboard that Twyla had bought several years ago from an antiques shyster in Sellwood. The blow split her lower lip, and a streak of blood slid down her chin.

'Jesus *Christ*!' she shrieked, when her brain finally comprehended what had happened to her. 'What in the hell is *wrong* with you?' She wiped gouts of hot cereal from her eyes and nostrils with trembling fingers, then pressed a napkin against her bleeding lip. 'Are you fucking insane? You ought to be locked up, you son of a bitch!'

Rex said nothing for a long moment, but only watched as she furiously daubed milk and cereal and blood from her face. A sickle of blond hair hung loosely over Rex's eye, giving him a slightly demented look, but he otherwise appeared to be in control of himself. He stood up suddenly from the table, causing Twyla to cower in a corner of the dining room. 'Sweetheart, I'll thank you not to insult me with your eyes in the future, okay? Next time it won't be a bowl of cereal. It'll be a brick.' He turned to leave.

'Lewis Kindred did this to you, that fucking bastard!' Twyla shouted, spitting blood. 'He's turned you into a fucking maniac! You can't sleep, you can't hold a decent conversation, you can't even behave like a civilized human being. I hate him! I *hate* him!' A sob shook her, and she steadied herself against the dining-room table.

'So you hate him, do you?' said Rex, turning to face her again. He folded his arms. 'That's very interesting. Do you hate him because of what he did to me, or because of what he did to you?'

Twyla fled into the kitchen. She tore paper towels from

a roll on the wall and pressed them to her face and front, still sobbing. 'I hate him because of what he did to you,' she answered finally, her words muffled in paper.

Rex stepped into the kitchen behind her. 'I don't believe you. I think you hate him because he had the poor taste to survive after you dumped him, way back there in Vietnam. Not only that, he survived getting his damn legs blown off, didn't he? Then he had the gall to come home where you might actually see what he'd become . . .'

'That's bullshit, Rex!'

'Sweetheart, I think not. Lewis Kindred survived everything you and the war could throw at him. And now he's a living, breathing reminder of the fact that you're a self-centered airhead who can't be trusted out of sight.'

'Doesn't it mean anything to you that I've stayed with you all these years? Do you think it's been easy for me?'

'Now that you mention it, yes, I think it *has* been easy for you. I've given you all the coke you can push into your face, all the booze you can drink. I've given you clothes, cars and trips to Provence, for Christ's sake. I've even put up with your lousy poetry-writing for more than twenty years.'

Twyla whirled toward him, her hair stringy with cooked cereal and milk. Her right eye was puffy, already beginning to blacken where the rim of the cereal bowl had bruised it. 'You don't have any right to talk to me this way! I know about all your women on the side, Rex, and I know how you keep yourself entertained on your fucking business trips, so don't talk to me about being untrue and untrustworthy. As for my poetry, it's something I *care* about, which you couldn't possibly understand, because you don't care about anything except selling coke and playing poker. You're a criminal, a common dope-pusher. The only thing you do well is wreck people's lives.'

Rex grinned dangerously. 'I don't force people to do drugs. If my clients don't get their snorts from me, they'll get them from someone else – maybe from someone not as understanding when they get behind in their payments.'

'Yeah, you're a real prince.'

'I suppose you think it doesn't take talent to be a good drug dealer – is that what you think, you graceless cow? You think it doesn't take brains? Well, here's a flash for you – the stupid ones end up in the joint, or they end up dead. I've been in this game for more than two decades, and in case you haven't noticed, I haven't spent so much as one night in jail. I haven't even gotten a parking ticket, for Christ's sake. And I don't recall that you've ever turned your nose up at the money I've given you, tainted as it was with human misery.' He turned on his heel and strode to the front closet, from which he hauled an anorak.

'You hate him, too, don't you, Rex?' Twyla called after him. 'You hate him as much as I do.'

'What if I do? I have my reasons. Lewis Kindred is an arrogant, condescending asshole. He's like you – he can insult you with his fucking eyes. On top of that, he cheated me out of half a million dollars.'

'What do you mean, *cheated*? He beat you fair and square, because that's what he does, Rex – he wins at poker. You ought to know that after all these years.'

'You can think whatever you want, but I'm telling you he cheated. He had some kind of good-luck charm, a ball of red glass that looked – well, never mind that. After the game he tossed it to—' Rex held up. No need to mention

Millie Carter, actually. 'Forget it. The bottom line is he couldn't beat me without help. You can take it from me, sweetheart – your old boyfriend is a cheat.'

'So why don't you get rid of him? You have ways of getting rid of people, don't you?' She hurried into the living room and caught him by the arm. 'I mean it, Rex. The guy is ruining our lives. Look at what's happening to us . . .' Rex studied her face and cringed. She looked like something out of a bad movie. She was fat, hung-over, coked out. Could she really believe that the two of them had a future together?

'Sweetheart, it's happening to *you*, not me. I'm not the one who's addicted to cocaine and booze. I'm not the one who's let my body go to hell. I'm the same guy I've always been.'

'Not true, babe. Lewis has stolen something from you, and I'm not talking about money. He's been stealing it for years, a little at a time. It's your self-respect. I've watched you become obsessed with beating him at poker until you've excluded everything else from your life. Even after you beat him once, you couldn't give up – you let him goad you into a rematch. Now he's got your money . . .'

'It's half a million bucks, Twyla. I don't like taking a hit that big, but it's not a catastrophe for me, okay? I can afford it.'

'That's not the point. Lewis Kindred is destroying you – destroying *us*. There's only one way you can put a stop to it.'

'Have him killed, you mean?'

'Sure, why not? You know people who could do the job. What about Mase and Spit? Those two reprobates would do anything you told them.' She sidled up close to him. Angry tears had left streaks of mascara on either side of her nose. 'You need to be free of him, Rex. You need to get that twisted, ugly cripple out of our lives once and for all. Kill him, for God's sake, so we can get our lives back.'

Rex pulled her hand off his arm. 'I'll deal with Lewis in my own way. Now if you'll excuse me . . .' He checked himself in the mirror inside the closet door, as he habitually did, before leaving the house.

ii

Rex punched the buttons on his cellular phone as he drove away from the Sellwood Bay Club. As a telephone rang in Mason Benoit's townhouse in northwest Portland, he thought about what Twyla had said only moments ago. The bitch was obviously beyond hope if she thought that killing Lewis Kindred would solve their domestic problems. That was cocaine talking, Rex knew. Prolonged use had warped her perceptions. Lewis Kindred had nothing whatever to do with how Rex felt about Twyla, but Twyla couldn't face the ugly truth. Rex knew now that he couldn't stand living with her much longer, and the only question that remained was how to get rid of her gracefully.

She was right on one count, however, he admitted grudgingly to himself. He did indeed hate Lewis Kindred enough to kill him. But this wasn't what he planned to do. Killing was too good for Lewis.

A woman answered the phone on the other end, her voice dreamy with drugs or booze or both. One of Mase's little sluts, probably. 'Put Mase on,' Rex ordered, and Mase came on the line, sounding full of piss and vinegar, a real top-of-the-morning guy.

338

'I'm on the C-phone, so watch your mouth,' said Rex as he turned north on Macadam Boulevard, heading toward the center of town. Gauzy clouds hid the summits of Portland's tallest business towers and apartment buildings. 'I want you and Spit to meet me at the Metro on Broadway as soon as you can get there. I've got a little chore for you guys. Whether or not you fuck it up will determine whether you keep your jobs. And no heavy metal, okay?'

Benoit acknowledged the order. Heavy metal was code for guns.

iii

Metro on Broadway was a few steps below street level, directly across the street from the Portland Hilton in the heart of downtown. It consisted of a large common area crammed with tables, ringed by eight or ten walk-up kitchens that served everything from sushi to gourmet pizza. The crowd at midmorning was light and Rex had no trouble finding a table in an isolated corner.

Mason Benoit and Spit Pittman arrived together. Mason still sported a bandaged wrist, but Spit had dispensed with his head bandages, leaving visible sutures and hideously colored bruises. They spotted Rex immediately and joined him at his table.

Rex got down to business. He wanted Benoit and Pittman to do two simple things, one of which was find an elegant racially mixed woman named Millie Carter, whom he described in great detail. Then, if possible, he wanted them to relieve her of a certain object, a globe of red crystal about the size of a billiard ball.

'This Millie bitch is the one who wanted to be your walking-talking, good-luck charm, am I right?' asked

Benoit, running the fingers of his uninjured hand over the bandage on his other.

'That's right,' Rex confirmed. 'She's says she's new in town, which may be true, because I can't find her name in any of the local phone books.'

'And may I ask what's the significance of this ball of red crystal?'

Rex started to answer the question, but held back. How would it sound, he wondered, confessing to his underlings that he actually believed in good-luck charms? Truthfully, he wouldn't have believed in such a thing himself, if he hadn't seen what he'd seen two nights ago at the Fanshawe. After the game, after humiliating him with his demand for payment within an hour, Lewis Kindred had pulled the mysterious red ball out of his pocket, tossed it several times into the air, and flipped it to Millie. *'I'd say your good-luck charm performed admirably,'* she'd replied, gazing at Lewis with her witchy eyes. Lewis had then said something, but Rex couldn't remember what it was and didn't care. What was clear to him was that Lewis had used a charm to win the game, which was the same as cheating. It was also clear that Millie had somehow been involved. Rex could try to explain all this to Benoit and Spit, but he doubted that he could make them understand any of it. You had to be there, he told himself, to appreciate the red ball. You had to feel the electrical tingle in the air and the resonance that came from Millie or the object itself. Rex had since decided that he wanted the red ball for himself, and Millie too, if he could get her. It only seemed fair that he should have them, after what he'd suffered.

'Just get the damn crystal for me,' he replied. 'If Millie won't give it to you, I'll approach her myself, assuming you can locate her for me. One way or another I want to get my hands on the thing, the sooner the better.'

'You've got it bad for this bitch, don't you, Rex?' Mase chuckled, grinning a shiny grin. 'Which do you want worse, the bitch or the crystal ball?'

Rex didn't dignify the question with a response.

CHAPTER EIGHTEEN
Like Panicky Bats

i

After the poker rematch, Josh Nickerson buried himself in schoolwork and extracurricular activities. He spent at least four hours every week night doing homework. He put in extra hours at the high-school newspaper. He filled out his college application forms and gave his room a thorough cleaning, much to his mother's happy surprise. On Saturday evening he took Laurel to a movie and afterward treated her to a meal. On Sunday he acquiesced to spending the afternoon with his father and sister at the Oregon Museum of Science and Industry on the east shore of the Willamette, the first such 'custody visit' he'd allowed in several years.

On Thursday morning, October 1, a full ten days after the rematch, he woke up feeling guilty for not having contacted either Lewis Kindred or Nicole Tran in all that time. He scolded himself for not keeping the promise he'd made to Lewis – *'Whatever happens, I'm going to be here for you . . .'* What if Lewis had needed someone to talk to in the wake of all the craziness that had befallen him, someone to help him get his head back together?

Josh remembered too that Nicole's father had begun behaving strangely again. Josh felt as if he'd neglected Nicole as well as Lewis in his energetic effort to crowd out the memories of Millie Carter, her orb of red crystal, and all the bizarre happenings leading up to the night of the rematch. Equally troubling was the fact that neither Lewis nor Nicole had contacted *him*.

He vowed to set things right, starting right now.

'Joshua, come back here!' his mother called from the kitchen as he headed out the door of the apartment. 'You know the rule in this house – no one leaves without eating breakfast.'

'I'll eat an extra-big lunch, Mom, I promise. Right now I'm late for something important.'

'What about *me*?' his sister piped up, poking her head through the door of her room into the hallway. 'I need a ride, y' know. What am I supposed to do – hitchhike to school?'

'Kendra, chill. I'm just going down to see Lewis for a few minutes, that's all. I'll leave for school at the regular time. If you're in the car, you can have a ride.'

'Oh, you're *soooo* good to me,' Kendra retorted, tossing her pretty head.

Josh clomped down the rear stairs of Sloan House and entered the dusky passage to Lewis Kindred's apartment. A beam of cold sunlight slanted through the cut-glass door in the foyer but the passage to Lewis's apartment seemed dark and chill.

Accustomed as he was to barging right in, Josh tried the doorknob and found it locked, then remembered that Lewis had gotten jumpy and had started locking the door after Rex Caswell's no-necks had attacked him. Lewis had given him a key, but Josh had left it in his room this morning. When he raised a fist to knock, someone jerked the door open so quickly that air rushed past him into the opening, fanning the hair on his head.

He felt the blood drain from his face when Millie Carter stepped around the edge of the door, grinning as if she'd known that he was about to knock. She looked as if she'd taken huge pleasure in scaring the bejesus out of him. A long robe of hunter green velvet surrounded her, sweeping to the floor in elegant folds, but one bare thigh poked through the folds, suggesting that she was naked underneath. Though the light was thin, indicating perhaps that the shades were drawn in Lewis's apartment, Millie's blue eye caught the color of the robe and shone almost green, while her brown eye gleamed with a reddish caste. Her teeth were as white as ever.

'Josh, it's so nice to see you,' she said in her silken voice, her vowels elongating in the Southern way. 'Lewis and I were just talking about you.'

'I – uh – is Lewis here?'

'Yes, of course, but I'm afraid he's indisposed at the moment. Why don't you come back this afternoon after school? You'll be going to school today, won't you?'

Josh's stomach felt as if it might try to crawl up through his throat. *Indisposed?* What the hell was that supposed to mean? Suddenly all the fears and anxieties he'd tried so hard to suppress for the last ten days broke out of their cages and fluttered through his mind like panicky bats. 'Uh – yeah. Right.' He gulped audibly. 'I'll come back later.' He pivoted away and plunged toward the cold sunlight in the foyer of Sloan House, needing that sunlight as much as he'd ever needed anything in his life.

ii

'I talked to Greg on the phone last night,' said Kendra as Josh swung the old Escort out of the parking lot of Gavin Dell School. Kendra called their father by his first name as she called their mother by hers, which Josh knew made her feel *very* grown up. 'He thought it was really cool that you spent the day with us last Sunday. I told him I thought you had a good time at the museum.'

Josh joined the queue of cars waiting to turn onto Barnes Road, which would take them on a circuitous route through wooded hills back to downtown Portland. The day had become gloomy. 'I'm glad he thought it was cool. I just hope he doesn't expect these little outings to become a habit.'

'Isn't it about time you stopped hating him so much? I mean, we're not little kids anymore, and he *is* our dad. And he *is* paying our way through the most expensive private school in the state. It seems to me that it wouldn't kill you to show a little gratitude.'

Josh didn't want to talk about his hated insurance-executive father, and he didn't want to ignite Kendra's red-haired temper by confessing that he'd accompanied her and Greg to the museum for no other reason than to prevent himself from dwelling too much on certain things. Besides, he was intensely worried about Lewis at the moment. He'd been able to think of little else but Lewis and Millie Carter all day, his brain furiously hatching theories that would explain why Millie had been in Lewis's apartment this morning, undressed and looking oh-so-domestic. None of the theories was comforting. 'Look, can we talk about this later?' he pleaded. 'I've got a lot on my mind right now.'

His sister gave him a reproachful glance with her huge

green eyes and made a production of digging through her backpack for a book to read on the way home. Upon arriving at Sloan House, Josh pulled into the front drive and let her out at the main entrance. Then he drove down the block to Nicole Tran's house.

Nicole answered the bell after what seemed a long time, and Josh's heart sped up when he saw her. She was lithe in white denims and a bulky red sweater, her radiant black hair resting in graceful swoops on her shoulders. Her eyes were deep and brown, and though she smiled when she saw him, he could read hurt and tension in her face. Things weren't good in the Tran household, he knew instantly.

'God, Nickster, I'm glad you're here,' she said, pulling the door wide. 'You're probably pissed I haven't called you, huh? It's my dad. He came home in the wee hours a couple of weeks ago, so sick he could hardly stand up. My mom and I managed to get him upstairs to bed, but he's been flat on his back ever since.'

'Are you *serious*?' breathed Josh, following her into the paneled hallway that led to the kitchen. 'He's been in bed for two weeks?'

'Maybe not that long – I don't know, I've lost all track of time.' Seeing the exhaustion in her face made Josh want to take her in his arms and hold her. 'Up until a few days ago, he'd hardly been able to keep anything down. Even now he can't handle anything stronger than apple juice and a little fruit.'

'What does the doctor say?'

'He won't let us call a doctor, not even the Chinese acupuncturist he normally goes to over in Vancouver. My mother won't leave his side, so I've been cooking their meals and taking them upstairs on a tray. My schoolwork's in the toilet, as you can probably imagine.'

'Where's your mother now?'

'Up there with him – where else?'

'Who's running the janitorial company?'

'The foremen, I guess. They've been calling at least six times a day, needing decisions on one thing or another, but Dad won't take their calls. I don't know how much longer things can go on like this.'

'Nicki, you've *got* to call a doctor. Anyone who's so sick he can't get out of bed for that long needs professional help. Apple juice and fruit aren't going to do the job, okay?'

'I can't disobey him. He's my father.'

'But the guy can't be in his right mind. He needs someone to do his thinking for him. Otherwise he could die, Nicki. You know that, don't you?'

'Yes, I know that.' She twisted away from him and sat down on a tall stool next to an island counter in the kitchen directly beneath an overhead rack of dully gleaming pots and pans. Gray daylight filtered through a tall window, and the only color in the room seemed to be the red of her sweater and the pink of her cheeks. 'Nickster, I need to say something.'

'Say it. I'll shut up and listen.'

'Except for my face, I may not seem much like a Vietnamese. I don't have an accent, and I don't observe Buddhist holidays. I dress like every other middle-class teenage girl in town, and I love pizza and the Trail Blazers. But the fact is, I've got a lot of Vietnamese in me, having grown up with a mother like mine. For that matter, my dad is very traditional in some ways. I'm *their* kid. What I'm trying to say is, I can't just do what my father has forbidden, not even when I know I should. I'm not like a lot of Asian kids who think it's cool to trash everything their parents stand for. If my dad tells me not to call a doctor, I can't call one. Can you understand that?'

Josh nodded. She'd only confirmed something he'd known for years. Studying the tiled countertop, he asked whether she had any idea what had made her father sick. Knowing this, he offered, might enable her to doctor him herself, within certain bounds.

'There *is* something. He has a weird burn right in the middle of his forehead. It eventually scabbed over, and it looks almost healed now. He had it when he stumbled in that night.'

'A burn? What kind of burn?'

'I don't know – how many kinds of burns can there be? I asked him how he'd gotten it but he won't tell me.' She reached out and caught Josh's hand. 'Nickster, he seems scared of something. I don't know what it is, because he won't talk about it. Now I'm scared, too.' She squeezed, and he detected the shudder that ran through her. 'I'm scared of his being scared, can you believe that? It sounds perfectly crazy, doesn't it?'

'No crazier than everything else that's been happening to us for the last month or so.'

Nicole let go of his hand and slid off the stool. 'Come on. There's something I want to show you.' She led him out of the kitchen and up the rear stairs of the house. When they alighted on the second-floor landing, she pressed her finger to his lips, telling him to be quiet, then signaled him to follow. They proceeded a short distance down the hallway to a heavy door of dark-stained oak, which Nicole opened with a key that she took from a pocket in her white denims. They slipped inside, and she eased the door closed and locked it behind them.

The grayness of the afternoon diffused through a pair of shuttered windows at the far end of the room, providing barely enough light for Josh to make out trappings and furnishings. An ornate wooden desk presided at the center of the room, and behind it sat a rattan chair with a flared back that reminded him of a peacock's tail. Bookshelves lined the walls, crammed with volumes that appeared both old and new, hardbound and paperback, thick and thin. At one end was an alcove with a low altar, upon which sat a jade-colored Buddha, rotund and smiling, with joss sticks clustered around it. Flanking the Buddha were lower altars, on which stood framed photographs of people who Josh supposed were ancestors of the Trans. Here and there lay groupings of small tables and cabinets that held clutters of carved Asian gods, ceremonial fans and candle holders, brightly colored lamps and lanterns. Among them were statues of Jesus and the Virgin, both of which seemed wildly out of place amid the swarm of Oriental paraphernalia.

'What is this place – some kind of Asian cultural exhibit?' Josh whispered.

'It's my dad's study. What I want to show you is over here.' Nicole tugged him toward a low table, where sat a stoutly woven wicker basket that was cubical in shape. It looked handmade. 'You should be here when he cranks up the traditional Vietnamese music on the stereo,' she whispered, 'and then you'd get the full effect. You'd swear you were in an office on Tu Do Street in Saigon.'

'I've never been on Tu Do Street in Saigon, so how would I know?'

'Use your imagination, like I do.' She opened the basket and carefully took out what appeared to be a small lacquered box with a hinged lid. 'I'm not sure what this is – maybe a jewelry box or something. My mother has one similar to it, but she keeps old snapshots of her family in it. I think they're fairly common in Asia.' A Vietnamese artist had painted meticulous miniature portraits of notable personages on the lid, some of whom Josh recognized. Among them were Jesus, Shakespeare and Sun Yat Sen. Josh was certain that another face belonged to Victor Hugo, of all people, right next to an Oriental gentleman that he was willing to bet was either Lao-tzu or Confucius. On the sides of the box were mystical scenes in which monkeys featured prominently.

'Unusual mix of people,' Josh observed, studying the portraits. 'I didn't know that the Vietnamese were into Shakespeare and Hugo.'

'The paintings probably have some religious significance – Cao Dai, I think. All these people – Christ, Shakespeare, Sun Yat Sen and all the rest – are Cao Dai gods. The priests contact them in seances and ask for their wisdom about how to live. My mother once explained it all to me – she had an uncle who became a Cao Dai priest. Big scandal in a Buddhist family.' She opened the lid, and what was inside caused Josh to flinch. It was a small marble of bright red glass. This object was totally unlike Millie Carter's much larger orb, however: It appeared to be completely lifeless and inert. It cast no filaments of light around the room and had no living protoplasm swirling inside. 'Remember when I told you about the sound I've sometimes heard at night after Dad comes home and locks himself in here – the thumping sound?'

Josh nodded. He recalled her saying that the thumping was very rapid and prolonged, almost machine-like.

Nicole closed the lid of the box and shook it back and forth several times so that the marble thrummed against the lacquered sides of the box. 'That's the sound,' she said, her eyes wide in the half-light, 'except when I've heard it before, it's been much louder and faster.'

Josh wrinkled his brow, thinking. He took the box from her and shook it himself several times, taking care not to do it too loudly. 'You're absolutely sure about this?'

'I've never been more sure of anything in my life. The lacquer gives it a tone that's very distinctive, and I'd know it anywhere. I just can't figure out how he makes it happen.'

'Didn't you say that he moans or chants when the sound starts?'

'Right, but it's always been in Vietnamese, so I can't understand what he's saying. Sometimes it goes beyond moaning, Nickster. Sometimes he sounds terrified, and hearing him makes the hair stand up on my neck.'

When Josh peeked into the wicker basket from which Nicole had taken the lacquered box, the hair stood up on *his* neck. Resting on the bottom in wads of insulating tissue was a stumpy semiautomatic pistol, its barrel coldly dark, its grips made of pearl-colored plastic. He reached in and forced his hand to close around it, brought it out – an ugly thing that looked bluntly lethal. He held it close to his eyes to examine it carefully, squinting. 'Chinese characters etched on the barrel,' he said, turning it over carefully. The thing was heavy and slightly clumsy in his hand. 'Christ, it's loaded, Nicki.'

Lewis Kindred had taught him how to handle the old service .45 that he kept in the drawer next to his bed, and this pistol was of similar design. Josh found the tiny button that discharged the ammo clip from the handle, and the clip dropped into the tissue in the bottom of the wicker box with a soft thud. He then pulled the slide back, ejecting a bright brass cartridge from the chamber. The thing skittered across the Oriental carpet, and the slide stayed back, locked in the open position, meaning that the gun was now harmless. Josh spotted Western printing near the trigger guard, and he was just able to make out a serial number followed by 'K-54.'

'I have no idea why he keeps that thing in here,' breathed Nicole. 'I'm glad I've never touched it – I didn't realize it was loaded. It gives me the god-damned creeps. Put it away, okay?'

Josh scarcely heard her, so deep in thought was he. Hadn't Lewis shot Gamaliel with a Chinese-made K-54 pistol – one that had pearl grips? This couldn't be the same weapon, could it? Why *should* it be, for the love of God?

'Nicki, does your dad know you've been in here?'

'Are you kidding? I sneaked his keys out of his pants pockets after Mom and I put him to bed. I didn't work up the guts to actually let myself in here until a few days ago, and then I made sure that both he and Mom were asleep before I did it. I hope to hell they're asleep now.'

'What did you do – just start rummaging through all this stuff?'

'More or less. I was hoping to find something that might shed some light on what has happened to Dad, some clue about where he's been going at night, or who he's been seeing. I don't know exactly what I was after. This study has been a part of my dad's life that's a mystery to me, and I needed to come in here and experience it. Once I got in, I went through his desk, then moved on to the file cabinets. Then I started on the trunks, and I finally got to this old basket.'

'Find anything else of interest?'

'Not really. A lot of Vietnamese stuff – things from temples and pagodas, even rubbings from grave markers. The desk is full of what you'd expect – pens and pencils and stationery. It's strange, though, that Dad would collect so much religious junk, because he's never seemed like a religious man.'

Josh picked up the cartridge from the floor, pressed it into the clip, and pushed the clip back into the handle of the pistol. Then he released the slide, and it sprang forward, loading a round into the chamber. 'It's loaded now, Nicki, like it was when I took it out of the basket. Remember that if you ever take it out again. I'm going to put it back where it was, okay? – then you put the box and the marble back the way they were. Let's do it and get the hell out of here.'

iii

They sat for a long while in a double chair-swing in the rear porch of the old Queen Anne house, swinging lazily back and forth, saying little and listening to a breeze whisper through the yellowing elms and maples that shaded the Trans' backyard. Josh remembered that when he and Nicole were in the third grade, they'd built a tree house in the ancient maple at the rear of the Trans' property. For several years the tree house had functioned as their refuge from the hassles of the outside world, a place where they could talk and read and bitch privately about things in general.

Josh rose from the chair-swing and ambled down the steps of the porch, following a curved stone path leading toward the old maple, which reared yellow and brown against a bleak sky. Staring into the mass of paling leaves, he wished that he and Nicole had such a place today, now – a retreat where they could hide and feel safe. This was an impossible wish, he knew, because the older you got, the less safe you became, and the more likely you were to die in an accident or become excruciatingly sick or lose someone you loved. Life unfortunately followed the rules of mathematical probability, and the rules weren't pretty. If you were lucky, you got old and decrepit, like the D'Arcys who lived on the first floor of Sloan House, or like Josh's mother's mother, who lived in a rest home and no longer recognized her kids. There was no such thing as safety; no good could come from wishing for it.

Josh searched in vain for some trace of the tree house, running his gaze along every branch and trunk of the tree, but saw not so much as a protruding rusty nail.

'My dad took it down about three years ago,' said Nicole, drawing alongside him. 'The planks were starting to rot, and he was afraid some little neighbor kid would climb up into it and fall through.'

Josh glanced at her and smiled. She was doing it again – reading his mind. No one in the world knew him as well as she did. 'Guess what: I came over here today to say I'm sorry for not getting in touch with you for so long. I even had my excuse ready. Want to hear it?' Nicole nodded. 'I've been trying to stay so busy that I don't have time to worry about anything, especially anything associated with Millie Carter. I've been spending every spare minute on school stuff, and I didn't come up for air until today. It occurred to me that I hadn't talked to you in a long time, or Lewis, either.'

'Has it worked – staying busy, I mean?'

'Sort of. Before leaving for school this morning, I

thought I'd drop in on Lewis to say hi.'

'And how is he? Winning half a million dollars hasn't turned him into a jerk, I hope.' She managed a grin.

'Nicki, I didn't see him. I knocked on his door, but . . .' This was hard. Josh suddenly felt like a little kid who'd lost his best friend. '. . . Someone was there. Sh-she told me that Lewis was indisposed . . .'

'No way it was Millie Carter,' Nicole whispered, shaking her head. 'It wasn't Millie Carter, was it?'

'It was.'

They stared at each other for a long time as the wind rattled the leaves in the old maple where they'd once built a tree house.

CHAPTER NINETEEN
The Tempest in His Eyes

i

When Lewis felt his Action Power 9000 tilting back, he instinctively leaned forward toward the computer screen, but relaxed again almost immediately, knowing that he was in capable hands. The wheelchair pulled away from the computer desk, turned and headed toward his bedroom.

'Hey, I've got work to do here,' he protested weakly, laughing. 'I'm already a week behind on that personnel manual, and it's for one of my best clients!'

'What I have in store for you will be much more fulfilling than any old personnel manual,' cooed Millie Carter, maneuvering the heavy motorized wheelchair through the bedroom door. For some reason she enjoyed pushing Lewis in the chair, even though he could easily drive himself around in it without help from anyone. 'It seems to me that you're winning enough at poker these days to justify putting your computer into mothballs. Besides, you should be devoting your energies to selecting your next target, because at the rate you're going, you'll soon outgrow little old Portland, Oregon, as charming as it is.'

This was true. Lewis had played poker nearly every night since his big win against Rex Caswell, and the results had been the same, though not as spectacular. He'd played in posh downtown hotels, in the back rooms of ancient saloons in Northeast Portland, and in smoky card rooms on the Washington side of the Columbia. He'd played with local high-rollers, professionals, amateurs, and well-heeled out-of-towners. He'd played anywhere he could find a game except the Hotel Fanshawe, where he could never again play cards, he knew. With Millie at his side and the orb in his pocket, warm and throbbing, he'd been unstoppable, having won something like $75,000 since the night he took Rex Caswell for half a million. So Millie was right: An income of this magnitude, coupled with his substantial mutual fund portfolio, meant that his desktop publishing business had become something of an anachronism almost overnight. She was also right that he couldn't go on winning like this much longer and expect to be allowed back in the local action. He would soon need to sally forth in search of fresh victims, maybe north to Seattle, then up to Vancouver, B.C., or south to the San Francisco Bay, where you could always get into a rich game if you knew the right folks, which Millie did, she assured him. Eventually, he supposed that he would hit the Mecca – Las Vegas, where he could win enough in six months to live like a smiling pig for the rest of his life.

Life had more to offer, though, than hot card games and money, even for a man with a bad arm and no legs, a truism he'd rediscovered with Millie. In the eleven days since she'd first shown up in his bedroom, having somehow crept in as silently as a shadow, he'd ceased to ask himself, *Why?* He'd stopped asking himself what she could possibly see in him, a ragged old Vietnam vet whose radically truncated body was a mass of shrapnel scars. He'd simply accepted her explanation about wanting a man who used his mind for something more than deciding how many six-packs to buy for the weekend or whether to bet against the Dallas Cowboys next Sunday. And she'd said something poetic about 'the tempest in his eyes,' where his feelings swirled and spun like tornadoes – anger and love and compassion, but especially *anger*. Millie loved men who could muster righteous anger, she'd whispered one night, and Lewis's anger was the most righteous she'd ever found.

He lay on his bed now, propped on pillows, naked and unashamed of his stumps and scars, watching her undress in the quiet glow of the lamp on the table next to his bed. She'd gone out today as she had most every day since that first night, apparently to her own place, wherever that was, and had returned wearing a long burgundy shift with a wide belt of finely tooled leather. The tubular shift literally undulated when she moved, clinging to her muscular body and giving tantalizing hints of the features that lay beneath the soft cotton cloth. Around her neck she wore an elaborate necklace of brightly lacquered charms molded in clay – jungle animals, miniature roses, sunbursts, stars and crescents.

The leather belt fell away. She carefully laid aside the necklace. She pulled the dress over her head, slowly, languidly, revealing high-cut panties and a bra of matching red satin. In this light, had he not known her, Lewis wouldn't have been able to discern whether she was a lightly complected black woman or a well-tanned white woman, not that such distinctions had ever mattered to him. What mattered was that she was a woman. She'd given him what he'd long ago given up hoping for, wishing for.

After tossing the dress aside, she playfully shook her dreadlocks, which dangled and jounced like ropes over her shoulders. She stared at him a moment with her wildly mismatched eyes, her full lips parted, her broad nostrils flaring with every breath. Lewis wondered if she saw him as he actually was, a double amputee and a hopeless cripple, or if she was seeing what he might have become if a mortar round hadn't taken so much of him away. Her eyes gave no clue.

She reached behind her with one hand to unfasten the blood-red bra, twisting slightly, giving him a quarter-profile of her proud breasts and the curvature of her back. Suddenly the bra was gone, flung away, and Lewis thrilled again to the sight of her brown areolae, perched like dollar-sized hillocks on her breasts. Her taut nipples reminded him of olive pits, and he longed to take them in his mouth and suck them, lick them, and bite them gently while coaxing them to hardness. Last night she'd taken his cock in the cleavage of those breasts, squeezing it between them and heaving up and down furiously until his orgasm thundered like a summer storm.

Her hands slid down her sides and dipped into the indentations just above her hips, converging on the flat pan of her abdomen. One long finger toyed awhile with her navel, a tan nodule that stood out slightly from the surface of her skin, and slipped beneath the band of the high-cut panties to the mound of black hair that grew where her legs met her torso. Lewis's breath became short and rapid as the bulge in her panties shifted, suggesting that her finger had gone where he desperately wanted to go, inside her, and a soft sigh escaped her mouth as if to confirm this. After a long moment of preparing herself thus, she pushed the panties below her knees and stepped out of them.

Lewis could not suppress a shiver of delight as she stood upright before his bed, long-limbed and dusky, showing him every inch of herself and glorying in his hungry stare. She raised a leg and planted a foot on the mattress, revealing a trace of the pink orchid in her groin, allowing him to imagine what he wanted to do with it. He beckoned to her, and she lowered herself onto him slowly, deliberately, allowing her nipples to play in the hair of his chest. Her hips settled against him, and his good hand found her buttocks as her hands found his cock, hard as a railroad spike. Spreading her thighs wide, she took him into her a fraction of an inch at a time, her pelvis gyrating in lazy circles, until she'd taken him wholly, all the while kissing him with parted lips, probing his tongue with her own.

ii

The orgasm opened a doorway into an alternative gestalt where reality mixed with memories and dreams. As his genitals pumped life-stuff into Millie, warmth spread from the center of his body to the tips of his extremities, right down to the phalanges of his hands and feet. Every fiber of nerve tingled, and every square inch of skin prickled as his consciousness expanded. Suddenly he and Millie were walking arm-in-arm down Montgomery Street from Gander Ridge, the evening air cooling their faces, their shoes whooshing through fallen leaves.

Thirteenth Street, a left turn, down to Jefferson.

Left again.

A short hike across the bridge that spanned I-405,

while beneath them a ribbon of red taillights streamed in one direction and a river of white headlights rushed in the other.

Down into Goose Hollow they went, laughing quietly now and drinking in the night air. Behind them reared the towers of downtown Portland like bejeweled spikes against a purpling sky, while ahead loomed the wooded hills of Washington Park, spangled with the lights of expensive homes. Lewis wondered if he'd died and gone to heaven.

They walked into a torrent of congestion. People were everywhere, bright-eyed and rosy-cheeked from the autumn chill. There wasn't a parking space to be had, but this wasn't a problem for Millie and Lewis, because they'd *walked*. They were *pedestrians*. Lewis gloried in the impossible yet undeniable reality that he had legs and feet, that he was wearing tan Rockport walking shoes and white athletic socks, and that he was *walking* around Goose Hollow with a gorgeous woman on his arm. As if that wasn't enough, his left hand was as supple and strong as his right one, and the ringing in his ears was gone. He was a whole man.

The human currents flowed from all directions toward Civic Stadium, where banks of floodlights cast a yellow aura high into the evening sky and recorded light rock blared from a mammoth sound system. The Reverend Billy Graham was in town, and Christians had rallied from every corner of metropolitan Portland by the thousands to hear his message. Every few hundred feet stood an official representative of the Billy Graham Crusade handing out pamphlets on the salvation of one's immortal soul.

Lewis accepted one of them and tossed it into the next

trash bin he met. Millie laughed when she saw him do this, and asked why he hadn't at least read it. 'Because these people don't know what the soul is, much less how to save it,' he answered with a grin. 'I doubt that anyone does.'

They walked on, giggling like a pair of high-school kids, but somewhere in the deepest folds of Lewis's mind lay the uneasy suspicion that someone was following them. He tried to banish the feeling, but couldn't resist glancing over his shoulder twice or three times. He saw no one.

They ate a light dinner at the Cajun Café in the heart of quaint Northwest Portland. Their table was next to a window on the street, which allowed them to watch the passersby and wonder aloud whether they were poets, sculptors, songwriters or hookers. Lewis washed down his blackened redfish with two pints of Bridgeport Oktoberfest, and, gazing at Millie over snifters of brandy, remarked that her skin was the color of café au lait. She merely smiled and toyed self-consciously with a dreadlock.

They walked back toward Gander Ridge, past Civic Stadium where Billy Graham's sermon had just ended. The neighborhood reverberated with the strains of 'Just As I Am,' the Reverend's trademark theme-hymn. Those who'd already been saved streamed out of the stadium into the streets, creating a traffic jam of biblical proportions. Lewis and Millie veered away from the stadium, hoping to avoid the worst of the congestion. Again Lewis suffered the skin-crawling sensation of being followed, but when he turned to scan the area behind them, he saw only serene-faced Christians.

Millie pressed herself close to him, and he felt her warmth through the layers of his anorak and sweater. 'There's nothing to be afraid of, Lewis,' she said softly. 'Relax and enjoy yourself. You were made for this.'

Lewis began to feel less uneasy. He followed Millie's advice and basked in the joyous miracle of owning two legs again, of simply strolling around town on a fall evening.

Suddenly he halted, pulling Millie off balance. At the intersection ahead, a cluster of senior citizens waited for the traffic light to change, all of them bundled against the autumn chill in expensive-looking winter clothes, all sporting pink and blue badges that said, *We're praying for Greater Portland!* Prominent among them, taller by inches than all the other women and several of the men, was Lewis's aunt Juliet, her face narrow and white, her silvery hair cropped close.

When she saw him, her eyes widened stupidly and her mouth fell open. A shade of pure, potent horror passed over her rouged cheeks as her brain processed what she saw – her nephew, the double-amputee who'd rejected Christ in favor of Godless humanism, standing on two legs, with a woman of color holding his arm.

Amazingly, she maintained her composure and walked with her friends across the street to a chartered bus that waited with its engine idling, Billy Graham's huge face grinning on the side. A long line of elderly Christians waited to get aboard. Juliet glanced back at Lewis several times while crossing the street, several more times once she'd gotten into line. When her eyes met his, Lewis's heart fluttered, and he heard his aunt's voice in his head, pronouncing with divine authority that every miracle has its price.

iii

Lewis awoke just after dawn to a squawking argument that occurred in the trees outside his window among Sloan House's resident family of crows. He rubbed his crusty eyes and edged off the mattress into his wheelchair, then reached down and unplugged its batteries from the charger. He piloted the chair from the bedroom into the bathroom, where he used the handrails on the walls to position himself on the toilet in order to take his morning whiz. This done, he got back into his chair, washed his hands and face, took his bathrobe off its hook on the door and threw it over his lap to hide his stumps.

Next stop, the kitchen – whence came the smells of strong coffee brewing and good things frying. Millie had risen at least an hour earlier than he, and had made breakfast, just as she'd done on every other morning since she'd come to stay.

'I have a tray for you in here,' she called from the studio. 'If you would be kind enough to bring the coffee pot with you, we can both have a fresh cup.' Lewis smiled to himself. Believer in equality for women though he was, he had to admit that these Southern women certainly knew how to take care of their men. He could become accustomed to this kind of treatment, if he wasn't careful.

He brought the pot into the study, where Millie had set an exquisite-looking omelet for him, together with bacon, toast, and a wedge of melon. She sat in the armchair next to the window, her robe of hunter-green velvet swept around her, a vision of feminine charm in the soft light of dawn. Her mismatched eyes seemed almost luminous in the gray of the morning. 'You're spoiling me,' Lewis told her, topping off her cup. 'I'm starting to wonder how I ever got along without you, or if I ever could.'

'You're a man who deserves some tender loving care,' she answered, raising her coffee cup in salute. 'I feel privileged to be the one to give it.'

Lewis tackled his breakfast with gusto, savoring every bite. He couldn't remember ever having eaten an omelet this good, and said so. Millie replied that her secret was mayonnaise beaten in with the eggs.

'I'm glad my internist can't see me now,' said Lewis, chuckling around a bite of bacon. 'There's more cholesterol in this meal than I'm allowed for the whole month.'

'Cholesterol isn't something you need to worry about anymore, Lewis. Our kind have more important things to occupy our mental energies.'

'Is that so?'

'Trust me, and enjoy your breakfast.' She smiled angelically, set aside her tray and got up from the armchair. She wandered toward the low bookshelves that stood against the inner wall of the studio and stooped to eye one book or another. 'Tell me, did you dream again last night?' Lewis had previously described the dreams that attended their love-making, and she'd listened appreciatively, nodding as if she understood from firsthand experience how vivid and full of texture the dreams were.

'As a matter of fact I did dream last night. And it was great, as usual. Except—' The part about meeting his aunt Juliet came back to him, and it gave him a chill.

'Except what?'

He set down his fork, having lost his appetite. 'Nothing. We'll talk about it some other time, okay?'

'Okay.' She turned back to the books on the shelves, and he watched her lips move as she mouthed the names of the authors. Nietzsche, Dewey, Foucault, many others

– the names of the greatest thinkers in history among them. 'Lewis, why does all this matter to you – this philosophy? What does it do for you?'

'It helps me decide what to believe about certain things that I think are important.'

'What sort of things?'

'Oh, like what qualifies as truth and what doesn't.'

'And what qualifies as good, I suppose. And evil, too.'

'Those, too.'

'Why are they important to you?'

'They're important to all of us, or at least they should be,' he replied, carefully thinking out each word. 'Knowing about these things can help us decide how to live together as a society, what kind of institutions to build and what kind to get rid of. Philosophers help us decide what we want to be, it seems to me.'

She smiled with a hint of irony, her eyes glittering with intelligence. 'The answers you're after are really very simple, Lewis. There isn't any truth – only what people *say* is truth. And that can change on a daily basis. The same is true of good and evil.'

Lewis had heard such pat assertions many times, and they annoyed him, especially when they came from people so young. 'Well, if it isn't Thoroughly Postmodern Millie?' he said sarcastically, saluting her with his coffee cup. 'As long as you're handing out answers to cosmic questions, can you tell me if the soul actually exists, and if it does, what it's made of? That one has bothered me for a long time, and I'd like to get it cleared up.'

She turned away from the bookshelves and walked a few steps toward him. 'There's no need to be snide, Lewis. I'm only trying to help you. You see, I too have spent a great deal of time and effort looking for answers.

Of all the philosophers I've read, the only one who came close to providing a useful answer was Schopenhauer, and I suspect he stumbled upon the answer without knowing why.'

'*Schopenhauer?* Care to enlighten me?'

'The *will*, Lewis. Schopenhauer emphasized the *will* as the center of existence, the force behind all movement. He was right.'

'Whose will?'

'Yours, mine. Ours. The only ones that count.' She moved to the opposite wall and studied the framed photographs that hung there, paying particular attention to the ones of his family. 'Are these people your parents?' she asked. 'I see a strong family resemblance.'

'Yeah, I'm a chip off the old block. The one below is my brother, Ken.'

'And who are these men?' Her finger touched the frame of a group picture that showed Lewis in the midst of his closest Vietnam buddies.

'The tall ugly one making the peace sign is me, believe it or not. The little blond fireplug is Danny Legler, the skinny black one is T. J. Skane, and the big black one is Jesse Burton. The guy in the cowboy hat is Scott Sanders. They were all in my platoon in Vietnam.'

She backed away from the wall a step, viewing the photos from a longer perspective. 'They're dead, aren't they – the men in this picture, and your parents? Your brother is dead, too, isn't he?'

Lewis bit his lower lip, surprised at the grief that stirred to life somewhere near his heart, even after all these years. 'Yeah, they're all dead, except for Jesse and me. He's very much alive and living in Chicago. How did you know about the others?'

Millie ignored the question and turned to face him, her eyes hard and urgent. 'You should get rid of these pictures, Lewis. The dead aren't of any use to anyone, and it's not healthy for our kind to dwell on them.' She whirled and snatched the three photographs off the wall, leaving behind three ghostly rectangles where the paint had faded around the picture frames. 'Life is for the living, and you would do well to remember that.' She strode into the kitchen, apparently meaning to dispose of the photographs in the wastebasket under the sink.

'Wait just a damn minute!' shouted Lewis, chasing her in his wheelchair. 'I care about those pictures! I care about those *people*! You don't have any right to—'

'I'm only doing what's best for you, Lewis. I'm trying to give you the benefit of my own experience. The dead should be left alone, avoided. You'll understand this someday.' She tossed the pictures into the basket, and Lewis heard a shattering of glass.

'You bitch! Those pictures mean something to me!' He halted his chair in the center of the kitchen. 'You can't just throw away the memories of people you love. Who the hell do you think you are, anyway?'

She went down on her haunches before him and gripped both arms of the wheelchair, letting the velvet robe fall away to reveal her bare thighs. Staring intensely into his face, she said, 'Lewis, listen. It's time for me to leave you. I've done all for you that I can, and you've got to do the rest on your own. Don't worry – it will come naturally – I doubt that you could stop it if you tried. All you need to do is relax and let it happen.'

'Leave me? Are you saying it's over between us?'

'I'll see you from time to time, of course, and we'll share our experiences and memories like two old friends . . .' Her face darkened with what Lewis took to be regret. She lowered her eyes. '. . . But I can't say any more right now. It would only confuse you. You're confused enough as it is, I can see.' She kissed him suddenly, then stood up and strode from the kitchen down the hall to the bedroom.

Lewis motored after her, pleading with her to tell him why she must go, and failing in that, why she'd even come to him in the first place if she hadn't intended to stay with him. And what had she meant, he demanded, about having done all for him that she could, and that now he must do the rest? The rest of *what*? She said nothing more until she reached the front door of the apartment, having put on her burgundy shift and a white raincoat, her overnight bag in her hand.

'Lewis, you asked me whether the soul is a real thing. I can tell you that it is. It's real, and it's made of energy – nothing less, nothing more. I suspect that the real question on your mind is whether the soul survives the death of the body, so I'll answer that for you, as well: Yes, Lewis, the soul survives. It's made of energy, and it survives. Good-bye.' With that she pulled the door open and went away.

CHAPTER TWENTY
A Miracle from Hell

i

'God, am I glad it's Friday, or what?' exclaimed Kendra Nickerson as she climbed into the passenger's seat of her brother's trashy old Escort. 'After the week I've had, I *need* this weekend in a major way. I've had no social life at all since school started, and all my teachers are total homework freaks . . .'

Josh switched on the radio in order to preempt a rehash of Kendra's travail during the past week and wondered how he himself would get through the coming day. He'd slept hardly at all last night, knowing that in all likelihood Millie Carter was only a few yards away in Lewis's apartment, one floor below the Nickersons'. The very thought of Millie and Lewis in bed together, doing what men and women do in the night, made his skin crawl.

Hard rock blared from the radio, causing Kendra to switch to KINK, which played contemporary pop and jazz, both of which Josh hated, but he lacked the energy for an argument.

He turned onto Gander Circle as a newscaster wrapped up a story about a night-time curfew for juveniles that the Portland police had announced to curb gang violence.

Josh was about to gripe that the Crips and Bloods were ruining the lives of everybody under twenty-one when he caught sight of Millie Carter walking along the sidewalk about half a block ahead, her white raincoat visible against the gray morning. He slammed on the brakes, bringing the Escort to an immediate halt on the damp pavement.

'For God's sake, Joshua, what're you *doing*?' demanded Kendra, her green eyes snapping angrily. 'Are you trying to kill us both? Why are we stopping, anyway? We're going to be late for—'

'Shut up.' His tone was steel-cold, his face set like sculpted ice. Kendra shut up. Josh watched Millie Carter walk briskly down Gander Ridge, her rusty dreadlocks swinging and jouncing with every purposeful stride, until she arrived at her black Jaguar, which was parked on the street near the intersection at the base of the hill. From this distance Josh could barely see her, for the fog had crept up from the valley below and now roiled like smoke among the houses of Gander Ridge.

'Joshua, who's that woman?' Kendra asked timidly. 'Do you know her? Why are you behaving . . . ?'

'I said shut up.' Kendra flinched, and drew her arms more tightly to her.

Josh saw the Jag's taillights switch on, saw the sleek black car glide away from the curb. He made a snap decision, then turned off his own headlights. With the fog as thick as it was, he figured that he could follow Millie without her knowing it.

ii

The house was a Mediterranean-style villa that stood behind a protective phalanx of hemlocks and cedars on a hillside in Northwest Portland. Its tiled roof had once been red but had darkened with the relentless build-up of coniferous needles and cones over decades. The eight-foot stucco wall that surrounded the property appeared similarly neglected, inasmuch as the stucco had crumbled away here and there, exposing ancient bricks.

'Whoever she is, she must be rich,' Kendra declared sourly as Josh halted the Escort near the entrance gate, which was barred with wrought-iron. A moment earlier, the bars had parted to admit the black Jaguar and had closed behind it, apparently remote-controlled. 'Can we go to school now? We can still get there before second period if we cruise. I don't mind telling you, Joshua, that I'm not exactly ecstatic about being taken on a wild goose chase.'

Josh ignored her and got out of the car. He approached the gate and peeked through the bars, leaning cautiously around the stucco wall. The Jaguar sat in the drive, looking starkly out of place in the seedy, overgrown surroundings. Despite the enveloping greenery, Josh could see enough of the house to know that it had indeed been grand in its day, but he could also see that it had fallen on hard times. Mounds of needles and leaves covered the grounds, broken here and there by colonies of weeds. Ivy grew in a ragged riot over the front entrance and completely covered the doors of the four-car garage, meaning that its doors hadn't been raised in years. The windows of the house were dark and bleak, the stucco gray with decades of neglect. The place looked deserted.

Josh got back in the car and drove past the gate, following the wooded lane as it curved around the hillside. Occasionally the foliage broke to afford a foggy vista of the valley below. Josh stopped the car at a point where the lane switched back around the hill in its descent, got out and gazed upward through a soft rain. Above him, besieged by ivy and holly near the crest of the hill, was the stucco wall that surrounded Millie Carter's crumbling villa.

If someone wanted to enter the property unseen, he said to himself, he could do it here.

iii

The silence in the aftermath of Millie's departure was deafening. It lay on Lewis Kindred's heart like a stone, almost as heavily as the loneliness that had thudded down on his world at the moment she walked out of his life only hours ago. The ringing in his ears had grown so loud that at first he didn't hear the doorbell, and when he finally did hear it, he decided not to answer. But the caller persisted, and he gave in.

He was totally unprepared to see his aunt Juliet standing on the other side of the door, angular and tall, her face as gray as the morning except for the patches of rouge on her cheeks. They stared at each other wordlessly for nearly half a minute until Lewis nudged his wheelchair into reverse and motioned her in. She sidled past him into the living room and sat on the edge of the sofa, stiff-backed and straight, as if poised to launch herself at the door under the slightest provocation.

'Can I get you anything?' Lewis asked, endeavoring to be civil. They hadn't parted amicably after Juliet had refused to lend him money to pay his poker debt to Rex Caswell, and Lewis felt inclined to patch things up. She was, after all, his only living relative.

'I attended the Billy Graham Crusade last night,' she

said in a voice that crinkled like tissue.

'It must've been nice for you. You're lucky it didn't rain.'

'It didn't rain because many of us prayed that it wouldn't.'

'Well, there you have it – the power of prayer.'

'I *saw* you,' she added, getting quickly to the heart of the matter. Her pasty face began to twitch in places, and her eyes enlarged to a point at which her irises were surrounded with white. 'You were with some Negro woman, and she was fawning all over you, right there on the sidewalk outside the stadium.'

To Lewis it seemed as if the temperature in the room suddenly dropped twenty degrees, and he gripped the arm of his chair to keep from shaking. 'You're mistaken, Juliet. I didn't go out last night.'

'Don't lie to me! I saw you, and you saw me!' She eyed the stumps of his legs, which lay hidden beneath the striped bathrobe he'd shrugged into before answering the door. Without warning she reached out, pulled the bathrobe aside and gasped upon confronting the naked gnarls of flesh and bone.

'J-Juliet, please,' Lewis protested, pushing the skirt of the robe back into place. 'I don't know what you think you saw last night, but—' But what? His voice caught, and he forced himself to swallow. He *had* met his aunt last night, but the meeting had occurred in a dream – a vivid, fully textured and nerve-wrackingly realistic dream, to be sure, but a dream nonetheless.

'How did you do it?' she demanded, thrusting out her chin. 'Have you gotten artificial limbs without telling me? Is that what you've done, Lewis – gone up to the veterans' hospital and gotten yourself fitted with wooden legs?'

'You know as well as I do that I can't use prosthetics, Juliet. The muscles in my back were too cut up by shrapnel. I would never be able to maintain my balance.'

'Then *how*? How could you have been *walking*?'

Lewis stared stupidly at his aunt, shaking his head in jerky sideways movements to deny the mind-bending truth. If she'd actually seen him last night in Goose Hollow with Millie, then he hadn't been dreaming at all. And this meant . . .

'Lewis, you know I believe in miracles. I've prayed for miracles all my life, and I've seen them happen more times than I can count. I've seen people healed of addictions and afflictions of all kinds. I've seen others turn their lives around with the Lord's help, turn their backs on sin and become living, breathing witnesses for Him, which is nothing short of miraculous.' Juliet's upper lip whitened and became moist as her emotional pitch heightened. 'So when I saw you last night, I didn't think for even one moment that I was hallucinating, because I've never doubted that the Lord could give you back your legs in the twinkling of an eye, if He wanted to. After all, He healed a paralyzed man in Capernaum – told him to take up his bed and walk, and the man did just that. And if He was able to create the entire universe in six days, then He'd certainly have no trouble making you a whole man again. What I saw last night, though . . .' Her breath seemed to go out of her, and she paused to take another, slow and deep. 'What I saw last night wasn't God's work.'

Lewis looked away and stared at his ficus tree, which loomed against the window. Rain tapped diffidently against the glass, casting squiggly little shadows on the leaves. 'What you're saying is crazy, Juliet. You're getting yourself all worked up over a mistake. I tell you, I didn't go out last night.'

'Don't play games with me, Lewis! I'm not crazy, and you know it! I saw what I saw, and what I saw wasn't from God. Not every miracle comes from heaven, unfortunately – some come from Hell. God doesn't work a miracle and then undo it. Last night you had legs, and your left arm looked perfectly normal. Today you have no legs, and your arm appears as full of scars and as stiff as it's ever been. Do you know what this means, Lewis? It means that the Devil has touched you, that whatever miracle you've experienced is something unholy, something unclean. The Devil has given you a miracle and taken it back again for a reason that I don't even care to know. And he won't be satisfied until he's taken your soul!'

'For Christ's sake, stop it, will you?' He whirled and glared savagely at her, fully expecting his loathing of her hyper-religiosity to well up from his gut and spew from his mouth in a blast of barely controlled invective, as had happened countless times in the past. But it didn't happen this time. The loathing didn't come. For a crazy moment he actually envied her naive fundamentalism. More than this, he appreciated for the first time that his aunt really did love him, that she was reaching out to him in the only way she knew. He tried to imagine how it must terrify her to see evidence of Satan's touch on the only family she had left. Lewis's eyes suddenly smarted and started to water. 'I-I'm sorry. I didn't mean to scream at you . . .'

'Don't worry about *me*, Lewis. Worry about your soul

and where you'll spend eternity. Give yourself to Jesus before it's too late. Pray with me now, and we'll ask the Holy Spirit to minister unto you . . .'

'Juliet, please. You know I can't do that.'

'But you *can* do it, Lewis. In Matthew eleven, twenty-eight, the Lord says, "Come unto me, all ye that labour and are heavy laden, and I will give you rest." All you have to do is say, "Lord, here I am. Take my sin away and make me yours." If you pray that simple prayer, you're guaranteed a life that won't end, not even when you die.'

'Juliet, will you shut up for one minute and listen to me? This isn't a problem that can be solved by prayer—'

'Oh, but prayer can solve *any* problem, Lewis. If you're worried about that Negro woman, don't be, because even if she's Satan's vessel, she can't stand up against the power of prayer. She might be a demon sent from Hell, but she's no match for the Lord. Scripture says, "Thou believest that there is one God; . . . the devils also believe, and tremble." That's the secret, Lewis – believe! If you believe, the devils will tremble.'

'She's not Satan's vessel, damn it, and she's not a demon sent from Hell! How can you judge her when you haven't met her?'

'I'm sorry. I shouldn't've jumped to conclusions. I'm just trying to . . .'

'I know what you're trying to do, and I appreciate your concern – really I do. In fact, it's been a long time since I've told you how grateful I am for all you've done for me over the years, letting me live here, installing all the special equipment in this apartment. Since Mom died you've looked out for me, and I'll admit that I've often taken it for granted. I haven't been the best nephew,

Juliet.' He moved the chair close to her and reached for her hand, but she drew back from him, as if she feared diabolical contagion. Lewis ignored this. 'I hope that someday you and I can get closer, Juliet, but right now—' He massaged his brow, rubbed his eyes. He swallowed to prevent his voice from cracking. 'Right now I'm going through a bad time, okay? I'm pretty sure I can handle it myself, but I need to be alone. I hope you'll understand if I ask you to leave.'

Juliet's gray face became even grayer, except for the patches of rouge. Something in her eyes told Lewis that she verged on giving up all hope for him. 'I understand,' she answered flatly. She stood up, squared her shoulders, a soldier of the Lord who'd done her best and failed. At least for now. 'I hope you'll call me when you've finally become desperate enough, Lewis. And remember that little prayer. The Lord is as close as that little prayer, if you need Him.'

iv

Mason Benoit and Spit Pittman arrived at Rex Caswell's floating house shortly before noon. After Twyla had given them each a screwdriver, as was the custom, Rex said, 'Twyla, sweetheart, could you excuse us? We have business to discuss.'

She'd just lit a cigarette and had eased herself into a huge leather futon, a book of romantic poetry open in her lap. 'Since when aren't I good enough to sit in on a business discussion? I already know enough to put you slime bags away for fifty years apiece, so what does it matter if I hear more?' Her right eye had a vivid purple bruise beneath it that her sunglasses couldn't quite hide, and her lip was still swollen – marks left eight days earlier by a flying bowl of Cream of Wheat.

'Sweetheart, I'm only going to ask you one more time. Then I'm going to throw you off the upper deck of this house into the Willamette. Would you *please* excuse us?'

Twyla hoisted herself out of the futon and climbed the stairs, cursing blackly under her breath, the cigarette dangling from her lips. She wore a bulky flowered muumuu that obscured the excess poundage around her middle, but it couldn't hide the pallor of her skin or the fact that she was developing jowls. Her unwashed hair was stringy and limp. The smell of gin radiated from her. Rex didn't resume talking until a door slammed upstairs, indicating that she'd shut herself safely out of earshot.

'Okay, what did you find out about Millie Carter?' he asked Benoit.

'She's moved in with your old homey, Lewis Kindred,' answered the black man matter-of-factly.

'*What?* You've got to be shitting me!'

'Sorry, my man. I'm just telling you what we found out, that's all.'

Rex bolted to his feet and strode to a panoramic window that fronted the river. He stared a full minute at the far shore, running the fingers of one hand through his blond hair and shaking his head as his anger built. 'What in the fuck does she see in him? The son of a bitch doesn't even have any legs! He doesn't even have two good hands!' He turned back to Benoit and glared at him through slitted eyes. 'Are you absolutely positively fucking sure about this? She's actually living with him?'

'It certainly looks that way,' answered Benoit as he picked a piece of lint from the cuff of his custom-made silk shirt. 'We staked out Kindred's place three fucking nights in a row – cold nights, I might add – sitting in the car across the street from his apartment, waiting for her to come out. But she never came out until late the next morning. A couple of times she went grocery shopping. Couple of other times she went somewhere for some clothes.'

'But how do you know what they were doing in there? How do you know their relationship isn't platonic?'

'Rex, I'm telling you those two are an *item*. Kindred never goes anywhere without her. They've shown up together at card games all over town, and Kindred has been winning big-time. They arrive together, they leave together, they go home to Kindred's apartment, and the babe doesn't come out till the next morning. I'm sorry, but I can't make myself believe that they're spending all that time playing Mr Potato Head.'

Rex swallowed most of his screwdriver in one gulp and scowled furiously at no one in particular. 'You say he's been winning big-time?'

'That's what we hear. Plays almost every night – east side, west side, Vancouver. He's been so good that people are starting to avoid getting into games with him. Hey, I'm surprised you haven't heard about this. You're supposed to be hooked into the poker crowd.'

'I've been out of circulation for the last couple of weeks.'

'Understandable. If Kindred had done to me what he did to you, I'd be a little embarrassed to show my face, same as you.'

Rex ground his teeth so hard that his jaw muscles rippled. 'What about the crystal?' he asked. 'Did you get it?'

'No,' answered Benoit, after trading glances with Spit.

'Why the hell not?'

'Rex, think about it. Why would the bitch give it to us, anyway? We're a couple of perfect strangers to her. Besides, you said you'd approach her yourself, if we located her. Well, we located her. You can find her any evening at Lewis Kindred's apartment. I'd advise calling first.'

Spit guffawed loudly when he heard this, almost spilling his screwdriver. He fell abruptly quiet, however, when Rex glared at him. 'You're absolutely right, I did say that I'd approach her myself. Maybe that's exactly what I should do. I should've known better than to give the job to you jerks.'

'Rex, you gotta chill, man,' Benoit protested. 'We did what you asked us to do, right? We found the half-breed bitch. If there's something else we can do for you – something within the realm of feasibility, that is – all you've got to do is say it. We work for you, okay?'

Rex closed his eyes and breathed deeply as his hatred for Lewis Kindred rose in his throat like bile. In his mind he relived the countless times Lewis had condescended to him, humiliated him with snide little comments, treated him like shit. His brain replayed the episodes like a VCR on fast forward, but lingered on those in which Kindred had scooped Rex's money from the poker table, smirking malignantly as if to say that he'd won because he was *better* than Rex, not merely a more accomplished player but a better man, a more worthy human being. *I've got no legs, and I'm still more man than you are*, that loathsome smirk had said. And now, to top it all off, Lewis had taken Millie Carter away from him. Rex suddenly felt a longing to inflict harm on Lewis Kindred, but he dared not do it directly, because any harm worth doing would draw the attention of the cops, and their attention would gravitate immediately to Rex, given what had happened eleven days earlier at the Hotel Fanshawe. Who had a better motive to hurt Kindred than Rex Caswell, having just lost half a million dollars to him? This meant that Rex needed to be circumspect about it.

'There *is* something more you can do for me, Mase.' He sat down in his favorite chair and gazed intensely at the vaulted ceiling, his head tilted back. 'I assume you wouldn't balk at the chance to settle accounts with Kindred for what he did to you in Old Town the other day. How's your wrist, by the way? All healed?'

'My wrist is fine. Like I said, we'll do anything that's within the realm of feasibility.'

'And how about you, Spit? Would you like to settle up with the old dirtball who worked you over with the pipe?' Spit's small eyes brightened, and he nodded. 'Then that's what I want you to do,' said Rex, leaning forward and tenting his fingers in front of his face. 'Put the major kibosh on that old derelict friend of Kindred's, but this time use your heads. Do some planning, and make fucking sure that nobody but *nobody* can get back to me with it.'

'Are you saying you want that old dude to die?' asked Benoit, his forehead wrinkling. 'You actually want us to pop him?'

Rex swallowed. 'I want you to send the old rat-fucker up in flames. I want you to hurt him so badly that Lewis Kindred will never sleep again. Do you hear me?'

'Yeah, we hear you, Rex,' said Spit, chuckling. He smacked a hammy fist into a palm. 'We'll toast him for you. By the time we're done with him, he'll look like he belongs under the sneeze-guard at Tony Roma's.'

'You've never told us to do anything like this before,'

said Benoit in a low, cautious voice. 'We'll need to bring in some dudes from out of town, since Spit and I have a history with the guy, and the cops are likely to check us out if something ugly happens to him. I know people in L. A. who'll be glad to help, but it'll cost you some change. Are you sure this is what you want?'

'It's what I want,' Rex replied. He knew that his hatred had blinded him and rendered him less than his normal cautious self, but he didn't care. Sometimes a man needed to act according to what he felt, or he might tie himself in knots and strangle himself. 'Hey, if you don't have the stones for it, I'll get someone who does.'

'We've got the stones for it,' Mason Benoit assured him. 'I just want to make sure you know what you're asking. Once we get somebody popped, he stays popped. There's no undoing it, right?'

'Just fucking *do* it!'

Benoit put his hands on his knees, stood up, and buttoned his jacket around him. 'No sweat, Rex. No sweat at all.'

v

Lewis called Tommy Iadanza shortly after one in the afternoon and asked for a ride downtown, and Tommy was only too happy to oblige. Tommy asked how the hell Lewis was. The Fanshawe crowd had missed him at last Monday night's game, he said, and they'd all started to worry a little. Lewis apologized for staying out of touch for so long. He owed his friends better than this, he confessed. Tommy said he would pick him up in an hour.

Lewis bathed, shaved, and made himself as presentable as he could. He put on a newly laundered button-down sport shirt, a crew-neck sweater of Oregon Ducks green, and a fresh pair of khaki slacks, the cuffs of which he tucked neatly under the stumps of his legs. Then he went to the computer desk in his study, opened a drawer, and took out the orb, the only thing that Millie had left behind.

The sight of it, the feel of it against his palm, roused a perplexing mix of feelings and memories. In one compartment of his mind he felt certain that evil swirled around the thing – the evil of a nightmare creature named Gamaliel Cartee, whose stock-in-trade was trickery, torture and gruesome murder. Two decades ago Lewis had believed that the orb was the vehicle through which Gamaliel had sought to gain some sort of control over him. Even now he couldn't suppress the notion that by tapping the orb's powers to win at poker, he'd breathed the fumes of hell.

In another compartment of his mind, he associated the orb with Millie – weird, wonderful Millie – who had touched him in a way that awakened hungers and hopes that he'd long ago given up for dead. Though she'd spent less than two weeks with him, Millie had made him a whole man again. She'd taken his hand and led him into a sensual paradise, a place where he never felt crippled or impeded or incomplete. Through her he'd found a dimension of himself that represented all he'd aspired to become before a mortar round mutilated his life.

But even his experience with Millie had a dark aspect that defied reason, an almost Faustian element that caused him to fear not for his immortal soul, but for his sanity. He couldn't explain how his aunt had seen him in Goose Hollow, walking on two good legs. What he'd assumed to be an excursion to a realm of vivid, highly textured dreams seemed now to have been some sort of transcendental episode during which his most ardent wish had become material reality. He'd yearned desperately for legs, and lo, while fucking Millie, he'd somehow grown legs. His arm and hand had healed. His battle-damaged ears no longer rang. His body had felt like that of a twenty-year-old.

Lewis had read enough psychology over the years to appreciate the distinctions between neurosis and psychosis, to know the symptoms of schizophrenia. A schizophrenic mind loses contact with the real world and manufactures its own reality, one that seems as actual and as immediate as any normal sensory feedback. For many schizophrenics, the manufactured reality is a terrifying one that radically disrupts their lives. Lewis knew that he could not possibly have grown legs that night, but a huge part of his mind insisted otherwise. And this morning his mind had told him that Aunt Juliet had indeed seen him in the body of a whole man – something he knew wasn't possible. The only explanation that made any sense to him, the one that reconciled the conflicting realities in his mind, was schizophrenia.

How long, he wondered, before the disease progressed to the drooling, blithering stage? How long before it reduced him to cowering in closets to escape the relentless biting of the butterfly-lizards? Or loitering on street corners, picking invisible French fries out of the air? In all probability it was only a matter of time, he concluded, before his worst nightmares became as real to him as the air he breathed, which meant that he needed to make good use of the time he had left.

vi

The waiting room of the Veterans In Progress Center wa
standing-room-only, but Lewis and Tommy didn't nee
to wait long. Audra Fallon soon poked her head throug
the inner door and ushered them into her office. She gav
Lewis a huge hug and asked where the hell he'd been fo
the past two weeks. Good counselors were scarce as hen
teeth, especially counselors with Lewis's background, sh
said. And why hadn't he returned her calls? Didn't h
listen to his answering machine anymore?

'Audra, I'm sorry,' he said, opening the old Samsonit
briefcase he'd brought along. 'I should've called. Thes
last few weeks have been tough ones – I won't bore yo
with the gory details.'

'Oh, but I *love* gory details,' said Audra, smilin
sweetly and positioning her bulk on the edge of her desk

'Maybe some other time.' He took a letter-size manil
envelope from the briefcase and handed it to her, causin
her broad brow to wrinkle with curiosity. 'I want th
Center to have this,' he said. 'I know that cash contribu
tions are a little awkward, but don't worry – it's no
ill-gotten.'

'Don't believe him,' quipped Tommy Iadanza, hi
basset-hound face stretching into what passed for a grir
'It's the proceeds from a string of whorehouses he own
throughout the Pacific Rim.'

Audra opened the bulky, bulging envelope and gasped
She withdrew several packets of hundred-dollar bills and
turned them over before her eyes, apparently havin
trouble believing that they were real. 'Lewis, there's go
to be ten, fifteen thousand dollars here.'

'Twenty thousand on the nose,' said Lewis, smilin
sadly. 'I've had a lucky streak in poker lately. I figure

you could make better use of the money than I could.'

Audra placed a palm against her cheek, her face slack with shock. 'I-I don't know what to say. The money couldn't come at a better time. But I've got to wonder whether—'

'Audra, don't even think of trying to talk me out of this. It's what I want to do. It's also what I need to do.'

'Whatever you say, Lewis. I just want to say that what you've given in the past – your time, your skills, your caring – these are all priceless. The money's nice, yeah, but it's no substitute for *you*.'

Lewis dropped his stare to his stumps, unable to look her in the eye at this particular moment. 'That's something else I need to talk to you about, Audra. I won't be doing any more counseling, I'm afraid. I'm not the kind of person who should be telling someone else how to get his life together . . .'

vii

They found Dewey just where Audra Fallon had said he would be, at the south end of Tom McCall Park, his wheelchair braced against the rail so that he could stare at the bleak Willamette River, which lapped at the cement wall twenty feet below. Lewis's heart fell when he saw him, for Dewey looked achingly alone and desolate, like a tragic sculpture in dark stone. Passersby gave him nary a glance as they strode past on their good legs, or glided by on their costly mountain bikes. Only the pigeons and gulls paid him any heed, for he'd apparently shared with them whatever he'd had for lunch. The pigeons continued to waddle around Dewey's chair, patrolling for missed crumbs and hoping for more.

Dewey straightened up and turned when he heard the

whisper of Lewis's Action Power 9000 as it drew near. 'I'd know the sound of that contraption anywhere,' he said, offering his hand. Tommy shook it, and then Lewis. Dewey's handshake was uncharacteristically weak, indifferent.

'How's it going?' Lewis asked, trying to sound cheerful. 'You've been behaving yourself, I trust.'

'I'm soldiering on, same as you.'

In the weeks since Lewis had last seen him, Dewey had lost noticeable weight. The whites of his eyes had yellowed even more, and he slumped in his chair like an old man. Lewis felt guilty for having missed his usual Wednesday rendezvous with him, and apologized for doing so, but Dewey only looked away.

'I've got something for you,' Lewis said, opening his briefcase. 'You won't want to take it, I know, but I'm going to give it to you anyway.' He tossed a bulging manila envelope into the black man's lap.

'What've you got that I could possibly want?' Dewey tore at the end of the envelope with cold, stiff fingers. The day was raw and breezy, and he should have been wearing gloves. He gaped at the contents of the envelope, his whiskered jaw falling open.

'Looks like your scrounging days are over, sarge,' laughed Tommy, clapping him on the shoulder. 'There's twenty thousand bucks there – enough to take care of you for a long, long time, if you handle it right.'

Dewey scowled at the money and folded the envelope closed. 'Where'd it come from?'

'I've been on a lucky streak in poker,' Lewis answered flippantly. 'Bunch of high-rollers from out of town made the mistake of thinking they could bluff me.'

'Then it's your money, not mine.' Dewey tried to hand

it back, but Lewis wouldn't let him.

'Negative. I want you to have it. Before you get all pissed off and insulted, let me tell you what I propose. I'll give the money to Tommy here, and he'll take care of it for you. No sense carrying this kind of scratch on the street, right? You'd last about ten minutes in Old Town before some fucking *chiva* dealer put a switchblade in your ribs. Anytime you want some of it, go to Tommy at the Hotel Fanshawe down on Third and Salmon, and he'll give you as much as you want. He'll act as your bank.'

'Except I don't pay interest,' Tommy put in, winking.

'That's all there is to it? No catches?'

'No catches,' Lewis confirmed. 'But I'm going to suggest something to you, Dewey: Let Tommy invest the money for you. Let him help you find a place to live—'

'I've already got a damn place to live.'

'I'm talking about a roof, Dewey. I'm talking about three squares a day and some help for your pain. You need to get in out of the cold and rain, and you need to quit pounding down a fifth of bourbon a day.'

'Anything else I need to do? Maybe I need to quit cussin' and start washin' behind my ears? Maybe I need to trim my fuckin' toenails every week?'

'Don't get mad. I've already told you there're no catches. The money's yours. If you want to spend the rest of your life sleeping under the Burnside Bridge and eating out of fucking garbage cans, then have at it. I'm only trying to give you a shot at something better, that's all.'

Dewey stared a long moment at the river, saying nothing. A hundred feet away, a brightly painted stern-wheeler insinuated itself next to the pier, looking like an artifact of the last century, while a crowd of dark-suited executives chatted and sipped drinks inside its glass-paneled salon. At length he opened the envelope and fished around in it for a hundred-dollar bill, which he handed to Lewis. 'I'll take the money under one condition,' he said, his voice scratching like a nail against slate. 'You bring me another cat, one who looks like Big Sister. That C-note ought to cover it. Don't worry about tryin' to find one as smart as Big Sister was, or as nice looking, either. All she needs is to be warm. The nights are starting to get cold around here.' Then he folded shut the manila envelope and handed it to Tommy.

viii

After watching Dewey roll south along the river in his chair and disappear among the traffic going into and out of Old Town, Lewis and Tommy retired to the Huntsman's Bar and Grill for a beer. They sat quiet awhile, sipping their mugs of Bridgeport Oktoberfest and staring at the ancient photos on the walls, each lost in his thoughts.

'Are you going to get him a cat?' asked Tommy at length.

Lewis nodded. He planned to pick up a cat from the Multnomah County Humane Society tomorrow and take it to Dewey right away – one that looked as much like Big Sister as he could find. It seemed important not to wait.

'Something's bothering me, Lewis,' said Tommy, scratching his jaw. 'The way you were talking to Audra and Dewey was like you're planning to join the French Foreign Legion. That business about not counseling vets anymore – not being the right kind of person and all that – what the hell was it all about? I mean, here you are, giving away money by the fucking truckload and acting like you're tying up loose ends, getting ready to die – it's enough to make your friends worry, know what I mean?'

Lewis chuckled dryly. He assured Tommy that he wasn't planning to die anytime soon, but beyond this he didn't know exactly what to say. How do you tell a friend that you're going off your rocker?

He hoisted his Samsonite briefcase onto the table, opened it, and withdrew the final manila envelope. He tossed it across to Tommy and grinned when he saw his friend's basset-hound eyes become round as dollars.

'What the fuck is this?' Tommy asked.

'I could say, "Open it and find out," but that seems a little overly melodramatic, so I'll just tell you. It's twenty thousand dollars, coin of the realm.'

Tommy blew out a sigh of total, exasperated shock. 'Lewis, have you gone completely off your knob?'

'In a word, yeah. But let's not worry about that, okay? Just take the money and do something good with it. Use it toward the kids' college, if you want. Or put it into restoring the Fanshawe. Or better yet, take Carlotta to Venice like you've always wanted to do. I don't care what you do with the money as long as you take it.'

'Lewis, this goes beyond—'

'The *hell* it does, Tommy. It doesn't go beyond all the years you've put up with me, hauled me around with my fucking wheelchair, carried me up and down stairs, included me with your family and friends. It doesn't go beyond all the good conversation we've had, the jokes we've shared – even the shitty ones—'

'Lewis, I can't take this.'

'You don't have a choice, man. The money's yours, no strings. You'd do the same for me, if I asked for it. Subject closed.'

ix

Before heading back to Sloan House, they made a final
side trip – this one to the Hawthorne Bridge, which was
only a few blocks from the Fanshawe. Tommy walked
alongside Lewis's chair in a light drizzle, asking no
questions, apparently confident that his friend would tell
him what this was all about in his own good time. When
they arrived at the midway point across the bridge,
Tommy finally said, 'If you'd wanted to go across the
river, we could've driven, you know. We could've taken a
nice dry car.'

Lewis halted and dug into his anorak for the orb, which
he brought out and held a moment in his hand, staring at
it. Tommy exclaimed under his breath when he saw the
thing. 'Remember this?' Lewis asked with a faraway
look.

Tommy nodded as an eighteen-wheeler thundered
across the bridge, flailing them with spray. Over the
fading thunder of the truck he said, 'You gave it to Millie
Carter on the night you clobbered Rex in the rematch.
She called it a good-luck charm, as I remember.'

'You have a good memory.'

'What the hell is it made of? Why does it shine like
that?'

Lewis's lips tightened as he gazed away toward the east
shore of the river, unable to answer Tommy's questions.
Above the vista of urban clutter hung gray webs of rain
clouds that hid the horizon beyond, where he knew
Mount Hood stood like a sentinel. He wished he could
see the volcano now, for the sight of it might have given
him confidence that what he was about to do might save
him. He remembered that he'd once trusted Nui Ba Den,
the Black Virgin of Vietnam, and she'd betrayed him. So

393

the gods and goddesses of volcanoes owed him something, he told himself – if he could only make himself
believe in them. Deities never do anything for folks who
don't believe in them, he supposed. Then he reared back
and flung the orb as hard as he could away from the
bridge and followed it with his eyes until it disappeared
with a tiny detonation of spray many stories below.

CHAPTER TWENTY-ONE
Listening for Noises, Looking for Sin

i

Josh began another near-sleepless night listening fo
noises from Lewis's apartment, where he feared tha
Millie Carter was working some kind of evil magic on hi
friend, the nature of which he couldn't imagine and didn'
want to. Though he lay stone-still and barely breathed, h
heard nothing beyond the ordinary. Finally he got out c
bed, switched on his computer, and booted the Demo
Beef story.

Reading through the draft, he quickly reached th
conclusion that this story was no longer about Demo
Beef or the bizarre death of Ron Payne, but about Milli
Carter and her wicked red orb, as well as Lewis Kindre
and Josh Nickerson himself. The story had acquired eeri
elements that caused it to read more like a cheap horro
yarn than a piece of investigative journalism. There wa
Millie's supernormal physical strength, for example
There were her rustling blue shadow and her disturbing
mismatched eyes. There was her uncanny ability t
penetrate beyond locked doors and walk out of second
floor windows without getting a scratch. Then there wer
the orb itself, which made its bearer invincible in car

games, and the strange collection of artifacts that Nicole had found in her father's study, which included a pearl-handled Chinese-made pistol like the one Lewis had used in an attempt to kill a monster many years ago in Vietnam.

Josh confronted the bleak realization that this wasn't the kind of meaty, real-world stuff that a fledgling investigative journalist could write about and expect to be taken seriously by anyone other than the editor of the *National Enquirer*. Owing to his own direct involvement, the story lacked an objective viewpoint, meaning that the piece was a journalistic failure before he'd even finished a draft. Yet, he continued to lay down the facts as he knew them along with suspicions and conjecture, finding that with every keystroke his commitment to the story hardened. Someone needed to tell it through to the end, he felt, though he had no idea how or when the story would end. He resolved to be that someone, to discover the whole truth about the bizarre Millie Carter – not only to warn the world about her, but also to find some way of fighting her, maybe even beating her.

When his clock radio came on at seven A.M., he discovered that he'd dozed off with his finger on a key, causing the computer screen to fill up with question marks.

He ate breakfast alone, since his sister was sleeping in after a late date and his mother had gone to the Mult-nomah Athletic Club for an early workout. Halfway through a portion of microwaved French toast, Josh decided that he needed to talk with Lewis, even if it meant risking another encounter with Millie. With him still was the shock of meeting her at Lewis's door two days earlier, together with a sinking feeling that had washed over him, as if the battle had started without him and was already lost.

He hurried out of the apartment and thumped down the rear stairs of Sloan House. Reaching the first landing where the stairs curved sharply to the right, he happened to glance out through the tall, diamond-paned window that faced the cluster of high rises in the center of the city. A block away, just visible at the end of a corridor of pines and oaks, a Tri-Met bus had halted. Lewis Kindred had driven his Action Power 9000 onto the power lift at the door of the bus, and the lift was rising slowly. Josh watched as Lewis maneuvered the wheelchair through the door and the bus pulled away. Resting his forehead against the windowpane, Josh blew out a sigh of both frustration and relief. Lewis was apparently functioning with some degree of normalcy, which was reason to be encouraged. Still, Josh was antsy as hell to talk with him.

As he slowly climbed the stairs again, he mulled a notion that had come to him again and again since he'd followed Millie to the seedy old villa in Northeast Portland. To act on that notion entailed unconscionable risk, he knew, but *not* to act had become equally unconscionable. Lewis himself had often said that nothing worthwhile ever happens to someone who takes no risks. Josh thumped back down the stairs and headed for Nicole Tran's house.

ii

He parked the Escort on the shoulder of the narrow road at the base of the hill and leaned out the window, his face turned upward toward the stucco wall that curved along the crest. 'That's where we'll go over it,' he said to Nicole, who was crouched over to lace a hiking boot.

'We'll leave the car here, where it won't make anyone suspicious.' He reached beneath the seat for his trusty Coleman flashlight, which he slid into a side pocket of his bulky flannel sport shirt, then checked the other pocket to ensure that he had his notepad and a ballpoint. Nicole had dressed appropriately in old jeans with holes in the knees, a dark cable-knit sweater and a navy breaker. With her long black hair tucked under a knitted watch cap, she looked like an elfin cat burglar. 'Sure you're up for this?' he asked her one more time.

'I'm up for it only because I can't let you do it alone,' she answered, glaring at him. 'But I want to go on record that I still think it's a stupid idea – and a dangerous one.'

Josh grinned crookedly and put on his Twins baseball cap – backwards, naturally. He was glad that she'd finally relented and agreed to come along, because he doubted whether he could've mustered the courage to do this thing on his own. She'd always made him feel brave and capable. With Nicole beside him, he felt as if he could do damn-near anything.

Persuading her hadn't been easy, though. She'd felt a need to stay close to her father, who was still far from healed of the strange malady he'd suffered the past several weeks. But Nicole's mother, bless her heart, had insisted that she go out for a change of scenery. 'Go with Nickster!' Mrs Tran had commanded in her clipped Vietnamese accent, shooing her daughter out the door. 'You're young! Go out and breathe the air. Have fun for a change!'

As they strolled together around Gander Circle, breathing the tart morning air and feeling the tingle of mist on their cheeks, Josh had explained to Nicole that he needed to find out who Millie Carter was. He needed to discover her background, where she'd come from, how she lived – not merely to flesh out the story he was writing, but to arm himself against her. *Know your enemy*, someone famous had once said (or had it been Lewis?).

A person's household possessions said much about him, as every investigator knew, and this was precisely why Josh needed to get into Millie's house. He needed to check out the photographs on her walls, the back issues of magazines she read, the medicines in her cabinet, and—

'And the brace of rottweilers she keeps to guard against people like you,' Nicole had thrown in. 'You realize, of course, that breaking and entering is a crime, and that we're close enough to eighteen to be tried as adults, assuming the rottweilers don't eat us. We could go to prison.'

But they wouldn't get caught, he declared simply. Yesterday's reconnaissance had told him that Millie parked her Jag in the front drive of the villa, and that the garage hadn't seen any use for years, judging from the ivy that overgrew its doors. Ergo, he would check to see whether the Jag was present before deciding whether to 'penetrate' the house. Nicole had scoffed, but in the end, she'd agreed to come along, and Josh had detected a glitter of excitement in her eyes.

iii

Climbing the hillside to the stucco wall took longer than Josh had expected, for yesterday's rain had slickened the ground and made the going slow. When they reached the top, their hiking boots were caked with mud, their jeans soaked from slogging through rain-heavy sword ferns and low bushes. They stopped a moment to catch their breath and gaze over the valley below, where industrial Northwest Portland sprawled beneath a thin haze.

'Think anyone has seen us yet?' Nicole wondered aloud, her lips tight with misgiving.

'I doubt it,' Josh answered. 'No cars have come by.' Just then a large white Mercedes glided past on the roadway below, its tires sighing on the damp asphalt. Josh and Nicole stood still as mannequins until it disappeared around a curve. 'One of the neighbors, no doubt,' Josh speculated, trying to sound confident. 'No way they could've seen us, so there's nothing to get excited about.'

'You hope.'

They went over the wall with the help of a young oak tree that had grown just outside it. Josh hoisted himself into the vee from which a branch grew away from the trunk, then eased himself onto the top of the wall where a mason had mortared pieces of broken bottles and jars into the surface. He cautioned Nicole not to cut herself.

After alighting on the ground inside the wall, they made their way into what was once an Italianate garden but which decades of neglect had reduced to a hodge-podge of ragged hedges and legions of weeds. The ground was spongy with untold seasons' worth of decaying leaves and needles. Moss grew thick on the aged terracotta statuary, and a colony of blackberries had taken over the fountain. A flagstone walkway wound from the garden toward the house, which seemed to cower in the dusky shade of hemlocks and cedars, its bleak windows offering no encouragement.

A covered veranda swept across the rear of the structure, where some earlier occupant had dumped disused furniture and derelict appliances. A trellis had long ago rotted away and collapsed onto an old refrigerator, which stood with its door open, like a mute beggar. After circumnavigating the house to ensure that the front drive was empty of Millie's Jaguar, Josh and Nicole crept onto the veranda and halted next to a splintered armoire. There was no sound except the rustle of a breeze in the foliage and the squeak of branches against stucco. They moved through the obstacle course of dilapidated armchairs and sofas to the rear door, which was securely locked.

'Now what?' whispered Nicole.

'We try the windows.' These too were locked and heavily curtained. They climbed an exterior stairway at one end of the veranda, and found themselves on an open second-floor deck, empty but for mounds of yellowed needles and moldering leaves. Glassed-in French doors fronted what appeared to be a large sitting room, though the glass was so dusty and stained that they could hardly see through it. The French doors were locked, as were the windows that flanked them.

'I suppose we could break the glass,' Josh said absently, glancing around in search of a suitably heavy implement.

'*No!*' hissed Nicole. 'What if there's an alarm system? The cops would be here in a New York minute.'

'I suppose you have a better idea.'

'I have an idea – I'm not sure it's a better one.' She went to the far end of the deck, scissored over the railing and edged close to the wall. Leaning away from the railing, she was just able to swing a foot onto a second-floor window casement. Stretching, she grasped the upper edge of the casement and pulled herself aboard the lower edge, kneeling precariously against the window-pane on one knee. Josh held his breath, fearing that she would lose her balance and plunge into the unkempt thicket of junipers below. But she didn't fall, thanks to her lithe frame and a gymnast's sense of balance. She reached slowly downward until her fingers found the edges of adjacent windowpanes and pulled upward. The window slid open and Nicole rolled through it into the shadowy room beyond.

Josh let out his breath, his upper lip frosty with sweat. Before he could turn around, one of the French doors creaked open behind him, revealing Nicole's grinning face. 'What're you waiting for?' she whispered. 'Let's get this over with, okay? I'd just as soon not be here when Millie comes back.'

The room was bare of furnishings except for a dusty sofa with herniated knots of upholstery bulging through rips in the cushions. The floral wallpaper had faded to near colorlessness, though occasional rectangles of brightness betrayed spots where pictures had once hung. Josh and Nicole passed through the room into a balcony that overlooked a long interior hall, where daylight filtered in through dingy windows to create an appropriate dreariness. A chandelier festooned with webs hung from the ceiling, its brass lanterns green with tarnish. A long Persian runner stretched beneath the balcony into the front entrance, covered with dust and grime except for a comparatively clean strip down the very middle.

'Are you sure she actually *lives* here?' whispered Nicole, scowling at the general state of dilapidation. 'This place is the pits.'

'No, I'm not sure, now that you mention it,' Josh confessed. 'All I'm sure of is that she came here yesterday. I suppose the house could belong to someone else.'

'Oh, that's just great! That's really special, Josh.

You're telling me that we may have broken into a house that doesn't even belong to Millie Carter.' Nicole shook her head incredulously. 'We might as well see what's downstairs, now that we're here.'

They tiptoed down a curving staircase to the main hall, each cringing whenever a step squeaked or an inadvertent footfall echoed off the surrounding bare walls. They found the dining room, which adjoined the main hall, and beyond it another room that had many built-in shelves, most sagging precariously – a library, once upon a time. Both were empty of furniture. At the rear of the ground floor was a large kitchen, where cupboard doors hung askew on their hinges and rodents had left their scat among baseball-sized dust bunnies.

'Look at this,' whispered Nicole, having wandered back into the hall. She pointed to the Persian runner with its strip of comparative cleanness. 'Somebody walks down the middle of this rug on a regular basis.'

'No shit, Inspector.'

'And she turns here, before getting to the kitchen . . .' She pointed into a short adjoining corridor, where the parquet wood flooring had a path that was similarly free of dust and grime. '. . . and goes into that room.' A pair of walnut doors stood shut, their brass handles gleaming softly in the sparse light. *No tarnish on the handles*, thought Josh, *because someone uses them every day* – a realization that roused a tingle on the back of his neck.

'How much do you want to bet that the room is locked?' he asked.

'A large pizza at Pizza Oasis says it's not,' Nicole replied, arching an eyebrow. 'Care to do the honors?'

Josh swallowed and shrugged, tried not to look scared. He walked slowly to the doors, put his hand on the cold brass, and pushed. A metallic clink stung the silence of the empty house, and the door swung inward, creaking softly on its hinges.

'You owe me,' whispered Nicole with a sly wink. 'I'll want at least six toppings, including anchovies.'

'You're sick,' Josh replied, trying not to smile. 'Anybody who would ruin a gourmet pizza with anchovies should be locked up.'

He stepped into a high-ceilinged room made gloomy by heavy brocaded drapes that denied the daylight. As his eyes adjusted, he saw that this room appeared thoroughly lived in. To his left was a massive stone fireplace, its mantel paneled in walnut, its firebox heaped with ashy fragments of a still-warm log. Half a dozen ornate armoires stood against the outer walls, one with its doors open, revealing a collection of women's clothing. Here and there were exquisite old chests of drawers, and in a far corner sat a lady's vanity well laden with cosmetics, lotions and perfumes. Pieces of luggage lay open on the floor, costly looking stuff made of good leather, lined with heavy satin. Articles of clothing lay on padded sofas and chairs, as if their wearer had slipped out of them and simply cast them aside. A large round table squatted before the fireplace, attended by an authentic-looking Tiffany floor lamp and six high-backed chairs.

'So this is where she lives,' breathed Nicole. 'It's a little messy, but at least it's not filthy like the rest of the house. No stereo, no TV, though. I'd go crazy.'

'It doesn't make any sense. Why have a mansion if you're only going to use one room?'

'It has a temporary feeling, don't you think? – like a hotel room. It doesn't look as if she's even finished unpacking.'

Josh tried the light switch next to the door, and the Tiffany lamp lit up, flooding the room softly. 'She apparently does some reading, and maybe some writing,' he remarked, eyeing the stacks of file folders and envelopes on the table. He poked though a jumble of papers, among which were bank statements and bills for credit card purchases. 'This is Millie's place, all right – these bills came to her by name, and to this address. *Jesus* – Nicki, look at this . . . !' Millie Carter's checking account balance at First Interstate Bank in Portland was fifty-six thousand dollars and change.

'She's definitely not hurting for money,' said Nicole, reading the statement carefully.

'And look at *this* – statements from mutual fund accounts, stockbrokers . . .'

'From all over the country. Houston, Las Vegas, New Orleans . . .'

'God, she's rich! Nicki, she's a fucking millionaire!'

'I don't see why that comes as a surprise to you. You don't live at this address unless you've got plenty of money.'

'But why doesn't she fix the place up? I mean, why let a mansion like this fall down around your ears if you've got the greenies to make it nice?'

'Some people don't concern themselves with such things,' Nicole answered, her brow furrowed in thought. 'Some people have more important things to worry about than their physical surroundings.'

She busied herself checking out the clothes in several of the wardrobes and pronounced them on the cutting edge of fashion, as well as extraordinarily high quality, then did likewise for the jewelry in the vanity.

'She may not care about her physical surroundings,'

Josh remarked, 'but she sure as hell cares about what she wears.' He continued to peruse the papers on the table and, having done this, pawed through one of several valises stacked on the floor nearby. 'Here's a letter from the realtor who sold her the place,' he announced, holding aloft a sheaf of paper. 'They closed the deal early last winter. Listen to what this guy says: "Though the villa is in some need of restoration, I can guarantee that it will satisfy your requirement for privacy." *Some need of restoration* – can you believe it? She paid cash, almost five hundred thousand dollars. And look – the letter was sent to an address in Las Vegas, which must be where she lived before moving here.'

'I can't believe this place is worth that much, considering the condition it's in.'

'Are you serious? The land alone is worth that much, Nicki. She could subdivide this property into four, maybe five regular-size lots, I'll bet. She could make a killing.'

'So excuse me for being no real-estate expert.'

They poked around, neither of them knowing exactly what to look for. Josh occasionally jotted notes in his little spiral book.

Suddenly he started to choke noisily and Nicole rushed over to him. 'Nickster, are you okay?'

He waved her off, but his face was bright red. He'd opened one of the valises and had pulled out several sections of newspapers, each of which had a hole clipped in a page. 'I don't believe this,' he rasped, having not quite recovered. He coughed again, took several deep breaths, and collected himself. 'Look at these, Nicki.'

She took the section of newspaper that he held out, but didn't see anything particularly frightening about it. 'It's a newspaper that someone has clipped,' she observed,

sticking her fingers through the hole in the page ar
wiggling them. 'What's the big deal?' Josh handed h
another, and a third, and a fourth, all with similar hol
scissored into them. 'I'm sorry,' Nicole confessed, 'I si
don't see what the problem is.'

'Remember the newspaper clippings I got in the m
over the summer? They all concerned murders that had
striking resemblance to Ron Payne's. The first one car
in June, right after we got out of school, a piece from t
Atlanta Constitution about a night watchman who was
badly mutilated that the cops thought a big dog might'
done it.' He pulled a section of newspaper from t
bundle that Nicole held and pointed to the heading in t
top corner of the page. Sure enough, it was the *Consti*
tion, and the date corresponded to the clipping that Jo
had received in the mail – June 19,1992. 'I'll buy you *t*
large pizzas at Pizza Oasis if the clipping I got doesn't
this hole,' he added. Nicole's expression became sober

'The next one came a month later,' Josh went c
pulling out another section of newsprint. 'It was from t
Des Moines Register, and it was about a dentist w
picked up some babe in a bar and took her to a hotel. I
ended up in pieces, just like Ron Payne and the nig
watchman in Atlanta.' And this section, according to t
heading, had come from a July issue of the *Regist*
'Then, in August, I got one from the *Burlington Fr*
Press, in Burlington, Vermont . . .' – he showed her
clipped section of newspaper, pointing to the heading
'. . . about a sales manager of a car dealership, ripped
pieces in his hot tub. And a month later I got one fro
the *Sacramento Bee* . . .' – this one corresponded to t
final section that Nicole held in her hands – '. . . abou
windsurfing instructor from Lake Tahoe, found dead

his car outside Sacramento, California, more or less in the same condition as the others.'

Nicole drew her arms over her chest, as if she suddenly felt cold. 'What're you saying – that Millie Carter sent you the clippings? Why would she do that?'

'I don't have a clue.'

'Where were the envelopes mailed from?'

'The postmarks were from the actual cities where the murders happened, which makes me think – wait a minute! Let's do another take of her credit card bills.' Josh rummaged through the stacks of papers on the writing desk and pulled out billing records from Master-Card, Discover and American Express. He ran his finger down each list, occasionally circling an entry with his pen. 'Just as I suspected. In June she bought a round-trip ticket on United Airlines to Atlanta. In July, she went to Des Moines, Iowa. I can't find an entry for Burlington, Vermont, but here . . .' He shuffled a sheet to the top and made another circle with his pen. 'Here's a trip to Sacramento on Alaska Airlines. And the dates all match!' He laid the papers on the desk and stared at Nicole, his face pale, his fingers shaking. He felt slightly dizzy. 'That's three out of four, Nicki. She went to three out of the four cities where murders took place—'

'Murders like Ron Payne's.'

'She was physically there at three out of four, and I'd bet all my college tuition money that she went to Burlington, too, even though I can't find the record.'

'She might've lost that particular bill. People lose stuff like that.'

'You're absolutely right. Now the question is whether . . .' – he gulped – '. . . she actually *killed* those guys. You'll recall that I saw her in Ron Payne's apartment

the night he got killed. We can't assume she did the actu
killing but she was *there* – in each of the cities! And she w
here in Portland when Payne got snuffed!'

'We still don't know why she sent the clippings to you

Josh's mouth went dry as desert sand. His eyes start
to water and burn. He felt – humiliated, despairin
beyond redemption. But he didn't know why he felt th
way, unless he was unconsciously coming to grips with th
fact that he *meant* something to Millie Carter. He *mea*
enough to her that she'd sent him the clippings.

'Nicki, listen. The night Millie saved us from th
skinheads – remember how it happened?'

'How could I forget? I still dream about it.'

'She knew who we were. She called us the Dynam
Duo of Gander Ridge.'

'God, that's right! You asked her how she happened
come by when she did, and she said that it was
coincidence. She'd been *looking* for us!'

'And that means she knew us before we were ev
aware that she existed. I got the distinct feeling that nig
that she'd set the whole thing up, didn't you? It was li
she was manipulating us.' This thought chilled Josh all th
way down to his toes. His hand found Nicole's and th
stood silent for nearly a minute, staring fearfully into o
another's eyes. 'Let's finish up here and check the rest
the house,' he said finally. 'Be on the lookout f
anything else that might connect her to the murders. A
let's hurry, okay?'

Nicole went back to searching through the armoir
and the luggage, while Josh busied himself with th
contents of the valises. He found nothing else of mu
interest. It was Nicole who made the next startling fin
'This is unbelievable,' she breathed barely loudly enou

for Josh to hear. He dropped what he was doing and crossed the room to where she stood before a newly opened armoire.

'What's this, a war museum?' he asked. Scores of photographs lined the inside surfaces of the doors and shelves, snapshots taken of soldiers doing what soldiers do – lounging and loitering in foxholes and bunkers, marching or smoking and joking, playing cards, clowning and drinking beer, or, in a more serious vein, firing their weapons in scenes of combat. They were shirtless and ponchoed, helmeted and bareheaded, young and old but mostly young. Scattered among the snapshots were portraits in frames of various soldiers in various wars, swarthy men with strong faces and unsettling eyes, veterans of the Second World War, the First World War, the Spanish American War, even the American Civil War.

On shelves and in various nooks and crannies of the wardrobe lay more substantial artifacts of war. Ammunition clips and empty shell casings. Bayonets, several appearing to be very old. Sabers that looked older than the revolutionary war. Even a Renaissance-era cutlass.

On a horizontal rack hung a dozen or so military uniforms, one of which was a set of U. S. Army 'Class A's,' consisting of a forest-green jacket with matching trousers, gleaming brass insignia, and gold-threaded sergeant's stripes on the sleeves. Above the left breast pocket of the jacket were rows of ribbons and medals, and Josh recognized several of them, because he'd seen their mates on Lewis Kindred's old army uniform and Lewis had explained their significance to him.

'Whoever owned this one,' said Josh, pulling the uniform off the rack, 'was a Vietnam vet.' He touched a metallic badge that had a silver musket embossed on a blue field, encircled with an oval-shaped wreath. 'That's a Combat Infantryman's Badge. And this little yellow ribbon is a Vietnam campaign ribbon. This guy must've been some kind of hero – he's got a couple of Bronze Stars with Oak Leaves and a Purple Heart.' He placed the uniform back on the rack and pawed through the others, one of which looked like that of World-War-One-era doughboy. When he looked up at Nicole, he saw that her lower lip was trembling. 'You okay?' he asked.

'Nickster, did you see the nameplate on the first one?'

Josh retrieved the first uniform from the rack and held it up. Then he felt the sudden urge to fling the thing away and find a place to wash his hands. Above the left pocket hung a rectangle of glossy black plastic with 'Cartee' emblazoned in white letters. He quickly hung the garment on the rack again.

'That's the name of the man Lewis tried to kill in Vietnam, isn't it?' said Nicole.

Josh nodded, and without knowing it started wiping his palms on his jeans. 'Cartee,' he said, barely aloud. 'Carter. Cartee, Carter. Cartee . . .'

'I know what you're thinking. They've got to be related, right? Millie *Carter* and Gamaliel *Cartee*. Otherwise, why would she have his uniform?'

Josh forced saliva over his tongue and wetted his salt-dry lips. 'The names are too close for coincidence, that's for sure. I can't believe I didn't think of it before. And both Gamaliel and Millie have mismatched eyes -- or *had*. Maybe they were brother and sister. Or cousins.'

'How about father and daughter?'

'Hey, I'll believe anything.' His eyes found one of the photographs that hung on the interior surface of the wardrobe door. It was a faded color portrait of a striking man of indeterminate age, as young as twenty or as old as thirty-five, hard-looking in a lean way. He grinned broadly into the camera with dazzling white teeth. He had the features of an African and the complexion of a Greek or an Arab, and despite the fact that the picture had faded, Josh could plainly see that his left eye was brown and the right one blue. Just visible above the right pocket of his Class A's was his nameplate: *Cartee*.

Josh's head started to buzz as he stared into the cruel eyes in the portrait, as the gruesome reality sunk in and took hold. Regardless of Millie's precise relationship to Gamaliel, one thing was certain: She was a piece of the thread that had run through Lewis Kindred's life, beginning with his days in Vietnam. Now the thread had entwined the lives of Josh and Nicole and God only knew who else.

'Josh, you're right about wanting to write about this,' Nicole said solemnly. 'Promise me you'll do it, and that you won't let anything stand in your way.' She riveted him with her dark stare, reaching to him in a way she'd never done before. Without words she conveyed her belief in him and this touched him deeply.

He knew something now that had only been a fleeting thought before, one that had always slithered from his grip like a slippery, wriggling eel: He loved her, not as a friend loves a friend, but as a man loves a woman. He loved her with a pounding, insistent urgency. Whatever he'd felt for his nominal girlfriend, Laurel, and for all the other girls he'd dated, paled next to the blistering love he felt for Nicole. This was an epiphany, an awakening, an exhilarating plunge into an Arctic pond. Why hadn't he known it before? How could he have been so blind for so long?

'Promise me,' Nicole pressed. 'Write about it and make sense of it. It'll take someone like you to do it, Nickster. Not just anyone could.'

'I promise,' he said, his voice catching. He cleared his throat and said it again. He wanted desperately to kiss her, and was about to try, when—

They heard something, a thud in the distance, which – if not for the profundity of the silence of this house – they would never have noticed, especially at a time like this, when their brains were humming like motors. An old water pipe, perhaps. Or the thump of a tree branch against the roof. Or the slamming of a car door outside in the drive.

'We've got to get out of here!' Josh whispered, feeling a clutch of fresh fear. He moved toward the door, pulling Nicole with him.

'But she'll know we've been here!' Nicole said, gesturing frantically around at the strewn papers, the armoires standing open.

'Too bad! We don't have time to straighten up!'

As they entered the main hallway, they heard a clank of metal against metal, the throw of a dead bolt in the main entrance that clattered like a pistol shot through the empty rooms. 'Not that way,' breathed Josh, herding Nicole away from the front hall and the staircase. 'She'll be in before we can make it up the stairs.'

'*Where*, then?'

'This way!' He led her toward the kitchen, remembering a doorway that he'd supposed opened to a room that fronted the veranda. They passed quickly through a musty-smelling pantry and burst through a wall of cobwebs into a long parlor that was empty but for a pile of warped boards and an ancient snooker table standing on end against a wall. A glassed-in door on their left gave onto the veranda, where the derelict furniture and appliances were barely visible through the dingy windows.

Josh tried the door and found it locked, as before. 'Son of a bitch!' he whispered sharply. 'It's a dead-bolt lock that takes a key. We can't open it.' He stared at Nicole helplessly as seconds ticked by, as the scuff of footsteps echoed from beyond the pantry. Nicole stared back at him, her face whitening, her mouth contorting with near-panic. Her eyes silently asked, *What now?*

Josh pulled her back into the pantry, where they'd passed a descending stairway into what he'd assumed was the cellar. With the way to the front of the house blocked and the rear door securely bolted, the one remaining option was to hide down there in the dark. If they were lucky, Josh reasoned frantically, they would find an old coal chute with an opening to the outside, or an exterior entrance through a ground-level door, like many old houses had. But Nicole hung back when they reached the black maw of the stairway, her hand suddenly going cold in his. 'I can't go down there, Nickster.'

'Nicki, we don't have a choice! There's nowhere to hide up here!'

'I can't – it's too dark! It smells horrible—!'

This was true. An incredibly foul odor wafted up from the darkness below, a latrine-kind of smell that brought to mind human waste, unwashed skin, unbrushed teeth.

'Nicki, she's coming. We don't have a choice, I tell you . . .'

More footsteps came from behind them – curious footsteps that stopped now and then to listen with a cocked head, to stare around with hungry eyes for clues of intrusion, to sniff the stale air with flaring nostrils;

footsteps that knew someone had been here, that someone *still* was here.

A rustling came to Josh's ears, so faint that it hardly registered in his brain, but when it did register, he recognized it as the sound Millie's shadow made as it moved across the carpet in the Nickersons' apartment. Terror clawed at his belly. 'It's *her*. I know it.'

Nicole was whispering something, drawing away from the black hole that led downward. Josh couldn't afford to argue with her, lest his own terror seize him and transform him into a squealing idiot. He yanked on her hand and dragged her down into the darkness. With his free hand he reached into his shirt pocket and took out his flashlight, but he didn't dare to snap it on yet, because Millie might detect its glow from the top of the stairs. Nicole somehow did not let herself shriek in panic, but she trembled like a terrified newborn kitten, which Josh felt in her cold, cold hand.

With every step downward the stench became thicker, *warmer*. For a hideous moment Josh imagined that they would step off the foot of the stairs into a pool full of semi-liquid filth – stuff more vile than vomit, more poisonous than sewage, in which something huge and shark-like swam in patient circles, a meat eater. But he forced himself on, step after step, pulling Nicole after him until they reached the bottom, which was as firm as hard-packed earth, thankfully. He let himself breathe again despite the stink.

He snapped the flashlight on, and its beam knifed into the darkness ahead, revealing more or less what he'd expected. An antique-looking boiler hunkered in its corner on the right, from which led pipes along the ceiling in every direction to radiators in the rooms above. Stacks

of crates stood against sweating concrete walls, full of
household wares that long-dead people had probably
once thought valuable. And on all sides were piles of toys
and play-gear from childhoods long forgotten, judging
from the cobwebs and rust and mildew – tricycles and
bikes, a badminton set, a deflated football, a chipped and
faded rocking horse that would have looked at home on a
carousel, and much more. Josh oriented himself toward
an inner doorway at the far end of the room, and snapped
off the flashlight, causing Nicole to gasp and squeeze his
hand hard enough to hurt.

'It's okay,' he whispered. 'I'll lead you. Don't let go of
me, okay?'

'That's the one thing you don't have to worry about.'

He started forward into the pitch-blackness, keeping
the arrow of his mental compass pointed toward the
doorway, holding the flashlight far out in front of him
while clutching tightly to Nicole with the other hand. The
stink became noticeably stronger, the further they went,
until Josh needed to breathe through his mouth to keep
from gagging.

The flashlight contacted something solid, and Josh
tested it with his fingers, finding the splintery wood of the
doorjamb. As he and Nicole edged around it, his face
encountered a stiff spider web, and the terrified arachnid
scurried across his cheek into his hair. Somehow Josh
managed to swallow the scream that rose in his chest.
Once through the door, he peeked around it toward the
stairway from which they'd come, and saw only a pale
gray rectangle in a void of black, an island of thin light
spilling down from the rooms above. Now that his eyes
had adjusted, he was certain that he would be able to see
Millie if she came down those stairs. Frighteningly, he

had no idea what to do if that happened.

Above them the planks of old flooring squeaked and snapped – footsteps in the kitchen. Slow, searching footsteps. Another creak, closer; in the pantry now. Another, in the parlor that fronted the veranda. Then, nothing. Had Millie stopped to listen?

Josh heard a wheeze in the darkness behind him and tightened his hold on Nicole's hand, wordlessly telling her to be quiet, not even to breathe, if she could manage it. Another wheeze came out of the darkness, the beginnings of a cough. Josh squeezed again, and Nicole pressed herself against him, trembling.

'N-Nickster,' she whimpered into his ear, 'that w-wasn't me.'

Josh's heartbeat thundered in his temples. 'Nicki, please . . . !'

'Josh, I'm not kidding, it wasn't me. There's someone behind us . . . !'

A short scuffing was next, then a muffled grunt – almost the sounds of *struggling*. He heard breathing that wasn't his or Nicole's, for she was so close that he could feel the air from her nostrils.

'Nickster, turn on the light!'

'I can't . . . !'

'You've got to! I'm going to lose my mind and start screaming, if you don't. I can't stand this!' Her whisper rose in pitch, and Josh could feel the terror that had started to tear her mind apart. He had no choice. He raised the flashlight and positioned it over her shoulder, pointing it away from the rectangle of grayness at the stairs. He snapped it on.

The beam knifed across a face that he didn't believe at first, because it seemed so grotesquely out of context, so wrong for the here and now, a face that gazed into nothingness with empty, senseless eyes. It belonged to one of the skinheads who'd attacked them in the alley off Southwest Thirteenth Street, the one Josh had thought of as Fireplug. Slouching, head hung slightly forward, Fireplug literally looked dead on his feet, except for the fact that he was breathing and slobbering obscenely. Behind him stood his four pals in similarly witless conditions – Pimples, his face a dermatologist's nightmare, and next to him, the blond Hitler, scraggy and drooling, and behind him the two others. All five were bunched together in the dark like mannequins stored in the stock room of a department store, mute and motionless as if they'd been cast from wax.

Nicole clapped a palm tightly over her mouth and screamed into it, her breath whistling through her fingers like steam through a faulty gasket. Josh felt his bladder start to let go, but he somehow held it. His eyes collected more details and fed them to his brain, each generating a fresh twist of nausea. The stubble on Fireplug's face had grown out into an uneven beard, as had most of the others' whiskers. His brown leather jacket had collected a thick layer of dust. A spider had spun a web between the tip of Pimples's nose and the chrome swastika pinned to the flap of his army-surplus field jacket. All five thugs had dark stains on the fronts of their jeans, indicating that they'd voided themselves, which accounted for the stink. And all bore the marks of the drubbing they'd gotten two weeks ago at Millie's hands in the alley behind the Chef's Corner – contusions and scabbed-over cuts, abrasions from slamming into brick walls or asphalt paving.

Nicole clung so close to Josh that she seemed to be trying to climb into his clothes with him. When she spoke, her voice was a jagged hiss. 'What's wrong with them? Why are they just standing there like that?'

'I-I don't know. I think they must be under, uh—' His mind failed him momentarily, then clicked into gear again. '—*hypnosis*, or something.'

'But it looks like they've been standing there for *weeks*. There's dust all over them, and – *God*, it looks like fungus!' Josh beamed the light against Fireplug's cheek, where a splotch of discoloration suggested a colony of something fungoid or bacterial. Josh's stomach came dangerously close to violent revolution as he reached the conclusion that such things might indeed start to grow on your skin if you stood for weeks at a time in a dark, damp cellar.

'Millie did this,' he declared, his voice rising above a whisper. 'She put them under some kind of spell, or poisoned them – I don't know. She has powers, Nicki – I've told you that. She can come through locked doors, for Christ's sake. If she's on your side, you can win at poker, and if she's not . . .' He rubbed his eyes, fighting a burgeoning headache. 'It's not really so surprising that she can do something like this. Like I said before, she set us up in the alley that night – sicced these guys on us like a pack of dogs, then came riding to the rescue.'

'But *why*?'

'If we knew that, we wouldn't be here.'

Just then Fireplug coughed again and took a deep, rattling breath. As they watched, his vacant eyes turned toward them, and his head raised a little. His lips stretched slowly into a yellow-toothed grin, his eyes becoming homicidal slits. His body jerked, as if he was trying to break out of an invisible plaster cast.

'Damn,' whispered Josh, 'we've got to get out of here.'

'How? Which way? The stairs are the only way out.'

'Then we'll take the stairs.'

'But what about Millie?'

'Do you really want to stay here with these guys?' Josh hauled Nicole toward the mouth of the stairway, clicking off the flashlight as soon as they reached it. He hesitated a long moment to let his eyes readjust to near-total darkness, and during that moment he had second thoughts about climbing the stairs to face Millie Carter. How ludicrous it seemed, to think that they would have any chance of escaping her. She would probably do to them what she'd done to the skinheads or to Ron Payne or to those other poor guys about whom Josh had read in the newspaper clippings. A swell of regret rose inside him for having dragged Nicole along on this misbegotten adventure, for having been so stupid as to violate Millie Carter's domain and plan on living to tell the story. Now he would pay the price for his stupidity, but more tragic was the fact that Nicole too would pay. He clenched his jaw so hard that his whole face hurt.

'Josh!' Nicole's shriek jarred him, and he whirled with the flashlight, snapping it on. Fireplug stood scarcely a yard behind Nicole, having broken out of his spell somehow and moved after them. He'd pulled a long knife from his pocket and now held it forward in a jerky parody of a thrust, the blade having just made contact with Nicole's arm. Josh's rage exploded. He swung the heavy Coleman flashlight at Fireplug's head with all his might, felt it connect with bone-crunching force, and saw the lens dissolve in an explosion of glassy splinters. The light died, and Fireplug bellowed like a bull as he went down. Josh launched himself up the stairs while pulling the shrieking Nicole behind him, and he looked back only when they'd reached the top. Fireplug had crawled to the first step, his face awash in blood from the gash on his forehead, his hands clawing upward in a hopeless attempt to snag his prey.

'Are you hurt?' Josh asked Nicole. 'Did he get you with the knife?'

'It didn't even break the cloth of my breaker,' she answered, rubbing her arm. 'I'm okay, really. Let's just go.'

They turned left through the pantry and stole into the kitchen, trying not to let their hiking boots thud or scrape against the buckling tiles. They peered into the hallway before entering it, looking for any sign of Millie Carter, but saw nothing except motes of dust floating in the gloom. Having no choice but to press on, they moved slowly toward the front of the house, hand in hand. At each step the floor creaked and they feared that Millie would fly out of her hiding place to tear them limb from limb. They halted at the intersection with the short hallway that led to the room where they'd found her possessions, and traded fearful glances. If something was about to happen, this seemed a likely place.

Josh pressed his back against the wall and leaned slowly beyond the corner, going only far enough to get a look with one eye. What he saw nearly turned his blood to slush. Millie Carter stood outside the door of her room as if waiting for them, her head cocked quizzically so that her reddish dreadlocks splayed about her shoulders. Her eyes shone uncannily, as if they were themselves sources of light. She wore pleated tan trousers, a superbly tailored black blazer, and earrings made of large chromium chainlinks. Dressed as she was, she could have been a lawyer, or a banking executive or even a model, if not for her eyes and the grin that parted her lips to reveal teeth that didn't look quite human.

Josh tasted fear as he'd never known it, fear that made his scalp prickle. He exploded into a sprint toward the front hall of the house, holding tightly to Nicole's hand but having no time to tell her what he'd seen. Should they dash to the front entrance, where they might very well encounter a locked door, or bound up the curving staircase to the room with the French doors through which they'd entered? He chose the latter. Nicole was a fleet and sure-footed runner, fortunately, and she didn't stumble or even slow him, but actually overtook him on the staircase. Josh braved a glance backward when they reached the second-floor balcony, and he saw Millie in full pursuit, hauling herself hand over hand along the banister with her body stretched nearly horizontal, moving with a liquid grace that was almost eel-like.

They crashed into the room at the top of the stairs and headed for the French doors, their boots thumping and echoing against bare walls. From behind them came a *rustling*, a sound that could have been a billion flesh-eating insects in a cardboard box, or the sweep of Millie Carter's shadow over old wood. Josh had just pulled one of the doors open when she caught them. Nicole screamed as something razor-sharp sang in the air, the swipe of a claw. Josh caught a glimpse of Millie in another form – a thing so misshapen that her tasteful black blazer was in shreds, a thing with a head that was mostly mouth. He pulled Nicole out the door and down the exterior stairs into the veranda. Dodging a tumble-down trellis, he made for the garden with Nicole in tow, her whimpers piercing him, the sunlight nearly blinding him.

They found the stucco wall and somehow managed to

get over it, then plunged down the hill to the roadway below. They reached the Escort, scrambled inside it, and locked the doors. Josh fired the engine, slammed the transmission into first gear and popped the clutch, causing the front wheels to spray gravel.

'We made it!' he hollered jubilantly, thumping a palm on the steering wheel. 'We made it, Nicki! We're alive and in one piece! Do you fucking believe it?' He swung the little car around a curve, driving much too fast but needing to put distance between Millie's villa and themselves. He was drunk on adrenaline. 'I thought we were dead meat back there. When she caught up to us at the French doors . . .'

'She let us get away,' Nicole put in. 'You know that, don't you? She could've had us, but she let us get away.'

Josh slowed the car to a sane speed and glanced over at Nicole. His heart missed a beat, for she was as pale as an autumn mist, and she hadn't stopped shivering. She'd lost her watch cap, and her beautiful mane of raven hair no longer flowed down her back, but ended at neck-length in a cruel diagonal slash. Josh saw now that Millie's claw had made contact. He saw too that Nicole's breaker had a long gash across the shoulder, and that the seat in which she sat was drenched in blood.

CHAPTER TWENTY-TWO
Never to Die

i

This guy will be more than a match for Dewey, Lewis said to himself while filling out the Humane Society's paperwork. The twelve-week-old kitten had yellow fur like Big Sister's and similar greenish eyes, but there the similarity ended. In the first place, 'Little Brother' wasn't female, and in the second, he showed no inclination to spending two-thirds of his life asleep. With a high-pitched mewing that was cute for the first five minutes but grated on the nerves thereafter, he made known his wish to get out of the heavy cardboard carrier.

Lewis rode a Tri-Met bus south from the Humane Society shelter in Northeast Portland to a Max light-rail station and caught the commuter train across the river. During the ride, he mollified the kitten by poking a finger through an air hole of the carrier and letting him bite it. He endured the pain of needle-like kitten teeth in the interest of blessed silence.

He got off the Max on the First-Avenue side of the Skidmore Historical District, which teemed with a cheerful crowd of Saturday Market shoppers and sightseers. Keeping his eyes peeled for Dewey, Lewis drove his

Action Power 9000 through the maze of stalls, steering carefully around the milling shoppers and their darting kids, glad for the warm sunshine on his face. He checked Dewey's customary spot in the shade of a white colonnade, but found it occupied by someone else. After another complete circuit of the square, which produced no sign of Dewey, he crossed Second to the VIP Center, where none of the staff had seen Dewey since yesterday. Feeling uneasy, Lewis borrowed the VIP Center's phone and called Tommy Iadanza to ask whether Dewey had shown up to draw from the money that Tommy was keeping for him. Nobody at the Fanshawe had seen him, either.

Lewis spent the rest of the afternoon driving his wheelchair up and down the length of Tom McCall Waterfront Park, hoping to see Dewey. But the old veteran had apparently forsaken his usual Saturday haunts, and Lewis's unease grew.

He bought a can of Nine Lives at a 7-Eleven on the Esplanade and fed a third of it to Little Brother, then cleaned the kitty-poop out of the carrier with a handy-pack of Kleenex and headed back to Old Town. By the time he returned, the Saturday Market crowd had dissipated and the vendors had packed their wares and headed home. With the afternoon waning and a chill gathering in the long shadows, he cruised by the Salvation Army's Harbor Light, which had attracted more than a hundred scruffy, tired-looking men who waited patiently on the sidewalk for this evening's dispensation of charity. Dewey wasn't among them.

A pit formed in Lewis's stomach as he contemplated various possibilities. Dewey might have crossed the river for some reason, in which event Lewis could forget about finding him until he was ready to be found. Or he might have headed up Burnside into Northwest, which was a long pull uphill for a man in an unmotorized wheelchair but certainly not impossible. Or he might have gotten himself mugged. A *chiva* dealer might have slipped a blade between his ribs in order to rob him of his bottle. Or he—

'*L.T., is that you, man?*' The voice came from behind him among the men standing in line outside Harbor Light. Lewis's heart leapt, for it was an achingly familiar voice, but it wasn't Dewey's. '*L.T., wait up, will you?*'

Lewis pulled on the joystick to spin his wheelchair around, and saw a lanky, loose-limbed man quit his place in line and shamble toward him. The man wore street-dingy painter's pants, layers of moth-eaten sweaters, and a pair of cloggy workman's boots with fraying seams. His jaw was rough with stubble that looked like tungsten filings, his face the color of hickory. He stopped before Lewis's chair and bent slightly at the waist, pulling off his sunglasses and his Los Angeles Raiders cap. 'Don't you recognize me, L.T.? Take away twenty years' worth of wrinkles and gray hairs, and it'll come to you.'

And so it did. Lewis stared at the grinning face in disbelief. He'd last seen T. J. Skane twenty-two years ago in the Ho Bo Woods of South Vietnam, immediately after a rocket-propelled grenade had blown the young black GI off his track. T.J. was burning then, a dervish of fire that scorched the flesh from his bones even as Lewis watched. Lewis saw him go down, saw him cease writhing, and learned later from Lieutenant Colonel Gilbert Golightly that T.J. hadn't made it. On October 17, 1970, Specialist-4 T. J. Skane of East Los Angeles, California, had become a KIA – 'killed in action.'

Yet here he stood, a whole man, comparatively unscarred beyond the effects of life on the street, his 'Fro having thinned and grayed but his body sinewy and fit-looking for a man in his forties. And in his black eyes shone a simple joy for having stumbled onto an old pal after all these years, Lieutenant Lewis Kindred, his old platoon leader. The man who'd gotten him killed.

Lewis's mouth worked and yawned, but nothing came out. *It's drooling time*, he heard a voice in his head say. *The schizophrenia's catching up with you, bud. Better find yourself a reputable shrink and ask for some psychotropic medication. Otherwise, you're liable to start preaching sermons in Pioneer Courthouse Square . . . !*

'Who's your little buddy here?' asked T.J. sticking a finger through an air hole in the cardboard sack. Little Brother bit it, and T.J. yipped with mock pain. 'So, how you been, L.T.? You look pretty much the same, except your hair's a lot longer and a lot grayer. I heard about you gettin' your legs blown off, but somebody said you'd been doin' okay since gettin' back from the 'Nam. I hope that's true.'

Lewis managed to nod. 'A-And how have y-you been, T.J.?' he asked in a voice he himself hardly recognized. His vocal cords felt as if they were packed in dry ice.

The black man laughed and stuck his cap back on his head. 'I guess you could say I've been doin' okay, considerin' . . .' He glanced around him, indicating the Harbor Light building with the motion of his head, as if to say, *This is my life. This is where I live, which is nowhere and everywhere*. Still, Lewis heard no bitterness or anger in his voice, and his face seemed almost serene. 'I was hittin' the drugs and the booze pretty good when I got out of the army,' T.J. was saying, 'and I ended up in the

California joint for stealin' a mail truck and tryin' to sell it. Can you believe that, L.T.? – a fuckin' *mail* truck. That's how fucked up I was. I was gonna sell it and buy skag with the money!' He paused to chuckle in that infectious way he had, the way Lewis remembered. 'Anyway, I was never able to keep a job after I got out of the joint, and next thing you know, I was on the street in East L.A. with my hand out. Well, I'm tellin' you, man, East L.A. is no place to be out on the street – I mean, it's worse than the fuckin' Ho Bo Woods or the Iron Triangle. So I started travelin' around a lot, stayin' awhile here and there, tryin' to keep both halves of my ass together. I drink a little cheap wine now and then, mostly when the weather gets cold, but I'm no drunk anymore, and I'm sure as hell no junkie.' He folded his sunglasses and tucked them away. The sun had plunged below the West Hills and left Old Town in deep shadow. 'I never hurt anybody, L.T., so you don't have to be scared of me. I don't even hit up old friends for handouts.'

Lewis felt some fiber in his heart stretch to the breaking point as he wondered whether this was what T.J. would have become if he'd lived, an addict and a felon, a panhandler. Or was this grinning, good-natured man a fragment of a reality that Lewis had misconstrued all these years, a vision of the world twisted by the gnarled fingers of mental illness? He chose to believe the latter. T.J. had *lived*. Swallowing a sob, Lewis reached for him and caught his hand, found it to be a real hand made of flesh and bones, and surprisingly warm. 'I-I thought you were dead,' he said in a pinched voice. 'You and Danny Legler, and Scottie Sanders—'

'Well, I'm happy to say I ain't dead, L.T., and I'm happy you ain't either.' He shook Lewis's hand firmly.

'Know somethin'? For a white dude you were all right. I'm talkin' about the day you stopped that IPW motherfucker from thumpin' up on a little girl and her old granny – what was that motherfucker's name? I can't remember it – somethin' strange . . .'

'Gamaliel,' said Lewis, barely aloud. 'Gamaliel Cartee.'

'Yeah, that's it. Gamaliel, an Interrogator of fuckin' Prisoners of War, a fuckin' Eye Pee Dub-yew. That was one nasty dude, I don't mind sayin'. Anyway, I remember how you got in his face and told him to jack down, and how that old lifer – what was his name?'

'Markowski.'

'Right – Frank Markowski, the platoon sergeant. He tried to chill you out, but you weren't havin' any of it, and you drew your fuckin' forty-five and pointed it at Cartee's head and told him to let the girl go, or you'd blow his fuckin' brains out. I gotta say it, man, that was one of the best things I ever saw in my life. The motherfucker let the girl go, and the good guys won a round for a fuckin' change.' Laughing, he moved close and laid a hand on Lewis's shoulder. 'You didn't deserve what happened to you, man. I mean, if anybody deserves to have both his legs, it's you, L.T.'

Lewis bit his lower lip and struggled to keep the tears back. 'Thanks, T. J. I've told myself the same thing a thousand times, but it helps to hear it from you. I can almost believe it now.'

ii

They headed back toward the square, and Lewis offered to buy dinner at one of the walk-up kitchens in the New Market Theater. He'd been responsible, after all, for T. J losing his place in line at the Harbor Light. T. J. at first declined the offer, but Lewis could see in his eyes that he was hungry. Lewis insisted on buying him two slices of pizza and a large Coke, then found that he too was hungry, not having eaten since breakfast, so he bought a slice for himself. They ate where Lewis and Dewey normally had their Wednesday lunches.

Lewis was about to ask where his old friend planned to stay tonight, when T. J. suddenly said, 'It seems strange, meetin' you out on the street like this, L.T. Of all the people in the world, I would've never expected to see you on the sidewalk outside the Harbor Light. You've got a home to go to, right – a house, an apartment, somethin' like that?' Lewis nodded. 'Then why in the fuck ain't you there? It can get dangerous around here at night. You ought to be home, sittin' in front of the tube, sippin' on a beer.'

Lewis explained that he was searching for a Vietnam veteran named Dewey. Upon hearing Dewey's name, T. J. stopped chewing and stared at Lewis for a long moment.

'I know that old dude, L.T. In fact, I was talkin' with him just this afternoon, not ten feet from where we're sittin' right now.'

Lewis dropped his slice of pizza onto the paving stones. 'You *what*? You saw him here – today?'

'That's affirmative. He had himself a brown paper bag with a fifth of bourbon in it and a quart of milk, sittin' right over there beside that big pillar, just as content as could be.'

'Christ, I spent the afternoon scouring the neighborhood for him. I don't see how I could've missed him.'

'Hey, you better feed that little monster something,'

said T. J., pointing to the carrier perched on Lewis's stumps. 'He's makin' an awful racket!'

Little Brother was indeed mewing his head off, having smelled the pizza, so Lewis set the carrier on the ground, dug out the remainder of the Nine Lives he'd bought this afternoon, and fed it to him. 'How did he seem? – Dewey, I mean. Was he in good spirits? He wasn't sick, was he?'

'He seemed just fine, except he had an appointment he needed to keep.'

'What kind of appointment? Who was it with?'

'Said he needed to see a man about a cat, and that he had a long way to travel. Said he had to go to a warehouse up past the Broadway Bridge.'

Lewis wanted to know how long ago. T. J. estimated it to have been about an hour and a half, maybe two. Lewis retrieved the fallen slice of pizza and arced it into a nearby trash receptacle, then wiped his hands with a napkin. He apologized for needing to hurry off, but he was worried about Dewey.

'Man, I can't let you go up there by yourself,' T. J. protested. 'No tellin' what kind of trouble a man in a wheelchair might get himself into up in that neighborhood. I'm comin' with you.'

'I can't ask you to do that, T. J.'

'You didn't ask. I offered.'

iii

They crossed Burnside into Chinatown through a huge, three-story gate that was decorated with gilded Mandarin characters and guarded by a pair of massive lions carved from black stone. Darkness stole ashore from the river as they made their way ever deeper into the bowels of Old

Town, where lurked dealers of crank, crack and *chiva* (the street term for Mexican tar heroin). Loitering in the black pockets of alleys and doorways were the homeless, the addicts, and the child-whores who sold 'dates' for the price of a Big Mac and a hit of crack. Whenever possible, Lewis avoided their glittering stares.

By the time they reached Union Station, downtown Portland's only Amtrak stop, the Action Power 9000 had begun to run out of both action and power. Lewis's afternoon-long search for Dewey had depleted the battery.

'It's okay, man,' said T. J. 'I'll push you.'

'This thing is heavier than hell, T. J. I wouldn't hold it against you for going back to the Harbor Light. I can make it into the railroad depot and call a friend to come and get me.'

'Why should you do that? You've already got a friend.'

They continued north toward the Broadway Bridge, which was a skyborne river of vehicular traffic, with T. J. pushing the heavy wheelchair as easily as most people push shopping carts. The neighborhood gave way to an industrial quarter that was colorless for lack of neon and lonely for lack of retail traffic, where long expanses of chain-link fence guarded factories, warehouses, and parking lots for various industrial fleets. T. J. pushed Lewis along as if he knew exactly where to go, edging ever closer to the river, until they crossed Front Avenue near Terminal Number 1. They skirted a vast expanse of asphalt to the rear of a dock facility, where loading cranes towered against the night sky like colossal steel insects.

Lewis rode silently in his chair, his hands holding tight to the carrier with Little Brother inside it, his brain laboring. He decided to give in to the gestalt, knowing that the psychological configuration was greater than the sum of its parts, and that for this reason the vision defied logic and contradicted all rationale. Had the pattern begun with the first appearance of Gamaliel Cartee, he wondered – back in 1970, after a civilian bus struck an explosive device on the road to Trung Lap? Had the spectacle of mass death and gore so weakened Lewis's mind that his unconscious decided to manufacture its own reality, using phantasmagoric elements like red crystalline orbs and flesh-eating monsters to supplant the outrages of the real world?

He wondered how much of what he remembered since that moment had been real. That he'd lost his legs was certainly a reality, for the chair in which he now rode was beyond contention, its chromed frame cold to the touch, its tires hard and knobby. The stumps of his legs were likewise not a matter for argument. But what about T. J., who was pushing him with such determination and purpose – T. J., who'd fallen silent for the past several blocks as they penetrated ever deeper into the industrial blackness at the river's edge? Was T. J. simply another facet of the gestalt display, as Millie Carter must have been, as the two-legged Lewis Kindred himself must have been on the night he met his aunt in Goose Hollow?

How much of his life had been real?

Darkness closed around him, and the wheelchair began to jounce as T. J. pushed him ever faster along the graveled shoulder of the road they'd taken.

'Look, L.T., up ahead. You see what I see?'

Several hundred yards to their front, the road took a hard left turn at the riverbank, where a barrier of chain-link fence prevented anyone from venturing closer to the water. Someone had parked a car on the shoulder, and hung something dark and heavy on the chain-links.

T. J. sped up, his logger's boots crunching on the gravel, and despite the jouncing of the wheelchair Lewis was able to make out the figure of a man spread-eagled against the fence, his wrists and ankles chained to it. Two other men were in the process of dousing him with the contents of five-gallon cans. *It can't be gasoline*, said Lewis to himself. Nobody would do such a thing, not even in the heartless, utterly graceless world of the nineties, where kids carried Uzis and routinely gunned each other down in school yards.

But it *was* gasoline. One of the two flicked a butane lighter and held it close to the struggling man on the fence, and suddenly the world was bright with jittering flame. T. J. halted so quickly that Lewis nearly flew out of his chair. The two men threw their five-gallon cans over the fence and scrambled into the car, which Lewis could see was a plain Japanese sedan of some neutral color. Screams filled the night as fire bit flesh, and a starter wound and an engine gunned. The car sprayed gravel as it lurched onto the pavement and sped away, its taillights leaving bloody streaks across Lewis's vision. T. J. grabbed up the carrier with Little Brother in it which had slid onto the gravel.

Out of the writhing mass of flame came a voice that Lewis knew. It called his name. It pleaded with him to help, and Lewis *wanted* to help. He grabbed for the joystick, his sudden tears blinding him. The voice belonged to Dewey.

Lewis found the joystick finally, and the battery had just enough power to push the chair to within twenty feet of the struggling inferno – close enough to get a heaving lungful of the sweet stench of burning flesh.

He'd tasted that ghastly smell before. He'd watched T. J. Skane burn to a meaningless pile of charred sticks one afternoon in the Ho Bo Woods, and the smell had hung in the air like a curse, as it did now. He was watching Dewey burn away to nothingness, just as T. J. had, a human X with arms splayed like a crucifix, spindly legs similarly stretched below – *not* a figment of a schizophrenic fantasy, but a real happening, a horror beyond reason.

'*Do* something, T. J.!' Lewis shrieked, flapping at the night with his good hand. 'Throw dirt on him! Smother the fucking fire! We can't let him—'

More lights stabbed the night, white and red and blue, rotating beacons and headlight beams that cast harsh shadows across the walls of warehouses. Cop cars and fire trucks. Ambulances. Sirens shredding the darkness. Milling figures in uniforms, shouting orders to one another. Two-way radios crackling.

Lewis saw a man with an extinguisher spray a layer of foam on the motionless, silent form of Dewey; watched competent-looking people study the lifeless body and shake their heads; watched a pair of white-clad paramedics carefully take the body off the fence; watched TV news teams from four local stations shoot footage and conduct interviews of cops and firemen.

And soon, *too* soon, it was over. Night began to reassert its claim as beacons and lights switched off, as emergency vehicles left the scene. T. J. Skane, inexplicably, had vanished.

A young cop approached Lewis, his blond hair disheveled and his eyes too weary-looking for someone his age. He asked whether Lewis had seen what had happened. Yes, Lewis answered, his entire body having gone numb, though deep within him flickered an ember of rage. He'd seen it all.

iv

They sat in an interrogation room with sound-proofing tiles on the walls and a one-way mirror at one end. The room had a convenient electrical outlet, which enabled Lewis to recharge the battery of his wheelchair during the interview. He most assuredly was not a suspect in the murder of Dewey, the cops told him again and again. He was, however, a witness, and a potentially valuable one.

The young blond cop hung up the telephone he'd just used and pushed it across the table, out of his way. He lit a cigarette and blew smoke toward the ceiling. His nameplate identified him as L. McGillivray. 'The Salvation Army doesn't have a record of having served anybody named T. J. Skane,' he said matter-of-factly. 'They're pretty good about keeping records of these things. You're sure it was the Harbor Light where you met him, and not one of the other shelters?'

Lewis nodded and sipped the vile coffee that McGillivray had given him in a Styrofoam cup. Yes, he'd met Skane outside the Harbor Light. They'd eaten pizza together, because Skane had missed the dinner shift. Maybe T. J. hadn't gone to the Harbor Light before tonight, and maybe this was why the Salvation Army had no record of him.

'What I'm really wondering is where he disappeared to,' said McGillivray. 'The fire call went in almost immediately, thanks to the attendant on the Broadway Bridge. From his perch up in the bridge house, he saw the fire break out right away, and he was sitting at a phone.

437

That's why there was a truck on the scene within five minutes—'

'Which was more than enough time for Dewey to die,' Lewis put in, his throat aching, his stomach burning from the acidic coffee.

McGillivray sucked in another lungful of smoke and blew it out. 'Yes, Mr Kindred, I'm afraid that's true, and it's a tragedy. But my point is, where did Skane go, if he'd been pushing you along the road in the wheelchair? Did he run back the way you'd come? If he'd done that, then almost certainly one of our guys would've seen him, because that's exactly the kind of thing they look for – people running from the scene. If he'd run the other direction, *I* would've seen him, because that's the route I took. And as you know, I didn't see anybody running away.'

'Then maybe he's still out there somewhere. Maybe he's hiding in or around one of the warehouses. There must be a million places to hide in that neighborhood.'

McGillivray massaged his eyeballs through clenched lids and took another pull from his cigarette. 'You're right. And any minute one of the security cops who works out there is bound to see him and call us. In fact, it should've happened by now, it seems to me.'

'Jesus Christ!' shouted Lewis, pounding a fist on the table. 'Why don't you just come right out and say it? You think I made up the part about T. J. Skane, right? – that I know something more about this thing than I'm letting on? Well, I don't! I've told you everything I know, everything I saw. I don't know why T. J. took off, and I don't know where he went. I wish I *did* know, because his eyes are probably better than mine, and maybe he saw more than I did. I'm not holding anything back from you,

Officer McGillivray. I can't tell you any more than what I've told you, I swear it.'

'You didn't see what kind of car the suspects had, and you can't describe either of them, except that they were both males. Is that right?'

'For the nineteenth time, that's right!'

'And you don't have any idea where your friend, T. J. Skane, might've gone?'

'Right again. If I knew, I'd tell you. I hope you find him, honest-to-God I do, because he's got Dewey's cat. Do me a favor when you find him, will you? Call me. I'd like to get the cat back.'

McGillivray stared at him a long time with his tired blue eyes, slowly exhaling a cloud of smoke. 'I will, Mr Kindred. I'll call you, and you can get the cat back.'

CHAPTER TWENTY-THREE
Beyond the Call

i

Jesse Burton, PhD, had seen many substandard schools over the years, but he'd seen few that compared with Hancock Central Elementary in Sneedville, Tennessee. Throughout the building were spots on the cinder-block walls where the mortar had crumbled to let in the daylight. The teachers doubled as janitors, which accounted for the grime that coated the floors, desks, and fixtures. The school district had no money for books and crayons. To buy paper towels and toilet paper, the school held regular fund-raisers.

He wondered why the children all looked so happy, so full of pep. The teachers must be miracle-workers as well as part-time janitors, he thought. But gradually the truth dawned on him: These kids were young. The drudgery of substandard schooling had not yet worn them down or dulled their lively minds. *Give them five more years in this place*, he lamented, *and see how many are still happy and full of pep*.

The principal, a small black woman who wore the thickest horn-rim glasses Jesse had ever seen, led him down a flight of dusty stairs to the computer lab in the basement – a bunker-like room with ten archaic IBM PC 'Juniors' lining the drab walls. Only the first-graders, she told him, used the lab, since the only software the school possessed was the obsolete 'Write to Read.' Children who could read beyond the very lowest levels had little use for the application.

Welcome to Appalachia, thought Jesse.

The story was no rosier across town at the Hancock County High School. Here, the tiny library could neither afford to buy new books nor to participate in an inter-library loan program. Having only recently received her first computer for the library, a donated IBM, the principal hoped sometime soon to get software to run it, as well as some training. Until then, the computer sat untouched in a corner. Jesse knew that throughout the entire state of Tennessee, sixty-four percent of high-school teachers used computers in their classes, but here in Sneedville – a town of fifteen hundred in the heart of America's poverty belt – not *one* teacher used a computer.

The poor get poorer.

As he drove his rented car the seventy miles back to Knoxville, where he planned to catch a plane home to Chicago tomorrow, he dictated his thoughts onto tape: *The cause to upgrade education with computers is in big trouble, especially in poor schools. My survey shows that inner-city schools and rural schools just don't have the money or the training to acquire and maintain the machines. The sad fact is that computer-based education is perpetuating two separate systems of education in this country – one for the rich and another for the poor . . .*

As a black man who'd struggled most of his life to overcome the weight of poverty and disadvantage, he cared intensely for the kids who attended schools like Hancock Elementary and Hancock County High, whether they lived in desperate little towns like Sneedville or raging inner cities like South Chicago, where he himself had grown up. Education, Jesse believed, was the only effective weapon against poverty and the evils it spawned – drug and alcohol abuse, teen suicides, teen murders, teen parenthood, orphaned kids. Having clawed his way up from addiction and delinquency to earn a doctorate from the University of Illinois, he appreciated the difference that education had made in his own life, the hope it had given him, the means not only to make a decent living, but also to make a difference. That American society was failing to educate so many of its children properly both pained and angered him.

He drove into Knoxville on Highway 11 and followed the arrows to Interstate 40, which took him downtown, then followed more arrows toward Dickenson Island Airport on the Tennessee River. Before reaching the airport, however, he exited to the Holiday Inn where he would stay and work on his report until tomorrow's early-morning flight to Chicago. He turned in the keys to his rental car and checked the reception desk for messages, and was surprised to find one from Shandelle, his wife.

'Yeah, it's me, babe,' he said when she answered his call-back. 'What's up?'

A man had called several times for him, she reported, from out in Portland, Oregon, of all places. He had a slight foreign accent, and he sounded very upset. He'd insisted that Jesse return his call at the earliest opportunity and had left a number.

'I don't suppose he had a name, did he?'

Yes, of course he'd given his name, but it was a strange one – *No Bick*. Shandelle wasn't certain that she'd pronounced it correctly. She wanted to know whether the name meant anything to Jesse. *No Bick*, she said again, in case he hadn't heard her.

Dr Jesse Burton spent the next few seconds back in a place where red laterite mud clung to the soles of his boots and little blue mosquitoes tormented his sleep; where soul brothers did an elaborate 'dap' handshake and cigarettes came in mini packs of four; where land mines blew busloads of innocent people to pieces and men in crisp uniforms beat little girls half to death under the pretext of 'exigent need.'

Welcome to Vietnam.

ii

'Ladies and gentlemen, the Captain has turned on the safety belt sign, and we ask that you fasten your safety belts at this time for our descent into New Orleans . . .'

Jesse pressed his forehead against the pane of the porthole and gazed at the jumbled cityscape below, which ended abruptly at the shore of vast Lake Pontchartrain. The plane circled far out over the gray water and settled into its final approach, bouncing and lurching through the ever-present turbulence, slowly descending toward New Orleans Lakefront Airport. Jesse checked his watch when the landing gear skidded against the runway, and noted the time – 6:15 PM, Central Daylight Time, October 5, 1992. He'd gained an hour on the flight from Knoxville.

He filed out of the plane with the other passengers into the terminal and went immediately to a smoking section, where he hungrily lit up a Merit menthol. Smoking was

444

the one bad habit from his youth that he couldn't and wouldn't give up.

After finishing the butt he went to a cab stand outside the terminal, got into a cab, and gave the driver the address of a Howard Johnson's off Interstate 10 near the French Quarter. He rode with his window partially open, letting the humid Mississippi-River-Delta air wash over his face.

'*Shandelle, babe, I'll try to explain it to you when I get back,*' he'd told his wife on the phone before changing his flight reservation out of Knoxville. '*I swear it has nothing to do with women or booze—*'

'*Baby, I know that. We left all those bad old times behind. It's not that I don't trust you – it's just that I don't understand.*'

'*I know, I know. All I can say now is that this is something I've got to do. I guess I always knew that this day would come—*'

'*Will you call me when you get to New Orleans? Can you do that much for me? Otherwise I'll worry. You know me.*'

'*I'll call you as soon as I get to my hotel . . .*'

And he did. But he didn't fare much better in explaining to her why he'd come to New Orleans and not home to Chicago. Hell, he could hardly explain it to himself. An old friend from his Vietnam days needed his help, but he couldn't bring himself to describe what *kind* of help. On the telephone, No Bick had spoken the name Gamaliel, and had told him that Lewis Kindred had once again fallen victim to Gamaliel's kind of evil. No Bick had tried to intervene on his own to save Lewis, but had himself become a victim. Now he had nowhere to turn except to Jesse, whose whereabouts he'd kept track of since Vietnam. No Bick knew that Jesse cared what happened to Lewis, for hadn't Jesse carried him from the battlefield through a blizzard of withering fire and exploding mortar rounds? A man doesn't save another man's life and then stand idly by and watch him be destroyed.

Back in Vietnam, Jesse had helped No Bick dig into Gamaliel's background, contacting buddies who worked in division headquarters where personnel records were kept. Gamaliel had originally come from New Orleans, according to his file. A helpful clerk had even furnished the mailing address of Gamaliel's mother. All these years No Bick had kept the information that Jesse had procured for him, and today he'd given it back to Jesse over the telephone.

And Jesse had come to New Orleans.

But *why*? Shandelle pressed. What did he expect to accomplish there? How could she explain to their two teenage sons why their father hadn't come home from his business trip? Did Jesse expect her to lie for him?

He knew that he couldn't expect her to understand how Lewis Kindred had inspired him to become someone *good*, how countless times throughout the years he'd taken strength from the example that Lewis had set in halting the abuse of two innocent Vietnamese women. Remembering what this skinny young white guy had done and how he'd ultimately suffered for it, Jesse had found within himself the steel to rise above his own weakness, to kick addiction and dereliction, to pursue higher and better things. He'd become a crusader against injustice, and having become this, he could hardly turn his back on the injustice that Lewis now suffered.

No, he didn't want Shandelle to lie to their sons, he

said. She should simply tell them that their dad had gone off to help an old friend and that he would come home as soon as he could.

iii

Josh's eyes wandered around the hospital room, soaking up details. He studied the MediLogic patient monitor on the rack above Nicole's bed, with its spiky lines of green light bouncing across its screen, which signified her failing heartbeat, labored respiration, and weakening blood pressure. He studied the flowers in their pots on the window sill, on the bed stand, on the dresser – the unbearably cheerful offerings from her parents, friends and Josh himself. He studied Nicole's once-beautiful face, now yellowed by jaundice and tight with the agonal throes of some nameless, unspeakably virulent disease. He studied her hands, once so graceful and delicate, now knotted into claws.

Josh needed to remember every horrific little detail down to the color of the carpet and the pattern on the bedspread, because he intended to call up this scene in his mind again and again as his own worthless life wore on. He intended to relive this night's full blast of desolation and pain. Nicole's dying seemed incomprehensibly unjust, in view of the fact that he, the less worthy, would continue to live. He meant to suffer willingly for that injustice. He would pay the price for having dragged Nicole along to Millie Carter's house despite her well-reasoned misgivings. He would atone for having been blind to his own love for this girl, for having pushed it down and ignored it for so long, for having deprived them both of the joy it would have brought them.

Suddenly she reached out and gripped his hand, a feat

of will. She drew breath and moved her lips, trying to speak. Josh's eyes flooded, and the tears flowed into the corners of his mouth as he leaned close.

'It's okay, Nicki,' he barely croaked. 'You don't have to say anything.'

'Y-You owe me a large pizza,' she whispered barely above a hiss, so intense was the pain. 'We had a bet, remember? – about the door. You said it would be locked, and I said . . .' Pain pinched off her words, and she coughed excruciatingly. She'd adamantly refused to let the doctors increase the dosage of morphine, because she wanted to remain lucid up to the end. She'd told Josh that she wanted to look at his face while taking her final breath.

'Just get better, and I'll buy you a gourmet pizza every day for the rest of your life,' he managed, choking back a sob. 'In fact, we can have a wedding *pizza* instead of a wedding cake – how's that sound? We'll get a big one – like ten feet across, right? We'll get anchovies on it, and extra cheese . . .' Grief overwhelmed him; he lowered his head and cried.

Nicole lay still a long time, silent except for her raspy breathing. What was left of her raven hair spilled over a white pillowcase. Josh pressed her hand against his cheek, clenched his eyes, and tried to fathom how the last two days could have happened in a world that purported to be governed by the rational laws of science.

Nicole had suffered a deep slash across her left shoulder, as if someone had swiped at her with a sickle. Josh couldn't be certain of this, but he believed – based on what he'd seen out of the corner of his eye in a frantic fraction of a second – that Millie Carter had struck Nicki with a claw that was long and curved and razor-sharp. It had happened at the moment he and Nicki dashed through the French doors onto the upper deck of the villa. The blow had sliced through Nicki's long black hair, shortening it at a crazy diagonal, cutting through her clothing as if she'd been wearing paper. She'd bled profusely, and Josh had rushed her to the emergency room of Good Samaritan in Northwest Portland.

After suturing the wound, the emergency-room resident, an intense young man named Dr Kraus, had kept Nicole for observation, clearly disbelieving her and Josh's insistence that she'd cut herself on a rusty nail while squeezing between the slats of an old fence. Kraus had sarcastically observed that no rusty nail he'd ever seen was capable of shearing a girl's hair off while inflicting an eight-inch gash in her shoulder.

By four o'clock on Saturday afternoon, Nicole had worsened. Infection had spread from the wound throughout her body, carried by her blood. Her skin turned yellow and the whites of her eyes became orange with jaundice as the disease attacked her liver. Dr Kraus administered the maximum allowable dosages of every antibiotic at his disposal, then called in specialists who ran test upon test, looking for bacteria, viruses, malignancies, even death-cap mushroom toxins, anything at all. They found nothing. The antibiotics had no discernible effect on Nicole's condition.

By Sunday morning the disease had attacked her pancreas and kidneys. She developed pneumonia. Her pulse weakened. The doctors hovered over her with ashen faces, helpless, while her mother prayed at her bedside. Her father was himself too weak to visit his daughter's sickbed, which required that Mrs Tran divide her time between her husband and her daughter.

On Sunday evening, Josh's mother and sister arrived at Good Samaritan in time to hear Dr Kraus pronounce the situation hopeless, for the disease had so riddled Nicole's vital organs that total renal shutdown was inevitable within twenty-four hours. Nicki was dying, and she knew it, but she welcomed her visitors with what passed for a smile.

All through Monday she'd hung on, and Josh had stayed with her, even when her mother needed to go home in order to care for her father. But now, late on Monday evening, he could see that she'd used up her reservoir of strength, that she had only minutes left.

They were alone, though her mother was en route to the hospital, having received a call from the doctor. Nicole opened her eyes and smiled through the agony – a ground-glass grin that cut Josh to the quick. 'You promised that you would finish—' She cringed as new pain lanced through her, and Josh cursed the disease silently. *Let her talk, you son of a bitch! You'll get her soon enough as it is . . . !* '—f-finish writing the story,' she whispered. 'You'll do it, won't you, Nickster?'

'Nothing's going to stop me, I swear.'

'And you'll write m-more stories, won't you? Y-You'll become a writer. You're so good at it, you've *got* to do it.'

'I'll do it. I'll do it for you, Nicki.'

'For us.'

'For *us*.'

Her yellowed eyes filled with tears that ran in little rivulets down her cheeks. 'We had some great times, Nickster. I wouldn't trade a single minute of what we've had for an eternity with somebody else. I mean that – I really do. I-I guess you know that I've loved you all these years, huh?'

'I know. And I've loved you, too. I just wish—'

She touched his lips with a fingertip. 'Don't say it. I wish it, too. But it's enough that we have each other right now, isn't it?'

Josh couldn't speak. He could only nod.

'You won't forget me, will you, Nickster?'

He breathed. He breathed again before he found his voice. 'God, no. I couldn't forget you, Nicki. You'll always be my girl, right? And we'll always be the Dynamic Duo of Gander Ridge.'

Nicole's grip relaxed suddenly, and the frightening tautness in her face gave way. She exhaled and didn't draw another breath. Her gaze never left his, not even as death stole her smile.

CHAPTER TWENTY-FOUR
Pleasures of the Flesh

i

As Nicole Tran lay dying in Good Samaritan Hospital, Lewis lay awake in his bed, having tried and failed to take refuge in sleep from the madness of his waking life. The shock, the grief, and the anger over Dewey's horrible death weighed on him like an anvil strapped to his back, rendering him barely able to move even after two full days.

He'd simply lacked the strength to visit Nicki in the hospital. Cheryl Nickerson had phoned on Sunday afternoon to notify him of the girl's mysterious illness and the dire prognosis, but every time he tried to muster the energy to go out, his head swam with nausea and he became faint. Frustrated, he could only hope that Josh was bearing up, and that Nicki wouldn't linger too long in excruciating pain. His heart went out to both of them and their families.

Rain pattered against his windows, a sound that ordinarily would have nudged him over the threshold of sleep, but it didn't do the trick tonight. His brain refused to shut down, though he'd drunk four, maybe five bottles of Beck's. In one mental echelon, he concluded that his sanity was in tatters, that he couldn't trust his own perceptions, that Dewey probably wasn't even dead. After all, no perception within the dream-realm was truly trustworthy. You needed to take with a grain of salt everything you saw and heard there. Hell, Dewey might someday show up unscarred and full of piss and vinegar, just as T. J. Skane had done. It might happen tomorrow, or ten or twenty or thirty years from now.

But in another mental echelon he believed all he'd seen, that Dewey had in fact died a hellish death by fire. And he knew in his heart of hearts who was responsible for the outrage. As yet, he'd not decided that he himself must become a murderer in order to exact an appropriate vengeance, though this wasn't beyond contemplation, for Rex Caswell richly deserved to die, no doubt about that.

Lewis's thoughts gravitated to Millie, and curiously, this caused the mental fury to subside. Regardless of whether or not she was evil, she'd given him what no one else had the power to give. She'd made him whole, if only in his mind, if only temporarily. She'd *loved* him. She'd given him a taste of the life he could have lived if he'd not lost his legs, and regardless of what she was or wasn't, he would be eternally grateful to her. In the world where Lewis Kindred was a whole man, the simple joy of walking on his own two feet overwhelmed the issue of good versus evil.

He dreamed of her. They walked together in the rose gardens of Washington Park during a rainstorm, devouring the bursts of color with their eyes. Bloody reds, honey yellows, a hundred shades of peach and a thousand of orange. Against the grayness of the day, the color of the roses was delicious.

He asked her how much of himself a man could lose

and still be himself. A man didn't become someone else, did he, simply by losing, say, his legs? Or suppose that a man lost his arms *and* his legs; or suppose that he lost his entire body except for that section of his brain that housed sentience and intellect, assuming that doctors could keep that morsel of tissue alive in an appropriate vessel. At which stage of loss did a man lose *himself*?

Millie smiled at him with her wonderful blue-brown eyes. *Lewis, you never lose* just *your legs*, she said, *or* just *your body. You always lose more than you think you do. But no matter how much you lose, you're still you. Only one thing can truly change you into someone else.*

And that was death, wasn't it? he offered. Death changed a man's identity by simply wiping it out forever. Once you're dead, you're no longer *you*, right?

Wrong, she said, her smile dissolving.

As the dream knitted with reality, Lewis became aware of his aching bladder. He'd drunk far too much beer before turning in. He got out of bed and padded to the bathroom, stood before the toilet and pissed, leaning with one hand against the wall. Not until he flushed the toilet did he understand that he wasn't still dreaming, that he was actually standing in his bathroom on two good legs. He whirled to the mirror and stared dumbfounded at the reflected image – a man in his youngish forties, tall and slim, hairy of chest and slightly silvered around the ears. The gray eyes were warm and steady, the jaw only slightly scarred.

'Who are you?' he asked aloud. He discovered that his ears no longer rang, that his left arm was as good as his right. 'Who *are* you?' he demanded again, leaning close to the mirror. He ran his fingers over his cheeks, down his neck, across his shoulders. He pushed it down into his shorts, and his cock suddenly stirred with a tickling hunger.

He dashed out of the bathroom into the bedroom, his heart thudding crazily, expecting to find Millie there, but the bedroom was deserted except for the patter of rain. 'Millie!' He ran to the kitchen, to the living room and the studio, only to find that he was alone in the apartment, that she hadn't come back at all. How could this be happening, his brain screamed, without Millie? How could he have slipped into the dream-realm without her?

The answer came to him almost too easily. When a man makes love to a woman, he keeps a part of her with him, just as she keeps a part of himself. Their two bodies exchange not only sweat, but also the juices and oils of sex. Their minds touch, and each gives the other a fragment of something that represents his or her essence, some kernel of 'self.' Yes, he'd kept a part of Millie, and that part – whatever it was – made possible the change he'd just undergone.

Joy washed over him like a flash flood.

He discovered that he was ravenous, for he hadn't eaten today, or yesterday either. He got a sudden vision of himself sitting in a fine restaurant, a place with a great wine list and somber chefs who wore tall white hats. When had he last experienced a truly fine restaurant? he wondered. Too long ago, that much was certain. Few of his friends could afford such places, and until recently Lewis couldn't either.

He went to the closet and pulled out his best pair of Levis Dockers and slipped his strong, unscarred legs into them, one at a time. He put on his best sport shirt and shrugged into his favorite lambs' wool sweater. Casual gear, to be sure, but this was a Monday night on the

Upper Left Coast. No one would glance twice at him.

Then he remembered that he had no shoes, no socks, no footwear of any kind. He hadn't needed such things for more than twenty years, having lacked feet, but he had feet *now*, damn it, and he couldn't go out without shoes. He recalled again the night he and Millie walked down into Goose Hollow, and the exultation he'd felt upon looking at his feet and seeing a pair of tan Rockport walking shoes. He'd worn white athletic socks – not exactly chic, maybe, but comfortable. If the dream had produced footwear then, it could certainly produce footwear now, right?

He went back to the closet, pulled open the sliding door, and directed his attention to the area where Millie had hung her things while in residence here. Sure enough, a pair of tan Rockports lay in the corner at the far end of the closet, and with them several pairs of new athletic socks.

ii

Pazzo Ristorante was off the lobby of the plush Vintage Plaza Hotel on Broadway. Though nominally Italian rustic, the décor was in fact 'California modern,' which meant polished oak and marble, dark upholstery, and lots of potted plants. Several steps down from the reception desk lay the bar, where long windows offered patrons a lower-than-street-level view of passing pedestrians.

Lewis walked in on his own two feet, grinned at the maître d', and requested a table for one. For a shuddering moment he felt certain that someone had followed him, and he turned to stare through the glass doors of the entryway, but he saw nothing suspicious. Had he also heard something? – a half-familiar *rustling*, a sound from a forgotten dream or a previous life? No, he told himself. He'd heard nothing like that.

A pair of well-dressed women lounged at a far table, nursing fruity-looking drinks in skinny glasses. When one of them – a blonde in her early thirties – happened to glance up and lock stares with Lewis, he knew that he was indeed hungry, but not for food.

'On second thoughts,' he said to the maître d', 'I think I'll just have a drink in the bar.'

iii

The blonde woman was Megan Venton, a buyer for Nordstrom who traveled extensively in her work, enjoyed aerobics, and never missed an episode of 'L. A. Law.' She wore a long tan jacket with peaked lapels over a matching skirt and a white T-shirt with an expensive-looking gold necklace. Very *now*, Lewis thought, aching for her. *She's not my type. She can hardly put together a complete sentence. Yet here I am, having introduced myself and sat down, turning on charm I didn't know I had . . .*

Megan's brunette friend, a fellow buyer named Stacey Something-or-Other, recognized the chemistry afoot and departed, pleading an early day tomorrow. Forty-five minutes later, Lewis and Megan checked into the Vintage Plaza, using her American Express Gold Card.

'Drink?' offered Lewis, holding up a bottle of Scotch from the honor bar. 'We've got everything here from bourbon to aquavit.'

'No thanks, Zeb,' she replied, slinking close and slipping her arms around his neck. He'd told them he was Zebulon Councilman, and that he was the business agent for the American Association of Philosophy Writers,

AFL-CIO, out of Van Nuys. The bullshit had come off the top of his head, like water out of a tap, and Megan had lapped it up. 'I'm not up for a drink right now, but I might be up for something else. How about you?'

They kissed deeply, and Lewis savored the sweetness of her mouth, which might have had something to do with the syrupy drinks she'd had earlier. Without breaking the kiss they moved to the bed, which to Lewis looked big enough for four couples. They glided down onto it. His hands moved to her breasts and found that under the T-shirt she wore no bra. He massaged her breasts gently, while his hunger built to a level that almost frightened him. This was more than normal sexual hunger, he feared – more intense even than the craving he'd felt for Millie or for any other woman he could remember. What scared him was the growing certainty that he was powerless against it.

They broke their kiss in order to peel each other's clothing. 'You're married, aren't you, Zeb?' she whispered. 'That's why you wanted to use my credit card when we checked in. You don't want your wife to see the bill.'

'You're too smart for me, Megan. You read me like a book. I'm sorry – I really am.'

'Oh, I'm not mad that you're married. I think that adults should give themselves the freedom to do what comes naturally, don't you? I mean, why should we feel guilty about using our bodies in the way the good Lord intended?' She ground her pelvis against him and parted her legs.

'I couldn't agree with you more.'

'You'll wear protection, won't you? It only makes sense in this day and age.'

Lewis felt a bolt of panic. He hadn't bought condoms in over twenty years, and his face must have said as much.

'It's okay, Zeb. I've got some.'

She rose from the bed to fetch her purse, totally naked now, and Lewis watched her go, unable to take his eyes off her. She was tall and well muscled, smooth in her movements like a cat, thanks to her love of aerobics, no doubt. Her full breasts bounced tantalizingly with her every movement. The hair in her pubic mound showed her to be a true blonde. After rummaging a moment in her purse, she returned to the bed with a foil square in her hand. With practiced ease she tore it open and removed the condom from it.

'Let me do this for you,' she said, smiling lasciviously.

Lewis lay back on the bed and closed his eyes, grinning his poker grin but worrying that he might suffer an accidental orgasm if he let her handle the chore. Maybe he should think about baseball, he said to himself. It had worked when he was young. Megan gasped, causing him to raise himself on his elbows.

'What the *fuck* . . . ?' she breathed, covering her mouth with a hand. Lewis saw that his erect penis was almost five times its normal size, so long and thick that no normal woman could possibly accommodate him. He stared at it open-mouthed, not knowing whether to laugh or cry.

'I don't believe this!' Megan exclaimed. 'What *are* you, some kind of freak?'

She drew herself up to jump from the bed, but Lewis caught her and held her. He felt something spread through him, an excitement, an overpowering hunger that set his heart to thundering and his muscles to twitching. Megan's face contorted into a mask of raw panic as she saw the change creep over him, and Lewis thrilled to her look, her scent. He could smell her terror, and it was like an old dream that waited to be touched, to be prodded to life. He prodded it with his mind, prodded it again, and it burst forth in all its glory – bestial and brutal, the fleshy reality of a dream that belonged in hell.

Before Megan could scream, Lewis reached out with his mind and seized her will. She could do nothing now except cooperate. She couldn't struggle, couldn't scream, but could only breathe.

He hoisted her up on all fours and mounted her from behind, driving his monstrous cock into her up to the hilt. The throbbing and shuddering of her wounded body only fanned his excitement. Blood was suddenly everywhere, the smell of it tickling his nostrils, sharpening his hunger. Sweat poured off his forehead into his eyes, but through the blur he could see that his fingers had lengthened obscenely, that each had a long, curving claw. Megan's skin showed cruel red marks wherever he'd touched her.

The hunger burned and twisted inside him, demanding nourishment, even as his cock and balls sent signals of impending orgasm. Not knowing exactly what he was doing, he bent low and bit into the woman's left shoulder, ripping away meat with his newly sharp teeth. Blood filled his mouth, so rich and sweet that it nearly blinded him with pleasure. He chewed, swallowed, bent low for another bite, felt his jaws crush her clavicle. As each mouthful of flesh slid into his stomach, it produced a rush that made him want to roar his exultation to the stars and planets, for this was more than nourishment; this was power. Human flesh and human blood were the spoils of his victory over every disgustingly human frailty for which he'd ever suffered

– including the jingoistic and megalomaniac cravings and fears that had sent him off to war along with untold millions of others over countless generations; sent him off to be maimed and doomed to the life of an invalid. Eating flesh and drinking blood compensated him for the suffering, the hopelessness, and the baseness that countless others of his kind had suffered over a thousand generations.

His orgasm rocked him to near senselessness, and when he pulled out of Megan, he saw that he'd reduced her to a clutter of wet meat.

CHAPTER TWENTY-FIVE
The Fumes of Unreason

i

Jesse Burton had visited New Orleans many times during his tenure with the National Education Association. His search for Gamaliel Cartee's mother, however, took him far afield of the city's well-known landmarks. The New Orleans telephone directory contained no listing for anyone named Cartee at the address that No Bick had given him, so he had no choice but to rent a car and find the place. To help him, he went to a bookstore and bought the best map of the city that he could find.

Claudette Cartee lived in a crumbling tenement on a narrow side street, where every third or fourth upper-story window had a clothesline strung to a fire escape, a balcony, or another window. She was a wrinkled black woman with a Creole lilt in her speech, whose filmy eyes brimmed with a lifetime of hardship. To Jesse's surprise, she readily invited him into her cramped apartment with its peeling plaster and buckling floorboards, where the only sources of light were the cracked windows and a bare bulb that dangled from the ceiling on a fraying cord.

She hadn't seen Gamaliel since he joined the army in 1969, she said. He'd written no letters, made no phone calls home – actually, she couldn't remember whether she'd had a phone in those days or not. Gamaliel had simply vanished from her life, leaving her to wonder whether he'd survived the war, though her tone suggested that she wasn't really curious. Jesse specifically asked whether the U.S. government had ever notified her that Gamaliel had been wounded, killed, or missing in action. Her answer was an emphatic no.

Then she revealed that Gamaliel wasn't her natural son. The boy had come to her at the age of fifteen, she said, sent by her distant cousin Melusinne, who lived on the bayou outside Jean Lafitte, near Lake Salvador, some twenty miles south of New Orleans. Melusinne was a witch, she added almost as an afterthought, what old-timers on the bayou called a *sorcière*. If Jesse wanted to know about Gamaliel, she suggested that he visit Melusinne.

He requested directions to the place, and Claudette obliged. Jesse wrote the directions down carefully and read them back to her, for they were complex, and they involved roads and paths that sounded far off the beaten track. He didn't want to make a mistake and get lost in some remote, alligator-infested bayou.

What the old woman said next confounded him. If he was serious about consulting Melusinne, he needed to take some specific items with him, just to prove to her that he came with a good heart, that he was sincere about wanting her help. Lacking these, Claudette saw little likelihood that her cousin would give him the time of day.

ii

The area immediately south of New Orleans wasn't as rural or as backwoodsy as Jesse had expected it to be.

Scattered among the bayous and lakes were communities of contemporary homes, mini-malls, and commercial strips. He found a tobacconist in one such mini-mall and bought a cheap box of rum-soaked cheroots. He emptied the cigars into a trash barrel, for he needed only the box, or so Claudette Cartee had said.

He stopped at the next auto-repair outfit he came to, a Goodyear Automotive Center, and told the friendly man at the desk that he needed a single ball-bearing, that he would gladly pay anything within reason. This too he should bring with him to Melusinne, the old woman had advised. The man behind the desk looked at him with a cocked head and a raised eyebrow, disappeared into the shop, and returned with a marble-sized ball-bearing, which he tossed over the counter. 'Ain't no charge for this!' he said, laughing. 'Enjoy!'

Outside the community of Jean Lafitte, the countryside seemed more like what Jesse expected from southern Louisiana – lush stands of forest interspersed with shadowy swamps, long stretches of empty road, and quietude thick enough to put in a bottle. He followed Claudette's directions along a potholed asphalt road to a cluster of low gray buildings with sagging porches, one of which was a U.S. Post Office, another a bait-and-tackle store with a neon Budweiser sign in the window. The remaining buildings were houses, most of them bare of decoration and surrounded by junk cars and appliances. Here was rural poverty that approached Third-World proportions, thought Jesse, passing a hovel with several dusty black children sprawled on the hood of a derelict 1957 Mercury. He cringed when he envisioned the school they must have attended.

He parked his rented Chevy Lumina in the lot outside

the post office, stepped from the air-conditioned car into the densely humid air, and immediately heard the distant crowing of a rooster. He glanced around at the other three vehicles parked in the lot, all pickups with rifles or shotguns in their window racks. Beyond the lot, the town gave way abruptly to the bayou, where majestic swamp oaks and cypresses presided in their ragged cloaks of Spanish moss. As he watched, an egret gracefully skimmed the water and wheeled into the deepening afternoon shadow.

With his white dress shirt sticking to his back, he set out on the path that led southward from the parking lot along the edge of the swamp, as Claudette had instructed, carrying the empty cigar box in his hand and the ball-bearing in his pocket. Swatting mosquitoes became as automatic as putting one foot in front of the other, as routine as breathing. Occasionally the path forked, causing him to consult the slip of paper on which he'd jotted her instructions. The further he went, the thicker the gloom became, causing him to wish he'd brought a flashlight, not to mention a bottle of bug repellent. The return trip along this path would be a real adventure after the sun had gone down, and the afternoon had already begun to fade into evening. Eventually the path became squelchy with moisture, then downright muddy, and he resigned himself to ruining a nearly new pair of Johnston Murphy wing tips.

He came upon the cabin sooner than he expected to. It stood on the very edge of the bayou, enshrouded in a moss-draped swamp oak. A rowboat lay moored to a decrepit dock that had lost a third of its planks. The building itself appeared to be in reasonably good repair, and boasted electricity and a telephone, or so suggested the utility lines that led from the porch to a pole in the forest to his right. A late-model Isuzu Trooper was parked in front of a small attached shed, wearing a bumper sticker that read: COMMIT ACTS OF RANDOM KINDNESS! Jesse marveled that anyone could have driven a vehicle into this site, regardless of whether it had four-wheel drive.

The whine of insects seemed to intensify as he stared at the cabin, and he felt a darkness creep over him, a sense of misadventure more acute than anything he'd felt since his Vietnam days. Suddenly the door of the cabin swung open, and Melusinne stepped out with a shotgun in her arms.

iii

'I trust you haven't come with mischief on your mind,' she called out to him from the dusk of the porch.

Jesse raised a hand to wave. 'I'm here at the suggestion of your cousin in New Orleans, Claudette Cartee. I want to talk to you, if I may. It won't take long, I hope.'

Melusinne stepped out into the fading light of the afternoon, wearing a New Orleans Saints T-shirt, sensible shorts, and Etonic running shoes. Jesse had expected her to be as old and wrinkled as her cousin Claudette, which was a reasonable expectation, given Claudette's story, but the *sorcière* didn't look older than forty. She carried herself gracefully and proudly, despite being somewhat overweight. Her facial features were strong and finely drawn, her skin very dark, her eyes bright and lively. She wore her shiny jet-black hair pulled tightly into a teased bunch at the crown of her head. The Ithaca shotgun in the crook of her arm had a finely carved stock, and looked as if it belonged in a display case.

'If Claudette sent you, it's about Gamaliel, isn't it?'

A knot hardened in Jesse's stomach. 'Yes, it is, I'm afraid.'

Melusinne smiled. 'As well you should be.' She stepped to one side and motioned him forward, indicating the open door. 'Come in. I've got some iced tea made and a pot of gumbo on the stove. You might not be hungry, but you sure as hell must be thirsty. Hot and humid today – probably stay like this till mid-November. Whereabouts are you from?'

'Chicago. Name's Jesse Burton. I work for the National Education Association, but that doesn't have anything to do with Gamaliel Cartee, or why I'm here.' He entered the house, which seemed very dark at first, but his eyes quickly adjusted. On the walls hung just the kind of thing he would have expected to find in the house of a *sorcière* in the Louisiana bayou – the bodies and heads of dead animals, all expertly stuffed. There were cats of several varieties, a fox, an owl, a small alligator, a wild boar, and – Jesse gulped and flinched backward – the mounted head of a *man*, who looked to be in his seventies or older, though the wrinkles could have been attributable to post-taxidermic drying. The nappy hair was pure white, the skin a healthy black that looked startlingly alive. The facial expression suggested contentment after a life of toil, but the glistening glass eyes conveyed a certain restiveness that made Jesse's flesh crawl.

'That's my old great-granddaddy,' laughed Melusinne, closing the door behind her. 'He was born a slave and lived to the ripe age of a hundred and two. It was his wish to have his head mounted after he died, so his surviving kin could look at him and remember the things he taught them.'

'What kind of things?'

'The kind you're here to ask me about.' She winked and motioned him to a seat at the heavy oaken table in the part of the room that served as a kitchen. While she fetched glasses for iced tea, Jesse noticed a state-of-the-art stereo system along one wall, a Sony television set with a VCR, a respectable cloth sofa with a matching armchair. An interior door led to what he assumed must be a bedroom. Nearby were new-looking appliances, including the kind of refrigerator that Jesse's wife had lusted after but which they'd not yet been able to afford, the kind with an ice dispenser on the outside.

I'm in the wrong business, Jesse thought. 'How long have you lived here?' he asked, accepting a large glass that clinked with ice cubes.

'Honey, I've lived here longer than I care to admit, and longer than you'd believe. This property's been in my family since the Reconstruction, but I'm the only Cartee who cares about it. That's why there's nobody here but me. I guess you could say that I'm the only one with an interest in carrying on my great-granddaddy's work. By the way, you can smoke, if you want to.' She set an ashtray before him and took the chair opposite.

Jesse wondered how she knew that he was a smoker. 'You don't have much of an accent,' he remarked. 'I can tell you're a Southerner, but I don't hear much Creole.'

'I've lost it over the . . . years. I watch a lot of Yankee television. I travel. I suppose my cousin told you that I'm a *sorcière*.'

'She did. She also advised me to bring some things to you, said they'd let you know that I'm sincere.' He set the empty cigar box on the table and fished in his pocket for the ball-bearing, which he placed next to the box. 'For you.'

Melusinne smiled broadly. 'Oh, these aren't for me, Mr Burton. They're for *you*.'

'I don't understand. What use would I have for these things?'

'You'll find out soon enough. The fact that you brought them tells me what I need to know about you. Now drink your tea before it gets all watered down.'

Jesse sipped slowly from his glass and relished the wetness and cold on his throat. He couldn't remember when iced tea had tasted so good. He lit a cigarette, took a long drag and contentedly blew out smoke, feeling relaxed despite the fact that Melusinne's dear old great-granddaddy gazed down at them from his perch on the wall.

'Tell me,' said Melusinne, 'have you met Gamaliel personally?'

'I have. It was over twenty years ago in Vietnam.'

'Vietnam. Ah-*hah*.' The fact that Gamaliel had gone to Vietnam seemed to make perfect sense to her, but she didn't say why. 'You didn't play cards with him, I hope.'

'I'm afraid I did. Lost my ass, too, if you'll forgive the vulgarity.'

She laughed. 'I hope it wasn't a hardship for you.'

'It wasn't. A friend of mine won the money back for me.'

Melusinne grew serious and placed both hands on the table, palms down. 'He won the money back from Gamaliel – is that what you said?'

'Yes.'

'Were you present at this game?'

'Yes, I was. I think I can even remember the winning

hand – four sixes to beat Gamaliel's full house.'

'Did Gamaliel, by any chance, make a gift to your friend before they showed their hands? – it would've been a spherical piece of red glass, small enough for a man to carry in his hand.'

The memory of that night twisted inside Jesse like a snake. He remembered that Gamaliel had proposed an 'experiment' to Lewis Kindred, which entailed only that Lewis keep the crimson orb near him while they showed their cards. Lewis had won, of course, and won big. Afterward, Lewis had forced Gamaliel to take the object back, as if he'd sensed something unclean about it.

Jesse described the scene to Melusinne and all that had happened after the game, and after that night. He told her about the atrocity at Mama Dao's whorehouse. He told her how he and Lewis had subsequently conspired to kill Gamaliel, about the ensuing catastrophe in the Ho Bo Woods, where many good men died and Lewis lost his legs. Talking to Melusinne was something like an unburdening, Jesse found.

He admitted that after his conquest of alcoholism and drug addiction, the dark memories of Gamaliel had not receded into some lower dungeon in his psyche, as he'd hoped they would. No matter how hard he'd tried to put the madness behind him, it had periodically slithered to the surface of his consciousness, jarring him awake in the dead of night, or giving him a case of the shivering sweats as he sat in a meeting, or intruding into his thoughts as he played with his sons. He understood now that *fear* had always been with him, a nonspecific dread that swam in slow, patient circles beneath the veneer of his American-ideal life, waiting for the chance to thrust its jaws above the surface and take a bite out of his sanity. *This* was why he'd come to Louisiana instead of going home to his comfortable house and his loving family.

Lewis himself had said it on the night that he and Jesse stood in the darkness of the tank park in Cu Chi Base Camp, planning a murder: *'As long as Gamaliel exists, so will Vietnam. There'll never be a good place, Jess – not while he's alive. Not for you and me.'*

Melusinne rose from the table to stir the pot of gumbo on the range. After a long minute of silence, she turned back to Jesse and said, 'This friend of yours, this Lewis: He's the one who's in danger, isn't he?'

'Yes. I'm told that he has – ah – come under the influence of someone much like Gamaliel, a woman. She's got a brown eye and a blue one, and a shadow that—'

'When did you last see your friend?'

Jesse wrinkled his brow, thinking. 'I visited him in the mid-seventies, when his mother was still alive. He lived with her then. I didn't get back to Portland until 'eighty-two, just after I received my doctorate, and I went out there again a couple of years later on a business trip – 'eighty-seven, I think. That was the last time I saw him. We've written back and forth, of course, talked on the phone maybe half a dozen times.'

'Then it may be too late, Mr Burton.'

'What do you mean, too late? Too late for what?' Jesse's nerves jumped as some trick of the fading light told him that the eyes moved in the stuffed man's head on the wall. He stared a long moment at the face of Melusinne's great-granddaddy, and a ribbon of cold ran down his back.

Melusinne sat down at the table again, reached across it, and took both his hands in hers. 'Jesse, what I'm about to tell you – may I call you Jesse?' He nodded. 'What I'm about to tell you will be difficult to believe, though not quite so difficult for you as for someone else, because you've met Gamaliel. You've seen his shadow. You've seen what he can do with the orb. And you've heard your friend's description of what he can become. Even so, you're an educated man of the twentieth century, the kind who doesn't fear the dark or believe in ghosts. Am I right?'

'I'm not sure what I believe anymore. And I'm not sure what I'm afraid of. I remember my gran'mama sometimes talked about someone who wasn't a "natural child," as she called it, but I never really knew what that meant. I now wonder if she meant people like Gamaliel.'

'If you want to help your friend, you must believe what I tell you. You must accept it simply, without reservation, and without qualification. And you must do what I say. Can you pledge this to me – that you will *believe*, that you will *do*?'

Jesse gave his pledge, and Melusinne started talking. She told him that her family had suffered through an association with Gamaliel's kind for generations, perhaps because so many of her line possessed mental gifts that had led them to dabble in the occult. Whether such dabbling had actually attracted Gamaliel and his ilk, she couldn't say. All she knew was that Gamaliel had walked out of the swamp one day, and had knocked at her door – a gangling teenager who wore nothing but the filth of the bayou on his skin. Having heard stories of such beings from her old auntie and her granddaddy, she'd recognized him immediately for what he was. The mismatched eyes were a dead giveaway.

'What did he want from you?'

'Not much more than a place to stay for a while, a loan of some money for clothes, some food. He'd been in the swamp a long time, you see. He was ready to come back into the world.'

'But why had a teenage boy been living in the swamp? Where were his family?'

His parents were long dead, probably for many generations, Melusinne explained. Even though the kid looked young, he wasn't. 'You see, Gamaliel's kind lives a long, long time, Jesse. I'm not sure how long, or even if anyone knows exactly. But sometimes they get tired, and they need to go off and be alone, to sleep, maybe to hide – I can't say. It's like hibernation, you understand? Sometimes they need to go off and let folks forget that they even exist. They hole up in caves or bury themselves in swamps, and stay for years at a time. And when they come out again, it's as if the ageing process has reversed. They're like young kids starting out in a new life.'

Gamaliel's kind need the trappings of humanity in order to live among humans, Melusinne went on. Each needs a family, a background, a last name – what a spy might call a 'legend' – in order to function in society. The Cartee family and its antecedents in the Caribbean and Europe had met these needs for Gamaliel since long before anyone could remember. Why? She didn't know – perhaps because of some covenant struck long ago, or because of something as simple and elemental as fear. Who could say no to Gamaliel?

'It's not like we're a part of his life,' she hastened to point out. 'Gamaliel has always taken what he's needed from us and then gone his way, often to faraway corners of the world. After all, he doesn't really need us for much – just a jumping-off point, a place to start from. Like others of his kind, he makes money – a *lot* of money – and you can just imagine how he does it.'

'The orb. He uses the orb to win at cards.'

'Yes. Card games, or the stock market, or real estate. Or business ventures of various sorts. I suppose it depends on his frame of mind at any given time. The orb gives him the power to succeed at whatever he does. Ultimately, though, he ends up back in the bayou, where he hibernates. My old granddaddy used to say that he does this because he gets into so much hot water out there in the world, and that people find out what he is. As it turned out, I put him up here for a month or two, until he decided he wanted to go to New Orleans. I sent him to my cousin, Claudette, who kept him for over three years. They lived as if they were mother and son until Gamaliel went off and joined the army. From what I can gather, she never heard from him again.'

Jesse sucked his cigarette almost down to the filter, stubbed it into the ashtray, and lit another. He couldn't stop himself from glancing up at the stuffed man's head. For a horrible moment he thought that the old gentleman had begun to smile ever so faintly. 'Melusinne, I think it's time we get to the crux of the matter. During my tour in Vietnam, there was a string of serial murders—'

'Young women? Horribly mutilated?'

'Yes. Like I told you a minute ago, Lewis and I . . .' He cleared his throat, and took another sip of tea. The eyes of the old former slave had thoroughly unnerved him. 'We became convinced that Gamaliel was the killer, based on what Lewis saw at the brothel in Cu Chi City. He was certain that the . . . *thing* he saw in the act of killing that young whore was Gamaliel.'

Melusinne lowered her face and answered in an almost

prayerful tone. 'And that's why you conspired to kill him, yes. It *was* he – there's almost no doubt of that. You see, that's how his kind lives.' She looked up and stared hard at him. 'They kill. They eat human meat and drink human blood. Their lives go through cycles that nobody but themselves fully understands. During some periods, they need to kill only seldom, maybe every second or third year. In other periods, they need to kill at least once a week. I think it depends on . . . on . . .' The thought seemed painful for her. Jesse waited, his scalp prickling and his heart pounding. 'I think it depends on whether he's trying to reproduce.'

'Reproduce? They do *that*, too?'

Melusinne tightened her grip on Jesse's hands. 'Not like mortal humans, you can be sure of that. In a sense, I suppose it's not reproduction at all. You see, they don't bear young. The only way they can make another of their kind is to convert a human being.'

Jesse's heart skipped a beat. 'Convert a human being – you mean like a vampire might do? Is that what you're telling me? Their victims become—'

No, it wasn't like that at all. It was far more complex. Melusinne had never personally witnessed the process, but had only heard about it, mainly from her auntie and her granddaddy, and she doubted that either of them had actually witnessed it either. Her knowledge was less than perfect, but what she knew, she told him.

No ordinary human being could live the life of Gamaliel's kind. A suitable candidate was someone intelligent, resourceful, and *angry*. Gamaliel would gravitate to one whose anger was pure and deep, whose rage could be tapped to fuel the transmogrification when the right time came. An attractive candidate was one whose anger was righteous and unselfish, not self-centered or petty. Other than these, there was only one prerequisite: the candidate must have tried to kill the monster, not only proving that he possessed sufficient rage and the fortitude to kill, but also to achieve the necessary level of intimacy with the beast. To one of Gamaliel's kind, killing was the most intimate act possible.

Jesse cringed, for Lewis had indeed tried to kill Gamaliel Cartee by putting a bullet through his face. And Lewis had been a man who burned with righteous anger. Thus, Lewis had met the criteria of an ideal candidate.

Melusinne went on, saying that the monster would initiate the process by presenting to the candidate a gift, the crimson orb – regardless of whether the candidate had yet tried to kill him. If the candidate accepted, the orb would impart its evil energy to him, infecting him with it, giving him a taste of the powers in the offing. *Acceptance* was the key, because the change couldn't happen unless the candidate embraced it. And many did embrace it, Melusinne feared, for the orb enabled a man to achieve virtually anything he wanted – wealth, professional success, acclaim. The orb would give him power over his life, which was more seductive than the effects of any drug. Addiction to the orb was the first step.

As to what came next, Melusinne couldn't say. She had her suspicions, but she wouldn't voice them, since they could have been wrong, and no information at all was preferable to wrong information.

'So Gamaliel was trying to make Lewis into one of his own kind,' said Jesse weakly. 'That's why he tried so hard to make him take the orb back in Vietnam.'

'I know enough to confirm this,' she answered. 'Whether or not Lewis accepted the gift *then* may not be as important as whether he's accepted it from this woman you spoke of. He may have survived Gamaliel, but now the question is whether he can survive *her*.'

'She has the eyes, and she has the shadow,' Jesse said, remembering that No Bick had told him this on the telephone. 'There can't be much doubt about what she is, can there?' He rose to stretch his legs, which felt very old at this moment. He became intensely aware that he was no longer the strapping, powerful young dude he'd been in Vietnam. He'd grown a paunch and jowls. His hair had started to silver. He wondered whether he had the strength for what he was about to undertake. 'How do I fight her?' he asked, turning his back to the mounted head of Melusinne's great-granddaddy. 'How do I get Lewis away from her?'

Melusinne motioned him back to his seat as she herself got up. 'Wait here, Jesse.' She went to the front door and opened it, letting in a crescendo of insect music. 'I'll be right back. For your own good, I hope you don't touch anything.'

In the time required to smoke another cigarette Melusinne returned, her arms full of a curious cargo. She set a round baking stone on the table, similar to one that Jesse's wife used for baking homemade pizza. Onto the stone she placed a heap of dried sticks and wood chips. From a burlap bag she took a basketball-size clump of dark soil, which she'd apparently just spaded from the ground. As Jesse watched, she pulled apart the clump, until she'd liberated what appeared to be a small pouch made of oilcloth. Inside the pouch was an object that caused Jesse's breath to catch in his throat like a codfish bone – a miniature coffin of glossy oak, not more than five inches long. It had tiny brass handles and hinges long ago tarnished over. Carved into its convex lid was an intricate cross with the Sacred Heart of the Holy Virgin at its juncture.

'My daddy buried this a long time ago,' said Melusinne, her voice becoming low and husky. 'It was the work of my great-granddaddy, the one up there on the wall. My daddy made me promise never to disturb it unless I could be sure that the time was right, and I think it is. I also think that you're the right man to do this, Jesse.'

'Do what?' he asked, keeping his stare low, away from the mounted head on the wall.

'You'll see.' She placed the ball-bearing he'd brought into the empty cigar box, closed the lid, and handed the box to him. 'Keep this closed tightly. I suggest that you hold it against your chest.' She then began to scoop up the dirt in which the coffin had been buried, pushing it into a circle on the surface of the stone, humming a low and guttural tune that had no discernible musical pattern. After stacking the twigs and wood chips within the circle of dirt, she laid the miniature coffin atop the stack. She struck a wooden farmer's match, and Jesse noticed how far the sun had fallen as the match flared, for the room had darkened to a velvety texture that he suspected was peculiar to places like the bayous of Louisiana and the tropical fields of Vietnam. In spite of himself, he glanced up and detected the jittering reflection of the flame in the glass eyes of Melusinne's great-granddaddy. He could have sworn that the old man's eyelids were widening ever so slowly.

'There's but one way to kill Gamaliel's kind,' whispered Melusinne, lighting a stubby candle that she'd placed on the edge of the table. 'A mere mortal can't do it himself. You need the help of the dead.' Fear stuttered down Jesse's spine. 'Come close now. And keep the box tight against your body.'

He leaned forward, pushing his face reluctantly toward the mound of sticks with the tiny coffin on it, pressing the cigar box to his chest with both hands. As he did so, he heard a faint scratching. Something was inside the coffin. Something alive. He hoped that it was a small animal, a rodent or a large insect.

Humming her low, toneless song, Melusinne brought the candle to the mound and set the wood afire, as Jesse had feared she might. Incredibly, the scratching intensified, as if whoever or whatever lay in the coffin knew what was about to happen. Flames licked the slope of the mound and spread around it, yellow and white, shades of violet and blue. Puffs of grayish smoke spilled upward, spicing the air. 'Closer,' whispered Melusinne, beckoning. 'You must breathe the smoke and fumes. Don't be afraid, Jesse.'

But he *was* afraid. The scratching became frantic, and he worried that at any moment he would hear a tiny voice scream for mercy. And he feared what was happening to Dr Jesse Burton himself. Less than twenty-four hours earlier he'd been a normal, rational man of the twentieth century, a man with a family and a job. He'd grappled with real problems that lent themselves to analysis by computers, problems of numbers and budgets and allocations. He'd confronted the evils of poverty, ignorance, and uncaring politicians – *not* evil at the hands of monsters out of folklore. Now he found himself hunched over a table at the edge of a Louisiana bayou, watching a witch burn a miniature coffin and fearing that it contained a miniature human being who was no longer dead. *What the hell has happened to me?* his heart screamed.

The flames began to scorch the outer surface of the coffin, producing a tart smoke that invaded his nostrils and roused an itch in his sinus cavities. Melusinne's humming became a moan, a deep grumbling that sounded unnervingly masculine. Jesse stared at the coffin as the scratching became more frantic, and he knew that he was witnessing something unspeakable.

Suddenly Melusinne's eyes popped open and she ceased her moaning. Perspiration beaded her ebony face. 'Look beyond the *known*, Jesse,' she whispered urgently. 'Feel beyond yourself . . .'

Just then the edge of the coffin glowed orange, and a piercing squeal issued from it as the fire penetrated the wood. The varnish blistered and peeled. Fragments of molten satin dripped through gaps in the wood before curling and flaming into nothingness. The squeal rose to a shriek that sliced through the smoke to the core of Jesse's heart, shattering any hope that the occupant of the coffin was a small animal like a mouse or a rat, or even a baby alligator – *anything* but a human being. For the shriek was human, or close to it.

'. . . Turn your heart inward and outward. Inhale the message that seeks you!'

The reek of burning flesh flooded into his head. He'd tasted it before, in the Ho Bo Woods; he'd watched friends burn and die as tracer rounds laced the air around him, as mortar rounds dropped with bone-crunching detonations. This was the stench of a life snuffing out, and the colors it generated in his mind were those of hopelessness and insufferable pain.

The squeal died suddenly, and Jesse's eyes went to the wall where the old man's head hung on its mount. A milky fog hung in the air, soaking up the dancing light of the fire, but he could just make out the face, the eyes, the nappy white hair. The facial expression hadn't changed, but tears flowed from the dead man's eyes.

Suddenly the cigar box that Jesse held next to his chest began to pop and thud, as if the ball-bearing inside it had come to life. With each sound came a vibration that he could feel in his ribcage. The popping became more rapid and rhythmic, more powerful, and the box literally shuddered in his hands as the ball-bearing hurled itself against the rigid cardboard walls, producing a sound that was almost engine-like. Jesse could feel the ghostly energy resonate through his entire body. It warmed him, comforted him, opened his mind and heart to possibilities that he'd never before dreamed of.

'Look beyond the known, Jesse,' Melusinne repeated, her face streaked with the tracks of sweat and tears. 'Feel beyond yourself. Accept the message that seeks you . . .'

Suddenly the popping died and the ball-bearing rolled to a corner inside the cigar box, where it lay silent.

CHAPTER TWENTY-SIX
Killing Time

i

The manila envelope was identical to the four that Josh Nickerson had received from an anonymous sender throughout the preceding summer, the sole clue to its origin being the postmark – in this case, Seattle, on October 3, 1992. It had arrived on Monday, two days earlier, but Josh hadn't noticed it until now, for he'd spent Monday at Nicole's deathbed, watching her slip away.

ii

He'd spent the day after her death in his room, shunning all company and ignoring his mother's plea for him to eat something, anything – a granola bar, if nothing else. She'd begged him to talk to her and cry with her; to take advantage of the fact that he wasn't alone, that he had a family who yearned to help him shoulder his burden of grief. But he'd not wanted any help from his family, especially not from his father. The hotshot insurance executive had arrived at the apartment on Tuesday evening, summoned by his ex-wife to make a stab at doing whatever fathers are supposed to do at times like this, Josh figured. Greg Nickerson had pounded on the bedroom door without let-up for nearly thirty minutes, gently at first but ever more loudly as his frustration grew, a ham-handed attempt to spur his son to 'snap out of it.'

'You're getting a little old to be locking yourself in your room and crying whenever something goes wrong,' Greg had said, displaying his insurance-executive sensitivity. *'The only way to get ahead in this world is to square your shoulders and face your troubles like a man. Sitting around and sniveling in the dark never solves anything, believe me. Now, what do you say, Bud? – unlock this door and give me five, okay?'*

Josh had ignored him, of course, choosing to stay hidden in the darkness with his curtains pulled shut, cocooned in silence. He'd played no CDs, never turned on the television or the radio. He'd perused no magazines and read no books. He'd wanted no distraction from the pain, no intrusions into his impossible vision of a long and fruitful life with Nicole. If he concentrated hard enough, his heart lied, he might bring the vision to life.

He could almost see her, alive and full of energy, her Asian eyes flashing like gems. Throwing out smart-ass remarks like someone had put a quarter in her and pulled her handle. Making him laugh, making him think. Criticizing him when he needed it, patting his back when appropriate, guiding him ever upward. Josh would have done the same for her, of course. She too would have become a writer, he was certain – a playwright or a poet or a novelist. He would have encouraged her as she'd always encouraged him. He was confident that she would have succeeded hugely, if she'd lived.

How could she possibly be *gone*? The bitter truth of her

death seemed outrageous, out of sync with creation as Josh Nickerson knew it. He wanted no part of a world in which Nicole could actually die.

He envisioned being in bed with her, something that had never really entered his head until now. He visualized what they would have done together, her lithe little body pressed close against him, her strong legs wrapped around him, her tongue mingling with his. He tasted her, experienced her. Half asleep with this luxurious dream, he masturbated and awoke fully to a wrenching orgasm that fouled the sheets and blankets. Then he lay for a full hour and sobbed like a little boy.

iii

The envelope contained a newspaper clipping from the *Seattle Times*, dated October 3, Saturday. It described the gory murder of a forty-six-year-old lawyer aboard his sailboat at Seattle's Shilshole Marina on the shore of Puget Sound. A spokesman for the police said that the assailant had literally ripped the man to pieces, not unlike what a bear or a wolf would do to a prey animal. An initial examination of the scene by a forensics team suggested that the murder had occurred sometime the previous night, or Friday. The spokesman said that this was the most gut-turning homicide that anyone in the department could remember.

Friday night. Josh set the clipping on his desk, his mind clicking. *Millie Carter did this.* Why she'd gone to the trouble of mailing another clipping to him, he couldn't imagine, any more than he could imagine just who the hell Millie Carter was or what the fuck she wanted, other than to cause sickness and misery and death.

In his head, he pieced together the likely sequence of

events. Millie flew up to Seattle sometime on Friday, after Josh had followed her to the villa in Northwest. She located a victim – maybe picked him up in a bar, as she'd done with several of the others, or struck up a conversation with him on the street; who could know? – then went with him to his boat and tore him to pieces with her claws and teeth. She stayed the night in Seattle. After the morning paper hit the streets, she bought a copy, clipped the story about the murder, and mailed the clipping to Josh. She hopped a plane back to Portland, arriving scarcely forty minutes later. She drove home from the airport in her black Jaguar and caught a pair of intruders in her house. For some reason she let them escape, but not until she'd sliced open Nicki's shoulder, using one of the same claws she'd used to disembowel that poor asshole in Seattle, no doubt.

Josh seethed as he tried to imagine just how evil Millie Carter was: So evil that a cut from her claw caused an infection lethal enough to make you swell up, dry out, and die within two days. She was evil like nothing he had ever heard of or dreamed of.

A world without Nicki was damn-near unbearable, but a world with Millie Carter in it was even worse. A thing as evil as Millie Carter couldn't be allowed to live.

The LED readout on his clock-radio said 10:15 A.M.. Today was a schoolday, but he'd stayed out for the third day in a row. No telling when he would go back, if ever. School didn't matter anymore.

After listening for any sign that either his mother or his sister was at home, he carefully opened his door and peered out. Taped to the doorjamb was a Hallmark card in a peach-colored envelope, featuring a dreamy landscape executed in pastel chalks. He ignored the sappy

poetry and read his mother's penned note, which welcomed him back to the world of the living and informed
him of a casserole dish in the refrigerator that contained
scrambled eggs with onions, fried potatoes, and bacon
bits – one of his favorites. All he needed to do was to pop
the dish into the 'wave and blast it for sixty seconds. Oh,
and by the way, she loved him, and so did Kendra. *See ya
soon*.

Josh couldn't remember the last time he'd eaten –
Sunday, maybe? Almost four days ago? The thought of
food made him nauseous. He doubted that he would be
able to eat until after he'd killed Millie Carter.

iv

He let himself into Lewis's apartment with the key Lewis
had given him and found the place so quiet that at first he
thought no one was home. As he crept toward the
bedroom, however, he heard a rhythmic snoring that
could only be Lewis's. Josh halted and stood fossil-still,
listening for the breathing of another person, Millie, but
he heard nothing. He moved forward again, tensing
himself to whirl away and run, half expecting Millie to fly
out of the bedroom with her claws spread like giant
spiders, her mouth stretched into a slavering grin. Before
coming here, he'd walked around the grounds of Sloan
House and had checked the cars parked along Gander
Circle, looking for her black Jag, but he'd seen no sign of
it. Millie wasn't here, he was certain, but even so, he
couldn't shake the fear that she might be lying in ambush.

Lewis's blinds were shut, so his bedroom was dusky.
Josh went quickly to the low table next to the bed,
carefully pulled open the drawer, and took out the old
Colt .45. He paused a moment to gaze down at his friend,

who slept the sleep of the dead, face turned to the wall, a light blanket covering him. Something wasn't right, but he couldn't quite put his finger on it. He stood silent another thirty seconds, the pistol cold and heavy in his hand, staring down at Lewis through the half-light, wondering, worrying. His mind felt leaden and sluggish, as if his brain was deliberately filtering out certain realities in order to spare him the anguish it would cause.

I don't have time for this, Josh told himself. A chore awaited doing. He tiptoed toward the door and stepped on something that almost caused him to lose his balance and fall. Righting himself, and managing not to drop the pistol, he looked down at the carpet and saw that he'd tripped over a shoe, one of those casual walking shoes that middle-aged men seemed to like. Its mate lay less than two feet away.

Shoes. What did Lewis Kindred need with *shoes*?

He turned back to the slumbering form on the bed. Lewis lay in a tangle of blanket and sheets, the outline of his body obscured among the uneven folds, the ridges and valleys of cloth. From this angle, Josh could almost make himself believe that under the blanket Lewis had two good legs.

v

He left Sloan House through the rear entrance, which stood wide open. In the service drive was a huge United Van Lines truck, into which three beefy men were loading furniture, appliances, and cardboard boxes. Off to one side stood the landlady, Juliet Kindred, and the young stockbroker who lived on the second floor next to the Nickersons, chatting amiably in the cool late-morning sunlight. Josh surmised instantly that the guy was leaving

Sloan House. Josh didn't stop to chat.

As he drove into Northwest, he felt weirdly detached from the sights and sounds of the world around him. He felt detached from *himself*, as if he'd graduated to a plane of existence on which the familiar old Josh Nickerson didn't exist. He no longer cared about writing the story of Millie Carter and all her evil doings, for the time had come to *act*. He was no longer a mere observer, but a player, a victim. He'd tasted the sting of her evil. He'd lost Nicki, and nothing of his old life mattered anymore. Josh Nickerson had become someone else.

He parked the Escort where he and Nicki had left it on Saturday morning. He sat silent a moment, staring absently into the thicket that grew almost to the edge of the gravel. His hand went to the passenger seat, which was crusty with Nicole's blood. Hot tears pooled in his eyes. Anger constricted his chest. He raged.

He checked the pistol to ensure that it had a round in the chamber and that the hammer was in the half-cocked position, which was as good as engaging the safety switch, Lewis had taught him. After tucking the weapon into his belt, he got out of the car, checked for traffic in both directions, and sprinted across the road.

He trudged up the hill as Nicki and he had done four days earlier, fending off damp fronds of sword fern, battling through bushes and weeds. Here and there he noticed indentations in the soil that Nicki's boots could have made, and his heart weltered under fresh onslaughts of grief. He hauled himself into the young oak tree and went over the wall, then made his way through the tattered Italianate garden. He climbed the exterior stairs at the far end of the covered veranda. Using the butt of the pistol, he knocked out a pane in the French door, reached through it, and freed the lock. Whether anyone inside heard the commotion didn't matter to him. Just that quickly, hardly before he knew it, he was inside the house, a willing criminal who was armed and determined to commit a capital crime.

Down the curving staircase he went, into the front hall, where dust and grime on the windowpanes polluted the incoming daylight to create a netherworld of half-darkness, where filaments of spider webs fluttered lightly from chandeliers and light fixtures. He walked quickly into the foyer, squinted through the dirty glass of the doors into the front drive, and saw Millie's Jaguar with its chrome agleam in the sunlight. Holding the pistol tightly in his fist, he followed the Persian runner back toward the rear of the house, not caring about the thump of his hiking boots or the squeak of rotting floorboards. As he reached the juncture with the short hallway that led to Millie Carter's one livable room, he thumbed the hammer back and raised the pistol.

She waited for him just inside the walnut doors, wearing the same green-velvet housecoat she'd worn when Josh confronted her at Lewis's door last week. She stood next to the heavy round table, bathed in the soft glow of the Tiffany lamp, grinning at him with what might have been triumph or contempt – Josh couldn't read the glint in her blue-brown eyes. The sight of her froze him to the marrow of his bones, made his muscles go numb. She was beautiful, and Josh loathed himself for thinking so.

'I knew it would be you,' she said. 'I've waited for this moment a long, long time. I never had any doubt that it would eventually come.' She stepped away from the table and moved slowly toward him.

'*Why?*' Josh asked, his voice shaking.

'*Why*? That's the question of the ages, isn't it? Has it ever occurred to you that human beings are the only creatures on earth who ask it? Of all the sentient organisms on the face of this planet, there isn't one other that presumes a need to know the reasons behind events. Only human beings feel a need to know the *why* of anything. It sets them apart . . .'

'To hell with all that! Why did you kill Nicki?'

Millie moved to within an arm's length of Josh, close enough that he could smell her perfume. Her dreadlocks were the color of cinnamon. 'She was an encumbrance. She would've held you back, Josh. You didn't need her.'

'Who are you to decide what I need?'

'I'm the one who knows you. I know you better than anyone. More than that, I love you and your delicious anger. I've taken it upon myself to take your future into my own hands, quite simply because I *need* you. I've never needed anyone as much as I need you, not even Lewis.'

He began to feel dizzy. Images whirled and swirled in his mind like wind-driven snowflakes, put there by Millie, he suspected – wonderful images, frightening ones, sexy ones. This was another aspect of her power, surely – the ability to put things into the heads of others. How else could anyone explain how she'd manipulated both Lewis Kindred and Rex Caswell during a poker game in which she wasn't even a player? How else could she have manipulated five Nazi skinheads and then turned them into mannequins? Staring at her through blearing eyes, Josh saw her inhale deeply and tilt her head back, as if savoring the aroma of some succulent dish. Was she breathing in his anger and relishing it? he wondered. Was she feeding on it?

491

Something she'd said after the fight with the skinheads came to him: '*Never try to hold your anger in, Josh. Always let it out. Let it grow. Let it become strong and hard. Use your anger, and great things will happen for you.*' He sensed now that she'd had an ulterior motive in giving him this strange advice. She'd wanted him to feel rage so she could feast on it.

He mustered his will and broke out of the reverie. 'Why did you send me those newspaper clippings?' He pointed the pistol directly at her forehead. 'Tell me, or I swear to God I'll blow your brains out!'

'There's no need to threaten me, Josh.'

'*Tell* me!'

'I'm not sure I can. I knew that you'd seen me on the night of Ron Payne's rather messy demise, and I suppose that I wanted to connect with you in some indirect way. The time simply wasn't right for me to approach you straight on.' Her words flowed like Louisiana molasses, sickly sweet. 'And I did it to confuse you. To make you *angry*. It was a labor of love, Josh, I swear. You see, I'd been watching you for a long time. I'd pretended to be enamored with Ron Payne and that insane band, but it was really *you* I was interested in. By staying close to the band, I could stay close to you.'

'Why me? What have I ever done to you?'

'That's not relevant, Josh. As you've probably gathered, I had an interest in Lewis Kindred which goes back many years. We had unfinished business, he and I, which I'm happy to say we've concluded successfully. When I started watching him, I couldn't help but notice you, since you and he are such close friends. When I first got a whiff of your potential for anger, I knew that you were an excellent prospect, just as Lewis turned out to be.'

'You used the skinheads, didn't you?' Josh said, gulping. 'You used them in order to get to me. Couldn't you have picked an easier way? If you just wanted my help in giving the orb to Lewis—?'

'That wasn't the only reason! I needed to fan your anger, Josh. I needed to give you a reason to let it erupt—'

'So you could use it, right? You feed on anger like normal people feed on burgers and French fries!'

'That's not entirely true. I *sample* a person's anger before I move in on him in order to find out what kind of person he is. Not everyone passes the test. Ron Payne is a good example. He was a very angry young man, but his anger was selfish and pointless. By tasting it, I discovered that he was shallow and weak, not a good prospect. He turned out to be good for only one thing – a meal. Not like *you*, Josh.'

'That's the second time you've used that fucking word – *prospect*. Prospect for *what*?'

Millie's grin became wider, toothier. 'You'll find out the truth very soon. I might already have told you too much.'

'You killed the men in those news clippings, didn't you? And you're *still* killing. You fly around the country every month or so, and you kill someone – never in the same city twice, because you don't want to set a pattern. You killed those men, then you clipped the stories from the papers and sent them to me. And you killed Ron Payne.' Josh wiped sweat out of his eyes with his free hand and breathed deeply to banish the quiver from his voice. 'Is that what you have in mind for me? Am I a good prospect to become an animal like you – a cold-blooded murderer?'

Millie's nostrils flared, and Josh noticed a sheen of perspiration on her upper lip. 'You understand little right now,' she replied. 'In time you'll understand everything, and then you won't be quite so willing to condemn me.'

'Is that what you think?' Josh lowered the heavy pistol. 'I've got news for you, you filthy bitch. I'll always condemn animals like you, and I'll *never* become like you.'

'Then the loss is yours. You have such potential, Josh – you're strong, tough-minded, resourceful. Your anger is the kind that could *serve* you instead of destroy you, unlike the anger of so many others. You would do so well with the gifts I offer you.'

Josh felt exhaustion settle into him, and he turned to leave. He no longer wanted to become a killer. All he wanted was to regain control of himself and become the person that Nicole Tran had loved. The image of that person shimmered somewhere in his mind, and he struggled to bring it into focus. He remembered the promise he'd made to Nicole in this very room, that he would pursue and realize his dream of becoming a writer. 'I don't want anything from you,' he said to Millie, spitting the words. 'I don't want any part of you or the things you do.'

'Josh, don't go!' she commanded, reaching toward him. 'You had a purpose in coming here. You can't turn your back on it.'

'Can't I? Watch me.'

'I can give you what you never had with Nicki. I can give you what she could only give you in your dreams. You've dreamed of holding her body close to you, haven't you? – of putting your hands . . .'

She let the hunter-green robe fall to the floor and stood naked before him. Despite himself, Josh let his eyes devour her nakedness, starting with the lean slope of her shoulders, then continuing down to the chocolatey-looking areolae on her full breasts. A thin trickle of sweat ran between her breasts, over her ribcage. Her waist swept in graceful curves down to her hips, and her abdomen flowed into a dark vee where her long legs met her torso. She played with herself, kneading her breasts so that her nut-like nipples stood rigid, insinuating her fingers into the cleft below her pubic mound. Moaning softly, hungrily, she showed herself to him, beckoned to him.

'This is what you wanted to do with her, wasn't it, Josh? You wanted to kiss her here, and here. You wanted to run your hands over her body—'

Josh's eyes flooded as he remembered his dream of Nicki, and he felt his groin come alive. His anger rumbled as he remembered that he would never be able to live that dream with her.

'Do it to *me*, Josh. Come to me, and come inside me. Do to *me* what you wanted to do with her. It'll be good, Josh, I promise. It'll be so much better than anything you would've had with her. She can't compare with me, Josh. You'll be *glad* she's dead.'

His anger erupted, and Josh raised the pistol. He squeezed the trigger, heard a deafening *thud!*, and saw fragments of Millie's brain shower the Tiffany lampshade. She slipped to the floor and lay still in a spreading lake of blood, arms and legs splayed, harmless now, her perfect forehead ruined by a bullet. Josh stared at her almost disbelievingly, nausea gripping him and acid rising in his throat. He whirled away and fled to the sunshine.

CHAPTER TWENTY-SEVEN
Old Friends

i

Your wife ushers a man into your room, and he stands at your bedside with his hands clasped respectfully in front of him, bathed in the warm afternoon light streaming through your window. He's tall, bull-shouldered and black, but not as powerful-looking as you remember him. His closely cropped hair has a sprinkling of gray, and his cheeks have fattened and drooped. The decades have rounded him and left signs of wear, but he hasn't lost the marble-hardness of his black eyes, which makes him who he is.

'Specialist Burton,' you say finally, offering up your hand. 'It's good to see you again. Thank you for coming.'

Your visitor takes your thin Vietnamese hand in his huge, black one. You sense a kindness in his eyes that wasn't there before, but his handshake confirms that he's still strong, still a man to be reckoned with. He'll be a good ally.

He speaks your old nickname, No Bick, then apologizes. The nickname seems even more inappropriate now, he says, than it had in Vietnam. What should he call you?

You tell him that you took the name Paul Tran when you came to America, because you'd decided that using your real one would have been incautious, considering how close you would live to Lewis Kindred. In view of the mission you'd taken for yourself, you'd decided not to alert Lewis to your presence. The new name, you point out, preserves a piece of your old one, Tran Van Hai, but it's less foreign-sounding to Americans, which is good for business. An old friend like Specialist Burton, however, should simply call you Hai.

He nods, and tells you to call him Jesse.

Your wife has disclosed to him the tragedy that you and she have endured, the loss of your only child, your beautiful Nicole. Jesse offers his condolences. You can't say so with certainty, but you feel that Nicole died at the hand of Gamaliel's evil, and if not at his own hand, from one of the same species. You touch the remnants of the blister on your forehead and offer it as evidence of the potency of that evil.

You motion Jesse into a chair beside the bed, and your wife brings tea. You ask about his life, his work, his family.

When he asks about your life, you think for a long moment, then try to explain what happened to you in the years that followed that bloody day in the Ho Bo Woods, when Lieutenant Kindred murdered Sergeant Cartee, the day Lewis himself lost his legs. But how does a man put into words the thing that defines his life? Is it enough to say simply that you require a cause at the center of your existence, that you have a pathological need to raise your fist against some definable evil? No, it's not enough. You relate how you joined the National Liberation Front with the mistaken belief that at last you'd found your cause, only to discover that the Viet Cong and the North Vietnamese cared less about social and political justice than power. Then you sided with the Americans and the Saigon government, becoming a *Hoi Chanh* and a Kit Carson, but you found little goodness and no justice with them, either. Only once in your life had you encountered an enemy who was worthy of the commitment you yearned to make. That enemy was, or is, Gamaliel Cartee.

More than this, you'd seen goodness in Lewis – the kind that halts the torture of innocents, regardless of the consequences; that stands tall in the face of evil and resists its temptations, as Lewis had done during the poker game in the Triple Deuce motor pool; the kind that goes to battle with a monster like Gamaliel Cartee. At last, here was an alliance worthy of your commitment, your trust.

Jesse nods, a knowing look in his eyes. He understands the need to become a crusader, for he has discovered that same need in himself. He wants to hear more.

Following the fall of Saigon, you journeyed to the jungle north of Tay Ninh and visited a renegade priest of the Third Alliance between Man and God, needing to learn more about your enemy. What the old man told you horrified you, made you feel weak and inadequate, but you didn't shrink from your commitment.

'I knew early on that Lewis was the key to defeating Gamaliel,' you confess. 'I knew it when I saw Gamaliel after Lewis had shot him. When he handed me the pistol that Lewis had used, he said, "Tell him our dealings are far from ended. We have much to do together, he and I – much to do!" I remember those words as if I heard them yesterday.'

The old priest's instructions were brutally simple. 'He disclosed to me the signs to look for and gave me the tools I would need to conduct an adequate surveillance.' You point to the bed table, where you've placed a lacquered box with brightly painted Cao Dai iconography on its lid. The lid is open, and inside the box lies a marble of red glass. 'He gave me this, and told me that the marble would stir when the evil was near. He told me that I was to watch Lewis during the night in order to discover whether anyone shared his bed. If I ever found that he was indeed sleeping with someone, I was to ascertain whether that person possessed what he called the "telltales" – the mismatched eyes, the shadow of indigo. If the person possessed these traits, then it was too late for Lewis, because he would have been irreparably tainted.'

Jesse asks what this means. He looks very worried.

'It means that I must kill him,' you say. 'Killing him would be merciful, compared to letting him become one of Gamaliel's kind. I believe that Lewis would agree.'

Silence, long and painful. Jesse buries his face in his hands and shakes his head in tiny, jerky movements. You swallow, then begin to speak again. 'I came to America, to Portland, as you know, because I knew that this was Lewis's home city. I found him merely by consulting the telephone book. I took a job – more than one, in truth, and worked hard. I built my own business. I bought this house, which is less than a block from where he lives.' You lever yourself up onto your elbows and stare intently into your friend's face. 'I became a prowler, Jesse, what you Americans call a "Peeping Tom." From time to time, I prowled around Lewis's windows at night, watching him, trying to discover whether anyone was in his apartment with him. Sometimes I followed him during the day in order to see who he associated with. I even placed one of my workers – I own a janitorial company – inside Sloan House where he lives, in order to justify periodic visits to the building. Doing all this made a wreck of my family life, I'm afraid. My poor wife—'

You see that Jesse is staring at the lacquer box with wide, unblinking eyes, and you could swear that his black face is turning pale. He reaches over the bed and takes it from the table, turns it over in his hands and examines it. The marble rolls around noisily inside. How exactly does the marble warn you? he wants to know.

You take the box from him and hold it tightly to your chest. Meditation is the crux of the matter, you explain. Under the right conditions, the marble comes alive and throws itself against the inner walls of the box, often with great force, propelled by 'guardian spirits,' in the words of the old Cao Dai priest. The effect is almost engine-like, you say. The vibrations penetrate your ribcage and warm your entire body. You offer the theory that the phenomenon is actually psychokinesis, brought on by a certain subliminal awareness of the presence of another mind.

'Gamaliel's mind?' asks Jesse.

'His or the mind of someone like him.' The theory isn't really scientific, you admit, but it's more palatable to a rational mind than spirits and demons.

On the night of September 21, the marble went mad, you tell Jesse. Never before had the marble been so full of energy, so rapid-fire in hurling itself against the interior of the box. The intensity of the experience convinced you that Lewis Kindred was under deadly assault by a determined force, that the time had come for a showdown of some sort.

You armed yourself with a tire iron and the K-54 pistol that Lewis had used to shoot Gamaliel. You went to Sloan House and began your surveillance. Lewis came home to his empty apartment shortly after eight o'clock, accompanied by his young friend, Josh Nickerson, who also happened to be a close friend of your daughter. Several hours later Josh left the apartment and went home to the apartment directly above Lewis's. Hours passed, and the night grew chill, but you held your position behind the clump of azaleas outside the veranda that spanned Lewis's apartment, certain that a confrontation would occur before the night was out. A few minutes after one A.M., you saw a shadowy figure approach the front entrance of Sloan House, a tall woman with hair that shone like copper in the ambiance of the street lights. She took out no key, but simply put her hand to the door handle and pushed the door open, then disappeared inside. Your stomach fluttered, for you knew that without a key, a visitor needed to call a tenant on the intercom to gain entry. But the woman with the coppery hair hadn't done this.

More movement, this time inside Lewis's apartment, the mere flicker of a shadow in the window of his studio, which was the room next to his bedroom. *The woman?* you wondered. You waited for what seemed an eternity, then ventured out of your hiding place and entered the veranda. You tried the windows there and found them locked. You tried the other windows, the rear entrance, then the front entrance, and found them all locked. You returned to the veranda and took the tire iron out of the bag. You decided to smash the window and go directly to the heart of the matter. If Lewis was in bed with a creature who owned both a blue eye and a brown one, you would kill them both and try to escape. If he wasn't in bed with such a creature, then you meant to escape if you could, or to accept manfully the consequences of breaking and entering.

You raised the tire iron to strike at the windowpanes, but became aware of an angry red glow that ate up the darkness of the night like acid eats silk. Before you knew what was happening, the orb sailed around from behind you and took up a position between you and the window, as if to bar your way, hanging in the night air like a miniature sun and flinging its filaments of bloody light across your face and body. You'd seen one like it before, in the motor pool of Triple Deuce Mech in Cu Chi Base Camp, on the night that Lewis Kindred and Gamaliel Cartee played poker. You knew who it represented. As you tensed to strike at the thing with your tire iron, it attacked you, darting forward to press itself against your forehead. A shower of sparks erupted, blinding you. The heat seared your skin and lanced through your skull into your brain. Beyond this moment you remember only tingling pain.

ii

The sun has sunk below Gander Ridge, leaving a sky that's the color of a ripe cantaloupe. You and Jesse have finished talking for now. He gazes through the window, studying the intricate pattern of elm branches against the fading sky, occasionally coughing into a closed fist.

He has told you what he found out yesterday from a *sorcière* in Louisiana, and it fits with what the renegade Cao Dai monk told you years ago, that there is but one way to kill a demon like Gamaliel. Whether it's actually possible to call forth the dead to handle such a chore isn't something you want to debate right now. *Calling forth the dead* may be a metaphor for reaching deep into your own storehouse of mental capabilities to find the proper psychic weapon. In your study of Eastern religions and cults you've found numerous references to extraordinary mental phenomena, such as psychokinesis, the ability to move objects with thought, and physioplasty, the ability to contort one's body into monstrous shapes. Too, you've read case studies about forms of schizophrenia that can cause a person to believe that he is a monster – a vampire or a werewolf or a demon. Psychologists have documented cases in which patients behaved as though they were indeed monsters, committing unspeakable acts of murder and mutilation, even cannibalism.

Are Gamaliel's kind merely schizophrenics who have mastered psychokinesis and physioplasty? You hope that this is so. Hanging in a rear room of your mind, however, is the question of how Gamaliel rose from the dead after Lewis fired a nine-millimeter bullet through his head. You have found no explanation for *this* in your exploration of religions, cults, and psychology.

'We would be honored if you would stay with us,' you say to Jesse, breaking the silence. 'My wife will prepare one of the guest rooms for you.'

He protests. You have just lost your daughter, and the funeral is tomorrow. He doesn't want to impose on you in your time of grief.

'It isn't an imposition, Jesse. You are my brother now, my ally. I had planned to confront the evil alone, but this—' Your hand goes again to the blisters on your forehead. '—This has robbed me of my strength. I know that the battle will require much concentration and great mental power, but this sickness, whatever it is . . . I know that I'm not up to the challenge on my own. With you, though, I can do it. Together we have the necessary strength, of this I'm certain. Stay with us. Please.'

Jesse nods. He will stay. He will want to see Lewis, though, he says, and soon.

CHAPTER TWENTY-EIGHT
Only a Face

i

Twyla Boley lowered the Metro section of Wednesday's *Oregonian* and stared intently through the panoramic windows of the floating house, her mouth hanging open in shock. A moment later she raised the newspaper again and studied the police artist's sketch that accompanied a long story with the headline: *Police hunt suspect in grisly hotel murder.*

This was crazy. This couldn't *be*. The sketched face couldn't possibly belong to Lewis Kindred.

Just then she heard Rex's key enter the lock on the door. He was tall and immaculate, his blond hair tousled just so. He truly was a beautiful man, thought Twyla. Why wasn't her heart pitter-pattering the way it once did whenever she caught the tiniest glimpse of him?

'Rex, look at this,' she said, rising out of the leather futon. 'Tell me if I'm out of my mind . . .'

'Sweetheart, not now,' he said, moving past her toward the stairs. 'I have some phone calls to make.' He'd just taken a meeting with his main supplier, from whom he'd received a large shipment of cocaine. Now he would call Mason Benoit to summon his help in distributing the goods to his retailers, always a ticklish matter. Much money would change hands tonight, Twyla knew.

'Rex, for God's sake, you'll be interested in this. Look at this picture and tell me what you see. It'll take ten fucking seconds, okay?'

Rex halted before stepping onto the stairs, sighed, and turned around. 'How many times must I ask you not to use that kind of language around me?' His tone was that of an exasperated parent. 'You know how I hate coarseness in women.'

'Fuck that! Look at this picture.' She thrust the newspaper toward him, and he took it from her, shaking his head. The man in the sketch might have reached out from the newsprint and seized Rex by his hand-sewn lapels, given the look of shock on Rex's face.

'See what I mean? It's Lewis, isn't it? – the long hair, the pitted skin along the jaw, the nose, even the *eyes*, for Christ's sake. It can't be anyone else.'

'It says the drawing is from a description given by a woman in Pazzo Ristorante,' said Rex, his eyes narrowing on the print. 'It was her girlfriend who got killed. She didn't say anything about the guy being in a wheelchair.'

'He told her his name was Zebulon Councilman, and that he worked for some philosophy writers' association, or some such garbage.'

'I suppose that name means something to you.'

'Not the name, Rex, but the bit about the philosophy writers is *pure* Lewis. He was a philosophy major, you know, a real egghead. He loves philosophy almost as much as he loves poker. He was slinging bullshit to those girls, and they ate it up.'

Rex grew impatient and tossed the newspaper back

at her. 'Would you listen to yourself? You're saying that Lewis walked into a ritzy restaurant on a pair of legs that he doesn't even have and put the moves on one of the bar flies. He then walked her next door to the Vintage Plaza, stripped her naked, and tore her up into little pieces. Think about it, sweetheart: Does that sound like the Lewis Kindred we know and love – a guy who can't make it to a men's room without space-age technology?'

'Then how do you explain the face in this picture?'

'Sweetheart, police artists are notoriously bad. The resemblance is coincidence, that's all. This kind of thing happens all the time. The cops are forever picking up some innocent slob who looks just like a sketch they put out to the newspapers. Now be a good little bovine and mix yourself another Bloody Mary. I have work to do.'

ii

Throughout the evening, Rex tried to put the police artist's sketch out of his mind, but he couldn't deny that the damned thing did indeed look like Lewis Kindred. A *lot* like Lewis Kindred. Just how much was possible, he wondered, if a man had that red crystalline globe in his pocket? Did the crystal give its owner powers that went beyond the poker table? Did Millie Carter come with the crystal, or was it the other way around? Outrageous, half-defined speculations fluttered through his head, both scaring and exciting him.

After taking care of business with his retailers and securing the proceeds in several safes around town, Rex took Mason Benoit for a drink at the Benson Hotel in downtown Portland, one of his regular haunts. They sipped their brandies in an alcove off the wood-paneled lobby, their conversation covered by the background music of a live pianist.

'In case you're curious,' Benoit said, 'our old home-boys from California are safely out of the country. One is in Costa Rica and the other's in Cabo San Lucas. I've got ironclad guarantees that neither of them will set foot in the States for at least six months. With what you paid them, they should be able to live like kings.' He referred to the two men he'd hired to toast a homeless black veteran in a wheelchair, a man known simply as Dewey. 'That's one crime that'll never be solved,' Benoit went on. 'No clues, no surviving family to press the issue – just one less derelict to clutter up Old Town. The cops have bigger fish to fry.' He took a large swallow of his Courvoisier and grimaced. 'Can't say the same thing, though, about that slaughter two nights ago at the Vintage Plaza. The cops'll get that dude, mark my words. The city's in a fucking frenzy over it, have you noticed? – worse than when Ron Payne got himself done last spring. After all, Payne was a heavy-metal rocker, one of those wild-eyed hair farms who looked like he belonged with the Manson gang. But this little bitch at the Vintage Plaza is a different matter – nice-looking, respectable, every momma's idea of what her daughter should grow up to look like, every daddy's little girl. She gets herself lured into a hotel by some maniac and—'

'Did you see the police artist's sketch in today's paper?' Rex interrupted.

'Yeah, I did.'

'Who did it look like to you?'

'Promise not to fire me for being a lunatic?'

Rex nodded his promise.

'It's Lewis Kindred.'

Rex studied his glass, avoiding the black man's eyes. After a stint of silence, he said, 'I haven't given up on getting that red crystal, you know. When I *do* get it, I'm going to play one more round of poker with Lewis, and I'm going to take him for everything he has. In fact, I'm going to take him for everything that he's ever *hoped* to have. I may even call our home-boys from California back from their vacations and give them some work to do, depending on the mood I'm in. Or I may let Lewis twist in the wind for the rest of his worthless, poverty-stricken life.'

'What's the point of it, Rex? You lost some big bucks to Kindred, sure, but you're not hurting for money. Hell, tonight you took in more than ninety percent of what the white men in this town see in a year. You'll do the same thing in two weeks, and you'll do it again two weeks after that. Why do you care about mashing some pathetic middle-aged double amputee in a wheelchair?'

Rex ground his teeth and absently toyed with the gold bead in his earlobe. 'Nobody makes an ass of Rex Caswell and gets away with it. You should know that by now, Mase. Nobody – especially not an arrogant prick who doesn't even have a pair of legs to stand on. I've taken his shit for better than ten years, and I've had it up to here.'

Benoit blew out a weary sigh. 'Okay, I can dig that. But if you ask me, there's no way you're going to get the crystal from Millie Carter. I've never said this before, Rex, but she's one spooky bitch. When Spit and I were following her and Kindred around, I sometimes got the feeling that she could stare through solid walls with those damn mismatched eyes of hers. She's a good one to steer clear of.'

Suddenly Rex's face brightened. An idea hit him. 'Mason, you're absolutely right. I don't know why I didn't think of this before.'

'Think of what?'

'It doesn't make any sense to concentrate on her. I should be concentrating on the *kid*, Lewis's little pal – what's his name? Joshua! Josh, he calls him.' Rex slapped his hands together. 'For years I've been hearing Lewis talk about this kid, almost like he's his own son. To hear him talk, this Josh is going to be the hope of the twenty-first century. And Josh was at the Fanshawe the night of the rematch.'

'And you're thinking he probably knows something about the orb.'

'He was there when Lewis took it out of his pocket and tossed it back to Millie, right after the game. And there was something else, too – something I hadn't remembered until just now. Millie Carter had an *effect* on that kid—'

'Hey, she has an effect on everybody.'

'But not like this. You should've seen him. When we walked into the room, he took one look at Millie and went white as a sheet. There's a history between those two, I'm sure of it.'

'So, what's this got to do with the orb?'

'I'm telling you, Mase, the kid and Lewis are close. If either Millie or Lewis have the orb, that kid will have access to it. And something tells me – call it intuition, or call it knowing people – something tells me that Josh will cooperate with me. I'll use him to get the orb, and I'll worry about Millie later.'

'Sounds like a good idea,' said Benoit, signaling the waiter to bring another round of Courvoisier. 'Use the kid and stay away from Millie. I'm serious about this, Rex – that bitch is bad news. I don't know how I know this, but she can hurt a man. She can hurt a man real deeply.'

CHAPTER TWENTY-NINE
The White Eagle

i

The hunger woke him long after night had swallowed Gander Ridge. He sat up on the bed, swung his legs over the edge of the mattress, and planted his feet solidly on the carpet. For a long time he sat still in the dark, tasting the coarse pile of the carpet through the soles of his feet, loving the sensation. *You never know what you've got till you've lost it*, he mused.

> *This little piggy went to market.*
> *This little piggy stayed home . . .*

He wiggled his toes. He massaged the instep of one foot with the big toe of the other. He played joyfully with his feet, visualizing the miraculous articulation of tarsus, metatarsus, and phalanges, conjuring images and anatomical terms that hadn't entered his mind since his high-school biology class studied human anatomy – the components of the human foot. *Navicular. Os calsis. Cuboid . . .*

And thanks to the fact that the ringing in his ears was gone, he could hear a dripping faucet in the bathroom, a sound he'd grown to love, unbelievably. And his left hand was still limber and strong, his left arm as good as his right. He was whole.

The hunger growled and squirmed, telling him that it needed sating and promising some horrible, unknowable consequence if an appropriate feeding didn't occur soon.

He'd dreamed of Millie while asleep – a long, sweaty dream in which she'd approached his bedside and slowly peeled away her clothes, allowing him to devour her with his eyes. She'd knelt before him and let him lick her nipples to hardness, then encouraged his mouth ever downward, into her navel, then further down still as she arched over him, humping his face. Insinuating herself into bed with him, she'd kissed and licked him around his mid-section, and had taken one of his testicles into her mouth at the very moment his tongue slithered over the lips of her sex. For a rocking, primal moment, he was certain that an orgasm would thrust him into transcendental ecstasy, but it never happened. Rather, sounds intruded from the realm of the real, far away and metallic, the bleep of his telephone and the buzz of his answering machine. The dream withered. He heard his own recorded voice tell the caller that he couldn't come to the phone right now, but to please leave a message at the tone.

'Lewis, are you there, man? It's me, Jesse Burton, at – uh – nine-fifty in the evening. You've got to talk to me. I've come all the way from Chicago – make that New Orleans. I'm here in Portland. I've got to see you, Lewis. It's important . . .'

Vietnam is still chasing me, Lewis told himself. The voice was Jesse's, yes, and Jesse was Vietnam, just as the hunger was Vietnam. As Millie and the orb and Gamaliel

516

Cartee had all been Vietnam. *I've been slipping in and out of a psychogenic fugue, an alternative life that exists only in my mind. I don't really have legs, even though I can feel them and see them as plain as the nose on my face. In fact, I may not even have a nose or a face . . .*

He'd laughed out loud as the machine cut off Jesse's pleas . . . *or arms or hands. I may not even have a head. For all I know, I may not even be alive. Vietnam may have already eaten me . . . !*

How much of himself can a man lose before he becomes someone else – some*thing* else? he'd asked himself for the millionth time, and his laughter became hysterical.

ii

The White Eagle Café and Saloon on North Russell, the cab driver had said, was famous for straight-ahead live rock and roll. The establishment occupied a shabby brick structure in a dismal industrial quarter near the east shore of the Willamette River. A building that had once housed a brothel.

No punk or grunge at the White Eagle. No spike heads, skinheads, or Gothics. The crowd was a lively mix of middle-aged professionals, blue-collar types, and bikers – the common denominator being a love of good old-fashioned rock music played live and loud in a club.

The place was haunted, said local legend. Patrons occasionally complained of harassment in the men's room by a poltergeist, supposedly the spirit of a young prostitute brutally murdered around the turn of the century in an upstairs bedroom by a drunken john. A modern-day patron had reported that something had thrown him against a wall, while another claimed to have had his penis bitten. No one had established with certainty that the ghost was responsible for either attack.

In his college days, Lewis had been a frequent customer of the White Eagle, but he'd never encountered the ghost. Maybe he would encounter her tonight, he thought hopefully, flushing the urinal after emptying himself of his third pint of Widmere. He hadn't come to the White Eagle to meet the ghost, of course, but to troll among the unattached females that the place attracted. The cab driver had confirmed that the reputation of the place was as notorious as ever.

Lewis made his way from the rest room back to the bar, dodging couples on the dance floor, eager to get back to the business at hand. Halfway across the floor he halted to glance behind him, certain that he'd heard something among the layers of rock music that rolled forth from the stage – something unnatural; a rustling or a hiss that roused fear in his gut. But he saw nothing out of the ordinary among the sweaty dancers, no one following him or hiding in the shadows flanking the stage.

Kaycee waited for him on a barstool, a raven-haired beauty in fire-engine-red lipstick and the tightest Levis that Lewis had ever seen. He'd met her an hour ago, and she'd succumbed immediately to his newly acquired charms. Everything that came out of his mouth, it seemed, was magic to a woman's ear. *God, if I'd only had this power twenty-five years ago . . . !*

Kaycee Logan, her full name was. A dental hygienist from Gresham, which was an eastern suburb of Portland. Divorced at thirty-five. Mother of three, but you wouldn't know it from the tautness of her ass or the slimness of her hips. Lewis figured that within the hour he would be fucking her to death. Literally. And then . . .

well, he didn't want to think about it, even though his hunger was like a blast furnace.

'How 'bout I buy you kids a drink?' someone asked just as Lewis reclaimed his barstool. He turned around and saw a square-jawed man in his early forties, tall and raw-boned, easy blue eyes, wavy brown hair. The man would have looked comfortable in a wide-brimmed Stetson and cowboy boots, but instead of these he wore a well-tailored corduroy sport coat over a conservative button-down shirt – the gear of an affluent urban professional out for a night on the town.

Lewis suffered a thrill of panic. The man was Scott Sanders.

'*Doctor* Scott Sanders,' the guy said, beaming, as if he'd heard Lewis say the name in his head. 'I'm an osteopath these days. Got myself a clinic out in Beaverton. It's good to see you again, L.T. I mean that. I think about you a lot.'

Lewis's mouth dried as a scene from the distant past flickered to life in his mind, a scene that with the passage of decades hadn't eroded in vividness or the quality of detail. He saw red and green tracer rounds slashing the sky above the Ho Bo Woods, felt the crunch of incoming mortar rounds and rocket-propelled grenades, heard the chatter of automatic weapons all around him. Specialist Scott Sanders, a medic of Lewis's scout platoon, jumped into the clump of bushes where Lewis and Jesse cowered from the blizzard of hot metal that blew at them from all sides. Scottie's uniform was gory with the blood of a wounded GI to whom he'd ministered moments ago, just as Lewis's uniform was soaked with the blood of Gamaliel Cartee. '*Thought you were a goner, L.T.! Where you bleedin' from?*' At that moment, a bullet fired

519

by an NVA soldier ripped through Scott's chest and blew his heart out through his back. His face went instantly slack, and his forehead thudded on to Lewis's shoulder.

'You're dead,' said Lewis, having gotten control of his mouth at last. 'You're not here. I saw you die . . .'

'Never trust what you see, L.T.,' chuckled the late Specialist-4 Scott Sanders, slapping Lewis on the back. 'The eyes will lie to you every chance they get. Now, why don't you introduce me to your date?'

Lewis heard himself say Kaycee's name, then Scott's name. Heard himself describe Scott as a former rodeo-rider from Wyoming. All-around cowboy. Got drafted and sent to Vietnam, where he—

'Where I was a medic,' Scott interrupted. 'That's what got me interested in medicine. When the army turned me loose, I went back to school and stayed there until I made something of myself, as they say. I miss rodeoin', but my wife hates the smell of livestock, so I s'pose it's a good thing I'm into what I'm into. Ever been to a rodeo?'

Kaycee had. In fact, she *loved* rodeos, but she'd never met an actual cowboy before. Had Scott ever ridden a bull? she wanted to know. Or a bucking bronc? Scott explained that an all-around cowboy masters a wide range of rodeo skills, including calf-roping, saddle-bronc-riding . . .

Thus went the conversation until the band took a break, while Lewis's hunger raged like a fever, growing ever hotter and more insistent. Kaycee excused herself to visit the ladies' room, pronouncing her lipstick in need of attention.

'Fine-lookin' girl,' said Scott, saluting her with his whiskey glass as she clicked away across the dance floor in her tight Levis and spike heels. 'You're a lucky man,

L.T. I hope you treat her right.' He gave a knowing wink.

'Tell me,' Lewis said, clearing his throat uneasily, 'do you ever see anyone else from our platoon – I mean like Jesse Burton or T. J. Skane? Ever run into any of those guys?'

'I doubt that I see as much of them as you do, L.T.'

'Why's that?'

'Because I suspect that No Bick has sent them to you. Just like he sent me.'

Lewis's skin went cold. The background noise of the busy bar receded. 'You've seen No Bick, uh?'

'Haven't you?'

'Now and then, I guess.' Lewis swept his stare around the old saloon, wanting distraction, but he found none. The absurdity of Scott Sanders, standing next to him with his elbow on the bar, a drink in his hand, couldn't be displaced. The guy should be moldering in a coffin, six feet deep in some veterans' cemetery in Wyoming, but here he was, having become more or less what Lewis would have expected him to become, if he'd survived Vietnam. But he *hadn't* survived. He'd died in Lewis's arms. 'No Bick's here in Portland, you know,' Lewis said. 'The little son of a bitch stole one of my legs the day I got them blown off in the Ho Bo Woods. Took it somewhere and roasted it on a spit, then stripped the meat off and ate it. Probably ground the bones to powder and drank them with rice wine.' Lewis took a swig of ale. The hunger had raised beads of sweat on his forehead. 'Now he wants the rest of me. He creeps around my apartment at night, rattling at the windows, looking for a way in. He carries a pistol and—'

'Lewis, do you really believe all that?'

'Why the fuck shouldn't I believe it? I believe in *you*,

521

don't I? I'm sitting here drinking with you, listening to your voice – even though I know you're deader than dinosaur shit. I know what I've seen.'

'And I've told you – your eyes will deceive you every chance they get, and so will your other senses, if you're not careful. You can't take things at face value, L.T.'

Lewis became angry. 'Okay, why don't you tell me the truth, goddamn it? If I can't believe anything I see or hear, I'll let you be my eyes and ears. I'll believe whatever you tell me, I swear.'

'It's not that easy.'

'No, I don't suppose it is.'

'The truth is inside you, L.T., where it's always been, where you've always found it before.'

'The truth about what?'

'About what's right and wrong, good and bad – the only truth that counts. Remember the time you stopped Gamaliel Cartee from torturing a young girl and an old woman in – where the hell were we? Somewhere north of Trung Lap, I think. It was the same day that a big mine blew up a civilian bus and killed something like ninety civilians. The Old Man brought in Cartee to—'

'I remember, Scottie. Let's not relive it down to the last detail, okay?'

'You did what you did because of what was *inside* you. You knew right from wrong, and you didn't need any-body to define it for you, least of all the damn army. You didn't buy all that military bullshit about how it's okay to do something ugly and outrageous if it saves GIs' lives, or if it means fewer people get killed in the long run, or if it shortens the war. You knew that it was wrong to beat up a little girl and an old woman, period. You knew that no amount of rationalizing would make it right. And you had the guts to do something about it, which isn't true of everybody, I'm sorry to say.'

'I don't see what that has to do with the here and now.'

'I'll make it as plain as I can. You can't avoid taking responsibility for the things you let yourself do, Lewis, even in a dream. If you decide to let yourself become—' Scott coughed into a fist, a gesture that seemed profoundly unlikely for a ghost or the figment of a dream. 'Well, you know what I mean. If you let yourself become—'

'No, I *don't* know what you mean, damn it! Become *what*?'

Scott Sanders looked like a man who'd just received word that his brother had died. 'I'm talking about whatever killed the girl in the Vintage Plaza a couple of nights back. If you let yourself become *that*, you can't avoid living with the responsibility.'

Lewis suddenly felt wobbly, and he gripped the edge of the bar to keep from keeling over. 'That night at the hotel – it . . . it didn't really happen. It was all part of a psychogenic fugue, a dream. I can't be held accountable for what happened that night.'

'I wish that was true, L.T., but it isn't. If there's any hope for you at all, it lies in your freedom to choose goodness over—' He coughed again, obviously not liking what he had to say. '—over whatever it is you're about to choose.'

Lewis held tightly to the bar, grateful for the solidity of the stool beneath him. The room was tilting oddly, and the background noise echoed through his skull like some cheap soundstage effect. 'Hey, I don't have the ability to choose anything anymore,' he protested. Scott wrapped an arm around him to steady him. 'I'm a schizo, Scottie –

don't you understand? I have fugues and fantasies and dreams. I'm a sicko! I'm a fuckin' *victim*!'

'Not so,' whispered Scott, leaning close to his ear. 'You chose to do what you did to that girl, because you knew that this was what it took for you to become a whole man. Eating the meat and drinking the blood was the price of a permanent pair of legs—'

'You're lying!'

'You *know* I'm not! You knew the truth from the beginning, in your heart. Millie Carter gave you the first taste of wholeness, but to keep it, you need to do what she does, what Gamaliel does—'

'It's not true! It *can't* be true. She's not like Gamaliel, and I could never become like Gamaliel!'

Scott forced him around so that he faced the dance floor, where Kaycee Logan was striding across the glossy hardwood toward the bar from the ladies' room. Her hips lurched delightfully with her every step, and her ample breasts jiggled beneath her knitted top. She smiled when she noticed that both Scott and Lewis were watching her approach.

'So tell me what you feel when you see her,' hissed Scott in Lewis's ear. 'Make me believe that it's what a normal man feels. Tell me what you plan to do with her, Lewis, after you get her into bed tonight.'

Lewis's stomach cramped, nearly causing him to double over, but Scott held him firmly atop the stool. The sight of Kaycee fanned the hunger to white hotness, causing sweat to drip from his jaw like beads of magma. He couldn't deny what he wanted to do to her. He couldn't deny knowing that a bellyful of her succulent flesh and a snootful of her coppery blood would give him what he needed to maintain the body that he now wore.

Killing, eating flesh, drinking blood – this was the price of a real man's body, and he knew it. He'd *chosen* it.

'*No!*' He twisted and convulsed on the barstool, but Scott held him steady. 'I can't let it happen again, Scottie . . . !'

'I understand. I'll help you get through it, Lewis. I'll help you be strong . . .'

'What the hell's going on here?' asked Kaycee, arriving at the bar to find Lewis and Scott clinging to one another. 'Is this what I think it is?'

'K-Kaycee, I think you'd better go,' Lewis managed, his voice cracking. 'All of a sudden I don't feel so well.'

'I'm sorry to hear that,' she said, eyeing first Lewis and then Scott. 'Well, thanks for the drink. I hope you two are very happy together.' She whirled on her tall heels and clicked away, a pout on her face.

iii

Scott guided Lewis through the front door of the saloon out to the sidewalk, where a dense mist sucked up the light of the street lamps and turned every exhalation into a cloud. The night was dark and wet. Lewis leaned against the grainy bricks of the outer wall and breathed heavily, as if he'd just run a marathon, his clothes sopping.

'Wait here,' said Dr Scott Sanders. 'I'll call you a cab. Will you be okay for a minute or two?'

'I'll be okay.' Before Scott could duck back inside the White Eagle, Lewis caught the cuff of his sport coat. 'What about you? Are you coming with me?'

'Where I'm going, I don't need a cab.' He grinned in the way Lewis remembered and disappeared inside.

A minute turned into two minutes, then five, then ten.

Lewis concentrated on breathing, on keeping from collapsing onto the filthy sidewalk. Many times the heavy front door of the saloon swung open, letting people in or letting them out, but none paid any attention to the sick-looking man leaning against the bricks. His hunger turned to nausea. He shuddered to think what he would have done to poor Kaycee if Scott Sanders hadn't come along when he did.

Good old Scottie Sanders.

If there's any hope for you at all, it lies in your freedom to choose goodness . . .

Lewis realized that he was slipping down the wall, that the rough bricks were tearing at the fabric of his jacket. A familiar old squeal filled his ears, and when he tried to steady himself with his left arm, it crumbled under him. He went down hard on his ass, biting his tongue painfully, and sat for a full two minutes amid the cigarette butts and the used hypodermic needles before realizing what had happened.

The hunger was gone now. His head was clear. Gone too were his legs. Gone were the little piggies.

. . . and this little piggy cried wee-wee-wee . . .

Through a blur of tears he saw two sets of feet approach from the curb, a pair of huge wing tips and a pair of Nike cross trainers. He managed to lift his eyes, feeling as low as he'd ever felt in his life, a legless vet sitting helpless on a filthy sidewalk outside a saloon – the universal picture of degradation. He saw two faces, one belonging to a large black man and the other to a white teenage boy. His vision cleared as the tears fell away. He recognized Josh Nickerson, who himself seemed to be crying, whose youthful face wore the sorrow and guilt of a man much older. With him was someone he hadn't seen for years – Jesse Burton.

They lowered themselves on their haunches, took his hands in theirs. Lewis tried to smile at them. 'I have no idea what the fuck this is all about,' he said, his voice shaking. 'But am I ever glad you guys showed up!'

'We're going to take you home, Lew,' said Josh. 'Is that okay?'

'Are you kidding? I've never wanted to go home so bad in my life.'

'I've got your Action Power 9000 in the car,' Josh added. 'I'll bring it.'

'How did you—? I mean, why are you here?'

'Jesse called me,' said the boy. 'I'll let him explain everything.' He jumped to his feet and bounded away to fetch the wheelchair.

Lewis tightened his grip on Jesse's hand. 'How long has it been, man?'

'Too long. Sorry I haven't come before this.'

'No sweat, GI. We all have our crosses to bear.'

'I tried to call you earlier tonight, but if you were there, you weren't answering.'

'I couldn't answer. I didn't want you to see . . .'

'I know.'

'You do?'

'Lewis, listen to me. I'm staying with the Tran family who live down the block from your apartment house—'

'The *Tran* family? You mean Nicole Tran's family? You *know* them?'

'I do now. After I called, I decided to pay a visit to you in person. I was just leaving the Trans' house when I saw you—' Jesse swallowed, as if to prepare himself to say

527

something outrageous. 'I saw you *walking* down Gander Circle. Naturally I didn't think it could be you . . .'

Lewis chuckled bitterly and ran his good hand over the stumps that lay hidden in the cuffs of his Dockers. He picked up an empty Rockport walking shoe with a white athletic sock inside, and held it out for Jesse to see. 'You like these? They're comfortable as hell. You ought to try a pair, Jess. I'd give you mine, but I think your feet are too damn big.'

Jesse sniffed and looked away for a moment. 'I followed you,' he said finally. 'I jumped into my rental car and followed you down the block, because I couldn't have kept up with you on foot. You were going fast, L.T., faster than a normal man could've gone, I think. Maybe it was my imagination . . .'

'No, it wasn't your imagination,' Lewis said wearily. 'When I've got legs, I can walk faster than most people can run. Know what else? I think I could probably go up the side of a building, if I wanted to. Amazing, but true.'

Jesse related that he had followed Lewis down Gander Ridge and across the freeway to the campus of Portland State University. Lewis had headed north then, into the heart of the downtown business district. Somewhere near the Center for the Performing Arts, he'd hailed a cab, and the cab had brought him here to the White Eagle.

'I followed you inside,' Jesse continued, 'and watched you put the moves on that lady with the tight jeans. I thought about approaching you, but I was afraid of how you might react.'

'I don't blame you. I can be a very ugly guy when I've got legs. But hey, does that lady have a nice ass, or what? As I recall, you were quite the cunt-hound in your day.'

'You've had too much beer, L.T.'

'You may be right. Or hell, you may be wrong. It's quite possible that I haven't had nearly enough beer. It's possible that I need something much stronger.'

Jesse explained that he had used the pay phone inside the White Eagle to call Paul Tran, who was Nicole's father. Paul, unfortunately, was too weak to make the trip to the White Eagle, but he'd suggested that Jesse call Josh Nickerson, who was Lewis's best friend.

'Josh seemed like he knew me,' said Jesse, his eyes misting. 'He said you often talked about me and the others in the scout platoon. Said you've got a picture of us hanging on your wall—'

'Yeah, Josh knows you, all right. He knows T. J. and Leg and—' Lewis grabbed Jesse's arm and squeezed it hard enough to make the big man cringe. 'Tell me something, Jess. Tonight, inside the bar – did you see me talk to anyone besides the lady with the ass? He would've been a guy about your age, about my height when I have legs. He was a white guy—'

'Corduroy sport coat, right? Brown hair?'

'He's the one.' Lewis's grip on Jesse's arm began to tremble. 'Did you recognize him? Do you know who he was?'

'I didn't get close enough, Lewis. Should I have known him?'

'It was Scott Sanders. He kept me from becoming—' He fought to keep control of himself. The very notion that Lewis Kindred could become a creature akin to the one he saw on a dark night long ago in a Vietnamese whorehouse sickened him, appalled him. No way could he confess this just yet – especially not to Jesse Burton. 'He saved my ass, Jess. Someday I'll try to explain it to you. All I can say now is that he saved my ass.' His hand fell away from Jesse's arm. 'He told me that No Bick sent him to me – can you believe that? Even more strange, he said that No Bick sent *you*.'

'He was right. No Bick did send me to you. He's here in Portland. His name is Paul Tran now, and he lives just down the street from you. Nicole was his daughter . . .'

CHAPTER THIRTY
Life in the Pit

i

The following afternoon, a drizzling Thursday, Josh drove his Escort to the Mount Calvary Cemetery, rather than ride with his mother and sister in the family car. He and Nicole had covered so many miles together in this old rattletrap that he felt as if a part of her would always live in the passenger's seat, and he wanted to be alone with that part of her, if only for the few short minutes that the drive took.

The graveside service for Nicole Tran was a secular 'meditation,' led by a family counselor that her father had retained for the occasion. Long after the other mourners had trickled away, Josh stood on the edge of the open hole and stared down at the glossy mahogany coffin, feeling a vast emptiness inside him. Only when he heard the engine of an approaching backhoe, the gravedigger coming to fill in the hole, did he wander down the hillside toward the road.

Halfway down the hill, he turned back toward the grave, just as the blade of the backhoe pushed the mound of damp brown earth into the hole. A blast of emotion shook him, almost driving him to his knees, but someone caught him from behind and steadied him with strong hands. Startled, he whirled around and confronted the wrecked face of Millie Carter, mere inches from his own.

Josh's scream congealed in his throat. Frantically he tried to push her away, but she was far stronger than he, and she held him tight, her fingers clamping around his forearms like iron bands. Her face was a direful gray, the whites of her eyes a sodden yellow. She had a neat bullet hole in her forehead that Josh himself had put there, surrounded by scorch marks from the muzzle flash of a .45-caliber pistol fired at close range. She wore a white raincoat that she'd tied tightly around her, its hood covering her head but for a few hanks of dreadlocks that dangled over her face like snakes. On her feet were white sneakers, spotted with stains that might have been blood. Except for her eyes, which glowered brown on the left and blue on the right, she looked dead. She *smelled* dead, too, thanks to the putrefactive work of fungi and bacteria. Millie Carter was a walking dead woman.

'I have something for you, Josh,' she said, her throat rattling abysmally. 'It's something special – a gift for a very special young man.' Grinning with her white teeth, she reached into her coat and brought out an orb from which shot dazzling sprays of red light. She pressed it into his palm, and its warmth traveled up his arm to his shoulder, to his heart and his head, to every part of his body. 'It's yours now, Josh. Keep it, and use it. You've *earned* it.'

Before he could gather strength to protest, Millie let loose of him and whirled away, her feet barely skimming the wet green turf on the hillside.

ii

Without lowering the binoculars from his face, Mason Benoit said, 'Give me the phone.' Spit Pittman reached across the steering wheel of the silver BMW, snatched the cellular phone handset from its cradle, and pressed the button that dialed his boss's number. By the time he handed the phone to Benoit, Rex Caswell's phone was ringing in his sumptuous floating house.

'Rex, it's me,' said Benoit, bracing an elbow on the roof of the car to keep the binoculars steady. 'Spit and I are at the Mount Calvary Cemetery near Sylvan Heights. The kid and his family went to a funeral; and we—'

'A funeral? Whose funeral?'

'How the hell should I know whose funeral? Anyway, we followed them here. We're maybe two hundred yards from the grave, parked on the road. The kid stayed behind after everybody else left, like maybe he was real close to whoever died and wanted to spend some time at the grave.'

'Anyone see you?'

'No, it's dead out here, if you'll forgive the expression. It's a Thursday afternoon, and the weather's shitty, so that's no surprise. But listen to this, man. Josh walks away from the grave, like he's headed for his car, right? And who do you think dashes out of the trees and grabs him? – none other than the talented and lovely Millie Carter! It happens while I'm watching the kid with binoculars, and I can see everything that goes on . . .'

'Millie's out there at the cemetery? Right now?'

'No, she's not here now – I don't know where she is. But let me finish. The kid struggles with her like he wants to get away, and I can see why, because Millie looks like death-warmed-over. I mean, she looks like she belongs in quarantine. She doesn't let him go – just holds on to him tight, right there on the side of the hill with the rain coming down in buckets. And then – are you ready for this? – she pulls a ball of red glass out of her pocket and hands it to him. The kid acts like he doesn't want to take it, and staggers around for a few seconds, like someone has just hit him on the head with a baseball bat. Then, before he can give it back to her, Millie runs over the hill like an antelope, and that's the last we see of her.'

'Like an antelope? I thought you said she looked sick.'

'Rex, she looked worse than sick. But she ran like I've never seen anyone run before. If you want to know the truth, it gave me the fucking willies.'

'Where's Josh now?'

'Sitting on a damn gravestone in the rain, staring at the crystal like he's just lost the best friend he's ever had.'

Rex fell silent for a long moment, thinking. 'Is there anyone else around?'

'There was a guy here with some kind of tractor to fill in the grave, but he did his thing and split. Like I said, it's a Thursday afternoon, Rex. People don't visit graves on a Thursday afternoon in the rain.'

'Take it from him. Do it now.'

'You mean the crystal? Just like that – walk up and take it from him?'

'Make sure nobody sees you. And be nice about it, if you can. Offer the kid some money.'

'How much?'

'I don't give a fuck how much! Offer him a hundred dollars, a thousand dollars. I'll reimburse you, for Christ's sake.'

'What if he doesn't want to sell it?'

'Then *take* it from him. Listen, Mason, I don't care

how you do it – just get the goddamn orb and bring it to me. You understand?'

Mason Benoit understood.

iii

The managers of this particular cemetery only allowed gravestones that lay flush with the turf – metal and marble plates in the ground with the decedents' names and dates engraved on them. Josh sat on one, his knees drawn up to his chin and his arms wrapped tight around his shins. The rain had matted his auburn hair and penetrated his heavy wool hunter's jacket, but he felt neither the wetness nor the chill. He sat here because he needed to try to make sense of a life that was disintegrating before his eyes, and this seemed a good place to do it.

He stared unblinkingly across the hillside into the valley below, where lay suburban Washington County, which from this perch looked like a sea of cloud. Down there, he knew, were hundreds of thousands of ordinary people who lived blessedly humdrum lives, who had never encountered Millie Carter or her kind, and had never touched evil red orbs like the one he held in his fist. For them, reality was fighting traffic, paying credit-card bills, going to school and jobs and day-care centers, paper-training the puppy, whatever. Comparatively few of them had ever killed another human being. And not one, he was willing to bet, had killed someone only to see her alive again the next day.

His life had slipped into a pit, where the rules were different from the ones normal people live by. He could no longer count on creation to behave as he'd always expected, for here, in the bottom of the pit, a double amputee could grow his legs back, as Lewis Kindred had done last night. An orb of red crystal could make you unbeatable in poker. A beautiful black-white woman could transform herself into a beast with toxic claws.

And Nicole Tran could die.

It was insanity, he knew. Lewis Kindred had been right, surely, in believing that his war trauma had twisted his perceptions and warped his reason. The evils that had befallen Lewis over the years were merely the products of his sick mind. But how had Josh caught the sickness? he wondered. Or Jesse Burton? Or Paul Tran? Nowhere had he read that insanity was contagious. *And where does the sickness end and reality begin?*

Two men trudged up the hill toward him, both dressed in dark raincoats, one holding an umbrella. They were big men, but one was *incredibly* big and dumb-looking, the white one. The black man, impeccable in a beige cable-knit sweater beneath his coat, looked intelligent but not particularly friendly.

'You must be Josh Nickerson,' said the intelligent one, offering his hand. Josh didn't accept the handshake, but only sat still on the cold grave marker, hugging his knees. Something didn't seem right about these two, and he wished they would go away. 'Today's your lucky day, Josh,' the black man added. 'You're about to make some money.'

The orb throbbed slightly in Josh's hand, and grew noticeably warmer. He suffered a flash-vision of freshly shed blood pouring from a vat into a deep, dark pit, but he clenched his eyes and concentrated on wiping his mind clean. The orb grew warmer still when the black man bent low and smiled at him. 'Are you up for doing a little business with us?'

'I don't know who you are,' Josh replied weakly.

'Let's say I represent a man who's willing to relieve you of something you don't really want, and he's ready to pay you handsomely for it. I'm talking about the thing you're holding in your hand – that ball of glass Millie Carter gave you.'

'What does he want with it?'

'Seems to me that's his business, right? He asks no questions of you, and you ask none of him.'

Josh felt even sicker. These men were here about the orb, and life in the pit had just become more complex. He raised his eyes to those of the crouching black man's, and saw a glitter of something cruel and totally without feeling. 'Does he know what it can do? It's no ordinary piece of glass, you know. It can be dangerous.'

The huge white guy stepped forward and prodded Josh's butt with an athletic shoe that looked as though someone had urinated on it. 'Let's not waste time, kid. Our man wants to buy that fuckin' thing. You want to sell it or what?' Josh felt the blood drain from his face. He was about to say something – he wasn't sure what – when the black man reached into his raincoat and brought out an eel-skin billfold, from which he pulled a pair of hundred-dollar bills. He held them in front of Josh's face.

'Ever hear of "caveat emptor," Josh? It means that the buyer takes all the risk for any merchandise he buys. My employer knows all about caveat emptor. In fact, he practices that principle in his own business life. It means you don't need to worry about what this little ball of glass can do or what it can't. Once you've sold it, you're free of all responsibility for it. What do you say? – let's do a deal.'

The buyer takes all the risk, Josh thought. *I wish that were true.* He wondered whether the orb would allow

transfer of its ownership to someone other than the one
to whom the Millie-thing had given it. Interesting question, this. 'I won't sell it to you,' he said, causing the
white guy's muddy little eyes to narrow menacingly. 'I'll
give it to you.'

'Seriously?' asked the black one.

'Seriously. God knows I don't want it.' Josh pushed
the orb toward him, and he reached for it eagerly, but
when his fingers closed around it, his eyes grew wide
suddenly.

'Damn it, what's it doing?' he asked, dropping his
umbrella. A stream of red sparks shot out from between
his fingers, and he screamed, flipping the orb into the air.
The white man grabbed for it and caught it like a
baseball, but as soon as his hand closed around the orb,
he screamed at the top of his lungs. His hand became a
nest of sparks, and each tiny spark bored into anything it
touched, including the denim of his jeans and the leather
of his dirty athletic shoes, and the fabric of his raincoat.
He gyrated and twitched as if undergoing a violent
electrical shock. His tiny eyes rolled back into his head.

'Spit, drop the fucking thing!' screamed the black man.
'Drop it before it kills you!'

'I-I-I c-c-can't! I c-can't let g-g-go!' The orb hauled Spit
right off the ground to a height of six or seven feet. He
flailed helplessly like a man suspended by his thumbs
against an invisible dungeon wall. Sparks continued to
shoot out from between his fingers, streaming to the
ground like microscopic suns. 'H-H-Help me, M-Mase,
for God's sake! I c-can't b-breathe . . . !'

Mason Benoit whirled on Josh and grabbed him by the
collar of his sopping jacket. He hauled him to a standing
position as if Josh weighed no more than a stuffed animal.

'You're doing this! Stop it right now, hear me? Make that fuckin' thing let go of Spit, or I'll twist your fuckin' head off!'

'I can't! I'm not doing anything, I swear . . . !'

Benoit let him have the back of his hand, and Josh's head snapped to one side. He heard vertebrae pop in his neck, saw stars erupt behind his eyes. He tasted blood on his lip.

'You're controlling it!' Benoit roared. 'It's some kind of remote-control device! You can make it leave Spit alone! Now *do* it!'

'I can't, I tell you! I wish I could . . . !'

Benoit drove a fist into his stomach, causing Josh to fold up like a lawn chair. He buckled forward, choking and heaving, but Benoit hoisted him up again. Through tearing eyes he saw the flailing Spit fall abruptly to the ground, his hands released. The orb settled gently to the earth and lay like a harmless bauble in the wet grass, inert and lifeless.

Benoit maneuvered Josh into a hammerlock and held him. 'Nice going, you little shit. You've just pissed off the West Coast distributor of wholesale trouble. Spit – you okay?'

The muscle-bound hulk got slowly to his feet, gingerly massaging one hand with the other. 'I think so,' he answered. Josh saw that his scalp bore the scars of recent sutures, half-hidden by hair that hadn't yet grown out fully. Someone had apparently worked him over with a blunt object. 'What're we going to do with this little puke?'

'That remains to be seen,' answered Benoit, reaching into his coat for his cellular phone. 'Hold him. I'm going to talk to Rex.'

Spit took over the hammerlock while Benoit consulted someone who Josh assumed was Rex Caswell. He didn't hear the entire conversation, because Spit levered his left forearm so tightly against his shoulder blade that muscles and tendons screamed with pain, nullifying his other senses. Finally, Benoit folded up the C-phone and tucked it away. Spit loosened the hammerlock slightly.

'Okay, listen up,' said Benoit, standing squarely in front of Josh. 'You're going to pick up that ball of glass and put it in your pocket. You're going to keep it out of sight and safe, hear? Do it right now. Move!' Spit let Josh go, but stayed close to him as he walked the few steps to where the orb lay innocently in its bed of grass.

Josh hesitated a moment before picking it up, fearing that it might do to him what it did to Spit, but then he decided that this wasn't likely. Millie had meant the orb for *him*, just as Gamaliel Cartee had meant another orb for Lewis Kindred. It wouldn't harm him, at least not directly. He held it a moment to confirm that it would spew no fireworks and found that it wasn't even warm. As Benoit had ordered, he slipped it into the pocket of his baggy black pants.

'Now what?' he asked.

'We're going for a nice ride in my brand-new BMW,' answered Benoit, his eyes glistening with menace. He grabbed a handful of Josh's damp jacket and shoved him in the direction of the cemetery road. 'You'll be riding in the trunk, of course. I think you'll find it comparatively comfortable. Most people do.' From behind him came Spit's rough laughter and a metallic click that sounded like someone cocking a pistol.

iv

'Lewis, somehow I'm going to get you out of this,' vowed Jesse Burton as he pulled the door open to leave. 'Paul Tran and I will figure something out, I promise. Try to get some rest now, okay? And don't worry. I'll check back with you tonight.'

Lewis waved feebly from the living room, where he sat next to his beloved ficus tree, slumped in his wheelchair and looking like a character out of Kafka, he suspected. 'Thanks, Jess. Thanks for everything.'

Get me out of what? he thought, watching the door close. *Insanity? Hell?* He wondered whether Jesse meant to get him a shrink or a shaman. Or both. He wondered whether he had any realistic hope of ever resuming a normal life.

After Jesse had gone, he motored into the kitchen and fetched a Beck's from the fridge and drained half the bottle with a single chug. He belched and chuckled under his breath. Jesse and No Bick. What a combo. *Oops*, not No Bick these days – but *Paul*. Paul Tran. The former Tran Van Hai, trained sapper and political cadre of the National Liberation Front, cum *Hoi Chanh* and Kit Carson-advisor to the Triple Deuce scout platoon, United States Fucking Army. *And* devourer of severed legs, don't forget.

Not so, Jesse had insisted. Paul hadn't eaten one of Lewis's legs, and he hadn't followed Lewis from Vietnam to devour him, but to *save* him. To save him from the evil of Gamaliel's kind. And Paul Tran had summoned Jesse to help in the effort.

The story that Jesse had told him last night would have sounded ludicrous to anyone who hadn't lived in Lewis Kindred's skin for the past twenty-two years – a story that began with Paul Tran's visit to a renegade Cao Dai priest in Vietnam. Jesse himself had consulted a *sorcière* in southern Louisiana only a few days ago, where he'd learned some particulars concerning the creature whom he and Lewis had known as Gamaliel Cartee, a creature that ate human flesh and drank human blood.

The story didn't sound ludicrous to Lewis. Having seen what he'd seen and done what he'd done over the years, he was ready to believe almost anything. Even the part about 'calling forth the dead' to bring the tale to a successful conclusion.

Actually, Lewis no longer cared much about himself, for he'd given up on his own sanity. Vietnam had eaten most of his mind and soul, he felt, leaving precious little for him to hang any hopes on. So, what the hell? Let Paul Tran and Jesse Burton carry on with whatever mumbo jumbo they deemed appropriate. What could it hurt?

He had serious worries, though, about Josh. The kid had suffered too much. His young face had become a mask of pain and barely controlled panic. Lewis had studied that mask last night, after Jesse and Josh brought him home from the White Eagle. Josh had quietly listened to Jesse's account of his involvement with Paul Tran, grimacing now and again as if he itched to tell a story of his own. Several times he'd stared straight at Lewis, his green eyes brimming with a *knowing* that Lewis expected him to blurt out at any moment. But Josh had kept it in, bottled up like a restless genie. The kid had winced visibly whenever Jesse mentioned Millie Carter, and had nodded unconsciously upon hearing that Paul Tran believed that she was of the same kind as Gamaliel.

And today, thought Lewis, feeling an ache in his heart, *Josh is burying Nicki.*

Seventeen-year-old kids deserved better than this, especially a seventeen-year-old named Josh Nickerson.

Lewis motored back into his living room and halted before his window, beyond which gray October ruled. As usual in autumn, Mount Hood lay in hiding behind her veils of rain. He longed for a glimpse of her face, thinking that the goddess owed him that much, at least.

'And why do you think she owes you anything?' asked someone behind him, and Lewis knew instantly who it was. Though the voice seemed strangely hoarse, the Louisiana accent was unmistakable, as was the ability to hear his thoughts. With his heart pounding, he maneuvered his chair around to face Millie Carter, who had seated herself on the sofa. At her feet lay a small zippered tote, suggesting that she'd come prepared to stay.

She was impossibly sick-looking, a terror of rancid meat in a white raincoat. She'd wrapped a flowered silk scarf around her head, but something awful had seeped into the silk from her forehead and stained it. 'Really, Lewis. I *can't* look that bad. You should see your eyes – they're big as half-dollars.' She giggled with a sound that made Lewis squirm.

'Millie, what's happened to you?' he asked.

She shrugged theatrically, a parody of girlishness.

'How did you get in?'

'The same way you would've, through the door. As you should know by now, locks don't bother me much.'

'Why did you come back?'

'I was *drawn* back. By you. I sensed that you're struggling with yourself, Lewis, and I came back to help you one more time. I feel a responsibility toward you.'

'*Help* me? I don't understand.'

'You've resisted the hunger, and you've reverted

543

to . . .' She waved a hand at him contemptuously.
'. . . *this*. It must be horrible for you, having regained the
fullness of life in a whole body, and now being forced
to . . . well, you know what I mean. Fortunately you're
not beyond help. Another taste of me will put you on the
right track again.'

Understanding burst like a thunderclap in Lewis's
head, and he suffered a jolt of revulsion. He was certain
now that Millie was dead, and yet *not* dead; as Gamaliel
had been dead after Lewis had shot him, but yet *not*
dead. She meant to share her contagion with him.

Lewis gagged. 'Millie, please. Not this.'

She rose from the sofa with the silken movement of a
snake, loosening the belt of the raincoat. As she stepped
toward him, the coat fell away, leaving her naked. The
sight of her like this had once driven Lewis to sexual
frenzy, but not anymore. Now she was a walking carcass.

She probed his mind, which presented a challenge no
tougher than defeating a lock on a door. Lewis knew that
she'd always been able to do this; he'd done it himself to
an innocent young woman named Megan Venton to keep
her suitably silent and docile while he tore her to pieces.
To his horror, Millie seized that part of his will that
controlled his sexual nerves and muscles, and instantly he
was hard and ready.

'P-please, Millie. I'm begging you. Don't do this to
me.'

'Some day you'll thank me, Lewis. You're not thinking
straight right now, but after you've joined our ranks,
you'll look back on this moment and thank your lucky
stars that old Millie came back to you.'

Lewis reached for the joystick of the wheelchair,
meaning to pull on it and back away from her, but his

hand rebelled. It belonged to Millie now, just like the rest him belonged to her. She reached for his belt buckle and undid it. She worried his jeans and shorts down over his gnarled stumps, then grabbed a handful of his shirt and raised him up to her with one hand. 'I'm giving you a great gift,' she hissed. 'It's more than *power*, Lewis. It's beauty and health and near-unending life. You see, we have no cripples among our kind, no ugly ones or weak ones. We have no sufferers of hay fever or high blood pressure or AIDS, no depressives or neurotics, no sick of any ilk. We have only strong, beautiful specimens who can become anything they choose to become, for they alone control their lives.'

Lewis wished he could faint. Millie's stink was overpowering, her flesh clammy and slick with bacterial goo. She was a nightmare with a hungry brown eye and a heartless blue one. Lewis doubted that he could survive her embrace, that even if he survived, he would feel dirty and defiled until his dying day.

Millie lay down on the sofa, spreading her legs, pulling him over her. 'Isn't this what you've always wanted, Lewis – control over your life? You can confess it to me, for I've seen everything in your mind, and I know all there is to know about you. It's the reason you play poker, isn't it? – the reason you've worked so hard to master the game. Poker gives you the illusion of manipulating chance and making it serve you. Your daddy taught you that skill and self-control can defeat the tyranny of randomness, that it doesn't matter whether you're "lucky" or "unlucky." This may be true at the card table, but it's woefully untrue in life – *unless* you become one of us. With us, Lewis, you really *can* control chance. You really *can* make fate your servant. But only if you become one of us . . .'

Lewis felt himself weaken to the dream as images streamed into his mind from Millie's, but it wasn't the blissful kind of dream he'd experienced before while they were locked together in the throes of lovemaking. Millie's mind was a psychic receiver that picked up modulations of distant reality and focused them at whatever point she chose, in this case Lewis's mind. The subject of her psychic monitoring was Josh Nickerson. And the picture Lewis saw made him want to scream.

v

The car stopped and the trunk yawned open, admitting a wave of harsh daylight that stung Josh's eyes at first. Spit grabbed him by the upper arm and hauled him out, causing him to bump his head sharply against the trunk lid. The pain was intense, but he tried not to show it.

'We've got a real tough dude here,' chuckled Spit, pushing him toward an old sliding door of corrugated aluminum. 'He'll *think* he's tough by the time we're through with him!'

An alley, thought Josh, glancing quickly around. *Old part of town. Strange smell in the air like – hops. We're at a warehouse near a brewery.* He figured that these details might come in handy later, if not to tell the police, then to write the story of this adventure, assuming he lived through it. *Ever the writer*, he heard Nicki's voice say, somewhere deep inside his head. *Always collecting details . . .*

Inside the door was a cavernous room that smelled of dust and mildew, with high windows painted over to keep the place dusky even during the daylight hours.

Benoit and Spit led him to the far end of the warehouse, steering around broken wooden pallets and mounds of decaying cardboard crates. Spit unlocked a scarred wooden door that flaked eight or ten layers of old paint. Beyond it was a small room lined with gray concrete blocks and a single fluorescent light fixture in the ceiling. In the center of the stained concrete floor were two metal folding chairs, facing each other, one of which held an angular man who wore a stubby blond ponytail, a simple gold bead in the lobe of his right ear, and two-thousand-dollars' worth of Armani clothes. He had hazy blue eyes and an immaculate tan. Rex Caswell. On the floor beside his chair sat a long leather case that might have held photographic equipment, a musical instrument, or an expensive fly rod. Or it might have held a gun. Josh shuddered.

'Good afternoon, Josh,' said Rex Caswell. 'Welcome to my little warehouse. I don't use it for much more than a tax dodge these days, but who knows? I may fix it up, turn it into lofts for artists and poets. There's money in that kind of thing these days, as long you as don't really rent to artists and poets. Why don't you come over and have a seat?'

Benoit nudged Josh forward, and Josh sat in the vacant metal chair. Spit locked the door and left the key in the lock, a cobra-skin key packet dangling from it. Benoit bent low to Rex and whispered a long explanation of something into his ear. Rex nodded several times, and said, 'You're sure no one saw you.'

Benoit straightened up. 'Trust me. No one saw us.'

'Good.' Turning to Josh and leaning forward with an elbow on one knee, Rex smiled and said, 'You're probably a little bewildered by all this, aren't you?'

'No,' said Josh, his voice quivering a little. 'It's not bewildering at all.'

'No? Suppose you tell me what you think is happening here.'

Josh fetched the orb out of his pocket and found that it had come alive again. Rex eyed it with wonder as its innards shifted and swirled like miniature holograms of the galaxies, all in crimson. Flecks of red light leapt from its surface and flitted across the faces of all in the room. 'It's about this,' Josh said, holding the orb up. 'You want it. And I want to give it to you. But you think I'm playing some sort of game with it, that I can turn it into a weapon through remote control or something. You've brought me here to scare me into stopping the game.'

Rex pursed his lips and nodded. 'I'd say you've hit the nail on the head, Josh. You're a smart lad. Very smart. Now that you've defined the problem, how do you suggest we solve it?'

Josh did his best imitation of a smile, but it came out lop-sided and scared-looking. 'I wish I knew. I wish I could just hand it over and never see it again. But I'm not sure I can do that.'

'Well,' said Rex, planting both hands on his knees as if preparing to stand. 'I was hoping for something better from you, smart as you are. Since you can't come up with a suggestion, let me make one.' He picked up the long leather case next to his chair, set it on his lap, and pressed three latch buttons. He lifted the cover. Inside, nestled in plush red velvet, lay a short, ugly shotgun. Its metal parts gleamed an oily gray, its stock a flat black that looked almost like rubber.

'Josh, this is a Mossberg riot gun,' Rex announced, pulling the weapon from the case. 'The way this one is customized, you can set the choke to bring down an elk at thirty yards, or you can spray a pattern wide enough to take out a football team.' He opened a box of shells and started pushing them into the gun, then pumped one into the chamber with a sharp slapping of metal against metal. 'I've had this little baby a long time, and I was beginning to think I'd never have occasion to use it. But lo-and-behold, along *you* come, and – well, here's what I propose, my lad. Either you hand me the orb in such a condition that it doesn't hurt me, or I blow off one of your feet. Then you can be like your hero, the Stump-meister, and scoot around in an electric wheelchair. How's that sound to you?'

Josh's tongue felt like sandpaper. When he spoke, his voice cracked. 'Why would you do that to me? I've never done anything to you, have I?' He wiped frigid sweat from his lip. 'I only got this thing today – less than an hour ago. Your guys saw who gave it to me . . .'

'Millie Carter, unless I'm mistaken.'

'Yeah, Millie Carter. She just ran up and gave it to me in the cemetery. I don't have any idea how it works. I swear I don't.'

From the gun case Rex took two sets of ear protectors – large plastic earmuffs heavily lined with foam rubber – and tossed one each to Spit and Benoit. Then he took out a third set and put it on his own head, leaving his ears uncovered for the time being. 'Tell me something, Josh. Is this the same orb that the Stumpmeister used to beat me at cards a couple of weeks ago?'

'How should I know if it's the same orb?'

'For the sake of discussion, let's assume it's the same one. As I recall, it didn't hurt anyone that night, not even when Lewis tossed it to Millie. I was there, and so were you. We both saw it – Lewis tossed the crystal to Millie, and there was no fire, no sparks, no pain. But today, out at the cemetery, you tossed it to Mase there, and it burned him. When Spit got a hold of it, the fucking thing damn-near killed him. Why?'

'I-I don't know. I think it has something to do with—'

'*What* do you think it has something to do with?' Rex prodded him in the ribs with the muzzle of the Mossberg.

'I think it has to do with who it's meant for.'

Rex's handsome brow knit as he considered this. 'Are you saying that Millie meant for you to have it, and that it won't let anyone else near it?'

Josh nodded. He explained, though, that Millie once gave him an orb and told him to give it to Lewis, and that the thing behaved itself while in his possession. It seemed to know the intentions of the one who had it.

'In other words, it *likes* some people and not others?'

'No, I-I'm not saying that – at least I don't think I'm saying that. It's not a matter of who it likes. It's a matter of who *Millie* wants to have it. I'm sure it likes you just fine, Mr Caswell.' The orb suddenly started to vibrate in his hand and grew menacingly warm, as if it had taken offense at something said.

'Well, why don't we give your theory a little test—'

Mason Benoit strode forward, his hand in the air. 'Rex, wait! Be careful, man. You can't believe what the damn thing can do.'

Rex scowled furiously. 'You said it burned you! So why don't you have scars all over your hands? And the same goes for Spit! I don't see a mark on either one of you butt-heads.'

'It's not like regular fire,' Benoit tried to explain. 'It *feels* hot, and it burns like hell . . .'

'And it'll suck all the breath out of you,' Spit put in.

'. . . and it causes your muscles to go all spastic, like what happens when people are electrocuted. Have you ever read about that, Rex? – where some dude picks up a live wire, and the juice starts running through him, and he can't put it down. It's like—'

'Fuck all that!' Rex shouted. 'I don't want to hear any more from you idiots.' He turned back to Josh. 'Put that thing over here, Josh. I want to take a closer look.' Josh held out the orb hesitantly toward Rex, with it lying in his palm. Rex moved his face to within a foot of the thing, his hazy eyes narrowed on it, slowly raising a finger to it. Josh detected a slight rise in the orb's temperature and a slightly higher intensity in its vibration. The tip of Rex's finger finally made contact, which generated a warm throbbing sensation that Rex too felt, judging from the way his eyes widened. 'See that?' he called to Benoit and Spit. 'I'm touching it. I feel some vibration and a little heat, but that's all. No fire, no sparks.'

'Maybe it likes you,' offered Spit.

'How much do you know about its powers?' Rex asked Josh.

'Not much.' Josh tried to wet his lips with his dry tongue. 'I know it makes you lucky at cards, and I know it can hurt people under some circumstances. I don't have any idea how it works or how to control it.'

Rex laid the muzzle of the Mossberg against Josh's cheek. 'You better not be lying to me, you little shit, or I'll do worse than blow your foot off.' He gingerly plucked the orb out of Josh's palm with his free hand, using only a thumb and a finger, and held it suspended this way for perhaps fifteen seconds. Then he slowly wrapped his other fingers around it and gripped it tightly in his fist, a prize long sought and finally won. 'There it is, gentlemen – power!' he announced triumphantly. 'I can feel it coursing through me, warm and tingling and alive. You're looking at the next legend in the game of poker.' He brought the orb close to his face, and shards of crimson light escaped between his fingers and danced across his features. He closed his eyes, savoring the odd sensations flowing into his hand and arm, dreaming of the conquests that lay ahead, Josh supposed. Josh drew back, tensing for what he feared might come at any second.

And it came: a blinding flash and a thunderclap. Rex's hand became a ball of crimson flame, out of which spewed jets of tiny, dazzling-red pellets that exploded on contact with cement-brick walls, metal chairs, human flesh. Rex shrieked like an animal caught in a trap and convulsed backward onto the floor. Spit and Benoit flew to his side and hauled him up again as he thrashed and flailed. They screamed his name, asked what they should do, but Rex couldn't answer, for his body was in the grip of something like an epileptic seizure. The irises of his eyes rotated upward into his eye sockets, leaving gaping circles of white. He foamed at the mouth, gasped, convulsed. He writhed and kicked. But he didn't let go of the orb.

Josh bounded out of the chair toward the door, feeling the impact of pinhead-size pellets against his back and neck, not burning or stinging, but only *touching*. His hand closed on the key and twisted it. He threw his body against the door, forcing it open, then plunged into the half-light of the warehouse. He scrambled through the debris of broken pallets and shipping crates to the outer sliding door, only to find it securely locked. He whirled around frantically and looked for an avenue of escape.

Rex Caswell staggered into the doorway at the far end of the warehouse, having freed himself of the orb and now holding the Mossberg at the ready.

vi

As Millie pulled him ever deeper into her, Lewis's mental link to her strengthened. Just as he had no control over the muscles of his body, which at this moment drove his pubic bone against hers with autonomic frenzy, he had no control over the images that streamed into his brain via the mind-link with her, images gathered by her wandering psychic eye . . .

A dilapidated warehouse near the Henry Weinhard brewery in Northwest Portland. Josh running in a panic, dodging mounds of refuse; encountering a locked door, whirling, looking for another way out. And in the distant dusk of the place, Rex Caswell, armed with an ugly shotgun, advancing, his face twisted into a killing grin . . .

vii

Lewis could feel the heat of rage as Caswell strode toward Josh, kicking aside empty crates and boxes, swearing vilely with every breath. Lewis sensed too the burning pain in Rex's right hand, the one in which he'd gripped the orb only moments ago.

Clamor now from either side – Spit and Benoit on Rex's flanks, advancing on line with him toward the opposite end of the warehouse, kicking at the trash and cussing, their weapons drawn.

Josh also hears them and scutters along the rear wall, finds a door and dashes into a dark room that might have been an office long ago. Rusty file cabinets and ruined desks. Discarded IBM typewriters and wrecked chairs . . .

Sickly light pouring through a broken painted-over window with an expanded-metal screen on the inside.

But Josh sees that the wooden window frame is rotting away, and he knows that he can pry off the screen and escape through the window, if only he has time.

Josh casting around in the clutter, deliriously searching for an appropriate tool, hearing the approaching shouts of Caswell, Spit, and Benoit as they converge on the room.

Josh finding the amputated armrest of an ancient typing chair, leaping to the window and jamming one end of the steel frame into the screen.

Josh hauling back on the armrest with all his weight. Old wooden slats groaning and squeaking as they splinter and come loose . . .

Throwing aside the armrest, Josh attacks with his bare hands, mindless of splinters, and rips the screen away. He launches a derelict IBM Selectric through the window, blowing out old panes and frames, then flings himself through the opening, following the missile into the gray daylight. His cheek and chest slam against grainy asphalt. His knee collides with the typewriter that he has just thrown through the window. He staggers dizzily to his feet, gagging for breath, only marginally aware of the blood soaking through his shirt at the elbows. He wills his legs to move, his arms to pump – demands cooperation from his body in dashing toward the mouth of the alley far away, the soles of his shoes crunching over shards of glass, blood streaming into his eye from a slice on his forehead.

Rex reaching the window, his face a monster's and his eyes merely unthinking holes in his head. He sees Josh fleeing down the alley and raises the Mossberg, which he'd earlier planned to use only in threatening the boy, in frightening him and securing his cooperation in handing over the orb. But rage rules Rex now, blind and unthinking, the ripe fruit of years' worth of hatred and frustration. He squeezes the trigger. The barrel belches fire, and the boom! cannonades down the alley like an invisible bowling ball, bouncing off old brick walls and reverberating into the next block. Hot pellets rip into Josh Nickerson's left leg, upending him and scattering bloody bits of him against the side of a rusting dumpster . . .

viii

'Noooooooooooo!' Lewis screamed as an orgasm tore at his mind and body. He knew that what he'd seen was real, that Josh Nickerson lay wounded and bleeding in a dirty alley.

'That's good, Lewis, good!' hissed Millie, humping him greedily. *'Let your rage spill out, yes! Don't keep it in, Lewis! Let it burn! Let it burn . . . !'*

He understood now that his rage was the fuel that Millie needed to transform him. She'd shown him what happened to Josh in order to fan that rage. She reveled in it and drank it in, for rage was as necessary to her survival as human flesh and blood.

Then it was over, suddenly and brutally, as if they'd driven over a cliff together and slammed into an icy river. Millie pushed him off and he flopped on to the carpet, feeling utterly sick and defeated. She stood over him, glaring down at him with her mismatched eyes. When she spoke, her voice horrified him, for he hadn't heard that voice in more than two decades. 'You really are on your own now, Lewis. Whatever happens to you – whatever you become – depends totally on you.'

Lewis raised himself on his elbows and became conscious of his newly grown legs and feet. His left arm was straight and strong, and he heard no ringing in his ears. He raised his gaze to Millie, and what he saw made him shudder like a puppy in the snow.

She was changing. Growing taller. Lewis could hear the stretching of bones, snapping and creaking like the skeleton of an old wooden ship. He could hear the re-formation of muscles and skin, a wet sound that evinced notions of organs and tumors and festoons of diseased membrane. Her head elongated while her scalp retracted her dreadlocks like a million fishing lines on a million reels. Her ears enlarged and her brow became more pronounced. As her shoulders broadened, her chest flattened and hardened. Her trunk pulled in her hips, narrowing them and making them straight up and down. And out of her pelvic area grew a long, thick penis with a head that was almost blue, while beneath it appeared a pair of testicles. Coarse hair appeared on the newly sinewy belly and legs. The feet lengthened and widened.

Lewis saw too that the symptoms of death receded as the body grew and changed its sex. Bacterial pustules instantly dried and flaked away. The flowered silk scarf fell to the floor, revealing that the wound beneath it had healed. The skin became lustrous and firm again. All signs of putrefaction disappeared, except the lingering smell.

The one feature that didn't change was the eyes, the left one brown and the right one blue – sizzling, glaring eyes; full of mocking and yet . . . loving. *The eyes of a brother?*

This was no longer Millie Carter. This was Gamaliel Cartee, looking no older than Lewis remembered him. Lewis's chest ached as his heart labored under paroxysms of shock.

Gamaliel picked up the tote that lay beside the sofa and zippered it open. Inside it were a wine-colored jogging suit, socks, shoes, and a light jacket of black nylon – men's clothes, just the right size. He dressed as Lewis stared, as Lewis argued furiously with himself over whether he'd suspected this from the very beginning.

Millie was Gamaliel.

And Lewis was their brother now.

'I don't know if we'll ever meet again,' Gamaliel said, turning toward the door. 'If we do, I hope it's many years from now. By then you'll understand.'

'I understand now.'

'I doubt that. The day will come, Lewis, when you discover how pathetically naive you've been all these years. You'll develop a totally new perspective about the real and the unreal, about good and bad—'

'I have all the perspective I need. I know what I am, and I know what you are.'

Gamaliel laughed softly. He reached into the tote and took out a set of car keys, which he tossed onto an end table. 'The Jaguar is parked outside on Gander Circle. It's yours, Lewis. It's due for an oil change. I hope you enjoy it.'

'Wait! Aren't there things you're supposed to tell me? Like what my limitations are, hints on how to live among ordinary humans – all that sort of thing? For Christ's sake, you can't just walk out and leave me on my own.'

'Don't play games with me, Lewis. I know every trick in the book, believe me. As for the things you need to know – what can I say? I selected you because of your intelligence, your resourcefulness, your resilience, not to mention your proven capacity for killing. These qualities will serve you well in your new life. You're an inquisitive soul, and you'll soon find out all you need to know. You'll be good. *Very* good.'

'What about making another one of us – out of an ordinary human, I mean? How do I know when to do that? I'm not even sure I know *how* to do it.'

'Lewis, this is becoming tiresome. You're trying to keep me around because you'd like to take a crack at killing me. You'd do well to forget that – it can't be done, which you of all people should know. But to answer your question, I'll say that you'll know when the time is right to create another of us. There's no regular cycle for this kind of thing. When it's time to do it, you'll know it, and your instincts will tell you how. Search for someone who's capable of intense, righteous anger – someone like yourself. You'll be able to *smell* such a person, like I smelled you. War zones are good hunting grounds, because they're rich with anger and teeming with killers. I've spent many years in war zones, more than I'd like to count. In fact, I'm thinking seriously of going to Yugoslavia, where there's a great little war in the making.' He pulled the door open, but hesitated a moment. 'Have a nice life, Lewis. I'm sorry we didn't get an opportunity to play some poker. Maybe next time.' He stepped through the door and closed it behind him.

ix

'Tommy, the phone's for you!' shouted Carlotta Iadanza through the service window between the bar and the kitchen of the Huntsman's Bar and Grill. Her husband was tending bar this afternoon, because the regular guy had called in sick with the flu. Tommy snatched the telephone handset from its cradle next to the cash register and wedged it between his cheek and shoulder, freeing his hands for the preparation of a very dry Beefeater martini.

'Speak!' he said impatiently.

'Tommy, it's me, Lewis. I need a favor—'

'*Lewis!* How the hell are you, troop? I've been worried about you.'

'Sorry for not being in touch. I haven't been feeling too—'

'Hey, the VIP Center called yesterday. They're planning a memorial gathering for Dewey on Sunday in Waterfront Park. They're inviting the homeless folks down around the Skidmore District – I'm donating some food, as are some of the other restaurants in the area. Should be a nice event. I figured you'd be interested in helping, so I signed you up. There's a meeting tonight . . .'

'Tommy, I can't talk about it right now. Like I said, I need a favor. A small one.'

'No problem. All you need to do is ask – you know that.'

'I need Rex Caswell's address. He's not listed in the phone book.'

'Did you try the Yellow Pages under "Drug Dealer?" Or how about "Hairball?" Or maybe "Unredeemable Fuck-stick?" '

'I'm serious, Tom. I need to know where he lives . . .'

x

Rex hauled the designer suitcase out of the darkroom into his photography studio on the third floor of his floating house, placed it on the floor and opened it. For years he'd kept a packed suitcase ready, full of clothes, toiletries, spare cash, forged documents – he called it his 'dash kit.' A cocaine dealer could never know, after all, when his life might suddenly blow up in his face, requiring immediate departure to some remote and sunny clime that had no extradition agreement with the U.S. Every few months he recycled the clothing in the dash kit, just to keep it current. Going on the lam was no excuse for dressing like a jerk.

He checked the phony documents he'd paid dearly for several years back: passport, California driver license, social security card, credit cards (for show, not for use). Even phony pictures of a phony wife and kids. The documents said he was a management consultant named Roland Parker.

Everything was in order.

Except for Twyla, that is. Twyla was very much in disorder. She shambled through the door of the studio, clutching a tall glass that was a third-full of a screwdriver, a cigarette dangling loosely from her mouth. Rex didn't want to guess how much coke she'd sucked up today, or how much booze she'd pounded down. She stood before him with a fist planted accusingly on her hip, a strand of oily blonde hair dangling over one eye. Her muumuu looked as if she hadn't washed it in months. She looked like an unmade bed.

'Okay, I'm ready for you to tell me what's going on,' she announced. 'Enough of the bullshit, Rex.'

'Sweetheart, I told you: Something's come up. I'm going on a little business trip, that's all.'

'That's *not* all! Since when do you take the dash kit on a little business trip?'

Rex had no intention of telling her anything that remotely resembled the truth. Twyla Boley had become irrelevant to him. In mere minutes he would get into his

Mercedes and drive to an airport in Hillsboro, a distant western suburb, where he would meet Mason Benoit and Spit Pittman. They would each hand him a briefcase containing a total of a million dollars, money he'd stashed with this day in mind. He would board a chartered jet that at this moment was en route from its home airfield in Northern California. He would fly to a rural airport in central Mexico and lie low in some quiet little hotel for a month or two, then make his way even further south, maybe to Brazil or Martinique. He would live off his numbered Swiss bank account for as long as it took to plan and fashion a new life.

Never again would he see Twyla Boley, the woman he'd lived with for more than twenty years. Never again would he see Mason Benoit or Spit Pittman, who themselves would disappear into the wide world, handsomely flush with 'severance pay.' Never again would he see Portland, Oregon.

'You're leaving for good, aren't you?' Twyla said, her reddened eyes filling. 'Somebody's after you – the cops, some coke supplier you've shafted, some angry husband – and you're leaving. Just pulling up stakes and breezing out of here forever. That's it, isn't it, Rex? You don't give a rusty fuck what happens to me.'

Rex sighed. A part of him wanted to bash Twyla in the face for letting herself become what she'd become, an oily pig without style or grace, who cursed like a longshoreman and polluted her body with alcohol, nicotine, and drugs. But another part of him remembered what she'd once been – a strong and well-turned beauty, a poet and scholar who could quote endless passages of Dante Gabriel Rossetti. God, he'd loved her then, and he supposed that he would always love whatever small part of the old Twyla survived. It wasn't her fault, he knew, that he'd lost control of himself and become homicidally obsessed with gaining possession of a weird little ball of glass just so he could wreak vengeance on Lewis Kindred. He'd shot an innocent kid, for Christ's sake. If the kid lived, he would certainly tell the cops who'd shot him. And this meant that Rex Caswell must disappear forever.

Out with the old life, and in with the new. Good-bye Rex Caswell, hello Roland Parker.

'Look, sweetheart,' he began, 'I don't know how long I'll be gone. It may be—'

'Forever.'

'A long time. Things may get a little dicey for you. I'm going to leave you some money. Watch the mail for the next couple of days. You'll get a key to a luggage locker – I can't say where right now – but I'll put a note in with it, telling you where it is. Go to the locker and get the money—'

'How much, Rex? How much are you going to leave me?' Suddenly she was sobbing uncontrollably, and Rex felt his own eyes start to mist.

'A hundred large. I'll leave you a hundred thousand in little bills. Take the money, go south with it, and get some help with your chemical habit. You can still have a life, Twyla, if—'

'Oh, this is great! This is rich! The fuckin' drug lord is telling me to get help with my fuckin' drug habit! Know something, Rex? You have more guts than a meat-packing plant, telling me to get help with my drug habit just two seconds after dropping the bomb that you're leaving forever. You've got—'

The sight of Rex's face going ashen silenced her. Rex stared at an image he didn't believe, a reality too outrageous to be real, standing in the doorway behind her. Twyla whirled in slow motion and shrieked when she saw who it was.

xi

Lewis crossed the room on two strong legs and thrust his hand into Rex Caswell's throat. Rex fought savagely, and though he was bigger and more muscular, Lewis had no problem killing him. Lewis marveled at the way Rex's eyes bulged out of their sockets, so full of horror and wonder at the sight of the old Stumpmeister in the body of a whole man, and the way Rex's cheeks puffed up and turned beet-red, the way his tongue protruded and turned purple. Lewis marveled at the delicious sensation of piercing the flesh of Rex's throat with his fingers, finding the windpipe and ripping it out. The man of style went down like a discombobulated cyborg, geysering blood over the surrounding array of costly photographic equipment. Too bad about that Omega D-Series enlarger that Rex smashed in his death throes. And that Hasselblad Superwide camera that Twyla accidentally knocked from the shelf in her hysterical scramble to flee the room. But what would a dead man, Lewis mused, want with all this equipment, anyway?

He caught Twyla Boley by the hair as she reached the second-floor landing and dragged her into the spacious bedroom with its wide-angle view of the Willamette River. Out on the gray water a barge lumbered downstream, pushed by a huge tug. Gulls circled and wheeled in the rain. And Twyla Boley screamed as she'd never screamed in her life.

'It's okay to scream – no one can hear you, Twyla. Scream all you need to. This is the time for it.'

She fell quiet suddenly but for intermittent sobs and drew herself into a fetal ball on the expansive king-size bed with its polar-bear-skin spread, staring at him with mindless eyes. Lewis sensed that her drug-doused sanity was near to shattering, but alas, what did a dead woman want with sanity?

He slowly stripped naked. He knelt on the bed. Probing her mind, he found rejection of the truth. She couldn't make herself believe that this beautiful man spattered with Rex's blood could be the same one she'd seen in a wheelchair, whose legs ended crudely above long-gone knees; the one she'd once loved but had forsaken for a scum-sucker named Rex Caswell.

He found too her hatred for himself, though he couldn't understand it, for it seemed to have no rational cause. Had she come to hate him because she felt guilty over breaking her promises to him? He could only guess.

She spoke. Her voice was small, almost little-girlish. 'It *was* your picture in the paper. You killed that girl at the Vintage Plaza . . .' Lewis said nothing but only gazed deeper into her, looking for clues as to why both his and her lives had sidetracked so disastrously from what they'd dreamed of together. He found none. Only blank, irrational hatred. '. . . And you're going to kill me, too, aren't you?'

Lewis knelt upright and stared down at her. The hunger had begun to stir in earnest, and his cock was hardening. 'I never hated you, Twyla. Even after you wrote me that Dear-John, I didn't hate you. I was angry with you, yeah, but hate? – no. I wasn't capable of it. *Then.*' His voice had grown hoarse and descended. He could feel his jaws widening, his teeth growing longer. He watched his fingernails become hooks.

Twyla bleated like a sacrificial lamb. Lewis bent to her, his hunger yawning and roaring . . .

xii

Afterward, he showered in the late Rex Caswell's private bathroom, washing away both Twyla's and Rex's blood. From Caswell's wardrobe he selected something to wear, a conservative double-breasted blazer and a pair of light wool trousers. The clothes draped on him, having been tailored for a body-builder, but this didn't matter to him in the least.

While drying his hair he made a discovery that shook him. His left eye had turned brown, his right one blue. He recalled that Twyla had once told him that he had 'sensuous gray eyes,' so the loss was probably something to be lamented. Still, in return for a good pair of legs, it wasn't a loss at all.

He left the floating house through the front door with one of Rex's Burberry raincoats slung over his arm. Night was gathering in the east, and the manager of the Sellwood Bay Club had turned on the overhead floods so that residents and their guests could come and go without ending up in the drink. As he strode through the yellow cone of a floodlight, he experienced a feeling that had become somewhat familiar during the past several weeks, an inkling of being followed. He heard too the rustling that accompanied the feeling, a sound that roused the image of a plague of locusts, black against the sky. He'd heard the sound on the dance floor at the White Eagle and in the foyer of the Ristorante Pazzo. He'd heard it in Goose Hollow, just before he and Millie encountered his aunt amid the horde of Billy Graham enthusiasts. A hellish idea hit him, and he glanced down to his feet, now shod in custom-fitted calfskin that didn't quite fit. From the soles of his shoes his shadow sprawled in front of him over the planks of the dock, not black like the shadows cast by the hand rail, but a deep and iridescent blue.

CHAPTER THIRTY-ONE
Life Darkly Shaded

i

Josh Nickerson wheeled himself onto the deck that fronted the living room of his family's apartment, craving the few meager rays of sunshine that managed to dodge a horde of scudding clouds. He leaned back in his wheelchair with his face to the sky, soaking up the light and heat, wishing that this simple delight could go on forever. But it wouldn't, he knew, because nothing went on forever – not joy or sadness or grief or hope. Or life least of all.

The morning smelled tartly of rain and moldering leaves, for autumn was seriously under way now, and the grounds of Sloan House were ankle-deep in the reds, yellows, and browns shed by the majestic New England elms that surrounded the place. Josh loved the fresh air, the smells, and the colors, even the cackling of the resident crows. He loved the *aloneness*.

In the three weeks since he'd come home from the hospital, he'd gotten scarcely five minutes to himself. His mother and sister had waited on him hand and foot, doting on him, feeling the constant need to 'cheer him up' and take his mind off the fact that he'd lost a leg. Kendra especially had taken up the cause, bombarding him with well-meant but tiresome chatter, apparently believing that leaving him alone anytime he wasn't asleep constituted gross negligence. A day nurse had come in for the first two weeks after his homecoming, and after that, his mother took a week of family medical leave to stay home with him. Finally Josh had managed to convince his mother and sister that he was well enough not to require constant attention. He wanted to read, to listen to music, maybe even to write. He wanted to be alone.

Thus, on November 17, 1992, Cheryl Nickerson went to work in the morning as on any other day. Kendra Nickerson went to school. And Josh went hunting for sunshine.

As always happened when he closed his eyes these days, he found himself looking into the faces of Nicki and Lewis, both of whom had disappeared from his life and left vacancies more profound in some ways than the loss of his leg. He knew Nicki's whereabouts, of course – a muddy hole in a cemetery near the top of Sylvan Heights. With his own eyes he'd seen her go into the ground and the backhoe cover her up. Lewis, on the other hand, had disappeared without a trace on the very day Josh was shot. Later Josh had found out that Rex Caswell and his live-in squeeze had died horrible deaths mere hours after Josh had landed in the emergency room of Good Samaritan, where surgeons had labored heroically in a futile effort to save his mangled leg.

A burrowing worm of intuition told him that Lewis Kindred was somehow responsible for those deaths. Lewis had killed Rex for what he'd done to Josh, and had then fled. As to why Lewis had killed Rex's girlfriend, Josh didn't wish to speculate, because the possibilities were too ugly, too much like what had happened to Ron Payne and at least five other innocent citizens in every corner of the country.

Jesse Burton had visited Josh daily during the two weeks he'd spent in the hospital, and had become close to the Nickerson family. Cheryl was glad for his interest in her son, particularly since Jesse had sons of his own and could 'talk the lingo,' as she termed the way males conversed with each other. Moreover, any friend of Lewis's was okay in her book.

Jesse hadn't shared with her all he knew about Lewis, and Josh was glad of this, for he himself hadn't disclosed to the cops or anyone except Jesse the real reason that he'd ended up in Rex Caswell's warehouse almost six weeks ago. Rex had wanted the orb, a ball of red glass that could move on its own and burn people, that could make you a winner at poker. Knowing how ridiculous the truth would have sounded, he'd simply left it out and sent the police straight to Rex Caswell as soon as he regained consciousness in post-op. The cops had found Rex and his girlfriend dead, of course, the handiwork of – someone.

Within the past six weeks Jesse had flown back and forth between Chicago and Portland at least six times that Josh knew of, not only to visit him during his convalescence, but also to huddle with Paul Tran to discuss a strategy against the enemy, whom they referred to simply as 'Gamaliel's kind.' Lewis would return, Jesse was certain. Lewis would come back to help put an end to the evil. How Jesse could be so sure of this, Josh couldn't guess, unless Jesse, like himself, believed that no matter how radically Lewis might have changed externally, he was still a good man in his heart. Lewis could never become a Millie Carter or a Gamaliel Cartee – Josh knew this with as much certainty as he knew that the sun would rise tomorrow. *Faith*, he supposed this was, knowing that it wasn't one of Lewis's favorite words.

ii

After picking up his luggage from the baggage carousel at Portland International Airport, Jesse Burton went to a pay phone and called his wife in Chicago, as he'd promised he would do. She needed to hear from him often these days, especially now that he'd begun spending so much time in Portland, pursuing a matter that he'd described to her in only the vaguest terms. *Helping an old Vietnam buddy find himself . . . Being there for a friend who'd given him his first lesson in decency . . . Doing for a friend what he would expect a friend to do for him . . .*

Jesse knew that none of it sounded particularly compelling to Shandelle, and the fact that she put up with this strange behavior only whetted his love for her. He vowed that when this was over, he would take her and the boys on a long vacation to a place with bright sandy beaches and bathtub-warm surf. Sitting in the sun with his family gathered around him, he would try to explain why he'd needed to take a leave of absence both from his job and his home to spend his time and energies on people they'd never even met. He hoped he could make them understand without disclosing the whole of the story.

He and Shandelle talked a full ten minutes, saying many of the same things they'd said on the way to O' Hare early this morning. He assured her that he loved her, that he wouldn't forget to take his blood-pressure pills, that he wouldn't smoke more than a pack a day. Yes, he would call every evening, and no, he wouldn't forget his older son's birthday, which was coming up in a week. Oh – had she told him she loved him? Only six times since answering the phone.

He picked up a rental car and stowed his bags in the trunk. As he put his hand on the trunk lid to slam it down, he heard a strange thumping sound that seemed to come from inside a suitcase. The sound started slowly, but quickly accelerated to an engine-like pace, and Jesse's stomach started churning. *The cigar box . . . !*

He tore open the suitcase and snatched up the cigar box he'd procured in Louisiana, with the ball-bearing inside it. The ball of steel was in a frenzy, hurling itself against the inside of the box with force sufficient to raise welts on the outer surface of the stiff cardboard. The popping was loud enough to turn the heads of passersby more than a hundred feet away. As Jesse clutched the box in his hands, just managing to keep the lid closed by clamping both thumbs over it, the ball-bearing burst through a corner of the box and bounced across the asphalt of the rental lot, careening off the tire of an Avis Grand Am and rolling to a halt at the base of a chain-link fence.

Jesse raced to a pay phone near the rental check-in office. He called Paul Tran, and knew from the instant Paul answered that something was very wrong in the Tran household. The telephone picked up a sharp, staccato popping in the background, the source of which Jesse knew: a lacquered box with a glass marble inside.

'Paul, it's Jesse Burton! I'm calling from the airport – I just landed. My cigar box just—'

'Yes, Jesse, I know! It's happening! I think . . .' Jesse heard sounds of consternation on the other end, shouted words in Vietnamese. He didn't need to know the language to comprehend the terror in the voices of Paul

Tran and his wife. 'Jesse! You told me that the woman Millie gave an orb to Josh Nickerson, not so?'

Jesse confirmed this. It had happened on the day of Nicole's burial.

'Then it's Josh who's in danger! You must go to him now! Quickly! Do you have the key I gave you – the one that fits the front door of Sloan House?'

'I've got it, yeah! But I'm at the airport, Paul. It'll take me at least half an hour to get there, maybe more if there's traffic. Can't you—?'

'No, I can't go, Jesse. I'm still too weak. I have doubts now that I'll ever be well again. You're the one who must act. Remember the things we've talked about, and remember what the *sorcière* told you – look beyond the known, and feel beyond yourself. Accept the message that seeks you . . .'

Jesse heard the words and mouthed them silently, but even now, after all this time and talk with Paul Tran, he doubted that he knew exactly what they meant. He slammed the handset into its cradle and raced for the rental car, intending to set a record for the travel time between Portland International and Gander Ridge.

iii

Around noon the cloud cover disappeared but for an occasional charcoal-colored boulder that devoured the sun for a half-minute or so before passing on. Josh pulled off his heavy sweater and rolled up the sleeves of his shirt, wanting as much of the rare fall sunshine as he could get. He also rolled up the cuffs of his Levis, exposing the gray plastic cap on the stump just below his left knee. The stump was virtually healed, of course, but it was still tender, and would continue to be so for some time, the doctor had said. Strangely, he could occasionally feel an itch on the big toe of his left foot – a 'phantom itch,' which was actually a common complaint among amputees, he'd learned. Not for another month could he and his doctors begin experimenting with prostheses.

He took his Sony Discman from the saddlebag of his wheelchair and booted a Depeche Mode CD. As he was leaning back, he happened to catch sight of someone in the gazebo below, where he and Nicki had often sat together in the swinging love seat, talking about anything and everything. A thrill of grief raced through him when he remembered this, and for the millionth time since her death he wished that he could sit up in bed and discover that Nicki wasn't dead at all, and he hadn't lost a leg.

But Nicki *was* dead, and Josh's leg *was* gone, and someone *was* sitting in the swinging love seat.

She was young, not over seventeen, and dark-complected. Her hair, so black that it was almost blue, cascaded in a fashionable thatch over her shoulders. She wore a long tan reefer coat over a tunic sweater of nearly the same color, and white stirrup pants with tan high-top sneakers. Even from this distance Josh could see that she was beautiful, that she was slim and elegant in an almost fashion-model sort of way. He wondered who she was.

He remembered that the Nickersons' long-time neighbor, the young stockbroker, had moved away. Josh himself had seen the moving van. Weeks later, after coming home from the hospital, he'd overheard Kendra tell his mother about the 'new folks' who'd moved into the vacant apartment, a woman with a stepdaughter. Could *this* be the stepdaughter?

A cloud scudded quickly over the sun, and a crow cawed from its perch in a naked elm as the noontide darkened almost to dusk. The girl smiled at Josh, a shattering of white teeth. The crow glided toward the gazebo and flapped its glossy wings twice, three times to wheel and stall, to alight on the railing near the girl. It cackled again, then hopped to her outstretched arm, its wings spread wide to aid its balance. Josh watched breathlessly as she stroked the bird's head, whispered something to it, blew gently into its face. The bird stood on her forearm as if mesmerized, listening to her whispered words and breathing her breath.

With her free hand she reached up and slowly twisted one of the crow's wings, and Josh would have sworn that he heard the bones snap. Holding the poor creature with both hands now, she twisted the other wing – another snap. Then its right leg. Its left leg. And finally, grinning with feral amusement at Josh, she twisted its head completely around, then held the throbbing body up for him to see. A drop of blood fell from the crow's beak onto her coat, but she didn't seem to care.

If Josh had eaten lunch, he would have spit it up. He tore the headphones off and wheeled the chair around, wanting to be inside, wanting locked doors between himself and the creature in the gazebo. But maneuvering a wheelchair, he'd found, was sometimes like rowing a boat, especially when trying to squeeze through doors. After several attempts and several new scrapes in the woodwork, he got himself into the living room through the French doors. But as he turned the chair in order to close the door behind him, a dark shape rose from below and alighted on the rail of the deck.

It was the girl from the gazebo, having jumped to the second-story deck as easily as a normal mortal might take the first step on a stairway. She hopped nimbly down from the rail and strode toward him, and Josh just managed to lock the doors before she arrived. With his pulse hammering his eardrums, he backed into the living room, colliding first with an end table, then with a chair. Through the panes of the French doors he saw her raise a long finger to the lock, heard the dead bolt click as if someone had turned a key. The door swung open, untouched by anything seen.

She stepped into the living room, graceful and elegant despite the crimson stain on her coat, smiling prettily. Josh saw that her eyes were mismatched, brown and blue, as he'd known they must be from the moment she'd broken the bird's wing.

'Hi, Josh. I'm your new neighbor, Camilla. Camilla Cartier. I hope you don't think I'm rude . . .' She said the words lazily, unhurriedly, sweetening every syllable with Louisiana sugar.

'I know who you are.'

'Of course you do. I'll dispense with the pretense then. It's only for the benefit of others anyway.' She let the tan reefer coat slide off her shoulders and drop to the carpet. Her fingers began playing around the bottom edge of her long, bulky sweater. 'I'm sorry about your leg, I really am. Most unfortunate. Can you believe what a jerk Rex Caswell was? At least he got his comeuppance. In the final analysis, though, what happened to you is probably for the better. You see, the best specimens among our kind are those who suffered crippling deformities or injuries during their human lives. For them the transformation to our kind is especially joyful, since it lets them throw off all their old aches and pains and limitations. And so it'll be with you, Josh. Having lived without a leg, you'll be especially happy to have a complete pair of them again.'

The thought of having two legs again loosed a thrill. For a bright moment Josh's imagination ran wild, and he saw himself walking without crutches or an artificial limb, never needing a wheelchair and never worrying what others might think when they noticed his limp. Having lost Nicki, he'd doubted that he would ever again be interested in girls, but he knew now that life does indeed go on. Someday he would want a woman again, surely, but would she want him? Do women get turned on by guys with wooden legs?

The thing that now called herself Camilla pulled her tan sweater over her head, riling her hair and displaying the most perfect breasts that Josh had ever seen, small but firm and pert, the nipples standing tautly and begging for his tongue. She moved slowly toward him, her breasts bouncing with every step, and Josh suddenly had a hard-on that threatened to burst his jeans. Standing an arm's length from him, she unlaced her sneakers and slipped them off. Then she pushed her white stirrup pants down over her slim hips and stepped out of them, leaving only a pair of snow-white panties. She bent to him, kissed him, sending a pang through his young body. Moving her lips to his ear, she whispered, 'I have gifts for you. I want you to take them. I want you to *use* them.'

'What do you – mean?'

'You never got the opportunity to use the orb – old Rex Caswell saw to that. But don't worry. The orb always gives you another chance, and another one after that, if need be.' She drew away from him slightly and knelt on the carpet, then tilted her head back. A lump rose at the base of her throat and moved upward past her larynx, into her mouth. Her jaw unhinged like a snake's, and a dazzling arc of red peeked between her lips, its membranous rays flitting over walls, ceiling, furniture. With her mouth open impossibly wide, she tilted her head forward again, staring brown and blue lasers at Josh, and disgorged an orb into the palm of her hand. She held it out to him as her jaw reconnected. 'You've already fulfilled one of the requirements for membership. All you need to do now is to accept the orb and one other gift, as well. This.' She stood up again, and with her free hand pushed down her white panties.

Blood rushed into Josh's cheeks as the heat of desire consumed him. He stared hungrily at the thatch of black hair, his body already taking up the rhythm of sex. He would have given into the hunger, but he remembered what Millie Carter had said only minutes before he'd shot her. She'd referred to Josh as a 'prospect.' She'd meant for him to become one of her own kind, a creature who kills and kills and kills.

This was the piece of slime who had killed Nicki.

He launched a fist into her abdomen, knocking her backward. She merely stared at him in shock, her sweet face blank. Josh wished that he owned the legs to lunge out of the chair at her, catch her by the neck and jam his thumbs into her windpipe. She scowled at him. 'What do you think you're doing, you miserable little wretch?' she hissed. 'You don't seriously believe that you can hold me off, do you?' She advanced on him, her eyes blazing brown and blue, her lips curved into a snarl. 'I can get inside your head, if I want to. I can take control of your brain, your heart, even your *prick*, if I want to. If I want you to fuck me, then you'll *fuck* me!'

'Okay, why don't you do it? Why don't you take over my body and do whatever you want with it?' Josh worked the wheelchair backwards, steering around the sofa toward the center of the room. 'I'll tell you why – because you need me to be *willing*. If you force me, it doesn't count, does it?'

'Believe me when I say this, Josh: I can make life so miserable for you that you'll come to me willingly. I'm fully capable of that, you know. I've done it before – not a pretty thing to watch, but I always do whatever needs to be done. I can turn your world into a hell. By the time I'm finished, you'll be begging for my body.'

Josh tried to keep furniture between them, but the effort was useless. He'd nearly circumnavigated the living room, finding himself near the French doors again. He knew that even with two legs he couldn't evade a creature who could do a vertical leap to a second-floor deck from a standing position. 'You're wrong!' he shouted. 'I'll never want something like you. Just the sight of you makes me sick! I don't care what your body looks like – I know what you are inside. I know what you *do* to people!'

The doorbell rang, then rang again, and someone thumped heavily at the front door. *'Josh, are you okay? I hear voices in there! Josh, it's me, Jesse Burton! Open the door!'* The thumping resumed so furiously that Josh thought the hinges might break.

'Jesse, help me!' he screamed. 'It's Millie Carter. She's getting ready to—' Suddenly the muscles in Josh's jaw froze as if someone had thrown a bucket of liquid oxygen in his face. He felt the tentacles of Millie's mind probing his own, latching onto his control buttons. Revulsion erupted from his gut, but he couldn't stop the takeover.

Instantly he had a hard-on again, and Millie or Camilla or
whatever she called herself attacked his clothes, tearing
them off and flinging them aside. He could only watch,
horrified, appalled. The pounding on the door grew loud
enough to rattle his mother's precious vases in a hutch
next to the wall.

Millie pulled him from the wheelchair and flopped him
on to the carpet, then straddled him, her mismatched
eyes blazing and her mouth contorting as if it had a mind
of its own. Grabbing his cock she started to press it into
her, but at that very instant the living room door blew
open with a blizzard of splinters. Jesse had beaten it in
with the heavy old-fashioned fire extinguisher that the
landlady, Juliet Kindred, kept mounted in the corridor.
His face hardened into stone when he saw the spectacle
before him – a beautiful teenage girl, naked as the day
she was born, meaning to have her way with the boy on
the floor.

But Jesse didn't let appearances fool him.

iv

He looked beyond the known. He turned his heart both
inward and outward in order to inhale the message that
sought him.

And he saw the thing for what it was, not a comely
young girl with the face of an angel, but a vespertilionine
demon with hunkering wings and the virulent eyes of a
dragon. Fighting his terror, he launched himself at it,
uncertain whether he could damage it or even slow it
down, but needing to do something that might give Josh a
chance of escaping. He struck the thing at full tilt, like the
fullback he'd been in high school, and they crashed
through the French doors on to the deck with a gigantic

shattering of glass and wood. The thing somersaulted over Jesse while grabbing great clawfuls of his anorak, and Jesse felt himself being hauled upward. He managed to grab the thing by the throat as it hurled him over the rail, and it hadn't steadied itself, so Jesse took it with him.

v

'So let me make sure I have this right,' said the cop, wrapping up. Josh sat white-faced in his wheelchair, wearing sweat gear dragged hastily out of a dresser drawer, because he couldn't stand the thought of putting on clothes that Camilla had touched. An ambulance had taken Jesse Burton's body away. His mother had rushed home from her office and now sat close to him on a hassock, her arm wrapped protectively around him. 'The dead man, this Mr Jesse Burton, broke the door down to save you from a pervert who was trying to rape you. He wrestled the guy through these French doors here, out to the deck, and they both went over the side, landing on the flagstone patio downstairs. Is that right?'

Josh managed to nod.

'And you don't have any idea how the pervert got into the place?'

Another nod.

'And you can't explain why the pervert got away, while Mr Burton died of a broken skull.'

Josh's eyes filled with hot, bitter tears. 'It doesn't seem right, does it?'

'No, it doesn't,' agreed the cop, shaking his head as if he suspected that he'd heard only a tiny fraction of the real story. 'It doesn't seem right at all.'

vi

At ten o'clock that evening Lewis Kindred walked into the Huntsman's Bar and Grill off the lobby of the Hotel Fanshawe, wearing a new pair of baggy Levis, cowboy boots, a flowered Western shirt, and a stetson hat. Except for a few stringy old barflies who sat in their regular places under the stuffed moose head at the far end of the bar, the place was deserted of customers. Not much business on Tuesday nights these days.

Tommy Iadanza was busy taking an inventory of the liquor on the shelves that fronted the great arching mirror. When he glanced up and saw Lewis, he dropped his clipboard and groped for the countertop, blanching and looking near to fainting. The bartender, a rotund two-hundred-fifty-pounder named Huett (the regulars called him Baby Huey), rushed to his boss's side and shouted something about a heart attack, but Tommy waved him off and told him everything was okay. Baby Huey didn't recognize Lewis in these clothes, of course, not to mention the fact that he wasn't in a wheelchair with the cuffs of his pants rolled under his stumps.

After Tommy regained control of himself he came over to where Lewis stood, his face as white as newly washed wool. He looked Lewis up and down with his sad, droopy eyes. 'Talk to me,' he croaked, his voice having gone south.

'How about we get a table, maybe a couple of brew-skies?'

'No table, no brewskies. Just talk to me. You can start by explaining—' He leaned over the bar to get a load of Lewis's brand-new Justins, one of which Lewis had rested against the brass foot rail. '—The boots. Start with the boots, okay?'

Lewis sighed deeply and started to talk. He didn't stop talking until he'd told his old friend everything.

vii

Minutes before midnight.

Tommy wheeled Josh Nickerson into the card room above the Huntsman's, where Lewis waited at the huge green-baize table under a cone of lamplight, absently shuffling a deck of cards the way he'd done it since mortar fragments had ripped into his left arm more than twenty years ago – with one hand. When he saw Josh, his face tightened and his eyes misted, but he held back the tears.

Jesus, it was true, he said to himself. He hadn't dreamed it. There sat Josh with the stump of one leg resting on a wheelchair brace, maimed forever. Which meant that Lewis hadn't dreamed the part about killing Rex Caswell and Twyla Boley, either. *This thing just gets worse and worse. That's why we've got to end it . . .*

'I'll leave you two alone,' said Tommy, parking the wheelchair close to Lewis. 'If you need anything, pick up the house phone and I'll be here in a flash.'

'Thanks, Tom,' said Lewis. 'Remember if anyone comes . . .'

'Yeah, right. I'll send her up. Or him. Whichever.' Tommy ducked out, closing the door softly, as if this was a funeral parlor.

'So how's it going, mahatma? Hey, sorry – bad question. I guess I know how it's going. What do you young dudes call it – a "nasty hang?" I can't tell you how sorry I am about your leg.' He nodded at Josh's stump. 'It's not the end of the world, though. You know that, don't you? Life can still be good . . .'

'Are you aware that Jesse's dead?' the boy asked so

softly that Lewis barely heard him.

Lewis felt a current of new grief course through him. He shook his head. He hadn't known. He wanted to learn how it had happened, and Josh told him, detail by gruesome detail. Afterward, still cringing, Lewis remembered a pair of lines from an ancient Charlotte Brontë poem:

For life is darkly shaded,
And its joys fleet fast away . . . !

So it had been for Jesse.

Twyla would have been proud of him, he thought, blotting his eyes with the pearl-buttoned sleeve of his flowered Western shirt, no longer caring whether Josh saw him cry. Those were probably the only two lines of poetry he remembered, and he couldn't even say the title of the poem. He looked up again, and said, 'Thanks for coming tonight, mahatma. I needed you.'

'I almost wasn't able to do it. Mom was pretty definite about not letting me out, and she didn't agree to it until Tommy told her that you wanted to see me. That's the only reason she let me come.' Studying his hands, he added, 'We've all been pretty worried about you, Lew.'

'Yeah. I suppose I owe everybody some kind of explanation.'

'You don't owe me one. I know why you left.' He avoided Lewis's eyes. 'Rex Caswell and his girlfriend, right?'

Lewis nodded. 'I want you to understand something, mahatma. I haven't – uh – I haven't killed anybody since then. I won't say that I haven't wanted to, because – because the hunger has been strong. *Real* strong. I killed

Rex because of what he did to you and Dewey. As for Twyla—' A deep breath, a shake of the head. 'I killed Twyla because I needed to, because of what I've become. But since then, I've fought down the hunger. I went to Reno and played cards, because I figured I had to get out of Portland, and I didn't know where else to go. Won a fortune, too, which I'm sure doesn't surprise you, since you know all about the orb. As of two days ago, I'm banned from all card games in Reno. That's where I bought these clothes, by the way, in case you're wondering.' He looked away from Josh and shook his head, as if to concede the insanity of everything he'd just said. 'My problem now is that I don't know how much longer I can—'

The door opened, causing Josh to jump, and in walked the being who this afternoon had called herself Camilla, wearing a wine-colored jogging suit that was much too large for her. When she spoke, her voice was deep and masculine, the voice of Gamaliel. 'Don't let me interrupt you, Lewis. You were saying something about not being sure how much longer you can hold back the hunger. She alighted in a chair at the opposite edge of the table, planted her elbows on the green baize, and made a basket with her delicate fingers, into which she laid her chin. She batted her blue-brown eyes girlishly.

'You're wearing the wrong voice,' said Lewis sarcastically. 'Little girl should have little girl's voice. Big sergeant should have big sergeant's voice. For God's sake, Gamaliel, we can't take you anywhere.'

'You're in rare form tonight, Lewis. What brought you back?'

'You.'

'I'm flattered.'

'Don't be. I'm here to kill you.'

'May I inquire as to your motive?'

'I don't want you to get Josh. In fact, I don't want you to get anyone ever again. I don't want you to turn anyone else into whatever I am, and I don't want you to butcher any more innocent people. I think that about sums it up.'

'I see. But how did you know I had any designs on your young friend here?'

'You're not the only one with a psychic eye, you know. Mine probably isn't as good as yours, but it still works. I've been keeping track of you, and I knew that you would go after Josh the moment he was left alone.'

'You almost blew it, Lewis. I came this close to getting him this afternoon.' She indicated how close with a delicate finger and thumb.

'Like I said, my psychic eye isn't as good as yours, at least not yet. I'm glad that Jesse—' His heart fluttered, forcing him to steady himself. 'I'm glad that Jesse showed up when he did. That was no accident, you know. He knew what he was doing.'

'Ah, yes. Jesse Burton. I'll confess that he caught me by surprise, which is a very dangerous thing to do. But tell me: What made you think I would turn up tonight?'

'I knew you would follow Josh here, especially if he was to be the stakes in a poker game.'

'Then I was right! You *are* here to play poker! I think I'm going to enjoy this. I'm not clear on one point, though – the part about your killing me.'

'It's simple. We'll play five-card draw for money, as many hands as it takes for one of us to clean the other out. If I win, I kill you. If you win, you get Josh.'

When he heard this, Josh put his hands over his face and cringed.

'It sounds like the sort of proposition no Southern gentleman can resist,' said Gamaliel.

'Cut for the deal?'

'No. Let's ask Josh to do the honors. It seems only fitting, since it's his destiny we're playing with.'

Lewis turned to the boy, who looked brave despite the paleness of his face and the piercing innocence of his eyes. Lewis handed him the deck. With shaking fingers the kid shuffled the cards, allowed both players to cut. 'The game is five-card draw,' he announced. 'Nothing wild. Jacks or better to open—'

Lewis called Tommy on the house phone and requested the services of the house bank. Minutes later Tommy appeared with his chip bucket and receipt book. He sold ten thousand dollars' worth of chips each to Lewis and the stunning young woman who sat across from him, then quickly slipped out of the room.

The players anted a thousand dollars apiece. Josh dealt smoothly, and the cards whooshed across the green baize, five each to Lewis and Gamaliel, faces down. Lewis watched them alight in front of him, and felt as if he were playing a part in a movie, as if he was behaving according to a script. Unlike a real actor, though, he had no idea how the story would end.

Before he even picked up his cards Lewis knew what he'd been dealt – the same hand he'd seen on a dark night in Vietnam when he'd first played poker with Gamaliel, and again at this very table more than twenty years later when he'd meted out justice to Rex Caswell. It was the only hand that he could possibly draw, the script writer had decreed, a necessary symmetry. The deuce of clubs, three of hearts, four of diamonds, five of hearts, and jack of spades – a potential double-ended straight. He needed a six or an ace, and the odds of getting either weren't good in an ordinary game of five-card draw.

But this was no ordinary game, as the dealing of the cards had shown, for the odds against getting this particular hand at this precise moment were incalculable. Lewis had the red ball with him, which meant that he would win regardless of what he did. The red ball made him invincible. He *hoped*.

Gamaliel grinned slyly with his exquisite girl's mouth as he stacked his own hand neatly in front of him. 'Don't look so smug, Lewis,' he said in his deep male voice. 'The bauble can't help you now. You see, I have one, too. The best you can hope for is that our orbs will cancel each other out.' He winked. 'If I were you, I'd play poker like I've never played it before.' He bet a thousand dollars, and Lewis saw him but didn't raise. 'What happened to your trademark smile, Lewis? More important, why aren't you raising?'

Lewis ignored the taunts, discarded his jack and drew the six of hearts, as he knew he would, the capper to a six-high straight. Gamaliel drew one card, glanced at it and placed it squarely atop his neatly stacked hand, his face betraying nothing. 'With cards like these, I see no need to prolong the agony,' he said, his mismatched eyes glittering. He shoved his entire supply of chips into the center of the table. 'I'll raise you all I have, Lewis. Now that you've lost your smile, I wonder if you've also lost your nerve.'

Lewis's heartbeat thudded in his temples. If money had been the only issue here, he would have unhesitatingly seen Gamaliel's bet and waited for the showdown. But money wasn't the only issue. Josh Nickerson was the issue. Lewis had no intention of surrendering the boy, regardless of how the game ended, but he wondered whether he was strong enough to fight off Gamaliel if the beast won.

In the motor pool in Vietnam, Gamaliel had drawn one card to complete a full house, jacks over nines. Thanks to the orb, Lewis's six-high straight had become four sixes and a stray five, a winner. The same scene had played itself out against Rex last month. Could the orb deliver another victory now – against Gamaliel, who owned an orb of his own? Stinging sweat trickled into Lewis's right eye, but he didn't blink. He could feel Josh's worried gaze, but he stared straight ahead into the impossibly innocent face of the girl before him, a face that masked a creature beyond human imagination.

'I'll see you and call,' Lewis said, his voice having gone hoarse.

The Gamaliel-girl nodded her pretty head and started turning over her cards one by one. *Ten of hearts, jack of hearts, queen of hearts* . . .

Lewis's pulse became jack-hammer rapid. He became dizzy.

. . . *King of hearts, ace of hearts*. A royal flush. The strongest possible hand in poker. Lewis saw the corners of the girl's mouth widen into a grin. Another droplet of sweat flowed into his eye, turning the room into a blur. He blinked and lowered his gaze to his own cards, which lay face down. He fingered the top one and turned it over, saw that it was the nine of spades. The orb had transformed the hand into something, that much was evident, but not something that could beat a royal flush. *Nothing* beat a royal flush.

Suddenly the door opened to admit a stocky, middle-aged man whose yellow hair was going rapidly gray, what he had left of it. He wore a rumpled business suit that had probably come from K-mart and a tie that looked as if it had been cut from a jockey's suit. 'Guy downstairs says there's a game up here,' he said with a slow Midwest accent, beaming from ear to ear. 'Would you folks mind if an out-of-towner sat in? Name's Legler. Dan Legler, out of Grand Island, Nebraska, sheet-metal contracting. My company's bidding on some work up here in Portland, and—' His eyes connected with Lewis's, and his face lit up. 'Wait a minute,' he said, walking slowly toward Lewis's edge of the table. 'You look awfully familiar. Are you . . . ? Well, I'll be damned! It's the L.T.! Lieutenant Lewis Kindred, right? Can you believe it, after all these years—?'

The door opened again, and through it came T.J. Skane, wearing the same tattered clothes he'd worn when Lewis had last seen him, the same tungsten-filings beard, sunglasses, and baseball cap with the L. A. Raiders insignia. He grinned when he saw Legler, and threw his arms open wide. The men embraced like two long-lost friends, which they were – one of whom Lewis had watched burn to death; the other having ended up a legless, headless torso lying in the tall grass of the Ho Bo Woods.

And behind them came the osteopath from Beaverton, Dr Scott Sanders, former medic of the Triple Deuce scout platoon, immaculate in his Brooks Brothers suit and designer tie. This was a reunion of the dead.

Or was it? For a schizophrenic moment Lewis wondered whether *he* was the one who was dead, and these men were the living; whether his consciousness had arisen out of the ether through their remembrances of him. Why shouldn't this be so? Many cultures believed that immortality was possible only as long as the living remembered the dead.

The Camilla-thing glared at Lewis with its mismatched eyes, its face contorting hellishly, as if to incinerate him for contriving this trap. Jesse had told Lewis that Gamaliel's kind feared only the dead, and for good reason, Lewis had thought. The dead knew the suffering that Gamaliel and his race had inflicted on humanity.

Josh reached for Lewis and clutched at him, his eyes glassy with terror. 'They're your friends from Vietnam, aren't they?' he whispered. 'They're the guys from the scout platoon. I recognize them – T. J., and Scottie and Leg—'

'They're the ones,' Lewis said. 'Paul Tran sent them to us. They're here to kill Gamaliel.'

At this moment the Camilla-thing jumped to its feet. 'You can't be serious, Lewis! You don't think these miserable creatures can kill me!' Josh gasped as Camilla metamorphosed, not into the man-thing they'd all called Gamaliel, but into something for which human language lacks words. It had scales and razor-teeth and vespertilionine wings. It had dragon's eyes and tentacles bristling with claws. As its body shifted, it ripped the wine-colored jogging suit to tatters.

It thrust a six-jointed finger at Lewis, pointing, and shouted in a rumbling-lava voice to the gathered members of the scout platoon: '*He's* the one you should turn your anger on. If he'd been a competent commander, you'd all be alive today. You would have the bodies you're now enjoying for these few moments. You would have families, friends, and *lives*, if Lieutenant Lewis Kindred hadn't been so obsessed with killing me that he forgot about taking care of *you*!'

Lewis withered under the accusation, for it was true. The dead of the scout platoon had come to help him, but in a twinkling Gamaliel was turning them against him with the truth.

'Know the truth,' roared Gamaliel, laughing hideously, 'and the truth will set you free!'

The newly arrived veterans of the scout platoon began to change. Scottie Sanders developed a hump on his back that split the seams of his costly suit, and wriggling maggots appeared in his eyes. Danny Legler's florid face turned green and bulged with putrefactive gases, his silver-blond hair falling from his head in gobs. The skin of T. J. Skane's cheeks stretched tight as the flesh beneath it fizzled away, and his long hands twisted into claws.

Behind them, in the rectangle of the door, appeared Sergeant First Class Frank Markowski, beetle-browed and bristle-scalped, militarily correct except for the fact that a third of his skull was gone and a goodly portion of his brain had oozed all over his jungle fatigues. He grinned savagely with his bad teeth, a Pall Mall straight stuck to his lower lip. He leveled his M-60 machine gun at Lewis.

'I've waited a long fuckin' time for this!' he roared. 'Thanks to this little puke, I didn't live to see my grandkids born. I say, let's give him a taste of what we got because of him. Let's see how he likes being deader than a fuckin' dinosaur dick!'

Lewis expected a blizzard of 7.62-millimeter rounds to rip into his body, and he would have welcomed an opportunity to die like a conventional mortal man. But he couldn't let them hurt Josh. Josh deserved no piece of this hell.

Lewis leapt to his feet, facing the advancing foursome

of dead men. 'Don't hurt *him*!' he pleaded over the roar of Gamaliel's laughter. 'He never did anything to any of you. I'm the one who failed you, damn it! Don't you understand? If you need to kill someone, kill *me*!'

viii

For that one blinding moment, Josh was certain that they would kill Lewis, and himself, too. But he felt a tug on a remote corner of his mind, then a gentle probe. Light erupted behind his eyes, and his ears rang with the reverberations of Paul Tran's lacquered box.

Out of the light came Nicole, her raven hair shining, her eyes glistening with excitement. She smiled and handed him something – a silver orb, he thought it was, for the thing was too brilliant to look at directly. But once it settled into the palm of his hand, he knew that it was *power*. Prickling with its energy, he reached out for Lewis, and Lewis's bleary eyes came alive with the same power. Glorying in the energy it imparted, he reached for Lewis and found him. Lewis's eyes came vibrantly alive.

Jesse Burton stepped into the room, his eyes hard like black marbles, tall and strong in faded jungle fatigues. Bandoleers of ammo crisscrossed his chest, and a plastic peace symbol hung from his neck. He pointed his M-16 at the ceiling and fired a full clip on fully automatic, pulverizing acoustical tiles and causing a rain of plaster. Skane, Sanders, Legler, and Markowski suddenly evaporated into membranous squiggles of light.

Its allies gone, the Gamaliel creature turned on Jesse, but Jesse caught it by its scaly throat before it could raise a claw against him. Tingling with the power of the silver orb, Josh and Lewis joined the fray, scrabbling over the poker table. Josh ignored the pain in his stump, wanted only to lay his killing hands on Gamaliel.

And together he and Lewis *did* lay their killing hands on the thing, along with Jesse. And Nicole, too. Their heads rang with the din of the lacquer box as they fought it, as they tore out its eyes and heart, as they crushed its sinewy neck in their hands and beat in its skull with their fists. The Gamaliel creature disintegrated into gray flakes as it died, seeping through their fingers into a pile on the floor, killed less by their blows than its own fear of the dead.

Josh fell against the card table when it was over, gasping, and Lewis lay hunched beside him, his face slick. They were alone, the two of them. Jesse and Nicole weren't here. Maybe never had been.

Lewis carried Josh to his wheelchair and lowered him gently into it. Josh surprised him by catching a fistful of his flowered shirt and holding tight, not letting him go. 'I want to see your cards, Lewis.'

A weak smile. 'Why? You saw Gamaliel's. Nothing beats a royal flush. You know that, mahatma.'

'But you had more than the red ball working for you. You had this.' He held up the silver orb in his other hand, and its ghostly light danced against their faces. The thing seemed to radiate goodness. 'Please, Lewis. Let me see them.'

Lewis steered the chair around to the edge of the table where his poker hand lay face-down, except for the nine of spades. 'See for yourself,' he told Josh. The boy picked up a card and turned it over – the nine of diamonds. The next was the nine of hearts. Then came the nine of clubs.

Lewis sniffed. 'Not a bad hand, considering. Too bad that four of a kind doesn't beat a royal flush.' He managed a chuckle. 'Ever see such bad luck in all your life?'

'But there's one left,' said Josh, reaching for the last card.

'A stray, that's all, worthless as a fifth wheel.'

Josh turned it over anyway, and when Lewis saw it, his breath went out of him. The card was a nine, but its suit was a new one, symbolized by a glistening red ball that contained swarms of alive-looking matter. What was this – the nine of *orbs*?

'I don't believe it,' Lewis whispered, staring at the thing. 'I've never seen . . .'

'It's a nine! You had five nines, Lewis! Don't you see what it means?'

'But it's impossible to have five of a kind. There are only four suits, for crying out loud.'

'Nothing's impossible, Lewis – not when you have . . .'

Just then Tommy Iadanza burst through the door of the card room, his basset-hound eyes round with disbelief. He surveyed the ruined ceiling and clapped both hands to his head. 'Who in the hell shot up the place, for Christ's sake? I've got guests in this hotel . . . !'

Then he saw the condition of Josh and Lewis, and he remembered the artist's sketch that had appeared in the *Oregonian* weeks ago – the face of a killer who'd borne an uncanny resemblance to Lewis. He suggested urgently that Lewis and Josh get out before the cops arrived.

ix

Lewis pushed Josh in his wheelchair along the pedestrian walkway of the Hawthorne Bridge, which had a lacework of dirty yellow lights strung along its girders and cables.

He halted at the midpoint, leaned against the rail, and stared down at the bleak Willamette River, silently searching for something he couldn't name. Chilly rain fell, and the occasional passing truck or car roused spray that stung the backs of their necks. Neither said anything for a long while.

'What happened back there, Lewis?' Josh asked suddenly. 'Where did the guys from your platoon come from? And where did Nicki come from?'

'I don't honestly know, mahatma. If I were to guess, I'd say from inside our own heads. Paul Tran might've had something to do with it—'

'Like he empowered us, or something? Maybe cast a spell?'

'It could've been that, I suppose. Or maybe he reached out to us with his mind and opened up mental pathways that neither us of knew we had. Memories can be powerful, and maybe he gave us the ability to project them into the mind of someone else.'

'Gamaliel, you mean. We projected our memories of dead people into Gamaliel's head, and we made them behave like we wanted them to . . .'

'Except when he turned my own guys against me. I think what he did, mahatma, was turn me against *myself*. He preyed on my guilt without even knowing it. All he knew was that I'd done a bad job as a platoon leader, and I'd gotten a bunch of good guys killed. He pointed this out to T. J. and Scottie and Leg, because he thought they were real, but what he really did was lay a guilt trip on me.'

'So your mind changed those guys into – into something ugly? Is that what you're saying?'

'I changed them into things that wanted revenge

against me, and I might've let them have it if Jesse hadn't come back.'

'Jesse came back to *you*, and Nicki came back to *me*.'

'Yes. If I were a betting man—' He winked slyly, and Josh caught it, even though the lights of the bridge were at their backs. '—I'd say that old Paul Tran gave us the power to *call forth the dead* from our own minds.'

'What about Gamaliel? *He* was real, right? And Millie, and Camilla? They certainly didn't come out of our minds.'

'Oh, they were real, all right – as real as I am, as you are. But the evil that they did is *human* evil, mahatma – the darkest kind, yes, but no worse than the stuff we read about in the papers every day. I don't know whether Gamaliel's kind is a construct of our minds or whether they exist as the actual conscious entities we perceive them to be. I suppose it's possible that they're elaborate hallucinations that behave the way we expect them to. I do know this, though: they're *real*. None of us should ever forget that.'

Josh thought about this for a long moment, his forehead braced against the handrail. 'Why are there bullet holes in the ceiling of that room?'

'Guessing again, I'd say that either or both of us engaged in something called psychokinesis. Know what that is?'

'The power to move stuff with your mind, right? You don't have to touch something physically.'

'Right. To my knowledge, no one has ever demonstrated it in a laboratory setting, but it might explain the damage. If I were you, that's what I'd choose to believe, because the alternative is to believe in—'

'Okay, okay. That's what I choose to believe.'

Another long period of silence ensued as each contemplated the blackness of the river. The rain actually let up a little.

'It's good having two legs, mahatma,' Lewis said dreamily. 'I'd forgotten *how* good. But I can't afford them.'

'What do you mean?'

'The price is too high. I don't have what it takes.'

Josh knew what this meant, and the knowledge made his throat burn. He searched for Lewis's hand, found it, and held it tightly in both of his. 'You're not like Gamaliel, Lewis. You're good inside. You've taught *me* to be good. That must count for something.'

'Maybe it does. But the fact is, I chose the orb, and I used it. I let Millie use me. And then I actually killed people, and . . .' The thought was too vile, and he left it unfinished. He swallowed, shored himself up. 'I'm standing here on two good legs, while you're sitting there with only one. I don't think I can handle the unfairness of that.'

'I don't see what's so unfair about it,' Josh replied, choking. 'You spent twenty years with no legs at all. You said yourself it's not the end of the world for me. I'll get a plastic leg. I'll learn to walk on it. People do it all the time, Lewis. Life will be good.'

'Yes, it *will* be good for you, Josh.' Lewis touched the boy's cheek. 'Remember that and hang on to it. *Work* for it.'

He reached into the pocket of his jeans and took out an orb, which, in the feeble lighting of the Hawthorne Bridge, seemed nothing more than harmless glass. Josh wondered whether it was the same one that Gamaliel had originally given to Lewis two decades ago in Vietnam, and whether it had survived two dousings in the river but had found its way back, like a bad penny. The thought stuck like the thorn on a thistle.

'For the last time,' Lewis said tiredly. He hauled his arm back and hurled the accursed thing far into the night. Josh followed it with his eyes until it impacted the water many stories below. 'I still have one blue eye and one brown one,' said Lewis at last. 'And my shadow—' He glanced down at his feet and shuffled them, causing a faint hiss that Josh barely heard.

Josh ground his teeth to keep from whimpering. 'Your eyes will get back to normal,' he said, trying to sound hopeful, 'and your shadow will get back to being like everybody else's, and—'

'And my legs will wither up into stumps again, right? And my ears will start ringing like hell again. And my left hand will go numb and useless.'

'Maybe so. But so *what*? You'll be like you were, and that'll be great. You can help me deal with having just one leg. It'll be okay. You'll see.'

Lewis shook his head. 'No, it won't be okay. I'll tell you what'll happen. I'll get hungry again, so hungry that I won't be able to control myself. And I'll do what I did to that girl in the Vintage Plaza and to Twyla. And every time I do it, I'll come one step closer to becoming a full-fledged specimen of Gamaliel's kind. You saw what Gamaliel became tonight. That could be me someday.' He turned and cupped Josh's cheek in his palm. 'I've got to end it now, mahatma, while there's still enough of the real me to make it count.'

With that, more quickly than Josh could imagine, Lewis Kindred went over the rail of the Hawthorne Bridge and plunged into the blackness of the night.

Sobbing, Josh hauled himself out of the wheelchair and leaned over the rail, but he saw nothing that he couldn't have seen with his eyes shut tight.

x

On Wednesday, November 18, 1992, *The Portland Oregonian* reported that a body had washed up on Swan Island, downstream of the main urban bridges. It was that of Lewis Kindred, said the police, a double amputee and veteran of the Vietnam war.

Josh Nickerson read the story and wept for joy.